THE SCENT OF THE PAST

ALSO BY WAYNE BROWN

Poetry
On the Coast
Voyages

Fiction and Reportage
Landscape with Heron
The Child of the Sea

Biography
Edna Manley: The Private Years

Edited
Derek Walcott: Selected Poetry

THE SCENT OF THE PAST

STORIES AND REMEMBRANCES

WAYNE BROWN

PEEPAL TREE

First published in Great Britain in 2011
Peepal Tree Press Ltd
17 King's Avenue
Leeds LS6 1QS
England

ISBN13: 9781845231538

Supported by
ARTS COUNCIL
ENGLAND

CONTENTS

PART II

PART I

THE CHILD OF THE SEA

When I first met her I was sixteen and she was seven – not the most romantic juxtaposition of ages. But I'll tell you something I've learnt since. Grow fond of a little girl when you're that age, and it's a fondness you'll have till death do you part. At the time, I was friends with her brother, and she was a nuisance we had to put up with sometimes. I remember her, brown, pigtailed and knobby-knee'd, running away from us past the Savannah cemetery, surrounded by strange, burly, heavily panting men, trying like them to get from the five-furlong gates to the homestretch in time to see the horses we'd just seen start finish. I shouted, '—, come back here!', which alerted her brother, who pelted after her and snatched her up from the midst of that phalanx of galloping grownups and bawled at her, while she looked at me bright-eyed, and I knew she was thinking she mightn't marry me, after all – but I don't think she ever actually said it.

The marriage talk had started that summer down the islands: I was there with her folks for a fortnight. Somehow it fell to me to teach her to swim, perhaps because strangers cannot be as peremptory with little girls as older brothers can – or perhaps because only sixteen-year-olds really know the meaning of chivalry. For whatever reason, she lay on my hands in the water, and kicked her feet and splashed her arms, turning her head from side to side to consider the sky with one bright eye and then the next, until I got bored and threatened to dunk her, and call it quits for the day – whereupon the game would change. For five 'throwings-up' into the air ('But *high*! It has to be high-high-high! Or no deal.') she was ready to offer me, if not her heart in love, then at least hand in marriage, one fine day.

'When?' I'd say grimly, pretending to ponder her proposition.

'Soon's I'm eighteen.' Then, giggling at my scowl: 'Okay, seventeen! No, *pleeze*! Okay, okay, sixteen. I promise, sixteen! Sixteen-sixteen-sixteen-sixteen-*fifteen*!'

'Too long,' I'd say, in a voice of doom. 'It has to be now or never.'

'But I *can't* marry you now!' she'd wail. 'I'm only a little girl!' Dunk.

Her brother went away to study; we lost touch; the years passed. The next time I saw her I was twenty-four, she, fifteen.

This was at Las Cuevas. I introduced her to my girlfriend, adding, for no reason I can now explain, 'the child of the sea'. She had grown tall, with big hands and a fine frank face, and was just filling out. Something about her struck me very strongly, and to say it was her laugh – to say her laugh was like a delicious promise (of life, yes, but to whom? To herself?) – is to put it ineptly. But I cannot put it more clearly than that. I remember she laughed a lot that day. I remember: there were fights in the water, girls wrestling girls on the shoulders of young men, and our turn came to be paired off, she my warrior, me, her amphibian steed. But it didn't feel right; to her, either; and after the battle was over – we lost – we edged away from each other in the water.

And yet when her mother, not long after that, asked me to help her with 'O' level English, I did, and it was fine, and we were friends. She said: 'Why did you introduce me to your girlfriend as "the child of the sea"?' And – when I said I didn't know – 'I like that name, I feel that way, sometimes…'

Twenty-eight, nineteen: Jamaica. I was married and living there; she was just passing through on the way to art school in the States. I said: 'I thought you were going to marry me?'

And she, with teenage archness: 'You were the coward; not me.'

Thirty-two, twenty-three: a party in Cascade. She had grown beautiful: she, now, with a husband. I said: 'The years have been kind to you, my child.'

Her laugh was the laugh from long ago. She said: 'You don't know what a relief it is to find your fame hasn't made you any less corny.'

I smiled uncertainly. My fame? But she was only referring to a book of mine which had been moderately well-received else-where but which had passed unnoticed in Trinidad. I said, surprised: 'You know that book?' And: 'O you of little faith,' she said. When I caught up with her some time later and signed her copy, I signed it, *To the Child of the Sea*. 'I was hoping you'd sign it like that,' she said smiling. 'I still feel that way a lot of the time.'

Thirty-five, twenty-six. I heard she'd lost a child, in England. I should have written; but my own life was in a crisis of its own, and I didn't write.

Forty, thirty-one. Trinidad. I ran into her on Level Three, Long Circular Mall. She had flown in the night before. Her husband had gone on contract to Kuwait, and after this vacation back home she would be going out to join him there. Yes, they were childless; yes, she had been going to call me. It was necessary for us to have faith. It was necessary for me now to have faith.

I said: 'And you? You still have faith, after all that's happened?' 'Of course I do,' she said. 'And – look at me – so do you. Don't you remember, The Child of the Sea?'

I didn't see her again. Or, to rephrase that: I never saw her again. Last week I ran into an old school friend of her brother's and learned that she had died in London earlier this year; of cancer; at thirty-four. And frankly I find that hard to believe. That I should not have known.

But I'll tell you something.

I have known people so evil that, when they hated, a literal stench would come from them. And I have always known, subconsciously, I suppose, that such people would live a long dry time. But now I know it consciously as well. Because now the good ones have started dying.

A LION IN WINTER

I believe that one has to be seventy before one is full of courage. The young are always half-hearted.

(D.H. Lawrence)

An old man, Wilfred Douglas, died last month. He was eighty-eight and a widower, his second wife having died a year and a month earlier. That she should have beaten him to the grave was ironical: she was nearly twenty years his junior, and could have expected – as must he – to be the one destined for twilight solitude. But as it was, it was he who lived on, cantankerous and grim as ever, in the old 'fifties house in the Valley, minded from afar by a doting married daughter and, nearer, by an ancient hag of a maid who had been with him and his wife for donkey's years and whom he professed to loathe, but whom he could never quite bring himself to fire; in realisation of which she used to boss him around unmercifully, or try to. Even at eighty-eight – especially at eighty-eight – old Wilfred was not one of the more bossable characters you would ever be likely to meet, and they used to have some terrible fights.

'I hate that woman,' he would tell me confidingly, his pupils growing tiny and shiftless. 'One day, so help me. One day.' But that day never came.

The old hag's name was Christophene. That anyway was what he called her, and what, with promiscuous fierce mockery, she instructed me to call her when I asked her uncertainly if that was really her name. 'To you, sah? Dat is correct. My name is Christophene.' And she retreated to the kitchen, explaining angrily to the walls that she 'ent know what business all like him so have wid my name. I tell he call me Christophene? Dese young people too fresh-up wid deyselves.'

It was an ongoing battle between them, and I suppose I would have said that she hated him every bit as much as he professed to hate her, if I hadn't been in the vicinity and dropped in on him, unwittingly, the morning after he had his stroke, and seen the look on her face when she opened the door, and heard the broken note in her voice when she said: 'He goin' now, Missa Wayne.'

That, I realised later, was the first and only time she ever called me by name. On all the other occasions that I dropped in on him – which weren't that many, I have to confess – she would open the door, glare at me and say, without preamble, something like, 'He in de garden', or, 'He restin', whuh yuh wahn do?' or even, economically, 'Hm', infusing each remark, even that minimal monosyllable, with a mysterious but limitless contempt for both the visitor and the visited. Later, when he would bellow for her to come and offer his guest a drink, she would appear, glare at me again, and say: 'All it have is juice. You wahn juice?'

Whereupon, likely as not, a terrific brouhaha would erupt between old Wilfred and the crone, with him commanding her to 'give the man some rum with his juice', and her saying stonily that 'it ent have no rum', and him abruptly bellowing that the rum was behind the flour where she had hidden it, or rather where she thought she had hidden it, except that she was now so dam' old and forgetful she would hide things and forget where she had hidden them, and did she think he didn't know about the brown sugar, or that he was living with a blasted thief?

She would turn and give him a look of such pure hatred that her withered frame would seem to shrivel further.

'I hate that woman,' he would tell me, not caring if she heard; and once, hearing, she returned to stand in front of his chair, thunderstruck, and spit out suddenly that God would damn him for a blasted liar and a nasty man and that he would in consequence rot in hell; whereupon old Wilfred shouted back that the only fear he had of hell was knowing he would meet her there…

And so it went.

Now, I should repeat that the object of Christophene's vital loathing and comatose love was not himself an easy man. He wasn't easy when I first met him, twenty-odd years ago, and he didn't get any easier as he aged. Time, which mellows the wise, they say, furrowed his brow like a gridiron. He exploited to the hilt the license of old age – which is to say whatever it wishes, to whomever it wishes, and damn what people think – and the increasing passion with which he expressed his increasingly abrasive view of things had the perverse effect of salting and preserving his physical constitution rather than of wearing it out. His was an old man's body all right, towards the end; you couldn't look at the broken-down feet and bony shins, the knobby knees and swollen knuckles, the peering eyes and withered skin and think otherwise. But despite these, and the predatory arthritis that progressively tightened its talons in him as he aged, so that you got used to hearing his conversation interrupted by the passionate *non sequitur* of an expletive, and knew without having to inquire that he was cursing the enemy within – despite all these, it was a vigorous old man's body. In the days after his wife's death, that body grew suddenly enfeebled, so that he had to be helped in and out of bed and in and out of chairs by daughter or neighbour or the old crone; yet it wasn't two weeks before he drove them away, testily demanding to be left in peace and not 'put upon all the time by fools', and you knew that old Wilfred, or rather, something in old Wilfred, had decided not to follow his wife there and then, wherever it was she had gone, but to stick around a while longer, and take the bleak air of solitude, and maybe put to it a question or two. What those questions were I have no idea, far less what answers, if any, they might have elicited. But increasingly in his last year old Wilfred seemed to me – it was probably why, in retrospect, I went on dropping in on him – enigmatic, secretive, and somehow knowledgeable; and I have the irrational certitude that, in the end, old Wilfred died because he chose to die and not to hang around any longer in the familiar, sunstruck valley of our days.

No – old Wilfred died when he was ready, not before. And not after, either. And who will deny the self-possession of a life that times its exit with such circumspection?

I first met Wilfred Douglas in the late 'sixties. I met him courtesy his granddaughter, a staggering, brown-skinned beauty of twenty who shall be nameless, even though she later married a thick-ankled French Canadian and disappeared with him into the icicled North (where, if there is any justice in this world, she is today occupying the prime of her life with bringing him his after-dinner newspaper and slippers and helping him to find his pipe, amid moaning pines, and bitter winter, and wolves with eyes of coal). Old Wilfred had recently retired from his job as a senior civil servant and was filling his unaccustomed leisure time with pretending to grow things, and turning into a distinctly dirty old man. Small, tenuous and prematurely-withered citrus shoots appeared in his garden, each gratuitously girdled by a little teak paling fence; and Wilfred's winks in my direction, whenever his luscious granddaughter dropped in on him with me in tow, seemed discomfortingly leering to a young man.

'I won't ask you,' he said to me once in her presence, 'what your intentions are; you'd only lie' (wink). 'Well, I'd do the same in your place' (wink, wink). And, taking hold of his granddaughter's waist (bare midriffs were 'in' in those days) he kneaded her there in such un-grandfatherly fashion that the girl, only half in laughter, turned her head and wailed: 'Granneeee! Please come an' talk to Grandpa!'

I remember him taking me outside to show me with pride the little blight-stricken citrus. 'People think when you retire,' he said, 'life starts closing down.' (I remember feeling a dim, second-hand dread at the image of life *closing down*.) 'Well, they couldn't be more wrong. See? I've only just planted these. In five years the whole back of the house will be in shade.'

This wasn't exactly a logical speech – not to my young mind, anyway. I thought sagely – for all young men are sage – that Phyllis' grandfather was probably on the defensive about growing old, having retired and all that; and how embarrassing it was of him to be making now this little futile gesture of rebirth. I said dubiously: 'They look a little blight' to me.' But at that he laughed harshly. 'You don't know the strength of a lime tree, young man,' he said; and he turned away.

Another time – it was a Saturday night, and we had gone there, Phyllis and I, in the hope of being offered dinner before heading off to a big fête at Perseverance – we arrived to find him alone – Phyllis' step-grandmother (who, it should be remembered, had only just turned fifty, while old Wilfred was already pushing seventy) having taken herself off to some civic function – and in an obviously foul mood. He hardly grunted at us in greeting; but while Phyllis, availing herself of her genetic prerogative, sailed blithely in through the house and into the kitchen, there to coax, bully, and make a great show of helping the middle-aged crone into putting together a dinner for two from leftovers in the fridge, I found myself stuck on the verandah with Wilfred.

I cannot remember what we talked about – I cannot think we talked very much – but whatever it was, it must have made him angrier, for he abruptly terminated the conversation, saying: 'Anyway! Clearly none of this can be of any interest to a young sweetman with other things on his mind. Well, as you know, Mrs Douglas is out, and the old fool in the kitchen is deaf, blind and half-dead already, and as for myself, I can guarantee, for a small consideration of course, not to move from this verandah for the next hour or so. Even so! If you and my granddaughter decide to make use of the spare room for whatever reason, please have the good manners to lock the door.'

As the reader can imagine, this was so unexpected, preposterous – and *uncalled for*, I thought indignantly – that I actually stood up with a jerk, saying stiffly that I'd better go and see how Phyllis was getting on with dinner. But he only grinned sulkily; and when, later, I told Phyllis about it, she perplexed me by turning all moist and hurt on his behalf and asking me – not without dislike, it seemed to me – if I had ever thought what it must be like for an old man, married to a much younger woman.

I remember being slightly startled by that phrase, 'an old man', for till then I had seen him as someone growing old, which was not at all the same thing. But that was how I thought of him after that, as an old man; and the image overlaid and distanced him, in my mind.

Anyway.

Phyllis and I broke up. Phyllis broke up with me – or, to be more precise, behaved in such a tantrum-ridden way as to make it impossible for me not to break up with *her*, whereupon she played out, superbly, the part of the wronged party, you know women – and I stopped having any reason to drop in on Mr

Douglas. After that, for some weeks, I half-heartedly played the field (mourning awhile the loss of such perfection of feature and figure, and such imperious certitude over just about everything) and then I left and returned to university in Jamaica; heard, next, that Phyllis had married her neckless wonder from Quebec; and like that, bit by bit, I lost touch with the Douglases.

For the next fifteen years or so, in between spells in Jamaica, Jamaica again, England, and then Jamaica again, I lived in Trinidad on and off, but seldom thought of the Douglases, and never looked them up. A few years ago, hearing from a mutual acquaintance that Phyllis was back in Trinidad on vacation (no doubt with her lobotomised lumberjack in tow) I swung into the Valley on an obscure impulse, meaning to do no more (in the first instance!) than to discover whether they, the Douglases Senior, were still alive and still living where they had been. I actually drove slowly down the street where their house was, and caught a glimpse of a majestic lime tree in the back garden; but there was no one in evidence from the road, and I discovered I lacked the nerve to park the car and just walk in on them, after all those years. 'Let sleeping dogs lie,' I told myself sagely (a different, sadder sagacity) and I turned the car around and drove back out to the Main Road and dropped in on a current flesh-and-blood acquaintance instead.

Well, so it goes, you know?

After that more years passed, and Phyllis, I heard, had come and gone away again, when a friend gave me the address of a friend who, he said, could scrounge up a part I needed for my boat – and it was the house dead opposite the Douglases, down in the Valley.

There was no one at the boat-part owner's place. A note on the gate instructed tersely: 'Jennifer! Call Brian at Maxine this pm.!' It sounded pretty exciting, whatever it was. I turned away, with that depressed and pointless feeling we all get when it turns out we have journeyed in vain – and met the gaze of an ancient hag who stood motionless, peering at me from the pavement across the road. With withered fingers, she beckoned: come here.

I looked left and right, but there was no one else she could be addressing; so I crossed the road and stood before her enquiringly.

She looked me up and down distemperedly. 'You get big,' she said. And with that she turned away and, ignoring me, began emptying a small dustbin into a larger one that stood in its own corral against the wall, scrabbling at the reluctant contents of the former with a small stick she had evidently brought with her for that purpose.

I said, 'Christophene?' incredulity at this unannounced irruption of the past lifting the last syllable into a question. Not looking up, as though speaking to herself: 'Yeh, Christophene,' the crone said.

Show me the man who does not delight in the return of any loose end or scrap of his lost life, and I will show you a catamite of stunned adolescence, or a walking ghost. In happy inanity, I said again: 'Christophene! Well-well. After all these years! You mean, you still going strong? How the Douglases, they still around?' Meaning 'alive', but not wanting to say it.

The white-pepper head peeping out from the ancient head-tie did not turn. Peering rheum-eyed into the smaller dustbin, turning it suspiciously this way and that (as if, I thought, it were a putative gem, and she a sceptical jeweller), Christophene said crossly: 'De madam dead. De mister inside. Jes' de udder day he call you' name.'

This was too good to be true. 'Yeah? How come?' I said smiling.

The old crone straightened and looked me up and down with contempt. Then: 'As if you put out sumting in de paper get he vex,' she said airily. And she turned and teetered away up the drive, and climbed with difficulty, one at a time, the steps leading up to the verandah and, depositing there the now empty dustbin, progressed on into the house, leaving the front door open. I was still standing by the gate, undecided, when an old man in slippers, pyjamas and a dressing gown emerged from the dark oblong of the door and stood on the verandah frowning around him in the glare, and it was old Wilfred.

The intervening years – how many of them, fifteen, twenty? – had further darkened his skin and whitened his head. They had reddened his eyes and shrunk a frame that had once been substantial to ascetic medium height, and his gait had dragged slightly as he came out. But even so he looked okay, I thought;

looked a lot better, I must confess, than I thought he would, at his age. He caught sight of me as I advanced up the drive, put his hands in his gown pockets, and waited. I had got to the top of the steps and was already extending my hand before he spoke. Then he said: 'Nice to see you. Come in, come in. Look where the bitch left the dustbin. CHRISTOPHENE!' And, ignoring my hand (perhaps he didn't see it), he turned away and lowered himself with some difficulty into a morris chair. 'Siddown, siddown,' he muttered.

I said: 'Hey, it's been a long time, Mr Douglas!'

'Wilfred. You not a little boy anymore, you know. How old are you – forty, forty-five?'

I told him.

'Married?'

'Not anymore.'

'Children?'

'Two.'

'Boys, girls?'

'Two girls.'

'How old?'

It has never ceased to amaze me: the curiosity of the aged, and the peremptory, staccato, efficient way they go about eliciting from you the information they want. As though, aware of the clock running against them, they've decided: no more beating around the bush. I said:

'Eleven and twelve. I think. Or twelve and thirteen.'

Old Wilfred looked amused. 'Something like that, anyway,' he concluded. Then: 'Names?'

'Mariel and Saffrey,' I told him.

'Marian and what?'

'Mariel. And Saffrey. Like in saffron rice.'

'Unusual names.' Old Wilfred considered this for a moment. Then he said: 'Still! Kind of you to visit an old man. What'll you have to drink? CHRISTOPHENE!'

Here the old crone appeared, and one of the terrific quarrels I told about earlier ensued between them.

'And take the blasted dustbin with you!' old Wilfred shouted at her in parting. 'One day you'll forget yourself on the step and the cat will have you for dinner!' To me, he went on in a furious lowered voice: 'And then maybe I'll have a little peace around here for a change.' His eyes didn't twinkle as he said it.

After she'd gone in, I said conversationally: 'So how are you? I hear you took issue with something I wrote recently.'

Old Wilfred looked startled. 'How in the name of the Holy Ghost did you hear that?'

'Christophene.'

'That woman! One day, so help me... Yes, there was something, now you mention it. What was it? What the hell was it? Memory's a wreck... something about... a girl. Ah, yes. Jenny. You had no business walking away from Jenny; let me down.'

Don't ask me why, but I am always startled when people identify me too absolutely with the Wayne Brown who writes these columns. Complimented or cursed, my reflexive response (the others come later) is sheepish disownment – as though that other one, the columnist, might be my cousin, my brother, even my twin, but in the last analysis, definitely not me. Now, though, there was the countering pleasure of discovering that, unknown to me, old Wilfred had been keeping grim track of the meanderings of that other one's mind; and, fairly basking in his reflected glow, I laughed and said defensively:

'I was just a kid. And I had a car.'

'All the more reason,' old Wilfred said. 'You should have cleaved to Jenny.'

'Cleaved?' I said in mock horror.

Old Wilfred grinned. 'Cleaved,' he said self-satisfiedly.

'I see you're still a dirty old man,' I told him.

'And thank God for that,' old Wilfred said.

Rum and lime juice without bitters isn't the greatest drink in the world, but it is, indubitably, a drink. Sipping mine (which the old crone had contrived to deposit on the glass-topped side table without looking at either of us nor saying a word, until from the doorway through which she was retreating again there came an audible *steups*), I said, 'So. What have you been doing with yourself?'

He glanced at me sharply, and looked away. 'What have I been doing with myself,' he repeated, enunciating each word like a small potion of bitterness. 'A little reading. A little thinking. A lot of sitting around. What are old people supposed to do with themselves? Since Janice passed away...'

I said: 'I heard. How long ago was that?'

'Couple months. Nine weeks, to be precise.'

I was startled. 'I'm sorry,' I said. 'I didn't know it was so recent, I thought... Anyway. I'm really sorry. That must have been a hell of a blow.'

He nodded pensively. 'She was sixty-eight. It's the irony of things.' He glanced up. 'There was very little suffering.'

Here the old crone re-emerged and, ignoring us, began dusting the verandah balustrade six feet away – or rather, flicking at it with a cloth in a way that could only have aroused the sleeping dust and given it a free ride to other nearby surfaces. 'Christophene, stop that,' old Wilfred said. But he sounded tired, and she ignored him, until my host roused himself and bellowed at her – whereupon the crone spun around and babbled at him, a furious tirade the gist of which was that nasty people might not mind living in a nasty house, but she, Christophene, had her reputation to think of, and what would Mistress Marilyn (old Wilfred's middle-aged married daughter) say if she came and found the place like that, and who would she blame, not old Wilfred, oh no!

And suddenly I felt so sorry for him, old Wilfred, with his wife of forty years gone, and finding himself now, at eighty-seven, in this lonely death-struggle with the crone. But the latter's mention of his daughter had put me in mind, in turn, of *her* daughter, old Wilfred's granddaughter; and, to cover up the confusion of the first emotion, I asked him (after Christophene, calling all heaven as her witness, and all hell down upon his head, had nonetheless acquiesced in being driven back from the verandah):

'By the way, what news of Phyllis? Still happily married to the Canadian?'

Old Wilfred's pupils grew tiny. 'Still married. More than that it would be intemperate of me to say. She was here last year, you know.' And he glanced at me – more than a little archly, I thought.

Intemperate myself, I said: 'I don't suppose she ever mentions me...?'

'You don't-suppose right. Although I saw her reading your

column once. I think Marilyn sends them to her from time to time...'

Who can describe the silence that now descended upon the verandah, converging from two quite different directions upon the image of a long-gone girl? And what an odd trio we were, I thought: the widowed grandfather, by no means going gentle into that dark night, the ex-suitor of twenty years earlier, now striding morosely towards middle-age himself, while between these, at the apex of their thought, there danced the image of a brown-skinned girl, in short-shorts and a T-shirt and flapping sandals, and a tiara, yes, a tiara, forever lithe and lovely, forever twenty-one, imperious Phyllis, a coral bracelet on her wrist...

Old Wilfred said: 'She never understood these modern marriages. It upset her how they were always going wrong. I told her it was none of our business: another world. What do you think?'

It took me a while to realise he was referring, not to his granddaughter, but to his wife of half-a-lifetime; and then it took me a while longer to focus on his question. Then I said: 'Beats me, Wilfred. They say men and women are redefining their roles.'

'Is that what they say. And what do you say? I read your column from time to time, when the eyes permit; I know you think about these things.'

It was nearly noon, and the heat was getting oppressive, and the rum was beginning to make me feel odd. It occurred to me that old Wilfred must be pulling my leg; that with a forty-year marriage behind him he must know more about the subject of domestic contentment and strife than I, and the likes of me, ever would. Still – here he was, an old man, newly widowed, in pyjamas and dressing gown, waiting. I concentrated with an effort. Then I said: 'I think maybe we've come too clear of the clay.'

It was the first time I'd thought of it like that.

Old Wilfred was still waiting, so I went on and told him the story of Derek and his sculpture. Derek was a young sculptor I'd known in Jamaica in the late 'sixties. He came from the West Kingston slums and was illiterate, and his work was only just above that standard of sculpture that has done well for itself if it makes it to the craft markets of the tourist belt, thence to wind up on the cluttered sideboard of some effusive Minnesotan matron.

Then, one day, out of the blue, Derek did this sculpture in clay. It depicted an infernal lake or primordial sludge with human figures, male and female, trapped in it. Some lay face down in the undifferentiated muck; others were struggling to stay waist-high in it. Their postures suggested, variously, despair, lamentation, determination, struggle and hope; and in the centre of the sculpture, towering about the rest in a kind of backward arch, was the male figure of one who had heaved himself free to the ankles and was now preparing, so it seemed, for the one last herculean effort that would take him clear of the clay forever. And yet – and this was the staggering thing – neither victory nor elation showed in his features, but horrible anguish, inhuman suffering. Like a lightning rod bent and twisted by the bolts of God's wrath, he hung there, unable for the moment to rise any further, refusing to fall back, braced upon his solitary strength alone, levering upward through the corded muscles of calves, thighs, back...

It was a sculpture so unprepared by anything else Derek had ever done, that standing before it one felt oneself in the presence of an authentic miracle. And this intimation of miracle hardened when, the following week, Derek repaired to the university hospital for an antibiotic shot for some minor infection, and, not knowing he was allergic to penicillin (and no one asking), fell dead on the spot. He was nineteen.

'I've often thought since,' I told old Wilfred, 'that with his death already in him, Derek knew certain things. And that sculpture was one of them.'

Old Wilfred thought about this in silence for a while. Then he said: 'It's obvious from your columns, some of them, that you, as you put it, know certain things. Does that mean your death is in you?'

'I suppose it is,' I said. 'I suppose it's in all of us, to some extent.'

'It wasn't in me at your age,' old Wilfred said tartly. 'At your age life was just getting good.' And he drifted off into thought again. Presently he said: 'If I follow you, you're saying we may be getting too advanced for our own good. Not advanced, but... what's the word...'

'Evolved?'

'Evolved. Too evolved. Is that what you're saying?'

'I don't know,' I said. 'It's just a thought. I mean, you say "for our own good", but good may not be the same as happiness. I mean, it might be exactly the opposite.'

Old Wilfred looked arch. 'How can you talk like that? I thought happiness was the be-all and end-all of your generation?'

'It is. It is! Which is what makes it all very funny,' I said.

'It certainly does,' old Wilfred said. Then, rousing himself: 'What time is it? That fool should be bringing my pills. I suppose you know: those cigarettes are going to kill you.'

Now, I have to say I am pretty fed up of the new evangelists, the long-lifers with their anti-smoking zeal. I do not share their illusion of living forever, intend to be ill, not well, when I die; and as for the timing of the latter, I certainly have no desire to hang around past the stage where I can still pick up myself on a Sunday morning and take the *Lisa* out for a sail. Old age is not my Mecca, and in any case, writing is not a pensionable job. Gotta get outta here before the roof caves in, or is snatched away by some irate creditor of a landlord. So I merely countered old Wilfred (with no especial kindness, regarding his age) by saying brusquely: 'Well, that's me. And what's going to kill you?'

Old Wilfred looked thoroughly startled. He actually flinched away; and then his pupils grew tiny and shiftless, and he grinned. 'I see. Very good. Too-shay. Well, so long as you know.'

Here the crone reappeared with a glass of water and old Wilfred's pills. Neither spoke. Expressionlessly, she held them out to him. He took them, obedient as a child. The crone glared at me, and retired. Old Wilfred was saying crossly, '…a fortune in pills.'

It was time to go. I got up. Old Wilfred struggled with the morris chair, said, 'Blast!' and sat back down again. I offered my hand, but he slapped it away, and by dint of much struggling and swearing, eventually made it to his feet and stood, panting a little.

'Nice of you to come,' he said again, a little curtly, drawing his dressing gown around him. 'Keep on writing. And don't think too much about these things, you're still a young man. My God, if I was your age!'

'Well, take care of yourself,' I told him. 'Say hi to Phyllis, if you ever write her. And don't let old Christophene take you alive!'

Old Wilfred grunted threateningly. 'That'll be the day,' he said. And, shaking my hand, he retired without waiting for me to leave, turning at the door to sketch a parting wave that was more in the nature of a salute.

The door closed behind him.

Left alone, I went down the steps and along the drive, and crossed the road, and got into my car – all in a suburban silence. The note pinned to the boat-owner's gate was still urging Jennifer to 'call Brian at Maxine!' It was twenty to one and the car seat was scalding. Beyond the side of old Wilfred's house, between it and the garage, the lime tree stood, perfectly motionless.

From the road, the house looked empty.

If old Wilfred had petitioned me to come again, if in old age his loneliness had been abject, I don't think I would have returned to the old 'fifties house with its two warring geriatrics down in the Valley. The physical incapacities of old age are more easily borne – at least by me – than the teary witness of those whom life has broken; and I think I would have shied away from his need, had he expressed it, as from an intimation of some ultimate defeat waiting for us all down the soon-to-turn-drear road ahead. But old Wilfred had petitioned nothing of me. Rather, he had accepted my departure, that day, as unquestioningly as he had accepted my sudden reappearance, after all those years; and the dignity of his solitude, which left me free, enamoured him strangely to me, and made of his life a dim portent, by no means unpleasant, in my mind.

It was not that I saw in him proof that the battle could be won; for in that last unequal struggle, Death always wins. Nor had I had from old Wilfred any omen or sign that he had fallen secretly to brooding on that heavenly bliss the contemplation of which, some say, eases our transition from this enchanted world of sights and sounds into the stone blind, silently howling void beyond. No: to me, the happiness that resided in the thought of old Wilfred had less to do with his future than, selfishly, with my own. It concerned life, not death.

I saw in old Wilfred proof that character can prevail, though Time and the world hurl their increasing barbs at it. I saw that a broken-down body, 'a tattered coat upon a stick', could yet be a fit tabernacle for Mind; that Mind, its memory faltering, and words fleeing like deserters the marshalling of its thought, could yet retain its impersonality; and that the heart could endure the worst of horrors, the passing of its lifelong mate, and even the prospect of its own extinction – and be itself. I do not know if it is true that we are immortal, that Eternity is but a synonym for Time's cessation (the stopped clock ticking silently on forever, though its face is frozen) but I know that what I cherished in old Wilfred were not the mortal verities of pain and love, but something stonier, implacable, and unaging.

All this is hindsight, and perhaps it is inflated by the needs of one whose own future, as I write this, will assuredly be shorter than his past. But I think of old Wilfred cursing the infirmity that held him down in his chair even while he was struggling to rise, and I am sure that, in his own mind, old Wilfred knew himself to be something apart from his infirmity – as distinct from it as from the helping hand I offered him, and which he irritably slapped away. I felt for him the fondness of an old friend, but also the awe of a pilgrim for his guide. In his company I was aware of engaging in a sidelong listening (for what, I cannot tell) as though possessed of a third, incorporeal ear. And all of it was connected, obscurely, to his long-gone granddaughter, headstrong Phyllis, petulant and radiant and forever twenty-one, her image blurring after all these years to a presence, and beyond that to a mood, to the texture of a mood – and that texture in turn was like an intimation, a soft suffusing of the darkness ahead, a mystifying promise, an untellable surprise.

All this, I say, is hindsight. The dead have a quality that enjoins, even as it inures, us to them. They are our intimates in ways the living can never be. And certainly I was not thinking about old Wilfred (or the girlish shadow that abided, just out of reach, it seemed, in the dark of the house behind his back) with anything like the intensity the above paragraphs might suggest when I dropped in on him again, one windy afternoon a few weeks later.

He greeted me with the same unsurprise. Dressed in trousers, a pale blue and yellow T-shirt with a collar, and the same pair of bedroom slippers, old Wilfred led me through the house ('This heat is murderous') and out onto the back patio, which was in shade. There, to the pleasant distracted soughing of the lime trees, we sat and talked for a while. Old Wilfred, I remember, wanted to know what, in my view, was going on with the government, and I told him. But even as I spoke, I could see that my brief and bitter peroration was not impressing itself on his mind.

'I shouldn't have asked you that,' he said when I'd finished. 'I realise you don't like politicians; probably never will. Still. Politics is important.'

I have to tell you: disputing that premise has become something of a *cause célèbre* with me in recent months. I rehashed my main arguments for old Wilfred's adjudication, but his response was again tangential. He looked at me grimly for a few moments after I'd finished, and then he looked away. 'At any rate,' he said. 'It's up to you people now. Thank God, I'm out of it.'

I considered him. 'You mean that?'

Old Wilfred looked startled. 'Of course I mean it,' he snapped. 'You should have heard yourself!' Then, subsiding, he went on pensively: 'My generation did its bit. We were limited by who we were, what we came from. Just as your generation is, for that matter. Though it would surprise me to hear you acknowledge that. Well. No matter. These things are… I've lost the word…' And he trailed off into an abstracted silence.

I said: 'You look preoccupied.'

I was thinking the old crone Christophene had not yet put in an appearance, and wondering whether old Wilfred's distracted air might be due to his listening subconsciously for a clue to her whereabouts. But he mistook my thought and replied edgily: 'Preoccupied? I'm always preoccupied. What do you think: old people sit around all day doing nothing, with their minds blank?'

It was as close as I'd heard him come to self-pity, and momentarily it hardened me against him. 'I don't know,' I said brutally. 'I've never been old.'

'Try to remember that,' old Wilfred said.

I looked away. The lime trees were fine and resonant in the afternoon light and the breeze. Changing the subject, I said: 'I remember when you'd just planted those. They looked so blighted and frail at the time I didn't think they'd make it.'

Old Wilfred looked disoriented. 'What are you talking about?' he said irritably. 'Oh, those. Yes. Well. Lime trees are hardy things.' And he lapsed into thought again.

Presently: 'How's Christophene?' I said.

Old Wilfred glanced up, without much interest. 'The same,' he muttered. 'Always the same.' Then, rousing himself: 'By the way. Forgive my manners. What'll you have to drink?'

Truth is, I was thirsty, but a quick calculation told me that if I accepted his offer he might either bellow for Christophene (in which case an unseasonal uproar might ensue) or, failing that, have to struggle to get it himself; so I demurred.

This was a mistake. Old Wilfred read my mind as clearly as if I'd spoken it. 'So you say, then,' he said shortly. 'Mind if I have one myself?' And, struggling to his feet, he went painfully off into the house, returning in due course with a small oval tray of polished wood on which not one but two glasses clattered and shook. 'In case you change your mind,' he said drily, not looking at me, but with a slight rotation of the tray presenting what looked like a rum-and-water, and was. I took it, wry with defeat – then held my breath and watched (pretending not to) while old Wilfred achieved the considerable feat of getting the tray with its rattling glass down onto the table, and himself back into his chair, without spilling or breaking anything. 'Sorry about the coke,' he said. 'Marilyn brought a whole case the other day but it appears they're finished.' He glanced around, then resumed: 'You know what that woman does? Every time I go to bed – I have a nap in the afternoon, you know – she sits by herself in the kitchen and drinks the cokes. One coke after another – my God! What do you make of that?'

'Who, Marilyn?' I said, disbelievingly. It seemed an odd obsession on the part of his middle-aged married daughter.

'Marilyn! No-o-o!' exclaimed old Wilfred. 'Christophene, you fool! The old witch! Marilyn? Why on earth would Marilyn do such a thing? Christophene!'

'Maybe she's a coke addict,' I said.

'Who, Christophene? Nonsense!' Old Wilfred said. Then: 'Oh! I see what you mean. Yes. Very funny. Still!' – shaking his head – 'Seems a peculiar business to me. Sitting there, all by herself, drinking coke after coke after coke. I don't know... some sort of vitamin deficiency, wouldn't you say?'

'I suppose so,' I said. I didn't really want to think about it. It should have been funny, and so at first I had tried to construe it, with my lame pun. But for some reason the image of the old crone sitting by herself in the kitchen, old Wilfred asleep, methodically killing the cokes, struck me with a prescience of something akin to terror.

'Modern medicine,' said old Wilfred, with emphasis: 'Modern medicine could probably set her right in two-twos. It's extraordinary, the things they can do nowadays.'

I felt the afternoon trickling away into purposelessness. For reasons known only to himself, old Wilfred had locked me out from the world of his thought, this time around. Perhaps he was still angry at my condescension in having declined his offer of a drink. Or perhaps the old crone's absence, still unexplained, had had an unsettling effect upon him. Whatever it was, I regretted coming. I prepared to leave.

At the last moment he relented, saying, not without kindness: 'You must bear with an old man. I know, it's not easy.'

I took this as an apology and demurred in turn...

Five or six weeks later, I dropped in on old Wilfred again. It was nine, nine-thirty in the morning, but the crone appeared in the doorway to say stonily that old Wilfred was 'restin' ('Whuh yuh waan do?') and after hanging around on the verandah for a while, reading the *Express*, I got up and left.

After that, I became preoccupied with getting ready for my trip: I was going to the US, to a convocation of writers, for a few months. And it was at the eleventh hour that, almost as a kind of superstition, I made time to pass in at old Wilfred's before I left. Once again:

'He restin',' the crone said. 'Wait...' She warded me off with an upheld palm, and faded back into the house; from which presently she re-emerged clutching a small white envelope in both hands. 'Here. He say give you it if you come again an' he restin'.'

I took the envelope and bade Christophene goodbye. I put it

in my briefcase and forgot it there (I had a million things to do) and it was only weeks later and three thousand miles away that I rediscovered it. There, behind the pane of my eighth-floor apartment over the Iowa River with corn-haired coeds lounging on the banks, I opened old Wilfred's envelope and read:

'Apropos of our conversation – Chappie remarks: "The major religions available to industrial culture are all primarily built on the constraints of agriculture and pastoralism and the environment affecting it. Their symbols and rituals have, therefore, developed a major disconformity from the interaction forms of which they are constituted, supplemented by the strong emphasis, in each of them, on abstention, withdrawal – the individual's search for his religion's variant on perfection as the preferred interaction pattern. In addition, the composition of the contexts (agricultural and pastoral) from which the symbols have been filtered out are structured, particularly within Christianity, on the family as an institution, and the church as its communal expression. Yet the family, with all its emphasis on the control of sex and the procreation of children, is no longer the primary structural building block of society."'

This was the quotation; and beneath it was written, in the same spidery hand: 'Heavy stuff. But what do you think? Cheers! Wilfred.'

I didn't know what to think. To tell the truth, I didn't want to think. I put old Wilfred's quotation back into my briefcase and forgot about it, and like that it travelled with me all over the eastern United States, and thence to London, and thence back home to Trinidad – where for some weeks I was caught up in the activity of moving house and settling back, in pleasanter surroundings, to old routines. And it was only in February of this year, 'organising' my study (a euphemism for the tenuous sandspit of order I maintain on my desk, surrounded by the wild wastes of Chaos on the shelves) that I came upon it again, and one day soon after, on a whim, detoured into the Valley to see if old Wilfred was still alive.

Twenty past five. The afternoon light thickening to gold. The verandah of old Wilfred's house sunstruck, deserted, the light gilding the empty morris chairs and the bare white wall. The front door opening to my calling, a withered hand on the knob. The black oblong of the interior beyond her shrunken frame, a panel of yellow light at her feet. 'He in de garden,' the crone said.

She said it crossly, as if remarking a delinquency – as if old Wilfred were out there in the altogether, a withered satyr, sampling some forbidden fruit.

I was in a good mood. I said: 'Christophene! How come I've never seen you smile?'

I might as well have blasphemed horribly. The old crone shrank away, lifting her shoulders and drawing inward her flabby chest while a paroxysm of distaste contorted her averted face.

I laughed and walked in and through the house, leaving her so, and out on to the back patio. And there was no Wilfred: the garden looked deserted.

Then I caught sight of him. All but camouflaged by a croton, he was peering myopically up into the evening sky, as though patiently trying to decipher some message invisibly inscribed there. I followed his gaze but saw nothing: only the sky, gone high up and abstracted and pale, the air thinning out in between sky and earth: the pristine, still pallor of evening. I called, 'Wilfred, how you doing?' and started towards him.

I don't think he noticed me until I fumbled for his hand, and then he turned and looked at me without recognition. 'It's not there,' he muttered vaguely, shaking his head. His hand in mine was limp and cool.

The slight quiver now at his mouth, the shrunken cheeks and protuberant eyes with the black half-moons below them, the wrinkled parchment folds of his neck: he had aged fast in the seven months since last I'd seen him. Leaning on a walking stick, he was dressed in dark trousers and a white vest, and a black jacket that might once have fit but was now several sizes too big for him. I saw with surprise that he was barefooted: the splayed feet, paler than the rest of him, were gaunt and knobby in the dusty grass.

'I like your outfit,' I told him. 'What's the jacket for?'

'This?' He peered down at it. 'It's an old jacket,' he said vaguely.

'Anyway. How you doing?' I said again.

Old Wilfred looked at me blankly. Then, recognition startled him. 'Yes, yes, yes,' he said. 'Well, well. Kind of you to visit an old man.' Remembering, he looked around him in some discomposure, then drew himself up slightly and said with dignity: 'You must forgive me. I talk to myself sometimes.'

'Yeah? So do I,' I told him. 'More and more.'

Leaning on his stick, he considered me with wan amusement. 'That way we can at least be sure of a hearing.'

'And of not being misunderstood,' I added.

'Well, I'm not sure about that,' old Wilfred said. Then he added: 'My late wife Janice… did you know her at all?'

'Course I did,' I told him. 'You're forgetting, Phyllis and I used to come here all the time.'

'Phyllis?'

'Your granddaughter.'

'Oh, yes. Marilyn's second girl. She wasn't Janice's daughter, you know' – he meant granddaughter – 'She was mine. Last I heard she was up in… Calgary, I think. Lose track of the young these days if you don't keep up.'

I said: 'Wilfred, you never hear from her anymore?'

'Who, Janice? Janice is dead, didn't you know? Died a year ago this month. Cancer.'

'I meant Phyllis.'

'Do I ever hear from Phyllis? No. But that's quite okay, quite okay. Marilyn gives me the news from time to time.'

'And how is she – Phyllis, I mean.'

'God knows,' old Wilfred said. 'Now, you take this spot.' And he jerked his stick to two points of the compass over the grass at our feet. 'This was her favourite spot. She used to bring a chair out here and sit and read. Right here, with the croton at her back.'

I understood that he was talking about his late wife again. I said lamely, 'Yes. Well, it's a nice spot. This time of day the lime tree gives it shade.'

Old Wilfred didn't hear. He was gazing around him somewhat dismayedly at the grass at our feet, as if searching it for some long lost clue or trinket – perhaps an earring of his beloved's.

'Anyway,' he muttered finally. 'That's that, then.' And he squared his shoulders slightly and looked at me. 'Now we must go in. No point hanging around out here any longer; be dark soon.'

32

I offered my hand but he ignored it. Leaning heavily on his stick, he limped with difficulty back to the patio. There he turned himself around, felt behind him for the arms of the chair, found them, and, letting go of the stick (which fell with a clatter onto the terrazzo floor) lowered himself by painful degrees until he was sitting. It broke my heart, how old old Wilfred had got, in the short seven months I'd been away.

'Now, then,' he said. 'First things first. Call that woman.'

I didn't dare shout for Christophene. I went inside, and, as apologetically as I could, told the crone that Mr Douglas was asking for her. The old crone gave me a look that said in effect that my irruption into her solitude was the last straw; that by itself it had decided for her many important things; that now her mind was clear: someone must die. But she followed me quiescently enough back to the patio.

'What'll it be?' old Wilfred said to me.

I looked meekly at the crone. 'Rum and coke?'

'It ent have…' the crone began, but old Wilfred interrupted her.

'Yes, yes,' he said, tiredly and irritably. 'Now bring the man his rum and coke. Go on!'

The crone gaped at old Wilfred, thunderstruck. Then she let fly an incoherent cataract of abuse at him. I gathered that old Wilfred was harden, stupid, deaf, nasty, and evil, and talked to her as if she, Christophene, was a mangy dog in the yard, although it was he, not she, who was the dog, yes, and Lord of the flies, as the whole world would find out on Judgement Day – when she, Christophene, was going to laugh until she dropped, and show him no mercy: let him not even bother to ask. God was good, but He wasn't stupid. He wasn't a mangy dog like old Wilfred.

The really strange part of all this was old Wilfred's response. Through it all, old Wilfred never once glanced up at the crone – or at me, for that matter. Sitting in his chair, bare feet flat on the floor, one arm along each of the chair's arms like some bored and sullen pharaoh, old Wilfred stared expressionlessly out to where the shadows, guerilla vanguard of night, were now laying siege to the topmost branches of the lime trees. Around him might have been, not this crazed creature, but the somnolent sands of old

Arabia; through his mind might have moved, not this crescendo of spat spite and rage, but a silence as old as the sea's. So old Wilfred sat the while, unmoving and expressionless, while in the figure of the crone all hell beat about his white and skull-like head. And it was not until Christophene, her shrieked dissertation cut off at last by a gasping, racking cough – it was not until she had staggered away from us and back into the house that old Wilfred stirred, and looked around.

Then he said (and I shall never forget the urchin way he said it): 'Eric Williams was right, you know. Freedom is a difficult thing.'

I stared at him with awe. I wanted to crack up laughing, to jump up and shake his hand; I wanted to say, 'Hey Wilfred, let's cut this crap, go down the road and fire one down at Yachting.' Instead I heard myself say suddenly: 'Wilfred, tell me something. You not scared?'

'Of Christophene?'

'Of dying.'

Old Wilfred held my gaze grimly for a few moments. Then he looked away again. In the garden, nothing was stirring. The lime trees were now all in shade. Old Wilfred said nothing.

Trying too late to make amends for my indiscretion, I pressed on: 'I mean, you sit around these days, just thinking. What do you think?'

Old Wilfred inclined his head and, elbow on the chair's arm, applied two fingers gently to his temple. It was a strangely delicate gesture.

Here the old crone came out with my rum and coke. She neither spoke nor glared (nor, for that matter, did old Wilfred) but put the drink down on the table and retired – just like that. Far as I could tell, there wasn't even a remnant of animosity in the air. It was as if nothing, nothing at all, had transpired between them a few minutes before.

I sipped my drink. The crone had either put the rum in last or concocted a different drink: half a pint of rum with a dash of coke. I sipped again and decided it was the latter. I had concluded that my second question, too, had been deemed unworthy of a response, when old Wilfred began to speak; and when he did, the words seemed to attenuate out of an invisible trickle of dots, as though only the second part of his thought were being given voice. '…pain,' old Wilfred said. 'Pain all the time. It's a nuisance, that… The other part's ironical. So many of the things worth knowing, you only know them when it's too late. And even if you'd known them before – you wouldn't have been able to make use of them. Because there are no words… you see? You wouldn't have been able to tell… anyone. So there's that part. You're left with this thing on your hands. What else… You talk about dying. Well, it's a fair question. Everybody dies; everybody wants to know… Well, I can only speak for myself. The answer is: no, I'm not.

'You must understand: men always follow in this world. You are born, and you follow your parents. Then you grow up and you follow your career. Or your wife, or your dream, or whatever. The main thing is, you follow. You see? You always follow. But then these things pass; one by one, they all pass away. And something else comes along. And you follow it.'

I said: 'It? You mean, death?'

Old Wilfred nodded. 'It's the always-following, you see. Makes it easier.'

'Where, though? Surely you must think about little else? Follow – where?'

Old Wilfred's patience was wearing thin. 'But there's no point, you see,' he said, a trifle irritably. 'I've just finished telling you: there are no words for these things.' And he sat back and stared at the floor, as if examining a new and baffling prospect.

Then he turned to me almost defiantly, and said: 'I know where I want to go, though.'

'Where?'

'Wherever Janice is now. I think that would be… appropriate. Don't you?'

I turned to say that, yes, it was a nice thought. But I never answered old Wilfred because, at that moment, the Death's-head came and sat in his face, and glared at me.

How can I describe this? The sudden occupation of old Wilfred by this… thing! Austere beyond austerity, merciless beyond all mercy, terrible beyond the reach of human terror, transforming utterly the whitened head it had in a split-second seized and possessed, the Death's-head glared at me – horribly, O horribly! – from out of old Wilfred's eyes, and in its infernal writhing, baleful and aquiline, I saw Agony beyond agony, Knowledge beyond forgiveness, terrible, inhuman Will! Of goodness or evil there was none, of fear or courage, determination or hope, lamentation or despair – nothing! Beyond these, so far beyond these, that even to think to name them was in an instant to bang and flap away like a bursten tent amid the flying inchoate debris of reality; monolithic and triumphant, terrible and... *permanent*, the Death's-head glared at me; and as old Wilfred said, there are no words, but I saw, I saw. I saw in that instant the puniness of our lives by comparison with what waited at the end to snatch them away...

I flinched away in shock and dread; I dared not look at old Wilfred. I said, because I had to say something, I said – or rather, I heard myself saying – 'I almost forgot, I thought about your quotation...'

'What quotation?' It was old Wilfred's familiar voice, drear and irritable. I chanced a glance at him. The Death's-head had flown. Old Wilfred was as before, peering rheum-eyed at me.

'The quotation from that guy,' I said, still not quite trusting my voice. 'You know: the one you gave Christophene for me. About withdrawal and intervention, and the way the world is changing...'

'Oh, that,' said old Wilfred, without much interest... 'Yes, but that was a long time ago. That was when I was still...' And he lapsed into silence. 'Anyway,' he roused himself. 'So you thought about it. What did you think?'

'I think it wasn't written for me,' I said. 'I think like you I'm past that stage, thank God. It's up to them now, as you would say.'

Old Wilfred looked positively delighted. 'Is that true? Yes! Well, well. You see? Very good. Very good! Well, well.' Old Wilfred, I saw, was smiling like a felon.

Suddenly I felt close to him, closer than I'd ever been; and, at the same time, I knew it was time to leave. I put down my drink and rose, saying, 'Hey, Wilfred, I gotta go'; and when he began obediently struggling to rise, I took him by the upper arm, ignoring his bad-tempered protest, and practically hauled him to his feet.

'Good to see you,' he said, panting a little. 'I don't read the papers anymore, but I take it you're still writing? Very good. You must write and write. Write it all out. Write till there's nothing left that you *have* to write. Then, only then, you may stop.'

It felt like an oddly formal moment. I said: 'Now listen, Wilfred, I don't think you have anything to be ashamed of, so you probably don't have anything to be afraid of either. But remember what I said. Don't let Christophene take you alive.'

Old Wilfred looked grim. 'As to that, there's no chance, my friend. That much I can promise you. As to the first – well, all I shall say is, it's a good thing you don't know me better than you do.'

I laughed and let go of his hand, and made my way through the house, leaving him standing alone on the darkening patio. As an afterthought, I called: 'You want me to turn on the light?' and heard his faint reply: 'S'okay! Not to worry!'

But for the kitchen, the house was uniformly dark. I turned and saw the silhouette of the crone, standing motionless in the kitchen door, presiding silently over my departure.

And I let myself out and got into my car and drove away from the old 'fifties house in the Valley, and never saw old Wilfred again. I did pass around, one morning a few weeks later, but that was the morning – Christophene told me – after the night he had his stroke, and his daughter Marilyn and her husband had already come with the doctor and the ambulance, and they'd taken him away to the hospital. A few days later, I read in the paper that Wilfred Douglas had died; but though I would have liked to, circumstances intervened, and I couldn't make it to his funeral.

What I did though, was, a couple nights later, I sat down and wrote a long letter to his granddaughter Phyllis in Canada, recounting things I'd remembered about old Wilfred, pretty much as I've set them down here. I even phoned and got Phyllis's address from her mother, old Wilfred's married daughter.

Then I tore it up.

MR ALCINDOR

The first time I saw Mr Alcindor he was standing at the edge of a cliff gazing at the indistinct horizon and absently swinging a dead cat by the tail.

This was on a forested peninsula a few miles out of Port Antonio, a small town on the east coast of Jamaica safely south of the tourist belt. In the mid-60s I spent a few months there; and on this afternoon, armed with an envelope and directions from my landlady, I had gone on her behalf in search of Mrs Alcindor, her ironing woman.

My landlady's directions, I discovered, had been ingenuously understated: the designated road deteriorated and soon stopped altogether, yielding to a track which curved away downhill through the bananas like a despairing gesture. On the map I found her cryptic notation: 'Walk'. I parked my car and followed the track, damp, crumbling earth, down to and along a squelchy gully. There signs of human handiwork appeared: a corrugated zinc lean-to, a terraced vegetable plot; and once a dirt-coloured goat, tethered to a tree, erupted into a thudding, neck-jerking arc as I passed. Finally the track rounded a spur and rose diagonally up a steep and convex slope; and beyond this there levitated, as I climbed, a rear view of the head, the bare shoulders and torso, and finally the clean khaki trousers and rubber boots of the man I presumed – rightly, as it turned out – to be Mrs Alcindor's husband, and he was standing at the edge of the cliff gazing at the indistinct horizon and absently swinging a dead cat by the tail.

I cupped my hands and called, but the sea wind blew back his name. So I waited till I had gained the ridge, a few feet from him, then called again. He staggered and let go of the cat, and there was a pause while we both craned to watch the creature sail limply away and down to where a milky green sea moved uneasily at the foot of the cliff.

After it had disappeared, I said, 'Mr Alcindor?'

He was a broad, flat-faced man of about fifty, with no trace of grey in his hair; deliberate of movement, with small, unpeasant-like hands. His mouth, wide and without firmness, deferred to a pair of nicotine-tinted eyes which, perfectly shaped and too widely spaced in the flat brown board of his face, gave a first impression of placid ingenuousness which their busy pupils belied. Now he withdrew his gaze from the place where the beast had disappeared and glanced at me defensively.

'De wife cat,' he said; and he breathed heavily once – as if he had successfully pronounced in one breath a long and complex sentence. When I mumbled, 'Aha,' trying to sound as if this explained everything, he looked at me vaguely. ''Im dead,' he added helpfully.

I felt obliged to peer seaward again. He, perhaps deeming it prudent to see whatever I saw, did likewise.

Straightening, I said: 'Mr Alcindor?'

This time the sound of his name startled him to attention: his face opened and his gaze unclouded.

'Dat-is-me-what-mayst-I-do-for-you-sah?'

His voice was deep, yet without resonance. I soon discovered that he had this way of bringing forth each sentence *en masse* and then breathing heavily, once, in conclusion: as though for him each essaying of speech was a separate and risky event, a raid upon an untrustworthy silence, to be undertaken decisively, hastily, and with the prime goal of effecting a complete withdrawal with all his forces intact at the end, to where an implacable alert passivity waited to receive them. Listening to him, you might be forgiven for thinking that here was a man who had lived a long time in some dangerous terrain of the heart, where some preco-cious final silence had repeatedly to be beaten back, and impo-tence shielded by vigilance. When I explained my errand, his face fell into smiles. 'Ah, dat's nice,' he crooned; and he breathed.

I followed him along the cliff, then inland across the promon-tory. For a man of deliberate movements he covered the ground with surprising efficiency, and I discovered this was because the

39

pace he set himself conceded nothing to the terrain. Precipitous or level or claustrophobically overhung, Mr Alcindor plodded on. Once he paused and said inconsequentially: 'Yes we 'ave a nice likkle place 'ere. Nat big. Jessa likkle place.' And further on he stopped again, plunged his hands into his pockets, nodded to himself and concluded gravely: 'Yes…' Though whether this was meant to refer back, for emphasis, to his earlier remark, or connoted some new awareness on his part – or simply confirmed that Mr Alcindor had located in his pocket something that ought to be there – I could not tell.

His response to my polite query concerning his children was equally enigmatic.

'Oh, seven-call-it-eight,' he suggested; and since his concluding, trenchant sigh had the effect of quarantining off each utterance from further enquiry, I never did learn the truth about the titular eighth. 'An' five gran',' he added – and for the first time looked sheepishly proud.

Presently his 'likkle place' came into view: an unpainted shingle cottage of perhaps four rooms, its lovely grey-weathered boards ill-served by the motley amalgam of outbuildings it had apparently spawned over the years: a rusty zinc latrine-like cubicle; a bamboo lean-to; three decomposing chicken-wire coops or pens (all empty) with multi-material roofs; and, inexplicably, the burnt-out shell of a large, finned American car of the '50s which had mysteriously made its way to this pathless place to die, and now lay securely strapped in the hillside not only by its own dead weight but by a riotous mob of Earth's possessive tendrils as well. Out of the oblong gape where its windshield had been, a single whimsical lily lifted white petals to the sun.

'Mudder!' bellowed Mr Alcindor as we approached, adding in falsetto: 'Oo-oo!' *Sotto voce*, he confided: "Im prab'ly out de back.'

The response of the house was startling. As though at its owner's cry a gust of wind had fled through its rooms, the nearside window banged shut, while further along the wall another window almost simultaneously opened, disclosing the upper half of a plump and dark-skinned East Indian woman, who on seeing me immediately withdrew from sight.

'Shy,' confided Mr Alcindor. 'Nat to worry. 'Im will come out

40

when 'im is ready.' Raising his voice, he bawled: 'Me a'bring a fren'a Mistress Wilkshire t'see yuh!'

The house absorbed this piece of news in silence.

At the foot of the steps Mr Alcindor suddenly looked anxious. His eyes darted about as if to check what I had seen: an inspection which evidently had the effect of reassuring the inspector, for he relaxed, and his face when he turned to me was all encouraging smiles. 'So you like de likkle place, Missa B!' he exclaimed. 'Nice place. Nat big. Nat big.'

The strength of the day had passed, and I was thinking of getting back. But in the Jamaican hills you do not decline an offer of hospitality such as Mr Alcindor now laughingly proffered, and so we sat on his little verandah and watched the sunset bloom out of the sea. Mr Alcindor, grown amazingly proprietary, and almost verbose, on his own ground, discoursed with voluptuous, head-shaking sorrow upon The Hardships of Life on the Land; and, from that, switched without pausing to the subject of his children. Two daughters, the eldest, were in England; in Manchester, I think, or Merseyside. Both had married Jamaicans there, solid citizens: a miner, and a conductor of trains. This was more than could be said for the boys. He had had no luck with the boys. The elder, 'a bright bwoy in school', had turned bad and been caught, it seems; while the younger, the bad-foot one, whom the cow had stepped on as a child, had been lured south by a temptress and was now languishing in carnal contentment in one of Kingston's sundry slums. There was some talk of another boy, I remember, Joseph or Jonathan or Chuck, who apparently had emigrated to Houston and a post in the pharmaceutical field. But Mr Alcindor saved most of his superlatives for his youngest daughter: 'A bright gyul. A pritty gyul. Oh wotta pritty gyul. But difficult? *Difficult!* Dat one now favour de mudder.'

From the depths of the house, as if on cue, Mrs Alcindor called: 'Hector?!'

Mr Alcindor shook his head reassuringly. 'Nat me,' he said softly. 'De cat.' And, leaning forward and gripping my arm, he thrust his broad face into mine and hissed: ''Im doan know about de cat!'

This was startling news. I had supposed that what I had

witnessed earlier had been a casual sea-burial; now I wondered whether I had been an unsuspecting witness to the aftermath of murder. I retrieved my arm, and was about to make certain enquiries when: 'Alcindor,' said his wife's voice directly behind me. As I turned, she added: 'Excuse me, Missa —.'

'Brown. Wayne.'

'Jess excuse mih.' She looked worriedly at her husband. 'Alcindor, you see Hector?'

'Who, me? Hector? No missus.' Turning to me, he asked accusingly: 'Missa B, you nevah see a mangy brong-an'-white cat pass 'ere?'

Grateful for his phrasing, I shook my head.

''Im nat mangy,' Mrs Alcindor said sadly, and she wandered away into the house: a plump, pretty woman for whom child-bearing had evidently been a process of softening rather than attrition.

'Den Missa B,' went on my host, drawing back and consider-ing me archly along his shoulder. 'You are nat fram Jamaica?'

'Trinidad.'

'Ah. Trinidad. Well-well. Trinidad, eh?'

And, turning, he called this information back into the house. ('Nice,' came the laconic reply, along with the first sounds and smells of something frying.)

For the next minute or so Mr Alcindor elicited various facts and figures from the yet-unwritten Life & Times of the present writer. When, in response to his last cunning question – 'But you are married, don't it?' – I soberly shook my head, Mr Alcindor breathed, and fell silent.

After a while he said conversationally: 'Mih likklest one now, a likkle daughter, 'im is 'ere. 'Im will be glad t'see yuh.'

His meaning seemed so startling that I almost betrayed myself with a laugh; but Mr Alcindor placatingly explained that his Sonia, though a 'strang gyul', would be glad for a lift back to Port Antonio – where she was, I gathered, an apprentice nurse – and would in consequence, he was sure, be prepared to leave imme-diately, rather than staying overnight as she had planned...

And there begins a different story. I gave Mrs Alcindor her envelope, and dropped Mr Alcindor's 'likklest one', the 'difficult, pretty gyul', into Port Antonio later that night. She and I, we actually got involved for a while, until she left me for a young Kingstonian, a sallow Marxist in the PNP Youth League; and during our short-lived, passionate and unsatisfactory affair I saw Mr Alcindor from time to time. Once, at his request, I took a whole batch of photos of him. Mr Alcindor on his little verandah, Mr Alcindor leaning nonchalantly against the burnt-out, vine-wrapped car, Mr Alcindor 'working' in his fields. I didn't keep any, I gave them all to him. But I can remember my favourite one. It is of Mr Alcindor, collar up, hands in his pockets, like some American movie star of the 'fifties, looking handsomely at the camera with, behind him, the blue nothingness of sea and sky. I pride myself as an amateur photographer, but taking that shot something must have jarred my hand, for the whole composition is just slightly out of focus.

THE END OF THE ROAD

Elizabeth sighed. 'The road to Hell is paved with good sensations.'

'I heard it was good intentions,' I said.

'Nope. Sensations. The good intentions' road leads to heaven, never mind what they say. It's the good sensations' road leads to hell.'

'Then,' I said, 'you mean pleasurable, not good. If you mean pleasurable, say pleasurable. Don't say good.'

I was in a ratty mood. One of the few perks of my writer's job is I get to miss the rush hour traffic; but here I was, at the bottom of the Beetham at five on a Friday afternoon, in traffic jammed so solid you could probably walk on the car roofs from the fish market to Valsayn Park, torrential rain beating down, the windows up, the windshield fogged, the light outside like that of a London winter – and all because of Elizabeth.

Or rather because, an hour and a half ago, running into her in Abercromby's Bookshop, and learning that, like myself, she lived 'out east' and, as she put it, was 'carless in Gaza', I was intemperate enough to offer her a drop home. Whereupon I discovered that we had to stop at her solicitor's, 'just for a few minutes,' in St Vincent Street.

One full hour later:

'I know,' Elizabeth said gaily, dropping into the car seat beside me. 'I've just burned up all my credit. But I really didn't expect to be so long! I never knew getting a divorce was so complicated.'

Elizabeth, I should tell you, is a slim, very black, very beautiful woman, with fine hands, a long neck, and a Parisian air. Now pushing forty, she looks hardly changed from the laughing, elusive girl I'd known at UWI, Mona, long ago, when the world was young.

I hadn't really known her well then; we were in different faculties, different years. But being compatriots in a strange land gave us an unthinking kinship. Each knew who the other was. Crossing paths on the ring road we'd say 'hi'; finding ourselves at adjoining tables in the soda fountain we might exchange news about what was going on back home; and once, hearing a couple of my fellow-seniors discussing the Trini freshette – mainly, what a difficult catch she was turning out to be, and how, whenever one or another of the guys made his play, she'd laugh and move away – I remember smiling inwardly and thinking, 'Give them hell, kid.' One summer vacation, when I was returning to Trinidad and she wasn't, she approached me in the Students' Union and asked if I would deliver a package to her mother. I remember being surprised – as I said, we hardly knew each other – but I guess that by then I must have had a subconscious admiration for her, because I remember feeling flattered rather than discommoded by her request; by the light it showed me in, in her eyes.

But that was all. I doubt that two hundred words passed between us in two years.

In the early 'seventies I bumped into Elizabeth, in Lauzanne, of all places, and learnt that she was married to an Englishman who was something with the United Nations in Geneva and was pestering her to have a baby, which she didn't want. It wasn't a memorable encounter. The vivacity I'd remembered seemed strained and brittle and her UWI air of elusive animation was gone. In sanitised, pragmatic Switzerland, the camaraderie of compatriotism seemed irrelevant, and would have felt sententious had either of us indulged in it, which neither of us did. In any case, she had no plans for returning home; had no plans period, as far as I could see. I didn't meet her husband, and so could not imagine her real life, and afterwards that was how I thought of her: as connected to nobody and no place. In my mind, I classified her as a casualty: one of those misguided, determined West Indian women married to faceless, foreign men and eking out their years in anonymity in a wintry clime. And that was how she remained for me, till Abercromby's.

Now I learnt that, seven years ago, at the height of the oil boom, she had returned to Trinidad with her husband on vacation; and he, 'enchanted' with the country, had taken the daring step of giving up his UN job and starting a small business, out at O'Meara. They had settled down, still childless, not far from her mother's home in Arima. Hugh (Hugh?!) had done pretty well with his business, though, like most of his ilk, he was 'feeling the pressure' now.

And she? She was 'absolutely marvellous'. Doing absolutely nothing, a lady of leisure, in the middle of what, believe it or not, was only her third affair, and her first in Trinidad, in eighteen years of married life – just discovering what she had been missing all these years. 'You Trinidadian men!' Standing together like conspirators in the gloaming of the bookshop by a revolving stand of offerings from Picador, Elizabeth flightily volunteered this news.

'You probably know him; he's a high politician. Married, unfortunately. Or fortunately. But I'm not going to tell you his name, because you'd probably go and put him in the papers. Are you going to put me in the papers?'

She asked it with an air of mischief and no alarm. I said, 'Probably', and Elizabeth threw back her head and laughed.

'At least you won't be able to tell them about my beauty spot.'

'What beauty spot?'

'That's what I mean!'

I looked at her quizzically, but she broke it off with an arch wink and turned to finger *Rosshalde* (Herman Hesse).

Past thirty-five, only three kinds of women can flirt as wantonly as that: semi-nymphomaniac or passionately otherwise-involved or desperately unhappy women. I didn't know which she was, but her high-strung, talkative gaiety inclined me towards the second – although, maybe it was the third. I thought briefly about the high politicians I knew, and came up with an either/or/ or which, if I were to state it here (and there turned out to be no legal safety in numbers) would indubitably land me in court and lifelong penury.

We drifted side by side, more or less, along the shelves. In the end I bought *Portrait of a Sea Urchin*, a charming memoir of a West Indian childhood by an English naturalist. She, Elizabeth, settled for a Penguin Colette, *The Captive* – and then at the counter bought a copy of *The T&T Review* – which, for some reason, surprised me. On the steps down to the pavement I paused, half-waiting for her, half-measuring the force of the gusty squall now sweeping across: the forerunner, as it turned out, of the real rain. And that was when I learnt that she was carless in Gaza and, not knowing what I was letting myself in for, carelessly offered to drop her home.

Women in the act of sitting have this habit of sweeping their hands downward along their bottom, even when they're wearing tight skirts that don't need smoothing out; and that was the gesture with which Elizabeth, emerging from her solicitor's office one full hour later, deposited herself in the passenger's seat, semi-apologising and marvelling aloud at the unexpected complications of getting a divorce.

To this latter piece of news I didn't respond. Largely because I was in a thoroughly bad mood by then – but also because I had never met her husband and so had never really imagined her married – I merely glanced at her incuriously and started the car.

She took the rebuff. Settling back in her seat, she crossed her legs away from me, absently (or not so absently) tugging the hem of her skirt to nearly reach her knee, and looked thoughtfully out of her window – presumably at a leering vagrant fingering his crotch and clearly preparing to exhibit his all for the benefit of a pair of bank clerks, who, however, saw the danger and preempted it by crossing in front of my car to the other side of the street.

We got to the Twin Towers in silence. Opposite the South Quay Police Station we had a short sharp row, which ended with Elizabeth explaining appeasingly that she thought we went 'far back'; that even though she knew I 'hadn't really noticed' her at Mona, she had always assumed for some reason that I 'would be there' for her if she ever really needed me; and so I must forgive her now, but that was 'the misconception' under which she had thought it would be okay to keep me waiting, she'd never do it again – not that she thought she'd ever get the chance again – but she really hadn't expected to be so long; and anyway, I'd been 'nicer' at Mona; what had happened in the intervening years to make me such a 'stern disciplinarian'?

When a beautiful woman starts pressing all the buttons at once not many men can stand firm. Half-mollified (but only half) I said: 'Forget it. So! You're getting divorced?'

'That's the general idea.' Elizabeth smiled ruefully, looking straight ahead. 'If I can get him to agree. I never met a man like him; he's so stubborn!'

'The politician?'

'Of course not! Hugh!' Elizabeth laughed to herself. 'No, "he" doesn't know a thing about this. Be horrified if he found out. In fact, he'll drop me like a hot potato the day I tell him. Think of the scandal, the political fallout!' Elizabeth sighed. 'Don't worry, I know my limitations,' she said contentedly.

Bottom of Broadway. I forced a gap in the barely-moving eastbound traffic and joined the jam, three lanes deep, on the Beetham. There the heavens opened in earnest. Torrential rain pelted down.

Have you noticed, the rain falls whiter nowadays? Must be all those chemical pollutants in the atmosphere. That's my theory, anyway. Long ago, I seem to remember, no matter how hard it rained, the landscape stayed more or less in place. These days it's like a blizzard: all the car lights on, visibility reduced to zilch – what the hell is going on with this world?

'The road to hell,' sighed Elizabeth now, 'is paved with good sensations.'

After that part was over – 'So,' I said, 'you're leaving a twenty-year marriage for this politician guy? I thought you said...'

'Not for,' Elizabeth corrected me. 'Because of. It's not the same thing. Oh, but it's so delicious! All the hide-and-seek, I mean. Do you know, we never acknowledge each other in public? Even in the hotel lobby we pass each other straight. I think that's the part I'll miss most. All the cloak-and-dagger stuff.'

'Why are you telling me all this?'

'Okay, I'll shut up.'

'You know what I think?' I said. 'I think you're half-crazy with being unhappy.'

I wasn't being all that respectful; but neither had she been, parking me up for one full hour on St Vincent Street on a Friday afternoon, rain as for Noah coming. Women, they know you once, they think they know you for all time. Meet them twenty years later, and at once they give you That Look. In the interim you could have axe-murdered a dozen dowagers, invented the Grand Unification Theory, or been to the moon and back – you think they care? Let a woman become aware of a man when they're both, say, twenty – he'll still be exactly the same in her eyes when they meet again for the first time at sixty. Whatever he has done with his life since then, whatever he's become, whatever signs he shows of the wear and tear of the years – she'll brush all that off as a temporary aberration, or, likelier, a pretence. Women have no respect for Time. That's what I think, anyway.

Rolled-up windows. Fogged windshield. Rain like hailstones beating on the roof. Elizabeth, arm along the back of her seat, considering me fondly now. 'That's what I always liked about you,' she said. 'The way you hated being cornered. You always had to have a way out of every situation. The one time I saw you cornered at Mona, you turned mean as hell. Gosh, but you were mean! Do you know you had that poor guy from Barbados, what's his name, almost in tears? Bet you never knew I was watching the whole thing. Don't take this wrong, but I think after that I always had a little soft spot for you. Because you tried *so hard* to back out, and they wouldn't let you, and then you suddenly upped and turned on that poor guy. Well, you're cornered now and it's all my fault. So I suppose I'll just have to sit here and take it. So go on, tell me about my great unhappiness. Only please don't crash into anybody: I've problems enough, as it is.'

I said: 'You know what I hate about beautiful women? Your looks are something you're born with, no credit to you, and yet you let them dictate your whole life. You let yourself become that thing: A Beautiful Woman. No, really, think about it! If you had a hunch back and a potbelly and legs like two sticks you wouldn't be sitting here talking like that. Y'all beautiful women, you take such liberties because of your looks!'

'And you let us,' Elizabeth said complacently.

Traffic lights changing ahead, red to green: the Beetham Estate. A quarter of a mile in ten minutes. I checked the tempera-ture gauge; it was already halfway to 'Hot'. The ol' Hunter drives well, considering, but it likes to travel. It doesn't like to sit idling in one place.

A thought struck me, and I said: 'Does he know?'

'Does he know what?'

'Hugh. Does he know you're planning to divorce him?'

Elizabeth sighed again. 'Oh, I've talked to him about it so many times! But he doesn't believe I'm serious; doesn't want to believe. If you mean, does he know I've started seeing a lawyer, the answer is no.' She paused, looking uncharacteristically grim. 'He'll find out tonight, though. I'm going straight home to tell him. Then he'll believe. He'll have no *choice* but to believe.'

I said, noncommittally I hope (for life has taught me not to intervene in these matters), 'Well, I suppose eighteen years is a long time.'

But Elizabeth, absorbed now in the grimness of the coming scenario, wasn't really listening.

Then I saw her get a bright idea. 'Listen,' she said, turning to me, all bright-eyed and moist supplication. 'Will you wait and be there when I tell him? That would make such a difference, you needn't even be in the room, you could wait in the...'

'Who, me? Are you crazy?' I interrupted her. 'For*get* it! You never even thought that thought.'

The light turned red again; the rain gusted; inside the car it was already getting stifling. Elizabeth, looking at me, was meditatively testing her middle fingernail with her teeth.

'And stop that,' I said irritably. 'It won't work.'

Under the flyover at NP, the crash of rain on the car roof ceased suddenly – then started up again. I groped behind me on the back seat for a T-shirt and began wiping the fogged windshield.

'Here, let me do that,' Elizabeth said.

She was unexpectedly meticulous. She didn't swab the bunched up T-shirt about as I would have done; she folded it in her lap, many times over, and then wiped the windshield with long horizontal strokes, turning the cloth each time to a dry part. Watching her absorption I thought suddenly, 'Elizabeth, the housewife'. It was a side of her I had not imagined till that moment, and it gave me a whiff of the reality of her life in the intervening years, and of her marriage, to a man I had never met. A childless marriage; yet it had lasted eighteen years. Nearly half her lifetime. It occurred to me I knew nothing of Elizabeth's husband – nothing except that he was British, and had once wanted a baby Elizabeth would not give him, and at forty-odd, or so I assumed, had walked away from a cushy UN job to take his chances with a small business in Arima, Trinidad. Hugh. Hugh something. What a name!

'Hugh what?'

'Maxton. I'm Elizabeth Maxton. Isn't that something?'

She said it not looking at me, looking straight ahead through the windshield wipers at the crawling traffic and the rain. I felt she was playing to the gallery – that after eighteen years no woman could still find her married name a curiosity, worthy of comment. Or maybe her concluding question had just been a kind of wince; I don't know. What do we ever know of other people's lives, except the bare externals they can't help showing us?

I had never wasted a thought on Elizabeth's husband, and I didn't really want to think about him now. But the fact that he was about to be the recipient of a startling piece of news, delivered to him by this merciless beauty, his wife (while – if I had let her have her wish – I, a total stranger, sat and waited for her in a car outside of his house) made him now a figure of drama in my mind, and I found myself wishing I had a mental picture of him, or had at least heard his voice.

Still looking straight ahead: 'What are you thinking?' Elizabeth said.

'Nothing.'

'Then why did you ask that?'

'No reason.'

'Are you going to be like this all the way?'

'Probably.'

'I can take a taxi.'

'Sure you can.'

I turned into the Beetham Gas Station: Arima is a lot further than Santa Margarita and the temperature gauge was already on 'Hot'. Gas station attendants in this country, they make a big thing about opening your radiator. It's just bad mind, of course, or plain cowardice; but I wasn't in the mood to encounter either, so I didn't bother to ask. I propped open the bonnet, spun the cap and jumped back. The cap fell into the engine. A geyser of boiling mud shot straight upward.

Back on the road, I watched the temperature gauge drop slowly. Then I said: 'Look, don't take me on, okay? It's just that I hate traffic. And I'm not that big on rain, either.'

'S'okay,' Elizabeth said. 'Everybody's wrought up nowadays.' She didn't say it all that forgivingly; but then, as if in compensation, she uncrossed and re-crossed her legs in my direction.

'So!' I said. 'What's wrong with Hugh?' Adding mentally: 'That wasn't wrong with him for the past eighteen years, I mean.'

She looked surprised. 'Wrong with him? Nothing's wrong with him.'

'Then how come you're planning to leave him? I know it's not my business.'

'Oh, that's okay,' Elizabeth said. 'I never knew a writer who didn't snoop around. Like this guy I met in Mali once. Marc. He was a poet, from France. But he'd been living in Goa.'

The way she said all this, I felt sure the itinerant Marc had been either Mr First or Mr Second Affair. Women, they have this too-casual yet somehow resonant way of talking about their past lovers – as if they think that could fool you and me for a moment. Or maybe their intention is quite the opposite: to let you know.

'By the time he was finished with me,' said Elizabeth, wryly yet contentedly, 'I might as well have been made of glass. Totally transparent.'

I said: 'Why is it women like men who make them feel transparent?'

She glanced at me sharply. 'Maybe it's because we spend so much of our time not being really looked at at all. I don't mean leered at; I mean looked at. How many men, particularly in this country...'

I braced for a feminist tract, but unexpectedly she broke off and seemed to drift away into some private thought of her own. Ahead, a revolving blue-and-white light, two lanes of traffic laboriously squeezing into one: an accident. A white Sunny crumpled against the central divide; beyond it, at an odd angle, a

Galant, its trunk stove in. A raincoated policeman with a torch-light emphatically waving us on. The ant-queue of cars fanned out again into two lanes, began to move faster now; and still the headlights on everywhere, the blinding white rain beating down.

'You ever felt,' said Elizabeth dreamily, 'you had to do something – something difficult and unpleasant – something that would hurt somebody else very deeply – and not known why, only, you just had to do it?'

I understood that we had returned to Hugh. I said untruthfully: not that I could remember. 'Lucky you,' Elizabeth sighed.

Veering right under the flyover, the Highway ahead. 5:45, the rain crashing down. Still – twenty miles an hour felt like flying, after the stop-and-start purgatory of the Beetham. My spirits rose.

'You know how old I am?' Elizabeth mused.

'I could work it out.'

'I'm thirty-eight. Be thirty-nine in December: Capricorn. Christmas Eve, that's my birthday. In twenty months' time I'll be forty.'

'A good age,' I said, truthfully yet abrasively, since I knew it wasn't what she wanted to hear. 'Think of it. By forty the junk is over. The confusion, the melodrama, the Existential Despair; the wanting all the wrong things for all the wrong reasons, the making a total ass of yourself and not even knowing it. I look back at my life and my friends' lives, and I think, sometimes, that everything we did in our twenties and thirties was just another version of the little boy on the diving board, jumping up and down, saying, "Hey, lookit me, Ma! Lookit me!" On my fortieth birthday I suddenly realised I felt free, for the first time since I was about twenty-one. Take it from me, kid: forty's a great age.'

I didn't add that it was also a grim age – that at forty the first little aches and pains begin, and your hair starts turning grey in earnest, and things start tiring you that didn't tire you before: first intimations of mortality. I didn't add that at forty you start to understand, in earnest, what till then had been a negligible hypothesis: that one day you'll be dead, dead as a clod, and the traffic and the rain will go on without you, and the great sun coursing through the heavens, and the sleepless sea, and the morning sky. I didn't add any of that – or that, till recently, forty was the age most people died by, so that past forty we were all in a sense freewheeling, the fey beneficiaries of generations of better nutrition, better medicine, easier working conditions, healthier genes. A free ride down the years; think of that!

Elizabeth said: 'Do you know how old he is?'

'The Politician?'

'Hugh. Hugh's sixty-three. I lied when I told you he chucked the UN job. What he did was, he took his pension early, and we came here.'

I said: 'Elizabeth, I have to tell you. Women like you frighten the hell out of me.'

She didn't try to laugh this off. She said soberly: 'Well, I don't expect you to believe it, but sometimes I frighten the hell out of myself, too. I mean, I'm not proud of any of this, you know, Wayne. I just know I have to live.'

'Well, that's great,' I said. 'First you marry the guy and let him take you and show you the world. Then you deny him a child, which is your business; and if he didn't leave you at that point I suppose it's his business too…'

'…you're dam' right…'

'…then, when he's old, you bring him back here where he doesn't know a soul, and park him up in Arima. And now you're going to leave him because he's sixty-three and you "have to live"? Wow. It really has been a privilege knowing you, lady. No lie; it really has.'

'Please stop the car,' Elizabeth said.

Now, as the reader knows, there's this game men and women play. If there's a tiff and she gets petulant and says, 'Let me out of this car', you're supposed to say, 'Don't be silly', and more than that: you're supposed to withdraw, recant, start wheedling and coaxing and wooing her to change her mind. It's a game I, too, have played in my time, like any young man with chivalric ideas about himself. But I don't play it anymore. (That's another thing about turning forty.) If a woman says to me now, 'Stop the car', I stop the car. We're supposed to be equal adults, right? And who needs an abduction charge when they least expect it? I forced an opening to the left, pulled onto the breakdown lane outside of

Solo's, and stopped, leaving the engine running; white rain racketing down.

We both stared straight ahead, Elizabeth with her hand on the door lever. Then: 'You bastard,' she said.

I took this as a signal, engaged a gear, and edged back into the eastbound traffic. Besides me, Elizabeth was weeping quietly. 'I said I wasn't proud of any of this!' she cried. 'What else you want me to say?'

I said nothing. On impulse, I rolled down my window and hooked my arm over the door. To hell with the soaking, I thought. Some things are a positive pleasure compared to other things.

'You have no idea!' Elizabeth wailed. 'No idea!'

And suddenly it stopped, the rain, just like that, and we were moving again: a thousand, two thousand cars, crawling east under a sodden sky. So many nuclear families headed homeward in the dusk! So many private lives! And it was as if this was what the human heart had shrunken to, as if, in this alone, the shreds of nobility remained: this stubborn eastward-crawling in the rained-out dusk, this clenched determination to get home.

The Kirpalani Industrial Complex – closed. Glamour Girl. On the left, the first of the vendors' stalls, enisled by great puddles of muddy water, looking stoical and desolate, no cars stopping.

And then the Aranguez lights, not working, the eastbound traffic, three lanes wide, crawling steadily through. On the side road the cars were backed up. Kamikaze rainflies littered my wind shield. Beside me, the woman was saying tearfully: 'Can I explain? Will you at least let me try to explain?'

The Uriah Butler Intersection was a mess: the traffic lights were off there, too, and from all four points of the compass the leading cars had hurled themselves pugnaciously into the centre: a Gordian knot. By luck, I was still in the left lane. I squeezed left again and joined the queue fleeing north along Mt Hope to take their chances with the Main Road, shouting viciously at a would-be interloper on my right trying desperately, too late, to do what I'd done. That's one thing about driving in this country: it can turn a man into a beast. Beside me, in the gathering gloaming,

Elizabeth was saying: 'What gives you the right to sit in judgment, anyway?'

I started angrily to say something, but stopped. So many things in life depend upon one's mood at the time; and that mood, in turn, can depend upon such inconsequential things – like finding yourself driving at thirty for a change, instead of jammed bumper-to-bumper and fender-to-fender in the primordial chaos of the Butler intersection, the traffic lights down, night coming on, and not a single traffic policeman in sight.

I checked myself and said instead, a little tiredly: 'Everybody judges everybody all the time; it's a reflex. Like how we manage to drive in this country without crashing into somebody else every other second. People weigh their impressions twenty-four hours a day, even in their sleep. It's part of being human, what you call "sitting in judgment". Everybody weighs everything that comes to them. We don't do it consciously most of the time, but we do it.'

'And when you weigh what we're talking about now it tells you I'm the Lady in Red, right?'

I shrugged. 'All I know is what you told me. You're having this 'delicious' affair with some politician. You're planning to leave your husband, who married you when he was forty-five, and who's sixty-three now, and a foreigner in this country, and who hasn't done you anything, or so you say. But you're planning to leave him because you "have to live". What you want me to say: "Hey, wow, *right on*, go for it, baby"?'

Elizabeth was silent; she looked hurt again. I felt I was getting ready to dislike myself. I accelerated through the changing lights of the Priority, accelerated again through frank red this time, swerving east onto the Main Road – an enraged motorist slammed his hand on his horn and kept it there – and then I was safely ensconced in traffic once more, moving at twenty miles an hour, but moving.

As though talking to herself, Elizabeth mused: 'I wonder what you would say if I told you what I was thinking, a few minutes ago, back there?'

I glanced at her and returned to the road, just in time to brake for a wild man in a PX Cortina, swerving from right to left across me to go gunning, belching smoke, up the Maracas Valley fork.

'I was thinking,' Elizabeth said, 'I'm going to be too late to bring him his slippers, and he'll just be sitting there when I get home, looking poor-me-one and neglected, in those clompy working shoes you men adore, and he won't say a thing, he'll just "try to be brave", and I'll end up riddled with guilt – as usual.'

It took me a moment or two for this to sink in. Then I said: 'Aw, come on. Sixty-three isn't exactly geriatric. Why can't he get his own slippers?'

'Oh, he can. But he won't. It's one of our little "traditions". He comes home from work, and I bring him his slippers and say, something like, "So how was it today?" It's my own fault. In the beginning I used to bring them for him, quite naturally, you know, because he'd come home looking tired, or whatever. But then somehow, I don't know how, it became "a tradition". When I realised what was happening I tried to get out of it, but he made a big thing of it – you can't imagine! He said it was one of our traditions. That my bringing the goddam slippers had come to signify for him that the working day was over, and that he and his little Dox (that's what he calls me, it's short for "doxie", which I don't think is a very nice word, do you?) – that we were at home together, at last, again. Ta-ta-ta-ta!'

I didn't point out that her heraldic bugle-call could not possibly have emanated from the appassionato violin she sketched briefly, with both hands, in the dusky light. I was finding all this too hard to digest.

'So every evening of my life, little Dox here presents herself in the living room and says: "Here're your slippers, dear. How was today?" Or else he clomps about the house, all miserable and neglected, *clomp-clomp-clomp* siddong here, *clomp-clomp-clomp* siddong there, until I can't take it anymore and bring the slippers. I know, it's not a big thing; I mean, it doesn't cost me anything to walk from the bedroom to the living room with the blasted slippers. But still! I suppose you think I'm being unreasonable?'

I said: 'Little Dox?'

'That's me.'

'Little *Dox*?'

'I told you: it's short for "doxie".'

'You sure he doesn't mean, "ducks"? Is he from Yorkshire?'
'Very funny. You could have turned there.'
I had driven straight through the Curepe junction. I said absently, 'That's a No Right Turn'; but I wasn't really thinking about it.
'No, he's from Kent.' Elizabeth sighed. 'The Home Counties. My Hugh's a Home Counties' Man.'
A thought struck me and I said: 'So what do you call him?'
'Me, call him? Hugh.'
'That's it? Hugh? He calls you Dox and you call him Hugh?'
'Oh, stop it.' She cuffed me, but limply, on the shoulder. She looked almost happy again. For the first time since we'd left her solicitor's office, I was aware of her fine-boned beauty.
I said: 'Hugh and Dox. Dox and Hugh. Elizabeth, I have to tell you I'm having trouble visualising this marriage.'
I was hamming it up, playing for time; not wanting to look beneath the comedy of names at the awful thing she was showing me. How precious, and yet how frail, are our ideas of ourselves, how dependent upon things in themselves quite meaningless! The little ceremonies that uphold us, that reassure us that we are who we were; the little rituals in whose enactment we persuade ourselves that the world as we know it remains in place – how tenuous they had grown, in our time! Like the man who comes to work one day and finds that his boss has had his desk moved, from one corner to another corner of the office, and, for a long moment of existential vertigo, wonders whether his world had collapsed without his knowing it.
And the fragility of that world, the inextricable web of minutiae from which it depends!
For millennia, men and women had lived on the land, and their livelihood, and their livelihood's threat, lay in elementary, simple things. What had men and women to lose but their crops, their livestock, their villages, their lives? What had they to fear, except drought, flood, fire, unseasonable winter; some marauding leopard or belligerent tribe?
No more those essential simplicities! In our time, like a coral reef, a man's world had grown hydra-headed and brittle, and mortal threats to it, and to his idea of himself, lurked now in every

nook and cranny of his life. A moved desk in an office; an impending devaluation of his country's currency; some sudden revelation, a son or daughter hooked on coke; a flat tyre suffered by his wife, driving in the wrong place at the wrong time; his omission from some cocktail party list of invitees; a phone ringing with, at the other end of the line, his bank manager's secretary, or the IRS, or his wife... or his wife's solicitor...

'You could have turned there too,' Elizabeth said.

We had passed the university entrance. Night had fallen, damp and drear, and every street light irradiated a halo, and the tyres of the westbound traffic hissed quietly on the wet-black asphalt.

'We could take it higher up,' I said. 'Except that the busiest stretch of road in this country today is the highway between Trincity and the Piarco turn-off.'

'You're telling me,' Elizabeth said dreamily. 'Isn't it something. Everybody's leaving. My God! I thought the other day: it's like the drain hole in a sink – that same stretch you just talked about. You know, you pull the plug and all the water starts swirling around it?'

It was another housewife's image, and it recalled to my mind the spectre of an ageing Englishman waiting for us – in 'clompy' shoes – at the end of the road; waiting patiently (or fretfully, what did it matter?) for his young wife, his little Dox, to get home and bring him his slippers, so that they could be 'together again'; waiting, unaware that his world was caving in.

I said: 'You're not really going home to tell him?'

'Yes, I am.'

'Then,' I said, 'it's not just the slippers, right?'

'Well, of course it isn't just the slippers. I tried to tell you, but you wouldn't listen! You're just like him, in a way; you all never listen! You just jump up and say – whatever. It gets me so mad.'

St John's Road. Auzonville Road. Republic Bank, Tunapuna: the line of traffic slowing down, coming to a stop. Palladium Junction. On the pavement, two men threatening a short, square man with Down syndrome; he, believing it to be a game, shadow-boxing each man in turn, the men starting to push him roughly, from one to the other and back. I caught a glimpse of the short man's expression changing from animation to bewilderment, from bewilderment to alarm, and then to something like sorrow – and then we were moving again, the line of cars, and in the rear-view mirror I saw that one of the men had locked the man with Downs' neck and that the other was slapping his face, lightly but evilly.

Elizabeth said: 'It's not as if I didn't try to keep him young; Wayne, I tried so hard! But I failed. You see the first couple years back here? They were wonderful! They were like the happiest times we'd ever had together. But then, I don't know: the business got into trouble. It was, like, no sooner had he gotten it off the ground than it started going back downhill again. And then, suddenly, he just started turning old on me. But so fast! You ever seen a man age fifteen years in a year? Well, it was like that. One minute he was Hugh, and the next minute he was...' She stopped. 'He just wasn't the Hugh I'd known anymore...'

The Chinese Wok on the left, Eros on the right; and then Kentucky Fried Chicken; and then an open stretch on the left. I thought: at this rate I'll drop her off by seven-thirty, be home with luck by, call it quarter past eight.

Elizabeth said: 'When I saw what was happening I tried everything; it isn't as if I just sat and sulked. Wayne, I tried things I'd be embarrassed to tell you; things that even pleased' – she stopped abruptly.

'The politician?'

Elizabeth blushed angrily. 'And as you can imagine, he's been around. But it was no use. Listen, I can give you an example. There was a time Hugh needed a secretary, and I was always the one who helped him choose whatever little staff he needed from time to time: don't ask me why. Probably because he was a foreigner here, and I wasn't. Anyway – you know what I did! I chose the tartiest, wantonest, most painted-up little redskin barbie-doll I could find. I mean, this kid was walking jailbait, you could just take one look at her and know. Because I'd started thinking by then it was me, you know? That there was something wrong with me; that I was letting him down, somehow, in that way. And I'd reached a point, I was ready to try anything. So then you know what I did? I made an excuse and went off to Barbados for two weeks. You can imagine the state I was in, walking up and down Rockley Beach each day, being harassed by those blasted beach boys, not knowing what the hell was going on back home. I know: it was a stupid thing to do, but I went! I just had to do something, anything, to stop the slide. Stop him just suddenly turning old like that.'

I said: 'Ah, Elizabeth.'

'And you know what? It didn't work. He didn't even notice the child. I mean, I know men lie about that kind of thing, but just believe me when I tell you: Hugh couldn't fool me if he tried. And there was nothing. I came back and found an old man – the same old man I'd left alone for two weeks with this little Delilah, all the time in the world on his hands, and me safely out of the picture.' She stopped and thought. Then: 'You know what I think now?' she said, less bitterly than in a kind of wonderment. 'I think that once a man decides to get old, that's it. Nothing can stop him. He's finished; he's through.'

She gave a little laugh. 'For five years now I've been like his mother. Or his daughter, or his sister, or his maid. Everything except his wife. Hugh hasn't wanted a wife for years. So, say what you like – I think I held out pretty well. Because there were a lot of other men hanging around, you know – don't ask me why, there just always have been – and this one' – she inclined her head, as though the politician were sitting invisibly in the back seat, a silent audience to all we were saying – 'this one is the first. The first since Trinidad, anyway. The thing is, I know myself too well, Wayne. I'm thirty-eight. I'm not going to sit here and tell you he's the first – or be the last. Because that just isn't true – I know me! And I don't want to do that to Hugh.'

I was thinking: What a terrible thing is the human heart. What punishment it can give; what punishment it can take.

The traffic had lightened; the road was drying out; we were doing an easy twenty-five, driving through Tacarigua. I said: 'Has it ever occurred to you he might prefer that?'

She looked suddenly close to tears. 'Oh, Wayne,' she said. 'How could he? You forget, this is a small country. He'd be the laughing stock of everybody, all our friends. Besides, I told you: he doesn't want a wife anymore.'

'So you say,' I told her. 'My problem is, I can't imagine a man making a point of keeping on his working shoes, until his mother or his daughter or his sister or his maid brings his slippers for him.'

Though I don't know Arima at all, I've always had a special feeling about it; and part of this feeling is due, I think, to the approach to the town. Beyond Tacarigua, the Main Road (or so it seemed in a child's imagination) finally plucks up the courage to leave the protective shadow of the foothills; space appears for the first time on the left; and the traffic, as though responding to this intimation of vistas, drives more leisurely as well, space appearing on the road now, too. Ahead, Arima spreads itself after the long cramped chasm of the Main Road in what seems a luxury of spaciousness and serenity: the first real town to the east of Port of Spain. And the only one.

The latter meant that Arima was also a kind of terminus, a town at the end of the road (though the road went on, past Arima, through pasture land and into rainforest, and then out and along the wild Atlantic coast); and to Arima's remoteness in space was added a vague sense of its remoteness in time, a Sunday-supplement notion of antiquity which in my imagination has had the curious effect of subverting Arima's modernistic idea of itself as a city. Moreover, with its Spanish-Carib ancestry – with its girls who, when we were kids, had about them an unfamiliar, wanton beauty, and a reputation for being 'hot-blooded' – Arima was different.

Different, special: how much of this is fey or wishful thinking I don't know. I don't know Arima; and driving at night as I was doing now, concentrating on the road, I was unable to add more than a sensation of coolness, of the cool night breeze, to the store of qualities that made up Arima in my mind.

And yet, approaching the town, my mood began to lighten, until I had to remind myself where I was headed, and why: until I felt I had to keep this new mood in check. To the woman sitting beside me, I said, quoting the American poet Robert Frost: 'Whenever I get too happy, I think how little good my happiness ever did those near me.'

'What's that supposed to mean?'

She asked this measuredly enough, yet in a tone that conveyed a muted tension. We were nearing the end of the road.

'It means maybe we've always been more alone than we think.'

She was silent, looking straight ahead. In the darkness of the Hunter I glimpsed her immobility: a fine-boned beauty tensely rendered in black wood. It was that tension, more than anything she had said or could have said, that told me that her mind was made up; that no tentative line I might assay now could change it; that she was going home to tell her ageing husband that she was leaving him, after eighteen years; that, from here on to the grave, he would have to make it without her. Life is merciless, I thought; but I didn't say it. I couldn't think of anything to say.

Abruptly in the darkness Elizabeth softened (and I felt her soften before I heard her words). 'Poor Hugh.'

It was all she said.

'Well, they say life is merciless.'

I offered this casually – too casually – wanting to shunt the whole affair away into an aphorism, to wrap it up and put it behind me (it was, after all, none of my business); knowing there was nothing more, really, for me to say.

Elizabeth said wryly: 'You don't mean life; you mean me.'

I thought about this; and then I shrugged. 'I suppose so,' I said. 'Which way now?'

'Turn right at the lights and keep going.'

We were once more crawling in traffic. It was seven-thirty on a Friday night, and all the town's lights were on, and the pavements were teeming with pedestrians and vendors' stalls. Oysters. Doubles. Acra'n hops. Down a side road – narrower, less populated, less well-lit – a truck was parked at a tilt, its nearside wheels on the high pavement.

I said: 'Arima's busier than I thought it would be.'

'Friday night,' Elizabeth said. Then, unexpectedly changing the subject, she said impulsively: 'I think you forget I gave him eighteen good years. I think you forget, he was already middle-aged when I married him; that it was me who gave him a new lease on life in the first place...'

'...which you're taking back now, right?'

'Oh, that is mean. That is so mean!'

She controlled herself with an effort. 'All I mean,' she said tiredly, but not ready to stop, 'was that at an age when most men are settling down into gardening, or drinking in pubs, or sitting down in front of the TV every night – whatever it is middle-aged men do with their time – he was able to start again, because of me. I'm not boasting; I'm not saying I did him a favour, it wasn't like that. But still! Life is life; we both know that. So why are we sitting here pretending?'

'Pretending?'

'Pretending he didn't feel ten feet tall, travelling about the world with his exotic young wife at his side – this exotic young wife other men were always sniffing around, for some reason – other *young* men. Knowing he had nothing to worry about, because I never gave him anything to worry about – except twice, and that was different – and now three times; and he never knew a thing about those.'

And suddenly, as she was saying this, I felt sure that, whether she knew it or not, the truth had been exactly the opposite: that middle-aged Hugh (was he balding? Of course, he had been balding all along! I was suddenly sure of this detail) had never quite been able to believe his luck in landing Elizabeth; that however much, and with whatever justification from moment to moment, he told himself that she loved him, he must have known from the start (or quickly learned) that he would never have a hope of understanding her – his 'exotic young wife' who, not without tantrums sometimes, yet dutifully brought him his slippers each evening – and so, resigned to unknowing, seeing her desirability confirmed and re-confirmed, oh, endlessly, in other men's eyes (*young* men), his happiness no longer in his hands but consigned, all of it, to the inscrutable heart of a childwife he would never really know and could only ever take on trust, how habituated to dread he must have become, over the years! And what a toll on his courage it must have taken, this marriage of his, to one so different, one so young; and how he must have resented her and it sometimes!

And yet there was his name: Hugh Maxton. The name had about it a squat, unequivocal complacency. I recalled Elizabeth saying hopelessly, 'He doesn't believe I'm serious, he's so stubborn!' Was I inventing romance where no romance was, seeing danger and dread where only flat-footed complacency walked heavily about? In clompy shoes – I had forgotten about the shoes. But I didn't know now what to make of them. The shoes could belong to either scenario, either Hugh. I thought, not for the first time that day: What do we ever know of other people's hearts?

Beside me in the car, the lights passing in swathes across her face, leaving it each time dark but for the eyes, Elizabeth was saying: 'It sounds selfish, but it's not. I have a duty to myself now, to life – turn left here. I can't explain it; but I know what I mean.'

We had left behind an open dark space on the right and were driving south or south by east, between houses. I said: 'Listen. You don't have to go on. None of this is any of my business. Marriages break up all the time, for whatever reason; and I'm sure you know what you're doing. Just take it easy, okay?'

I'd hoped this last exhortation would soften what might otherwise sound like a rebuke; but it didn't. Elizabeth crossed her legs and said stiffly: 'I'm sorry, I've taken you a long way out of your way, and bored you with my troubles on top of it. But I really appreciate the lift. And it *was* nice to see you again, after all these years – re-establish contact, that sort of thing. Maybe we'll meet again sometime, when things… that's it there. The gate after the white wall. Not that one, the next one. Would you mind very much turning in? It's kind of dark…'

In the contemporary surroundings the house was a surprise. It was an old plantation-style house, raised off the ground with verandahs on three sides, and it stood well back from the road on grounds that must have been close to an acre. Many of its lights, including the verandah lights, were on, but there was no one in sight, although a jeep and a small red car stood side by side in the open, lit garage.

I drove cautiously up the macadam drive (as she had said, it was dark) and stopped, close to a corner of the house, in a pallid glaze from the eaves' light. There was still no sight nor sound of the house's occupant. And yet the front door from the verandah was wide open: a seeming recklessness that was like a dare, or a fatalist's uncaring, in these dangerous times.

With a quick, nervous gesture, Elizabeth ducked her head to peer up through the windshield at the house. She said, too softly for me to hear, something under her breath (it sounded grim); then, turning to me, a little distraught, she began: 'I really wish you would wait...'

I said: 'Elizabeth, don't start that.'

'Will you at least turn off your engine for a minute?'

'No.'

'Please turn off the engine – *pleeze!*'

I looked at her and shook my head. At the same time I heard, or fancied I heard, from deep within the house, the echo of shoes on wooden floor boards, approaching.

Elizabeth looked around her wildly; then she hissed: 'Will you at least do this? After you back out of here, will you park on the road and wait a while? Ten minutes. Just ten minutes. If I don't come out in ten minutes, drive off. Will you at least do that?'

It wasn't my imagining: measured and heavy, the shoes were approaching across the living room floor. Don't ask me by what process of mental gymnastics, in situations such as this one, we turn victims into assassins. I only know that I dreaded laying eyes on the owner of those shoes with an active terror; that, blameless and uninvolved as I was in the coming scenario, I would no more have faced the innocently emerging Mr Maxton than I would have changed places with him at that moment. I said: 'Okay, okay,' and Elizabeth swung the car door open and stood up into the night air with a jerky motion, and then I was reversing down macadam drive, not chancing a glance back at the house but reversing blind in pitch darkness, with the lit street beyond the gate posts my only guide.

Out in the road, I parked the car and killed the lights. Then I glanced at my watch: it was five to eight.

The road the Maxtons lived on was empty except for the occasional passing car. I became aware of a chill on the right side of my chest, where my damp shirt still clung to the skin, and I pulled the cloth away and blew warm air in between. I have always been mildly fascinated by this recycling of human energy, as when a man cups his chilled palms and blows into them air warmed by his lungs, his body warming his body, in effect. And now I thought with sour humour – referring to the middle-aged man whose face I had never seen, whose voice I had never heard, and whom in consequence I could not imagine now, standing in the brightly lit living room of the old house trying to comprehend what this sudden stranger, his merciless young wife, was telling him – I thought: 'His body will have to warm his body from now on.'

On the south wall of the house (I had seen it by the eaves' light as we approached) some previous owner, repairing an area of rot or filling in what had once been a door, had done so with plywood, spoiling the planking effect. Curious how you notice these things. I thought, addressing in my mind the still-hypothetical but imperilled Mr Maxton: 'So it was never perfect, after all. Not even at the start.' I don't know why I thought that.

Eight o'clock. The street lamp shone. After the heavy rains of dusk the night breeze was cold. A pair of speeding cars flashed by; then the road was empty again. What was I doing here?

The realisation made me feel like a fool. I didn't wait for her ten minutes to elapse; I started the Hunter and drove, angrily, the night road home.

In a small country, life can be strange. One Saturday morning, some months later, I sat at the bar at the Yachting Association in Chaguaramas, waiting for a phone call and listening meanwhile to two guys talking while I waited. The younger one – call him Ronnie – was telling the older one (whose name I do not know and so cannot reinvent) that if he was interested in real estate speculation now was the time to buy.

'Look at me,' Ronnie was saying – that peculiarly Trinidadian phrase, which without embarrassment instructs the listener to accord the narrator the status of protagonist in his own story. 'Right now I'm in the process of buying a big old house in Arima, on an acre of land – you understand what I'm telling you? An *acre* of prime residential land – for two hundred thou.'

'You joking,' his companion said, impressed.

'Two hundred thou,' Ronnie repeated with satisfaction. 'Five years ago, the land alone woulda cost twice that. Tell me how I could lose.'

'You cyar lose,' the older man said wonderingly. 'How you manage that?'

'Well,' Ronnie said, unabashedly preening now. 'You know how it is. Expatriate leaving.'

I pricked up my ears. 'What's his name?' I asked Ronnie, intruding without preamble upon their conversation (one of the perks of club membership, that).

Both men turned to look at me stonily.

'Maxton,' Ronnie said shortly; and he resumed talking to his companion. 'English fella; you know how it is. Come out here in the boom years to make a killing, and now the party over is time to split. Selling lock, stock and barrel for whatever he could get. You know dem English tesses; dey ent easy.'

I said impulsively: 'That's not why he's leaving'; and they both turned and looked at me again.'

'You know him?' Ronnie demanded.

'Well. Yes and no.'

I was going to say that, really, I knew his wife; but I thought that might get me an unearned admiring innuendo or two, and I didn't want that. I didn't feel like being one of the thongs of a whip lashing the retreating spectre of poor Maxton into the middle distance; so I didn't say anything more.

Ronnie was looking at me thoughtfully.

'I hear he an' the wife mash up,' he said to us, including me in the conversation now. 'I hear the wife is real hot stuff. Plenty younger than him, right?' He asked this, pointedly, of me.

I shrugged noncommittally.

Ronnie's companion said that all this old man-young wife business was a joke; that he didn't know how a man could be such a fool; that we could give him an older woman any day. 'You see me here? I happy wid dat. Dat way a man know where he stand.'

'An' he know dat he know!'

'An' he *know* dat he know dat he know! A man ent have to worry-worry all the time. What! Dat is chupidness, man!'

Ronnie wasn't ready to let me go. To me he said: 'You know the wife?'

I said: Vaguely. In another country. Long ago.

'Where's Maxton going; you know?' I asked Ronnie this as conversationally as I could.

He shrugged. I could see the subject was beginning to bore him. 'Back to England, nuh!' he said. 'What you think? Is a old man we talking about – not so? A old English fella. Well, then. Where else it have for a man like dat to go?'

CISSY THE DOBERMAN

Cissy the Doberman was three. She was a tan Doberman, slender, fine-featured and -boned, with an air of suppressed excitement, and comprehending, mischievous eyes.

In this, Cissy was the opposite of a doggy dog: she could be circumspect to a fault. When the big male, in large and imprecise happiness at his master's return, crashed against the gate (then rose onto his hind legs, stretching his neck, eyes slitted, to be stroked) Cissy would sit on the verandah watching, her gaze disapproving, stern. She would sit and watch while the man – staggering and cursing heartily under her noble mate's assault – closed the gate behind him; then, as he approached her, she would rise.

'Hi, Cissy!' he would call.

The sound of her name would set her a-tingle, and she might commence palpating the terrazzo with her forepads and bowing like a pony, while her stub-tail wagged in tense little flurries. But she would not come to him. He would have to go right up to her; and even then, at the last moment, she might turn and, claws skidding, sketch a six-foot sprint out of his reach, before prancing back to present her neck for the sinful pleasure of his scratching. And once this ritual of return was over and the man was on his way indoors, Cissy would invariably turn on the male, snapping and quarrelling and letting him know that he had once more lowered the tenor of the place by behaving like a slob.

Once, when the pair escaped – and gave the man and woman four distraught days of house-to-house searching, before turning up, early one morning, outside the white monastery which sprawled like a medieval town on the mountain ridge beyond and above their own – it was Cissy, not her fearsome mate, who bit the monk who solicitously tried to take them in. And driving home it was Cissy who sat in the passenger seat (while the male careened about in the back) looking primly out of the window and refusing the imprecations of her hugely relieved master, letting him know in this way that she would not easily forgive him for leaving the gate open, causing them to escape and spend four downright weird days and nights in the forest, and making her bite that strange man at the end.

Ah, she was a lady, Cissy! Watching her, the man, who had kept Dobermans all his life, thought he had never seen such a feminine female, nor such a classy one. The big male adored her, and would often intrude upon her prim and watchful quietude, prancing into a pre-pounce crouch directly in front of her face, as if to say, with happiness, 'Here I am!' He was one hundred-plus pounds to her sixty-five, so she soon learnt in self-defence to meet his charges as if they were mortally intended, and at such times would turn into a whirling dervish, snapping and biting him till he yelped or bawled, before – easily taking the pain into the spacious happiness of his love, since such a love is merely vivified by pain – throwing himself upon her again. In the end he might wind up pinning her broadside against a wall, grinning and whimpering while she rained bites on his shoulder and neck, but holding her there, holding her there, until she lost her temper in earnest and the tenor of her snarls suddenly dropped an octave. And then he would break it off and slouch sheepishly away – while she stood looking murderously at him, or dashed after him to deliver a parting, wicked bite – knowing he had once again forgotten himself and gone too far, and offended her, his impossible heart.

Other times, he would wander over to where she lay on her side, panting a little (for no reason you could see, unless it were the burdensome business of Being) and with an odd, proprietary humility begin grooming her. He might keep at it for what seemed hours, standing over her, the great muzzle gnawing and searching, while she lay immobile but with a definite air of being put upon, enduring his homage with female patience, but having to suppress a little irritation at him all the same.

At length, his inexhaustible selflessness would oppress the watching man. 'Stop that!' he might say suddenly, irritated; and the male, startled, would lift his head, and man and dog would trade complicated looks of brief sorrow and brief shame, while the object of their mute exchange took the chance to rise and hurriedly trot away, and flop down again in some impregnable place, behind a chair, against the wall, as if to say, 'Enough! No more.'

That she also loved him was less apparent. You would have to catch them in one of those moments when, from the verandah, the big male sounded the alarm – then tore off around the house (squealing with rage at not being able to get to *instantly* and kill the source of whatever scent or sound had triggered him: an iguana, a rat, a stray in the road, or some neighbour's itinerant gardener or guest) – and see Cissy lithe and terrible hurtling in his wake, not knowing the enemy but all ready to fight where he fought and joyously to kill where he killed.

Or else you would have to come upon them when, from sleeping side by side, the male rose and lifted his head to interrogate some scent, borne on the wind from somewhere down in the valley; and Cissy, too, would lift her head – then give it up and start licking his genitals, meaning, 'Forget it, come back here', while he stood over her, still elsewhere attending; until the woman, coming upon them, might say mock-scandalised, 'Cissy! What kind of behaviour is that?' or the man in passing heckled them both with a raucous remark, which might embarrass the male into moving away, but never fazed Cissy one bit.

Her first heat she took, predictably, as a betrayal. What was this strange agitation that would not let her sit still, she who till then had been the queen of Quietude? And the suddenly stepped-up harassing of the male, blundering, ceaseless, inconsolable, insufferable – she stood for him for a tingling moment, then spun on him snarling; stood for a moment, spun and bit. When by the third day the man saw that the male had no ebullience left, and that with him it was now only pain, he put Cissy on the lead and led her, oddly unprotesting, around the house to the laundry room. There he held her muzzle with one hand, and with the other around her waist supported her quarters, and, like that, man and bitch together staggered from the erring, frenzied bombardments of the male.

When at last they were joined the man released her, panting

himself; and he washed his arms in the sink and left, leaving them to their awkward tug-of-war. But long afterwards he would recall Cissy's gritted panting, and her air of deadly amusement, her sudden consternations and funkiness and secret gloating, and her evil eye.

After that she settled down and bore two fine litters, and amazed everyone by being an indefatigable mother. And the man remarked to the woman that it was a fine thing, how Cissy had turned from an irrepressible waif into the queen of the lawn.

Saying this, he relaxed into the assumption that the dogs had become a stable part of their lives, and that one day, old and arthritic, perhaps, they would limp down the verandah steps to sniff, with him, the dawning of a new century.

But then Cissy began vomiting.

She would eat her food as always, wolfing it down; then regurgitate it at once. After that, she would gingerly eat it again; and this time would keep it down. The man mused that she must be eating too fast; and he let it go. It wasn't for the vomiting but the conjunctivitis that had appeared in both her eyes that, one day in August, he took Cissy to the vet.

The vet prescribed steroids. Cissy's eyes cleared, but the vomiting and re-eating were becoming more frequent. By late September the conjunctivitis was back, too, and Cissy's coat had lost its sheen. When one afternoon the big male trumpeted then tore off round the house, and Cissy, instead of flying in his wake, contented herself with trotting anxiously back and forth on the verandah, the man told the woman he thought something was wrong with her; and they took Cissy back to the vet.

The vet mused: 'Distemper?'

But there were no symptoms of distemper, bar the eyes.

The vet said, 'Boy, this one is a puzzle'; and he gave Cissy some speculative shots.

'Just watch her,' he told them. 'If it's distemper you'll know soon enough.'

'And what if it's not distemper?' the woman asked.

The vet considered her thoughtfully. 'If it's not distemper,' he allowed, 'then she has to have a good chance. I mean, look at her; there's nothing wrong with her! At least, nothing *I* can see.'

And as October progressed, it was true, Cissy seemed herself, more or less. Regurgitating and re-eating had become the way she now ate, and she no longer hunted with the male. But she had been in heat in September; the man thought, though he could not say why, that she had conceived; and so he told the woman, and himself, that she was probably just having a bad pregnancy.

Then one morning Cissy stopped eating.

It was not a decision taken but a sentence imposed: she didn't know herself she was going to stop. She rushed her food bowl as usual, then stalled over it, her delicate muzzle briefly tracing the aroma's contours, before turning away with the glum air of one turned away, to watch the male wolfing down his. After that she wandered over to the brow of the lawn, and stood looking out over the bright and indistinct plains (while the male, not pausing to interrogate his luck, left his own meal half-eaten and hurried over to bury his muzzle in hers). And then she returned, glanced at him in passing, and went on up the steps to the verandah.

To the woman the man said, with more dread in his voice than he'd intended: 'Cissy's stopped eating.'

The woman looked up. 'Maybe she's upset,' she suggested. 'Why don't you try her with some milk?'

He tried milk; coconut water; stewed chicken. Each time Cissy sniffed, then turned away, with the air of one debarred. That afternoon she vomited bile.

The man put her food out next morning, hoping against hope. But in the interim, he saw she had grown used to the idea that that part of her life was over; and she barely glanced at the bowl. For a second day the male ate well.

The vet said: 'This is such a strange case!' And he stood back from Cissy, perplexed. When the man said he thought she was carrying, the vet palpated her belly. But he could feel nothing. And when the man insisted – uncertain himself now, but decid‐ ing to insist, since it was the one thing he'd been sure of, once – the vet said, 'Well, all I can say is, if she was, she's passed those pups.'

The man said to himself: no.

The vet put Cissy on a drip, explaining: 'Whatever's wrong with her, she'll just have to cure herself. All we can do is support her.'

On the white table, with the needle in her foreleg, Cissy seemed sphinx-like, graven. She looked around her gravely, magisterial, serene. Her head seemed more domed than usual.

'Bring her back tomorrow,' the vet said, 'and we'll give her some more. Let's do that for the next few days.'

It was startling, now that she no longer ate, how fast the flesh melted from her frame. Between them, the man and woman settled into a new routine: two syringes of milk every three hours, and the half-hour drip at the vet each evening. And they took turns asking each other if Cissy wasn't looking a little brighter. But that was only at first.

Now the finical choreography of departure began in earnest, the days coming and going like dull porters, each with its livid load. There was the day the big male stopped grooming Cissy, pausing over her and actually commencing gnawing, before giving it up and moving on. There was the day the man found she had retched and not moved, and was sleeping with her muzzle in it. There was the day he discovered the male out in the back, digging hole after hole under the mango tree. And there was the morning that, in the car port, Cissy lifted her head slowly and looked at him, and he saw that all the softness of expectation had gone from her gaze, leaving only a terrible, slow-appraising, stone gravity.

He had buried his own father twelve years earlier and knew that look. To the woman, he said: 'We're going to lose her.'

The woman looked at him uncertainly, still vague from sleep. Then he saw her decide to disbelieve him.

'We don't know that,' she said. 'Even the vet doesn't know. She may be trying to live for the puppies.'

The vet said, 'Listen. Take her down to the animal clinic at Mt Hope. Let them take some X-rays – I'll give you a note – see if they can find out what's going on.'

In the yard, the man said, 'Cissy.'

She struggled, pushing with her forefeet, and sat up. She was terribly thin now, but in the morning light she looked more fine-boned than ever; and as she delicately lifted her muzzle, inquiring of the air, he saw that she had grown beautiful. Merciful life, the man thought, that can make us shine so at the end.

In his arms she was a lightness, part Cissy, the other part a memory of Cissy. The Mt Hope scale showed she had lost 25 pounds. The X-rays showed two puppies.

The Mt Hope vets disagreed. One thought they might be alive; the other was sure they were dead.

The man said, 'They're alive' – ashamed of his sentimentality, but saying it anyway, since it was what he had. Then he added silently, 'If your X-ray hasn't killed them'; and wished he knew more about such things.

The two vets turned and looked at him.

Back home, the man showed the woman the X-rays, the little fern-curlings of the foetuses, and the woman marvelled and said, 'Who's a *brave girl!*' stooping to ruffle Cissy's neck. But next morning there was a brown sludge oozing from Cissy where she lay, and the vet said on the phone, 'She's trying to pass the pups, you have to take her in right away'; and he said he would phone the clinic himself.

In the car, driving downhill, the man had to brake, and Cissy slipped forward till her forehead bumped the floor, and the man saw with horror that she stayed so, and he stopped the car and lifted her back up. At the clinic he parked in the shade of a row of saplings, and carried Cissy across the glary asphalt to the cavernous reception area and set her down on the rubber tiles. He checked in with the receptionist, then returned to the divide near the asphalt drive, and sat on the floor against the balustrade, and Cissy lay curled by his side.

It was a sunny, breezy morning and the clinic was empty, and his car was one of only three cars in the car park, against the trees. Beyond them was more green, with the hum of the highway coming from it, and the Mt Hope lawns, still pale with dew, stretching away to the east. This is as good a place as any, the man was thinking, when there was a sudden struggle by his side, and Cissy forced herself to her feet and stood, legs splayed and panting a little, swaying. Her shoulder-blades protruded, her head was lowered, and she was peering out under the balustrade towards the saplings and the car; bracing herself and peering.

The man looked at her and he wasn't sure. Then he reached out and took off her collar with the lead, and said to her quietly: 'Go!'

She swung her head slowly and looked at him sideways, as horses do, and he saw the clouds drifting through her eyes.

The man said again, with pain: 'Go!'

She considered him; and then she let him drop. He saw his reflection fall from her eyes before she turned away. Head lowered, she faced front again, and the man saw she was trying to focus on the row of saplings, like a bull trying to measure through a red roaring the distance to an insolent matador. And for a long moment she stood so, bracing, swaying.

Abruptly she staggered forward, braced; staggered forward, braced again; and, like that, she passed into the glare of the drive, not so much trotting as falling forward, essaying the white crossing, and picking up speed, with her stiff-legged, drunken-sailor's roll, now blown sideways as if by the wind, now correcting and rolling back, the bull's head lowered, the row of saplings, he imagined, coming and going among the insolent clouds in her eyes, with beyond them, beyond the haven of his car, more tossing green, a roaring horizon, and all around her the towering heavens, with their silently exploding, slow-toppling sky, with their downrushing, churning sky...

She nearly made it across.

WAITING FOR JUMBIES TO CROSS

Vision is singular: in a crowd, the eye picks out a face, holds it, passes on, picks out another, flickers away. The Red Indian whom Wanda's gaze fell on, in the teeming western approach to the Savannah stage, was huge, swarthy and malevolent-looking. Long-striding, impervious to the opposing tide of spectators (which parted like the biblical sea to let him through) he was making straight for her, towering and unsmiling. There must be some mistake, Wanda thought.

Startled, she glanced for reassurance at the girl from the Tourist Board, but Marilyn Niles, inclining her head to hear something Wanda's husband was shouting into her ear, a small smile on her lips, did not see her. The Red Indian was almost upon her before she realised that his glowering gaze was fixed, not on her, but on the setting sun beyond her shoulder. She had a confused glimpse of a chest black-gleaming with grease, of something metal shining at his throat, of the diagonal of a strap – and then she was twisting sideways to him – too late. The Red Indian strode brutally between her and her husband. His arm struck wrenchingly across her breast, his swinging flask banged her hip bone and he was gone. She reeled away; saw, through the pain, her husband holding his own shoulder and looking almost thoughtfully after the departing, swinging headdress, and she cried in exasperation, 'Jer-ree!' Then they were with her, Jerry's handsome, still-boyish, crewcut face peering with concern into hers, him saying, 'Hey, Wanda, you okay?' and the pain beginning to subside, resolving into separate tendernesses, into a stinging flaring ache below, and the deep hurt over her heart.

'Of course I'm not okay!' she cried irritably, 'That – brute!'

'You got a good bounce,' the girl from the Tourist Board said sympathetically. 'Look' – she wiped her fingers on the upper sleeve of the blonde woman's blouse and held them up – 'Grease paint.'

'She'll be okay,' Jerry told the girl; and they both looked encouragingly at Wanda. ('He's apologising,' Wanda thought. She cupped the wrenched breast and leaned forward slightly, taking its weight in her hand, feeling for the depth of the hurt.)

'He didn't mean anything, Mrs Schulman,' Marilyn Niles said consolingly. 'He was just passin'.' Taking the older woman's silence for assent, she went on brightly: 'You know, we have a saying in this country: "You can't play mas' and be afraid of the powder".'

'But I wasn't playing mas'!' said Wanda irritably. It sounded petulant and childish as she said it, and she straightened up and looked around her, gingerly rubbing her hip bone where it protruded from the waistband of her hipster denims. 'I'm okay,' she said to her husband, and he smiled, relieved.

'She's better now,' he told the girl.

Marilyn Niles, looking at him, smiled. To the woman, she said, 'That's good. I knew it would pass.' Then she glanced away, amused. This was the third year she had hired on for Carnival as an escort with the Tourist Board; in three years, not one of the couples she'd escorted had had, as far as she could tell, anything like the absolutely fantastic time they tirelessly professed to be having; and yet, she supposed, they had all returned to their home towns in the States or Canada or West Germany, and been the envy of their friends with their terrific tans, their treasure troves of photographs, and their tales of an orgiastic tropical paradise; as this couple, no doubt, would, too. Well, that was okay by her. Everything was what you made of it, thought Marilyn Niles sagely.

And that was okay too. Her job was to show these people a good time, and if a good time was what they were determined at all cost to have, who was she to nitpick? Her only problem right now was keeping this one's interest in her short of the point where his wife would notice, take offence, perhaps even lodge a complaint about her to her employers; and she didn't think it would be a big problem.

At their first meeting, she had been routinely aware of her

79

effect upon Jerry Schulman. Lightly and cheerfully in the days that followed, she had let him come on, since that was part of the game, up to a point, since she had to admit that he wasn't exactly hard on the eyes, especially not by comparison with the odious, fat man from Arkansas she'd had the previous year, and since, most of all, to tell the truth, she had been first intrigued, and then animated, by the measured, cautious, slow concentration of the forces of his attention upon her, until now, five o'clock on Carnival Tuesday afternoon, she felt for the first time an instinct to draw back from him, not only for tactical reasons but out of self-protection.

Still – it wasn't a big problem. In fact, it wouldn't have been a problem at all, she thought, if he hadn't started drinking; but he had. Not a lot, not so that it showed; but slowly, steadily, like the way he'd been closing in on her; once he'd started, Jerry Schulman had gone on drinking. He'd been drinking now for three days, and was flushed beneath his tan, and there was a certain heavy watchfulness behind his boyish smile when he turned to her, and his shirt was unbuttoned all the way down the front. Still (and here Marilyn Niles' heart skipped lightly, as though at a pleasurable thought she had tossed her head) nothing untoward was going to come of it.

They were basically okay, these Schulmans, so far as she could judge, and basically okay with each other as well. In their early thirties, married for six years – she'd made a point of finding that out – that was no more nor less than you'd expect, she concluded.

Marilyn Niles had an ingenuously simple idea of marriage. She thought of marriage as a chalice from which the liquid of intimacy slowly evaporated, so that, full to the brim on the wedding day, its level sank imperceptibly but inexorably thereafter, until one day, fifteen or twenty-five years later, the chalice was empty, and husband and wife, looking up from the dinner table, each looked into a perfect stranger's eyes.

It was an image Marilyn Niles countenanced with fatalistic resignation, as though it represented a law of Nature. Her own four-year-old marriage to Charlie, she fancied, confirmed it (for wasn't his ardour that much less than it had been?) and while, fearing at first to hasten that slow slide, she had postponed having a baby, of late she had begun to feel the future coming upon her from another direction, and she felt that if she didn't have a baby soon, 'the time would pass'.

All these were vague premonitions. If anyone had asked her, she would have replied, truthfully enough, that she was still in love with Charlie and he with her, and that their marriage was still good, better than good. But no one could deny, it was not as it had been; and as for these two here, surmised Marilyn Niles, although their marriage looked to be basically okay, despite a li'l 'Carnival madness' on his part, one thing was as certain as the stars above, and that was that it was two years less-okay than her own.

She glanced at them, and met Jerry's intent look. Subconsciously she'd been prepared for it, but now it occurred to her, 'He was waiting', and the thought made her blush. To cover her confusion, she said: 'I think we better get closer. To the stage. I mean' – one of Edmond Hart's trucks came abreast of them and she had to cup her mouth and shout into his ear – '*I don't want to miss Charlie!*'

Yelled like that it sounded wrong, and she flushed again.

'We're looking forward to seeing your husband again,' Jerry bawled back obligingly, but the look with which he concluded the words complicated their meaning. She was glad when Sophie Johnson, a Bee-Wee counter clerk, came dancing towards her out of the last Hart section, to stand before her in a limbo crouch (feet spread, knees flexed, hands palm upward at her sides) crying jubilantly, 'Marilyn! O Gawd, chile, whuh yuh doin'?' Girl grabbed girl; hugged; pranced in a tight circle; and then Sophie Johnson let go and was gone, pausing once to clasp her hands between her thighs and shake her bottom at them (grinning back over her shoulder mischievously) before prancing off down the grass corridor, arms pedalling. To the Schulmans, Marilyn Niles said, with the bright inanity of a guide: 'Well! That's Carnival!'

Wanda gave her a neutral smile. To her husband, she said: 'So, what's the plan?'

'The plan,' Jerry told her, 'is to try and get closer to the stage and wait for "Jumbies", and after they come offstage we're all going to jump up with the band: you, me, Marilyn, and Charlie.'

'Who's Charlie?' Wanda asked.

Jerry looked at her oddly. 'Who's Charlie? Charlie's Marilyn's husband, for Chrissakes; don't you remember we met...'

'Oh. That Charlie.' She glanced around Jerry to see if an apology was required, but the girl from the Tourist Board had evidently not heard. 'Okay,' she said, 'I'm game. Let's go.' She smiled what she hoped was a brave smile, but he hardly noticed, and as the three of them began moving east again, making their way against the stragglers coming off stage from the Edmond Hart band, she slipped back into the private misery of her thoughts, and the strange torpor of bewildered helplessness they evoked in her...

Thought is active and purposeful, so it would be inaccurate to say, as they wended their way towards the exit ramp of the Savannah stage, with Jerry in the middle, holding each woman now by the hand, that Wanda was 'thinking'. Outwardly she seemed only subdued – a natural response, thought Jerry, glancing at her, to being struck like that by the monomaniac Red Indian – but inwardly, secretly, she was entirely passive. Wanda felt herself strangely at the mercy of all manner of inchoate and fragmentary sensations, emotions and images; and it was this novel sensation of helplessness, of being pinned to a wall and assailed by a world she could not begin to comprehend, that constituted the real misery she dared not let her husband see.

She had known of course, from the moment they met her, that Jerry was attracted to this child (for that was how Wanda thought of Marilyn Niles, a mere five years her junior, and married as well, but, unlike herself, still childless, and therefore still, in some obscure way, unpossessed) and at that first meeting – while she, Wanda, still felt like herself, and like Jerry's wife – she had appraised her, covertly and swiftly, as she had appraised more than one potential rival in the past. She had registered the wide mouth, gleaming cheek bones and tight black curls, the snub nose and elongated eyes, and she had glanced with envy at the younger woman's lithe brown legs in which, as yet, no varicose vein showed, not even behind the knees (the latter were the reason why she, Wanda, oftener than not these days, opted to wear slacks).

Yet at the first meeting, nothing about the girl had particularly fazed her. Wanda had known for many years that the world considered her a beauty, if in a slightly old-fashioned way, with her perfect mouth, squarish jaw, and wide-set almond eyes, blonde hair and fine throat (by contrast, this girl's neck was piggishly short and plump) and at thirty-two she had kept her figure. The varicose veins were her only blemish – that, and the slight, very slight, slackening of skin on her abdomen and breasts, something no woman, having given birth, could avoid. No – what fazed her was not the girl but Jerry's reaction to her. He was seeing something in the child she had not seen.

The thought frightened her. In this hot little country, so far away from Springfield, Illinois, from their house with the newly-painted wickerwork on the verandah, the musty attic Jerry kept putting off cleaning, the drained swimming pool out back – in this unfamiliar, bacchanalian place, bereft of all the habitual references of his life and hers (she even had trouble imagining clearly what Randy and Joanne, left behind with his parents, might be doing at any particular moment) she felt uncharacteristically unsure of herself. She watched with strange passivity, and growing dread, Jerry's deepening response to this girl, whose name she's been told but had forgotten, and now had the utmost difficulty in recalling, no matter how often she heard the name from Jerry's lips.

And as the days passed, and Jerry began drinking and went on drinking, slowly, remorselessly, it seemed, she had felt the texture of their lives together thinning out, had felt him withdrawing more and more of the deep roots of his nature from her and directing them, progressively, towards this negligible girl – and she had felt strangely powerless to act. Beset by incomprehension, bereft of support, she had become a spectator at a scene of untellable misery: the slow extraction of his life from their life, and the unexpected emptiness where once she had unthinkingly leaned for support.

Heat, noise. Her days lost sequence. Always the girl wore those fashionable, flared shorts with the cuffs. Lights, noise: each excursion into the evening darkness seemed the same. Always, it seemed, they ended up in this dusty arena; or if not, she couldn't tell where. The girl changed her shoes but not her lipstick, to match her shorts. Always her lipstick was the same dark red. Traffic, dust, lights, noise. People! Pulling the drapes in the hotel at night tight, tight! Speech between them becoming perfunctory, incomprehensible. 'I'm fine... wasn't that... didn't you... it certainly was... yeah... fine.'

She lay in the dark, a crystal vase, waiting to shatter. 'Jerry?... Yeah... Fine.' In the mirror, she probed her face experimentally with fine fingers. Her nights were limbos of suspension, presided over by the intermittent shudder of the air-conditioning. She slept badly, drifting in and out of sleep. Glare. Noise. Dust.

'Pardon?'

They were in the grassy walkway between the North Stand and the stage, and a band on a truck was approaching, and there was an inexplicable deep ache over her heart, and someone, Jerry, was holding her hand, and the brown girl in the shorts was looking at her expectantly. She saw they had stopped walking, and she looked around.

To her husband, she said, smiling: 'Here?'

He nodded. 'Marilyn says this is close enough,' he told her.

Like a ponderous boat pushing a bow wave of revellers before it, a McWilliams truck came towards them down the grass corridor between the North Stand and the stage. Wanda stood at a loss, watching it come, until the girl from the Tourist Board, taking her hand, led her over to a low concrete bunker-like shed roofed in corrugated zinc, on which a couple of young black men were already sitting. To Wanda's husband, Marilyn Niles said: 'Hoist me up.' Turning full-face to him, placing her hands on his shoulders like a child.

Wanda watched as Jerry, stooping slightly, took hold of the brown girl's waist and swung her up ('My, he's strong!' thought Marilyn Niles). Before she could protest he had done the same with her, though his hand on her bare waist pulled the skin tight over her bruised hip and sent a flash of pain through her so that she hissed: 'Owww!' Then he hoisted himself up into the narrow space between them. Wanda, flinching away from the sudden weight of his hip against the tender bone of her own, shoved against the young man in the fishnet vest sitting on the other side of her. She turned to him, smiling confusedly, saying, 'I'm sorry'; but the young man only looked intently into her face and she flushed and looked away, toward the empty stage (at the eastern end of which a band was massing) waiting for her husband's voice to rescue her, to rescue them both; looking meanwhile straight ahead, at nothing.

The bow wave of revellers passed below them. The truck, a slow boat inhabited by black-silhouetted, bellowing demons, passed, inches from their knees. A little boy, leaning outboard, banged a bottle with a spoon intently in their faces, looking back at them for some moments after he'd passed. The band burst onto the stage. Jerry shouted into Wanda's ear, 'Isn't it something?' and she turned to him with a sweet, drowned smile, which irritated him. In the corner of his eye he saw the unknowable brown girl lean forward, bending almost double to shout a greeting at a noble-looking middle-aged black man with a beard whitened with powder. Jerry saw the man, beaming, reach up and take her face in both hands and kiss it hard on the mouth, before moving on with a departing wave, not looking back; and he turned and stared at her face in profile, at the broad cheekbone, the snub nose, the full lips with their blood-dark lipstick slightly smudged, and at the little beads of sweat on her neck and on her forehead just below the hairline. He stared, and knew she was aware of him staring; but she refused to meet his gaze, and went on looking straight ahead of her with a vague smile; and, baffled, not knowing how to proceed, he drew back in uncertainty into himself, saying as an afterthought to Wanda: 'How's the hip?'

The bruise was already purpling. The childish gesture with which she showed it, tugging the waistband away from her flesh for his inspection, touched him with something like sorrow, and he mussed her hair briefly, saying, 'You're a brave girl.' Then Marilyn Niles leaned across him to say, 'You sure you okay, Mrs Schulman?' and he smelt her perfume and sweat, and her breast was hard against his arm.

On stage the figures in coruscating gold and blue chipped and pranced, or jumped, or merely walked, or, singly or in twosomes or threesomes, planted themselves and wined. In the flesh they

looked less exuberant, more exhausted, than they had on television earlier that afternoon. Except for the walking ones, there was
a curious air of determination about their movements, and on
their faces Jerry saw a slack-mouthed, lidded look, a suffused
daze, and here and there a secret, silly smile. 'They've forgotten
their faces,' Jerry thought; and here a young Indian girl, scantily
clad but for her cape, came and stood at the edge of the stage
directly opposite to him, shouting and gesturing at him, 'Leave
those two and come with me!' For answer he pulled his shirt-tails
wide with both hands, baring his belly at her in a gesture
simultaneously of challenge and helplessness, and she threw
herself down on the stage floor and writhed in a paroxysm of
feigned passion before getting to her feet and walking away from
him with a scornful look. At his side Marilyn Niles laughed and
laughed. 'You see everything at Carnival,' she told him. 'Any an'
everything you ever wanted to see: is right here.' This time she
held his gaze for a reckless moment, before looking away with a
little private laugh. Then she looked around her, businesslike. 'I
think Jumbies might be next,' she told him.

The day was fading; the stage lights came on; a light drizzle
began. The young men sitting next to Wanda fished behind them
and came up with a loose sheet of galvanise which they held over
their heads like an awning. The one in the fishnet vest offered to
hold an end over Wanda – offering this wordlessly, with an
inquiring, unsmiling look – but she shook her head, smiling
wanly: 'It's okay.' She caught his glance down at her breasts
before he looked away. It gave her a dull feeling, and she started
to wonder whether she shouldn't untie the shirt-tail knot under
her ribs and button up her blouse instead. But vaguely she
couldn't think why, and the ache over her heart intervened, and
the thought never completed itself. She sat slumped forward,
hands clasped loosely between her thighs, and tried to imagine
what her children might be doing at that moment.

'What's the time back home?' she asked Jerry suddenly.

Jerry looked annoyed. 'Well, what's the time here?'

She started to answer – then stopped and stared in dismay at
the band and disk of untanned white flesh where her wristwatch
had been.

'My watch is gone!'

The loss startled her momentarily out of her torpor. The Rolex had been a gift from Jerry four years ago. It had been intended to commemorate a double celebration: his promotion to branch manager of the insurance company in Springfield, and the birth of Joanne, their first child. She had worn it unfailingly ever since; had even told the child it would be hers one day. Now her wrist felt orphaned. She looked at the disk of white flesh, pale in the deepening gloom, and for the first time that day – for the first time since they had arrived in this hot and festive country – felt herself close to tears.

'Well, that's that, then,' Jerry said coldly. 'I told you you should have changed the band before we came.' And he turned away to explain, in answer to the inquiring, light hand on his knee, that his wife had lost her perfectly good Rolex watch.

'It's twenty to seven,' the man in the fishnet vest said to Wanda.

She turned to him in sudden gratitude, trying to make out his face. But it was shrouded by the galvanise, and in the deepening dark and the drizzle all she could see clearly were his eyes. She murmured 'Thank you', and looked away in confusion. The thought occurred to her that she had made a mistake in thus acknowledging him, but she couldn't think why this should be so. It occurred to her once more to button her blouse, but in a dullness of lethargy she let the thought go. The man said something to his companion, and they both looked at her. She felt them looking at her, and the dullness grew heavier. In a half-stupor, she gazed through the drizzle at the brightly-lit stage, from which the last of the coruscating figures were now draining, and thought: 'Now I've lost his watch.' When the man in the fishnet vest abruptly moved the galvanised sheet over her head, bringing her into the rainless dark of him and his companion, she didn't react.

Her hair was wet. With both hands she slicked it back on either side of her neck. The water trickled down onto her chest, cold, then warm.

Jerry was talking to Randy in his mind. 'Randy,' he said silently, seeing clearly before him the bright inquisitive face of the three-year-old, 'When you grow up you'll understand a lot of things. You'll understand how full of shit the world is. You'll understand how hard it is to be a man. Who made it so, I don't know. I came and found it so, is all I can say. But it isn't a small thing – not this and that. You can't say, I'll keep this and change that. It's a whole great thing wrapped up together. You have to take it all, or reject it all. I love you so much, little fella, you'll never know. But I've taken it for nine years now, all of it. I guess you could say I've given you a good start. I guess you'll have to admit that yourself, one day. Randy, I have to tell you about the world...'

He stopped. The child was vivid before him, with his tousled brown curls and broad and shining forehead, and his mother's wide-set almond eyes, staring and waiting for him to go on; but for a moment he could not go on. He didn't know what he was telling the child, or why. He didn't know how Randy had suddenly appeared to him, more real than his surroundings, brighter than the stage, more intensely apprehended, even, than this woman-presence sitting next to him, its shoulder pressed against his shoulder, its thigh against his thigh. He only knew that the pain in his chest, which had begun, quietly, from the moment he first set eyes on her three days ago, had gone on, growing stronger and sinking ever deeper into him, until now it was like a bloodbeat of anguish in the deepest part of his being, and he felt himself flushed and slowed with it, and strong with the power of anguish. Invisibly his skin crawled, the words were deep in his throat, the metal band around his chest tightened and tightened; and the woman-presence was there, pressed against his side.

Out of all that, and Wanda's loss of her watch, the kid had suddenly appeared before him. As though, with her betrayal of the Rolex, the last present he had given her out of sheer happiness, out of the exultation of his young manhood and the promise of a still-shining world, the skein of irritation through which he had come to see her abruptly burst, and beyond it was the kid, sitting splay-legged on the apron of the swimming pool with a plastic battleship between his knees, twisting around to look up, grinning at his approach, and he had known there were things he must say to him.

He said: 'Randy, you see, the world...'

The band around his chest tightened again. The kid was watching him, clear-eyed, waiting. In his anguish he felt portentous, huge. He said: 'Not the world, but society. Society is something different from a man. We live in society; but life is so short! Men understand things we cannot say. One day you'll be a man; you'll understand. I wish I could change the world they made for you, but I can't. You'll understand then. You'll understand your father. Nine years is a long time; I'm thirty-three, Randy. I'm not a kid, anymore. And I love you so much...'

He stopped, startled, feeling the woman-presence thrust against him hard. He was instantly, overwhelmingly aware of her – yet, turning to her, he was also aware, separately and distinctly, as in a drug trance, that a din of anticipation had risen in the dark stand behind him, and that a band had surged onto the entry ramp of the stage.

'Jumbies!' cried Marilyn Niles, thrusting her arms into the air, ten fingers spread. Twisting around like that, so that her arm was momentarily against his face, she cried heraldically again to the cavernous North Stand: 'Jumbies!'

Her wet cheekbone was six inches from his eye. He saw with startling clarity the mascara smudge, the tilt of her snub nose, the fine hairs above her lip – and below that, at the edge of his vision, the wide and blood-dark mouth, with its perfect teeth.

The band surged onto the entry ramp – and stopped. Out of the milling mass, indistinct in the gloom, stick-figures, two, then three, then four, advanced teeteringly onto the stage. The first two, eight feet tall, came long-striding down the northern edge of the stage, androgynously slender and sinuous in polka-dotted body stockings, black-on-white, white-on-black.

To Jerry, watching them approach in the strengthening light, they seemed heralds of a kind: twins, as the lit and dark sides of the moon are twins; and their meaning felt portentous and indecipherable. 'What are they supposed to represent?' he asked the girl beside him, raising his voice above the din: 'The age of unisex?'

'I suppose you could say so,' she shouted back gaily.

He saw that she didn't know and didn't care. He looked at her and felt for the first time a welling-up of enormous uncertainty; but it subsided, giving way almost at once to the tightening of the metal band around his chest. He tried once more to conjure up Randy, obscurely aware of something unfinished between them, but the image of the child, when it returned this time, was disaffected, blurred and far, and the feeling of urgency faded. Now a female figure on stilts came staggering towards him: a lurid, blue and yellow stick-female, its breasts and pubic triangle outlined in red, with a featureless, eggshell face, black holes for eyes. He smiled, uncomprehending, and, turning to Wanda, saw her sitting away from him, one of a trio (the other two were young black men whose features he couldn't discern) sheltering from the drizzle in the gloaming under a sheet of corrugated zinc. He nudged her, meaning to ask, 'Hey, you okay?' – and recoiled from the blank gaze she turned to him. 'Hey, you okay?' he asked her.

Wanda nodded, but coldly; as if – Jerry thought – he were a stranger who had presumed to intrude upon her solitude. Directing her gaze with a slight gesture at the female stick-figure still teetering towards them on the stage, he said conversationally: 'That's a terrific costume. Looks like a colour photo printed in negative; but see? There's no face.'

Wanda looked, not really seeing. Then Jerry saw her look. Placing the heels of her palms on the zinc roof behind her, Wanda leaned back, inclining her head to one side, and looked at the Queen of the Jumbies. Then she jerked forward, pulled her knees up to her chest, applied her cheek to her shoulder; and sitting so, hugging her knees and rocking slightly, she considered the lurid stick-female (now rising above them) with a wincing smile.

His wife was being difficult again. Jerry looked away. There was a truck approaching along the grass swathe, the din of its music rising, and Marilyn Niles' fists and shoulders were rolling to the beat, and she was shifting her weight from buttock to buttock, against him, away from him, against, away. 'Jumbies!' she barked. 'Jumbies!' Naughtily she dug Jerry in the ribs. 'Leh we get high wid de Jumbies,' she sang with the singer, laughing into his face. Jerry lunged for her mouth; as quickly she pulled her face away. 'Jumbies,' she sang softly, not missing a beat – not glancing at him anymore, still smiling, but with a sideways wariness of him now in her face; 'Jumbies,' she sang, fists, shoulders and buttocks rolling, against, away, against, away. 'You little bitch,' Jerry told her, and Marilyn Niles threw back her head and laughed at his adoration, and dug him remonstratively in the ribs again, just in case, looking away from him. 'Jumbies,' she crooned, everything rolling, 'Dese Jumbies is it!'

The truck came abreast of them and slowly passed, and in the reverberation of its crescendo they saw that the band was now on stage: a bobbing melee of black and white whose individual forms the stage lights weren't quite strong enough to render. They looked like a tossing sea under the moon, with the infernal stick-figures, waist-deep, rising from it; and towering above them all, Jerry now saw, was a near-naked, gleaming, brown-skinned figure with a winged Darth Vader mask for a face.

The Darth Vader figure advanced emphatically, stagger-striding, swinging its arms across its torso like a race-walker. Jerry was about to laugh with pleasure at the invention when the face drew nearer and he saw it was not what he had imagined. Not malevolence but anguish was what shone in the black eggshell face with its gaping eye sockets, its grid for a mouth, its diamond noseplate and barred forehead – not fury, but loneliness and torture. Hoisted aloft, the imprisoning mask came on, arms pumping, but with the head strangely lolling; and in it Jerry saw the crucifixion of his age, the merciless imprisonment of a man in his own life, and in the life around him, and in the inexpressive metal of the world he had himself made. He said in desperation, 'Randy, this is *it* – .' And stopped.

He had spoken aloud. Marilyn Niles, all motion, stopped dead, and gave him a hard look. 'What you said?'

'Nothing,' Jerry said.

She looked at him a moment longer, her fists and shoulders still frozen in mid-roll. Then: 'Oh-ho,' she said, mock-threateningly, as if he had nearly been a bad boy and aroused her ire; and she resumed her sedentary dancing, rolling her shoulders and shifting her weight from buttock to buttock, against him, away from him, humming, under her breath now, the Tambu song.

★

Now, though he didn't know it, Jerry had misconstrued Marilyn Niles' animation. It wasn't that she was any especial fan of the Jumbies' bandleader (she herself had played regularly with Garib before her marriage to Charlie) nor was it due to loyalty to her husband's band. What mattered to Marilyn Niles was that whenever Charlie caught sight of her – which would probably be before she saw *him* – he should see her having a good time.

A better than good time, in fact – for Marilyn Niles had obscurely sensed that her marriage had reached the stage where it would do her no harm at all to be seen by her husband, in the first flash of recognition, not as 'his wife', but as a woman animated and desirable in her own right, and not necessarily dependent on him for her happiness. If this was teasing, thought Marilyn Niles, it was teasing in a good cause; and so, the moment the band came on stage, the moment it was even theoretically possible that her husband's eyes might pick her out, perched on the little galvanised roof with her two charges, she had set herself in motion, fists, shoulders and buttocks all rolling – and her animation had instantly been increased to the level of something like exaltation by the effect it had had on this Mr Jerry Schulman of Illinois here. His hapless lunge for her mouth minutes ago had been like homage; and now, in the secondary realisation that with her husband near she could freely play with him and have nothing to fear, she revelled in the delight of her power.

Besides, there was something vaguely humiliating, Marilyn Niles thought, about being a tourist guide and having always to explain things that in your own life you took for granted. Now, in the moment of their release, she discovered a muted irritation and resentment at the role she had played for the past three Carnivals; and a little impulse of vengeance further heightened her exaltation; as though, sitting, dancing there for Charlie's eyes, and dancing up against this one here, the baffled force of him at her side like a homage or like a goad, she was also reclaiming her life: reaffirming her oneness with her people and their Carnival, which was her Carnival too, and putting a decisive distance between herself and her two charges, the insurance man from Illinois and his unhappy blonde wife.

Add to these that a young body in motion, as Marilyn Niles' was, insensibly increases its elation, and it will be appreciated that by the time that Charlie, from behind his mask, did in fact pick her out, Marilyn Niles seemed transported. So radiant, so more-than-herself she seemed, that Charlie's gaze went reflexively to the crewcut white man sitting pressed up against her, his face flushed, his shirt unbuttoned all the way, and – forgetting for a moment the unexpected good time which the young thing from the typing pool had shown him on the road, all the way from the cemetery to Memorial Park, and what vistas might thus open up to him, come Ash Wednesday morning at the office – he stopped chipping and said to himself, a trifle grimly, 'Well-well. We shall see what we shall see.'

The Jumbies were beginning to leave the stage. A slight strain had entered Marilyn Niles' sedentary dancing, and her humming had grown abstracted, almost inaudible. She had been scanning the stage without seeming to and not catching sight of Charlie; and the ghost of a question had begun intruding upon her exaltation with a wife's subconscious alarm. Where was Charlie? And what explanation could there be for his absence from the stage, other than some bacchanalian subterfuge?

She had faced the worst, and was preparing some gay dismissive explanation of his non-appearance for the benefit of her charges here, when a large, black and white, wedge-shaped mask thrust itself between her knees, and a deep voice said: 'Boo.'

Marilyn Niles gave a little shriek. Then: 'Charlie!' she cried. 'You beast!'

Charlie tugged off the mask as she leaned forward to take his head in both hands and shake it briefly in remonstration and relief. He was a young man of average good looks, lighter-skinned than she, with a neat Mugabe beard. In his face, the played-out, slack grin of the masquerader, come Tuesday night, was leavened by a certain alertness. Marilyn Niles saw it, and, throwing her arms around his neck, she laughed and nibbled his ear. 'We thought you were never comin'!' she cried. 'We thought some jumbie had got you, taken you off!'

Charlie grinned at her. 'How yuh doing there, Mr Schulman?' he said drawlingly.

Marilyn Niles laughed. With inexplicable gaiety, she cried: 'Jerry! You remember my husband!'

'Good to see you, Charlie,' Jerry Schulman said levelly.

'And Mrs Schulman?' cried Marilyn Niles to her husband. 'Say hi to Mrs Schulman, Charlie, she got a good bounce!'

Then they were down from the wall and, forming a wavering, unsteady line, pressed upon by bodies in front of them and by more bodies behind them, had joined the river of masqueraders winding westward across the Savannah in the thickening night. Jerry, with Marilyn Niles on one side of him – on her nearside shoulder her husband's wrist rested limply, in casual possession – was surprised to find on his other side, not Wanda, but a man in a fishnet vest, looking straight ahead, his hand around Jerry's neck. He leaned back and saw his wife beyond Fishnet, with another man on the other side of her; and for a brief moment he tried to catch her gaze and reassure himself that she was okay. But Wanda, looking down at her feet – she was dully trying to match her chip-step to those of the experienced feet on either side of her – did not see him.

Jerry looked straight ahead. Beneath his hand was the damp khaki of Marilyn Niles' blouse, and beneath that the thickness of her waist, and her own hand was light on his flank. In the dark he surged against her slightly, and felt her hand reflexively tightening on his waist, and the hand of Fishnet slipped from his neck; but it returned. He was about to shout something into Marilyn Niles' ear when the next thing happened. It happened quickly and all but invisibly, and it was over at once.

The line of six, with Jerry near the centre of it, began once more to sway to the left. Then it began to sway back to the right – except that Jerry, from a sudden lack of resistance on his left, discovered that Fishnet and by extension Wanda and her other companion were no longer there. Instinctively he lunged leftward in search of them – and in the same moment Marilyn Niles tightened her hand on his waist, spreading her fingers so that the tips slipped into the waistband of his trousers. Jerry surged back against her, so hard that she tumbled against Charlie and grabbed him for support – and it was over. In her ear, Jerry bawled, 'Wanda's gone,' and Marilyn Niles, ascertaining with a quick glance across his chest that this was so, yet postponed her reaction to this news to deal first with Charlie, whom she felt glancing at her on her other side. 'I stumbled!' she cried to her husband in explanation, but making it sound like a child's complaint. 'I nearly fell!'

Hardly were the words out than she believed them utterly herself. That was what had happened. She had stumbled and grabbed both men for support; that was all. Charlie mussed her hair, and she squeezed his waist. To Jerry she shouted, 'Not to worry, we'll catch up with her later!'

She knew this to be untrue as she said it, and the thought occurred to her that what was going to happen to Mrs Schulman before the night was over would indubitably get her, Marilyn Niles, in some serious trouble with her employers at the Tourist Board. And it was her lack of concern over this prospect that made her realise that her days as a carnival escort were over. She was going, Marilyn Niles knew now, to start a baby with Charlie soon. Yes, definitely. Not later than Easter.

And so they surged on in the bellowing dark towards the neon lights of the road, lurching, and stopping, and pulling from side to side as before, only they were three now where they had been six. Over their heads, intermittently silhouetted against the night sky, the gesticulating, hoarse figure of David Rudder shifted from foot to foot. 'We are children of Africa!' bellowed the truck into the surging dark. 'Children of Africa! Yay-hay! Yay-hay!'

THE RUNNER STUMBLES

Who says that Trinidadians are amoral; that they always, all of them, just grab what they can; that the winner takes all in this shameless Paradise, the damned die laughing all the way to the bank? Consider the cautionary tale of Sebastian, a Newtown, Tranquillity boy. And your brother.

My first meeting with Sebastian is associated in my memory with the noise of tyres on gravel. It was a sound the sea wind blew back until the car entered the lee of the house and it came: a malevolent swift crunching so abruptly near that you invariably experienced a pang of alarm before someone – usually my uncle – leapt to his feet exclaiming pleasedly: 'They're here!'

The house, our Balandra beach house, was a low-roofed, unpretentious affair of exposed block work and wooden Demerara shutters painted a gloomy, rainforest green. It squatted on a hillock near the edge of the cliff (too near, my aunt would vexedly tell our friends; Willie bought that hinge last month and look at it) with an acre and a half of undulating, coarse grassland between it and the road, hosting a claque of haphazardly tilted coconut trees, and a tea-coloured, scarcely-moving and definitely unhealthy ravine, which accompanied the gravel drive until, the latter climbing steeply to arrive at the house, it wandered off around the hillock in stupefied search of the sea.

My uncle had celebrated his promotion to director of a large Port of Spain firm by buying this place, which my aunt, with pardonable pride (since it was leavened by a kind of amused resignation) referred to as The Estate. And to The Estate we dutifully retired each weekend: the three of us and Aunt Eileen, a hearty spinster who grew ever heartier as the marriageable years slipped by, and ended up completely dominating my gentle aunt: 'Not like that, Helena; here, give me!' The remoteness and primitiveness of the place compelled us to travel like apprentice castaways – ointment for mosquito bites, Belgian blackstone for snakes and scorpions, kerosene for the lanterns and fridge, magazines for my uncle and Aunt Eileen; and for myself (since taking care of us sufficed to occupy my gentle aunt) a jam jar and an end of stale bread with which to entice, inebriate – and unfortunately, often to kill – the tiny translucent fish called 'millions' which shone in a nearby stream.

And once there we soon acquired the psychology of castaways ourselves, and spent the remainder of Saturday and most of the next morning secretly anticipating the arrival of the Sunday people.

These latter comprised the car load of jaunty relatives, or rather more restrained business associates, selected with strategic care by my uncle and informed of their selection by my aunt, whose musical voice and frank affectionate gaze few proved capable of resisting – though the initiated knew only too well that the diligent driving involved in getting them to and from our place would occupy such a large portion of their day as to make the effort hardly worthwhile.

Sebastian Senior was a business associate of my uncle's: through the car-window I glimpsed a sallow, unhappy-looking man seated motionlessly behind the wheel for a moment. Then the black Vauxhall expired with a rattle and four doors opened at once, disgorging its occupants, the youngest a gawky boy who immediately turned and began searching under the seat for something – perhaps that furtive tin.

Beneath the adults' cries of welcome and amazement ('Eh-eh, Bob?') we eyed each other cautiously. I must have been nine or ten; he, two years older; and in him a certain physical process must already have begun, for I distinctly remember having to look up at him.

His sister, a pensive beauty a year or two older than Sebastian, greeted my gentle aunt shyly, endured without squirming a terrific bear hug from Aunt Eileen, and followed her father inside. In the living room she at once selected a magazine and, ignoring everything else – the view that her parents were still admiring, the Spartan, strange surroundings, that mural of bright fish, me – sprawled on her stomach on the sofa and began turning the pages. I kept glancing at her as a nine-year-old might, frowning when once, perhaps feeling my gaze, she lifted her lovely head and looked broodingly at me before returning to her magazine with – O God! – a slight smile. My uncle's brusque commandment, 'You children go and play,' evidently didn't include her. She drew her thick black hair tight behind her head for a moment, shook it loose, and went on reading. Regretfully, and therefore curtly, I summoned Sebastian outside.

What emerged from that encounter? Very little, I am bound to report. Sebastian, no doubt feeling the natural resentment of a twelve-year-old consigned to the company of a kid, seemed preoccupied and remote. He merely grunted when I pointed out to him, as I had seen my uncle do to numerous apparently amazed guests, the boundaries of our land. The system of tarred wooden gutters, hoisted on knobby posts, which caught the rain from the roof and guided it to a concrete tank did not in the least impress him. And to my speculative suggestion that he should try his hand at selecting, from the following list, the disease most likely to emanate from our stagnant ravine – malaria, yellow fever, cholera, TB, polio, gangrene and the plague – he contented himself with replying scornfully, 'Gangrene is not a disease.' In due course we found ourselves at the cliff's edge.

It was one of those sunny, windy January days, and the sea, a tossing cobalt blue, showed little rushes of white all the way to the horizon (along which a toy ship, with infinite patience, was making its way). Nearer in, over the reef, white seabirds wheeled and dived, while at our feet, far below, among the rock slabs left bare and dankly glistening by the fallen tide, tiny black crabs or larger brown ones clambered, or scuttled and froze. The surge and withdrawal of the flat inshore water combed the seaweed to the left, then to the right, and then to the left again; and once, across one of the rare patches where the sea bed comprised pebbly white sand, a rock fish darted, and darted back.

Sebastian surveyed this scene and pronounced it 'okay'. Picking up a pebble, he took aim at a prominent slab of rock and threw, but the pebble fell short by several feet. I, eagerly following his example, overshot. 'Strong-boy,' muttered Sebastian. I flushed;

threw again; overshot again. Sebastian underhanded his next stone; it bounced squarely on the rock slab. I threw three more times, missing. 'Try underhand,' advised Sebastian; 'Here, lemme show you.' And he lobbed another pebble, which fell short. In quick anger he shied again, hard, and miraculously struck the rock slab again; his pebble bounced off it and flew. Three tries later I finally hit it too. The pelting petered out.

'I wonder,' mused Sebastian presently. 'Supposing you was to hold something like this... say a weight on a string. And say you was to spin it round and round, like this' – elbow against his ribs, wrist furiously rotating – 'and let it go!' – wrist stilled, palm upward, five fingers spread wide. 'You think you could reach that rock?' 'I dunno,' I confessed. 'You?' Sebastian frowned. 'Depends,' he said darkly.

It depended, I learnt, upon many things; upon the speed of your spin and the angle of release and the weight of the weight and the wind resistance; upon the strength of the wind and the wind's direction, and the length of the string; and chiefly upon something called your parabola.

'I suppose you think with so many factors,' concluded Sebastian (and I had to admire him for that word: factors) 'it'd be impossible to ever tell?' 'I suppose so,' I said dubiously.

'Well, you're wrong,' said Sebastian flatly; and leaving the matter there he stomped off.

I quickly caught up with him. Hey, could he swim? 'Course he could. Fast? Very fast? How fast? Faster than you, that's for sure.

Hey, could he climb a coconut tree, lessay that one over there?

When he hesitated, I ran over and began climbing it. I got quite high before sudden fright sent me scuttling back down. Sebastian glared at me. 'You must be younger than I thought,' he said pityingly. 'Only little-little boys feel they have to show off, show off, all the time.' And with that he walked away again, leaving me uncertain after all as to whether I had just won or lost a point, but inclining, as the day wore on, to the former view...

Five years later I had occasion to travel, in a chartered bus noisy with students, to a sports' meeting at Guaracara Park: a four-way clash between our school, St Benedict's, CIC and, I think, Presentation. We were along in the role of supporters: our athletes, including our track star, Galt, had already gone ahead by car.

My uncle had evidently found the company of Sebastian Senior unrewarding, for after that first visit we never saw them at the beach house again, and in the interim I had completely forgotten them. So you can imagine my surprise when, not long after our arrival at the track, I heard the name 'Sebastian' being repeatedly called in the CIC section of the stand, and, looking out onto a field bright with pennants, I recognised him, jogging in the company of three team-mates. 'Hey, I know that guy,' I said. 'His name's Sebastian; he came to our beach house once.' My class-mates considered this. 'Tell him about Galt,' one suggested; and, taking his own advice, he stood up, cupped his hands and bawled: 'Sebastian, you ever hear about Galt?'

'Sebastian, you dead!' bawled another.

'Sebastian, take some advice, boy – go home!'

The CIC boys, constrained less by the prowess of our Galt than by the presence of their presiding priest, glared at us; but Sebastian never once glanced up from the track. Perhaps he hadn't heard. A thought occurred to me and I looked searchingly around the stands, but she was not there, or else I didn't recognise her, after five years, among the gaily dressed fillies of the field. When the jogging foursome that included her brother came past again, I fell to studying him.

He had grown taller, of course, and was easily six foot, and slim. Jogging, he carried his head slightly back, which made him seem both arrogant and vulnerable. When his team-mates decided to end their warm-up with a short sprint (which brought a howl of derision from our quarter) Sebastian dropped out and looked up curiously at us until, realising that the jeers had redoubled and were now being directed at him, he grinned, shook his head and walked away.

His performance that day was – well, judge for yourself.

To begin with, in the hundred he false-started twice and was removed from the line-up by a disgusted starter. ('A big man like you, man?') No doubt rendered overcautious by this, he started last in the two-twenty and proceeded to run past five-sixths of the field, but was never in a position to challenge our flying Galt, who, as he approached the tape, swung his head sideways and lunged for it with his shoulder – a gratuitous lunge, since he was five yards clear. Our hero decided to skip the half-mile, and this race Sebastian won. He won it vengefully, too, by the brute ploy of immediately sprinting to the front and running the others into the ground. But this tactic, although it lopped several seconds off the schools' record and sent the CIC boys into a disgusting display of something like religious ecstasy, evidently found no favour with the tactician, judging from the way he slowed to a walk at the end and pushed the tape away angrily with his hands.

But it is the quarter mile that signals most vividly in my memory, and that first suggested to my schoolboy's imagination that Sebastian might be a young man of hidden depths.

The race began in confusion. What happened was that Galt, now, false-started fractionally and hesitated in anticipation of being recalled. In storming out, however, he had pulled Sebastian with him, the gun had gone; and in the second it took him to realise that no recall would be forthcoming and to accelerate again, Sebastian was at his shoulder, had snatched the lead, and the race was on. They pounded into the first turn; they sailed along the backstretch; they leaned, staggering slightly, into the final bend; and still Sebastian held that counterfeit yard. They straightened for home, and now you could clearly see the grimace on the face of Galt as he pulled out to make his run, and the odd look of drained dignity on Sebastian's face as he concentrated on keeping his form. And this montage held… held… held long enough for a sigh to sweep the stands at the realisation that nothing was changing; that nothing was going to change; that this was how it was going to end… and for jubilation to start finding its voice in the CIC section of the stands…

…and then Sebastian did an extraordinary thing. With the tape less than twenty yards away, he ran onto the inside of the track and stopped, leaving a disbelieving Galt bereavedly to spread his arms, breasting the worthless ribbon.

In consternation Sebastian's school mates closed around him and a general furore began; one glimpsed his enraged coach sprinting towards him across the field. And Sebastian?

Sebastian stood, hands on hips and head down, breathing hard.

Once or twice he wiped his nose with the back of his hand and looked around; then he began walking away.

'What happen, Sebastian, what happen?'

His reply sped stand-wards from mouth to mouth. 'I don't know,' he panted. 'I just thought, what the hell.'

It was a remark whose meaning I didn't even begin to grasp, until, a couple years later, I opened a West Indian literary magazine and found there, over his name, a short story entitled 'The Return'.

The opening paragraphs of this story relate in faithful detail most of the scenario of that race. There is the bungled start and usurped lead, the furious flight and chase, the sighted tape – and here fiction forks away from fact. The hero, 'Saunders', does not pull up; he goes on and wins; and soon after, leaving the hubbub behind, he flies out of the island to attend university in England.

In England, however, walking at dusk among 'snowy poplars', Saunders keeps remembering that race. He knows that, back home, 'Goodson' has resumed training; he knows that they will meet again; and he finds himself dreading his return to Trinidad and to the inescapable revenge race 'even now incubating in Goodson's wolfish heart'. This dread congeals into an obsession. Saunders begins to neglect his studies, to go running in 'weather fair or foul'. Soon he becomes the university's quarter-mile champion; then its record-holder; then record holder of the All England Under-21 quarter-mile. And yet he knows no peace, for well-meaning relatives or mischievous friends keep sending him news of Goodson's progress; and Goodson, to judge by his times, is improving as fast as he is. The prospect of the return, now less than two years off, becomes a nightmare. Saunders trains and trains. Finally he abandons his studies altogether.

The university warns; warns again; and then it acts! For protracted non-attendance at lectures and tutorials, Saunders is sent down. He returns to Trinidad in disgrace. And yet, in his heart of hearts, he is thankful. Now at least, now at last, the moment of decision has come. 'Grudge Race!' the newspapers blare.

It takes place, that race, on a glorious afternoon, an afternoon 'better suited to lovers strolling than to the stench of fear and sweat, the reeking red world of the arena' (Sebastian's prose, not mine); and Saunders – Saunders wins it narrowly. But that victory is celebrated hardly at all in Sebastian's narrative; he moves at once to Saunders' realisation, hardly less dismaying to the reader than to the hapless victor himself, that for him it was 'too late, too late'. Too late for justification or retribution. He had invested too much, too deeply and for too long in this race, and it had bequeathed him a ruinous posture – a posture of dread.

And so, like the Ancient Mariner condemned to retell his tale forever, Saunders must go on running, and go on winning, though every victory increases his guilt and dread, until what sobs at his shoulder is no longer McPherson of Marabella or Payne of Barbados or the barefooted Kittitian kid they call The Phantom, but the combined and terrible wrath of all God's avenging angels; and what they threaten is no longer mere defeat but sheer damnation should he lose. Exhausted, driven to the brink, Saunders comes to realise at last how 'a single lie, a single, snatched-at, fraudulent win, had condemned him to perpetual flight. Every race from now on would be the dreaded one. Every race would be a return.'

And yet it seems that there remains for Saunders this paradoxical solace – that his fear, in no way different from that ordinary human fear which bungles so many ventures, now lends wings to his runner's heels. His victories multiply, and in the eyes of the world his fame spreads.

But the Avenger is not yet finished with Saunders. Though he is now the world record holder, a pulled ligament forces him out of one Olympics and four years later a freak accident (a shipwreck) debars him from the next. And now it dawns upon the horrified reader that Saunders has come at last to pit his fear against the most intractable opponent of all: Time. At thirty-two Saunders begins to prepare himself again.

At first all goes well, or seems to. When he runs he wins, and the world, by now habituated to him, applauds as if by rote. But then, a mere three months before the third Olympics, Saunders, in his dingy training room in Jackson, Tennessee, picks up the morning paper and reads that a nineteen-year-old black American named Schaffer, a 'bronze young demigod from Houston', has broken his world record in Atlanta.

'With care,' wrote Sebastian, 'Saunders folded the paper. With care he laid it on the coffee table beside him. And then he stared sightlessly ahead. "I am old," he thought suddenly, "and now they want me to do this year what I could not do last year." And for a while he sat and thought of nothing. Then he gathered himself together, all his concentration, all his energy, all his nerve, and looked into the deepest part of himself, and saw plainly inscribed there that he couldn't do it. And again he let his mind lapse...

'Finally he shook himself, picked up his running shoes, and drove out to the track to train. For what else was there to do?'

Now, though (in a nice contrapuntal balancing of his protagonist's age) the author's youth betrays him into melodrama. Saunders, having won both his heat and semifinal, and in the final having held off for more than 400 yards 'the panting, grinning mask of the challenger' (not Schaffer, after all, but a totally unknown Nigerian named Clarke) collapses and dies within feet of the tape 'where waited, if not salvation, then at least one more respite, one more motel on the road to damnation.'

The moral of Sebastian's story is (much too) clear, and his style borders on the rococo. But the unrelieved melancholy of it, and the exacerbated sense of sin which it exhibits, I, for one, find startling, in someone so young.

So the next time you hear somebody saying angrily that Trinidadians 'don't give a damn', think of Sebastian, and beg to differ. Sebastian knew only too well why he pulled up in that four-forty; knew what demons of conscience waited like traffic policemen to arrest him at the tape, had he gone on. And where there is one Sebastian, surely there must be others?

THE LAST OF THE BIG SPENDERS

Metcalfe was not his real name, but for some reason everybody called him Metcalfe and I never found out his real name.

He was at Queen's Royal College around the time I was at St Mary's – a sleek dark boy, neither tall nor short, neither skinny nor fat, neither good-looking nor ugly; except that, quaintly even for those days, he wore his hair with a rigid part down the middle.

To tell the truth, I hardly knew him. But we knew the same girl, a reticent, pretty child (who shall be nameless, since I understand she is today happily married to a raving maniac, the Emperor of Jealousy and a sometime body-builder) and so we were awkwardly, sheepishly constrained whenever we bumped into each other on intercol sports' days, and saved our best intercollegiate taunts for other ears.

Metcalfe lived in Belmont, and rode a standard black Raleigh with no brakes and the handlebars reversed to a pair of horns – a purely flamboyant gesture, I suspect, since whenever I saw him riding he was carrying either a pile of books or a pile of records and so was proceeding 'no hands'. I remember him swinging nonchalantly into our mutual friend's drive – she lived in Woodbrook – and then, overdoing it, attempting to slip backwards off the moving bike – and Metcalfe and the records fanning out on the weedy swathe between the asphalt ramps, which was how, stingily, they built driveways in those days.

Fats Domino. The Drifters. Whoever it was 'and the Platters'. Those were the kinds of records Metcalfe hoarded and would bring, negotiating 'no hands' the sinuous curve of Serpentine Road, for his shy love's edification and presumptive delight. He would acknowledge my presence on her verandah with a burlesque of amazement, a spastic duck and peer along his shoulder simultaneously censorial and coy, and go on into the dark living room without breaking his stride, making a beeline for what we used to call the radiogram, seemingly oblivious of whether his young hostess followed him inside or not.

And it was only when the record had begun, and funky Fats or the falsetto Platters had settled down to assailing the verandah's ears with their urgent or plaintive news, that Metcalfe would start behaving like a normal human being in human company: cross his legs, crack a joke, look at you.

I would notice, but not think it worth remarking, that he never left with the records he had brought. And it was only later, much later, that I wondered whether, unknown to me, those records ever surreptitiously completed their round trip, Belmont-Woodbrook-Belmont – or whether, even then, Metcalfe was already a big spender, and was wont thusly to bring his culled treasures to the shrine of his reticent maiden, as knights errant, in other, more glamorous and tragical times, brought their wounds.

I left school, the girl's family moved, and I stopped running into Metcalfe. I heard he had got a job in the civil service; and then I stopped hearing about him.

Four years later, home on vacation from university in Jamaica, I bumped into Metcalfe at a fête at Harvard's. He had put on weight and looked sleeker and more peremptory, adult; and this despite the fact that, in addition to the figgy middle parting, he was wearing his collar up and a handkerchief spilling from his back pocket – something that by then seemed a vaguely retarded, teenage thing to do. When I laid eyes on him he was shuffling to the music with a miniskirted girl under each arm.

One looked half-Chinese; the other was, like Metcalfe, glossily dark; both looked sultry in a bored kind of way, as did Metcalfe (lips parted, eyes slitted): a triptych of smouldering boredom. I suppose they were digging the music, or had forgotten it. We acknowledged each other from a distance but didn't speak – as I say, I hardly knew him – and I would have forgotten I'd seen him that night, but for what happened next.

The music had stopped, and Metcalfe was standing, conferring with his girls, when I glanced across and saw him evidently dispatch the half-Chinese one to the bar. This was odd enough; and how he did it was odder. He took what looked like a huge wad of notes from his pocket and, without looking at it, handed it to her and at once appeared to forget her. You would have thought this vulgar ostentation on his part, except that the half-Chinese girl seemed to be used to that kind of thing, coming from Metcalfe. She accepted the wad without surprise and wandered off towards the bar, separating out the few notes she needed as she went.

'The ol' Metcalfe,' I thought sourly. 'The last of the big spenders.' That was the first time I thought that about him, and I suppose I was being envious. Both of his girls were beauties; and the wad-bearer, glazed with perspiration, seemed, as she walked alone, to give off a languorous, leonine light...

More years passed, and from Jamaica one night I boarded a BOAC flight for London. It was November, early winter, and London was bitterly cold. Frost formed on the windshields of cars and made sticky the park railings.

It was my first visit to England. I stood on a pavement somewhere in the West End and thought: There are ten million people in this city. I stood on another pavement, same city, and thought: A man would die in this cold if he didn't keep moving. This was to me a new and alarming thought: that Nature herself could wield such a cruel veto over inaction. From a London-based Jamaican anthropologist I borrowed an old duffel coat.

Weighed down by it, one night early in my stay, I was standing in Trafalgar Square, trying to decipher some newspaper's cinema guide in the light leaking from a cafeteria's window, when someone gripped my arm. Metcalfe.

'Ah-ha!' he said accusingly. 'So you here now! When you came?' He looked even plumper, sleeker, more peremptory.

'Two, three weeks ago,' I told him.

'Yeh?' He thrust his shining face towards me. 'Well, lemme tell you something. Dey say back home dat only Trinidad have carnival? Well, dey lie! London have carnival too. London is one big carnival.'

And with that – having, as it were, leapfrogged the years of our mutual oblivion for no other apparent reason than to transfix me on this freezing night in the middle of nowhere with this enigmatic news – Metcalfe hustled away, a muffled Trini moving fast through Trafalgar Square in the manner of a London spade: head bowed, shoulders hunched, hands plunged deep in his overcoat pockets, long-striding.

I looked at him in amazement. 'Hey, Metcalfe!' I called; and ran after him.

Metcalfe was moving fast; too fast for me, fresh from the West Indies, to keep pace. 'Hey, slow down nuh man,' I panted. 'Where you think you are, England?'

It was corny, but for some reason it cracked him up. He stopped dead, looked at me, and gave a wild laugh. Then he ducked his head, hunched his shoulders and strode off again; yet not now with the air of someone alone. Without checking, he seemed to assume I was at his shoulder.

I nearly lost him at the crossover from the Square to the road leading to the River. While I hesitated, Metcalfe, without pausing or looking left, plunged from the pavement and strode determinedly across the road amid the honking London taxis.

Eventually, risking life and limb, I followed him across. He hadn't looked for me, and I was relieved when, catching up once more, I found he had gone into neutral and was now coasting desultorily towards the Bridge.

'So,' I said. 'How long you here?'

He mumbled something.

What was he doing, where was he living?

I plied him with questions. Metcalfe mumbled and mumbled, and seemed set at any moment to frown. I was a newcomer in London; I wasn't aware that you should no more ask a spade these questions than you should ask them of a Vincentian fisherman on the north coast of Trinidad; and I began to feel my company was unwanted.

'Listen,' I said, slowing up and looking around. 'Which way is Piccadilly Circus?'

Without pausing or looking at me, he jerked a thumb back over his shoulder. 'So.'

I hesitated. I had more or less decided before Metcalfe appeared to try to catch Glenda Jackson and Alan Bates in *Women in Love*; but now, in the wintry air coming up from the dark river, London felt huge, forbidding, and too close. Each streetlight had a halo about it, and the road ahead merged with a dragonish glare. 'So what you doing?' I asked Metcalfe hopefully.

We – and, not looking at me, saying it casually as if it were already settled, he used to word 'we' – we were going to meet his girl and have dinner. His girl worked in south London, in a travel agency. Metcalfe turned sharp left and disappeared down the steps of an underground station. I followed, and soon saw we were heading towards an angular brunette, dressed apparently in nothing but an expensive-looking, mini-length fur coat and high-heeled, knee-high black boots, lounging by a newspaper kiosk. I had seen girls dressed like that in London and had thought, 'Their thighs must be freezing', and had thought, with awe: 'The ice-thighed maidens of London.' Metcalfe's girl had a thin straight mouth, a thin straight nose, gaunt, hollowed-out cheeks, and eyes with red in them – all of which probably makes her sound pretty unattractive to look at. She wasn't; she was okay. Better than okay, in fact, when she smiled at you. Her smile, like the smiles of certain French actresses, spoke of experience, tolerance, and an interest in you that was noncommittal but could become something more. 'The ol' Metcalfe,' I thought.

Metcalfe's introduction was less than cursory. 'Fella from school,' he told her imprecisely, jerking his head in my direction, leaving me to offer my first name, and she, hers. I think her name was Angie, or Josie; something like that. Her parents, I learned later, were mid-Europeans, and, though born in England, she had grown up bilingual.

'You got the thing?' Metcalfe asked her.

For answer she patted the bag hanging from her shoulder and smiled at him: she had 'the thing'. Three together, we re-ascended into the London night and winter.

Metcalfe called a halt at a steakhouse. I looked at the menu in the window and said, 'You must be joking; I can't pay that kind of money' – a remark which, for some reason, seemed to endear me to Metcalfe's girl. Amused, she took my arm in both hands and drew me in this way through the door. Metcalfe, expansive, followed.

I don't remember that we talked that much. Metcalfe ate his steak with concentration, pausing only to instruct me, 'Tell her about so-and-so' – so-and-so being, variously, J'ouvert, the idyllic beaches of Tobago, and a famous joke heard once in the crowded foyer of the De Luxe cinema after what would today be advertised as a 'sizzling sex double'. I had the impression he was in love with her, and was inviting me to tell her about him. Metcalfe's girl did, after all, have on something under the fur coat: a black, ridiculously brief mini. Metcalfe, his plump face shining, cocked his head while she leaned over to whisper something in his ear, then laughed and pointed his fork at me.

'Tell her about so-and-so,' he instructed.

That was the sort of dinner it was: forgettable; until the bill arrived.

The waitress, a snubbed and swarthy Mediterranean type with the look of a young woman prematurely past her prime, brought it over. But Metcalfe neither looked at the bill nor acknowledged my mumbled offer to pay part. What he did was what he had done years before. He handed the waitress a huge wad of notes without looking at her, and went on talking to us.

The waitress suspected a trick. 'What,' she asked Metcalfe icily, 'am I supposed to do with this?'

Metcalfe didn't even look at her; he looked at his girl, and Metcalfe's girl – Angie or Josie, but probably Angie – explained to the waitress that she should take whatever the bill was and return the rest.

Still the waitress hesitated, unsure whether she was being complimented or insulted. Finally, she ostentatiously selected out the requisite notes and tossed the wad with rude disgust back on the table. 'Keep a' change,' mumbled Metcalfe, not looking at her. The waitress, losing her temper, turned on her heel and flounced away.

For perhaps a full minute that wad of wealth lay on the table in full view. Metcalfe seemed not to notice it, and Metcalfe's girl, looking directly at me, seemed to be challenging me to mention it; so I didn't; I looked at Metcalfe. The Last of the Big Spenders, I thought; and suddenly I feared for him. The world as a rule does not repay such generosity or recklessness or faith, or whatever it was.

'Listen,' said Metcalfe suddenly as we left. 'You ever heard…?'

And he named some song by Diana Ross and the Supremes. I said I hadn't. 'Come and hear it,' said Metcalfe, the unlikeliest spade in London; and he hailed a taxi.

Metcalfe's flat was a long way away, in Highgate, and the meter ticked and rose. To my surprise Metcalfe's girl paid the driver, some exorbitant sum which Metcalfe seemed not to notice. He lived on the sixth floor of a modern apartment block, in a flat that was adequately heated and carpeted, with furniture that looked neither expensive nor cheap and was a lot less ugly than it could have been, and with a fine view out over level London. Metcalfe's girl disappeared into the bedroom, and Metcalfe, after first putting on Diana Ross for my benefit, followed her inside.

I didn't see him again. Nearly half an hour later, the music having long ended, Metcalfe's girl emerged, clad only in a towel, and said apologetically that Metcalfe couldn't see me, but that he wanted me to have 'this' – handing me the record in its sleeve.

I was irritated at being left alone for so long. I curtly declined his gift, and managed only a barely polite farewell as I left to Metcalfe's gaunt and wet-haired brunette (who gazed pensively after me from the lit oblong of the half-closed door).

I wish now I had accepted that record. Metcalfe, I heard recently, died last year – allegedly of some chronic lung ailment that grew unseasonably worse in the summer and killed him before the first freeze of winter. And though, perhaps uncharitably, I doubt this, and suspect his death had more to do with drugs than germs, I would have liked to have had his record to remind me of him.

As it is, I shall probably forget him. I hardly knew him, as I said; and already I remember him oddly and disjointedly, as someone blasé and unknowable, with that archaic middle parting in his hair – one of those odd Trinidadians who wander the continents under God-knows-what strange compulsion to go on giving away their music to the world.

THE LADY IN WHITE TERYLENE

In the mid-sixties, in Jamaica, I spent some time in Port Antonio, a small seaside town south of the tourist belt. I was in love, or had been, and was taking the cure, in the manner of the luxurious young – which is to say that, rejected beyond recourse, I had taken myself off to a rainy coast to 'think things through' and 'sort myself out' – but mainly to mope in soulful solitude for a spell. As part of this mood I often went for walks, sometimes quite late at night. And it was on one such nocturnal excursion that I met the young Trinidadian woman who – though I never saw or heard of her again – has, at odd intervals since then, exercised a strange influence on my imagination. Wherein I have thought of her, from the first, as The Lady in White Terylene.

Woo's, where I wandered morosely on the night in question, was a luridly lit, first-floor waterfront dive perched incongruously above the Harbour Mortuary. Perhaps because of its proximity to the frowning dead, the imperious roar of the god of the jukebox was there proscribed, and instead, side by side with the usual testament to the proprietor's right to traffic in spirituous liquors, a child's blackboard apologetically announced a menu: highly spiced curried goat-and-banana meals, mainly, and horrible, cold hamburgers. The lighting was merciless: naked red bulbs studding the celotex ceiling in a pattern of diamonds within diamonds; and there on a Saturday night you might loll at the bar, or pull out a chair at a formica table – plastic mats around a pyramid of ketchup, pepper and salt – and watch the livid couples mumblingly converse – or rise up in the demoniac haze and wander over to stand before the wall.

That, incidentally, was how you could tell the newcomer to Woo's. At some point in the evening, early or late, the companion of some pretty young thing might nudge her and whisper. She would look up, casting an appraising shy smile around the room; and then, a little jerkily perhaps, she would rise, self-conscious as the infernal faces turned, innocent of her own suffused face – and go and stand with him before the wall. The explanation of this mini-pilgrimage was to be found in the fact that the walls of Woo's were plastered with newsprint, with random pages from the lost newspapers of fifty years, so that upon them might be found a fair portion of the history of the race, not so much garbled as presented synchronously, with an Oriental disregard for time.

It was probably this experience of finding oneself in the red cathedral of history, rather than any impulse of deference to the upward-staring dead, that imparted to the clientele of Woo's a certain subdued air; that impelled the young thing abruptly to lean her head helplessly against her companion's shoulder and draw his protective arm around her waist: forlorn figures in the incarnadine haze, leaning together before the wall.

What did the walls proclaim?

'Elizabeth Regina! Flood Damage Put At; BITU Says Masses; Collie Smith Flies Home; Kennedy Tells Kruschev; Sobers to Play in South Af; Quads to Clarendon Mother; Sugar Heads Meet Postponed; Alcan Announces New; Garvey To Stand For; UWI Lecturer Deported; There Is A Man On The Moon! Churchill To Visit Jamai; Kingston Hit By; Court Rules United Fruit; Chamberlain Declares Pea. Jamaica Reaches Final; Jamaica To Host Com; Jamaica To Go It Alone! Jamaica Appeals For; Marley For U.S. Fes; Adolph Hitler Is; Nonsuch Nonpareil! Jamaica Is Tops, Says Tou; Five Killed In Sh; Jamaica Honours Its; PM Sees Bright Prospects; Welcome, Princess Mar...'

There was more, of course, much more – but who could sustain it? Soon it would all begin to whirl to cacophony, to a cackling volley of gibberish and pain... and it was a rare pilgrim who could endure for more than a minute or two in the light of Woo's maniacal walls.

The only mural relief was to be found in a far corner of the room. There someone – some enterprising publicity agent, perhaps, or else some prior proprietor with an interest in the local

113

cinema industry – had superimposed upon the stunned news a large poster announcing the imminence of *Battle of the Damned*: an experience, the subtitle warned, involving 'action from start to finish'. The turgid light imparted a totalitarian drabness to the depicted scenes, but it was still possible to deduce the pristine conception behind the dried-blood effect.

War roiled in the margins of the poster. A claque of dive bombers at top left confronted cata-corner a squat tank, which with muzzle erect was potently belching flame, while two small bands of men, distinguishable chiefly by their headgear, snarled at top right and bottom left. Their rage, however, seemed directed less at each other than toward the heart of the poster where, in an incandescent medallion or egg of light, a blonde girl stood. Shrapnel or those gladiatorial glares had ruined her white dress; she stood with one hand staunching the fall of fabric from her groin, while the other arm supported rather than concealed a pair of pathetically swollen breasts. But it was the expression on her face which startled. There the unknown artist had rebelled; there he had rendered his contemptuous dismissal of all the arguments of war. The girl's face was abstracted, calm. Lips parted, she gazed from the wall with a dreaming serenity no carnage could corrupt. Out of the midst of terror, out of the mobbing headlines, over the empurpled heads of the clientele of Woo's, those clear eyes beheld another glory, and she was elsewhere, not there in that strange place above a mortuary where the *Battle of the Damned* hung in the cave of history.

That, then, was Woo's. There both day and night were even-handedly excluded, there time itself yielded to a sanguinary haze. And it was there, on that rainy Monday night, that I came face to face, in suffused light, with the Lady in White Terylene.

'Hey, Sharks,' I said to the barman. 'You heard a' owl?'

I was in that portentous mood which alcohol tends to produce in a certain temperament and reluctant to ascribe to any inanimate source – the sea, the wind – an indeterminate low hooing I thought I'd heard.

He looked up from the sink, a mournful praying mantis of a man, with a mashed-in face made sad as a clown's by the droll cedilla of a scar beneath one eye. How he acquired the name Sharks is another, and perhaps apocryphal, story.

'I think I just heard a' owl.'

'Is possible.' He looked bored and amused.

'Check in the back,' I suggested. This advice elicited from him only a mirthless chuckle, so I swivelled on the bar stool and peered around for a prospective corroborator.

It was Monday night and the place was deserted, except for the solitary figure of a young woman who sat at the far end of the room, nursing a carmine drink and staring out of the black square of the window.

'Hey, Miss!' I called. 'You heard a' owl?'

I half-expected to be ignored, and was surprised when she turned her head and looked obscurely at us. 'You see,' I told Sharks. 'She an' me heard a' owl.'

He looked at me keenly. Setting down a glass, he undulated over from the sink, wiping his hands. 'You know who dat is?' he murmured.

'Who?'

'Ogunde-Davenport woman.'

'You serious?' And when, by way of answering, he slit his eyes significantly: '*That* is Ogunde-Davenport woman?'

I was intrigued. Though it had happened before my time, I had heard of course of the thwarted coup: of the arms cache, the marked maps of the city, the hopefully-worded manuals ('On assuming power, your first priority…'). There had been the body searches at the airport, the rumours of gunboats offshore, the hasty emigrations. Three of the accused had been incarcerated for life. Nigel Davenport, the son of a Methodist minister, ex-President of the Guild of Undergraduates of the Jamaican university, a young man who, in the scolding judge's opinion, 'in different company could have gone far', had been one of them. Some weeks ago, the Kingston Press had reported his escape, adopting the same scandalised tone in which it had reported his mid-trial assumption of his miscegenated title. ('My name is Ogunde-Davenport,' he had coldly told the Court. 'And I am not your friend.') And though as a foreigner I had been chiefly impressed by the residual awe of my informants, and had grasped

115

more strongly than any dramatic detail the sense of vertigo, which they all imparted, at having been caught unawares at the edge of unimaginable apocalypse, I could guess how, for someone like Sharks, the sight of this young woman here in Port Antonio must be like a stab – an adrenaline pang, twitching the corpse of an old wonder.

'Then tell me something,' I said sceptically. 'If that is Ogunde-Davenport woman, what she doing quite out here?'

His eyebrows shot up. 'Den master,' he breathed. 'Don't de man is *fram* Port Antonio? 'Im barn an' grope right 'ere. Yes, man! Ricketts? De sawmill man? Dat is 'im uncle – 'im mudder brudder!'

I peered again, squinting to pluck the tragic features from the infernal haze.

'Wonder what they did to him?' I mused.

'Did to 'im?' The barman was incredulous. In the lurid light his scar gave the impression of copious, one-eyed weeping. 'You nevah read was Inspector Jones what did the pre-trial interrigation? You doan know what dat mean? Ha, boy! Look 'ere. Dat was a straight case of Power Whap.'

'Power Whap?'

'Watch at dis,' said Sharks. He glanced around, then leaned on the bar to interpose a shoulder between us and the figure in the corner, while with a furtively oscillating forefinger he beckoned me to draw near.

'Arright,' he said, *sotto voce*. 'I am Inspector Jones. You are de culprit. I come in de cell, you sittin' dere. I have de ol' baton handy. I say to you: "Aw-haw, Mr Culprit! Dem say you plannin' coup wid dis Black Power. So – you like power?" Now, what you say?'

'Ah…'

'You doan say nutten. Because before you could open you' mout' I gone on. Hear mih now! "So you like power? Well-well. Look a lil power." *Whap*. Jes' a likkle tickle wid de baton: hear mih now! "You want power? Look power!" *Whap*! An' uh *likkim* wid de baton in 'im wais'!'

The barman leaned back and put his palms on the counter.

'Bwoy,' he said wistfully. 'You doan know Inspector Jones.'

I glanced around again. 'You think she would talk to me?'

'An' why not?' demanded Sharks indignantly. 'Don't 'im is 'uman like you an' me?'

'I dunno,' I said. 'She might want to be alone; you never know.' But the barman seemed abruptly to have lost interest. 'Cho, talk to de 'ooman, man,' he said sadly. And selecting a tea towel, a bottle and two glasses, he went inside, leaving the bar unattended.

I pondered the matter awhile. I have always been reticent when it comes to imposing my company on that inscrutable amalgam of hurts and hopes we call our fellowman; but the same spirits which had whetted my curiosity were dampening my reserve, and so, after hesitating for a moment longer, I went over and with a certain exaggerated gravity introduced myself and sat down.

She was in her mid-twenties, I guessed, slender and dark: of that mix of African and Indian you seldom see in Jamaica. White beneath its rose shimmerings, her terylene dress gleamed; and her hair, a mauve-black mane, framed a face with a thin mouth, soft recessive cheeks, and a pair of unexpectedly mischievous eyes. Looking at me with amused expectation, those eyes threw me slightly. I had prepared a corny line about the impropriety of drinking alone. Now I heard myself saying, with foolish surprise:

'You don't look Jamaican.'

'That's probably because I'm not.'

I stared at her. 'Wait, nuh!' I said. 'You from Trinidad?'

'Like you.' She smiled a little sadly, and I caught myself grinning in return. For a moment we were compatriots in a foreign land.

It passed though, the moment – and a shyness descended upon me. The Lady in White Terylene leaned back, crossing long legs, and looked out of the window.

Something made me turn to follow her gaze; but there was nothing there, only the sea contentedly lapping and the water-front lights lying along the water.

'On a clear day,' I told her, 'you can see Cuba.'

It wasn't true: Cuba was more than a hundred miles away, beyond the horizon. But the sharp, amused look the Lady in White Terylene turned on me invested my quip with a significance I had not intended; and it came to me in a rush that Ogunde-Davenport had already made good his escape, that he was already safely ensconced in Cuba, and that she knew it.

This intimation drew in its wake a fantastical James Bond scenario wherein the Lady in White Terylene, her hair lifting, ran out onto the rickety pier and jumped into a speedboat (waiting, rolling in its own wake) and was sped thence to some waiting ship or submarine, soon to be reunited with her subversive love. It was romantic nonsense, of course, but it was of a piece with the strangeness of the setting, and the strangeness of Sharks' story, and most of all the strangeness of her being here alone at this hour of the night, so far from home. And so, instead of instantly dismissing it, I put that scenario on 'hold', and looked at her speculatively.

She misread my gaze and lowered her eyes. Then, as if angry with herself, she looked at me and said defiantly: 'I know what you're thinking. You're thinking, what is this woman doing by herself in a place like this?'

Abruptly she was vulnerable. And it would have been kindness on my part to admit it, for she was right, after all. But kindness seldom enters into these matters. 'It's not my business,' I told the Lady in White Terylene.

If I'd expected her to flinch from that, I was wrong. She held my gaze, and after some moments we smiled.

'Well!' I said, thinking to concede from strength. 'Don't you find it's strange?'

'What?'

I gestured vaguely. 'This place. You.'

She made a show of looking sceptically around – then of looking with equal scepticism at me. 'No,' she said.

Okay, I thought: this was a game two could play. So I looked intently at her and said: 'You're a beautiful woman, you know that?'

'I know.' But the way she said it, with those alert, amused eyes, yielded nothing.

And suddenly I felt terribly hurt for her, alone and abruptly embattled in this strange place and fighting the good fight, and I didn't want to play anymore.

'Let me buy you a drink,' I said.

But she'd begun shaking her head before I'd finished. 'I don't want another drink.'

I stared at her. 'Listen,' I said in a sudden rush of ardour. 'I have to tell you this. If it's true what they say, he should have taken you.'

'Oh,' she said again, but this time wryly. Then: 'Well, don't blame *him*, if that's what you think. Blame me. I didn't want to go.' And she turned up her palms and grimaced.

On the tide of my confusion an obvious question floated by and I grabbed it. 'Then what,' I asked the Lady in White Terylene: 'What are you doing here?'

'Oh, I don't know.' With a pensive forefinger she wiped the condensation from her glass. 'Just saying goodbye, I suppose. I'm heading home. Well' – she amended herself – 'back to Trinidad, anyway.'

I registered the distinction and asked what she meant.

For some reason the question seemed to sadden her immensely. She turned and gazed out of the window, and I was afraid she was going to cry.

'Let's just say,' she said drily, 'I've come a long way from my roots.'

Outside, without warning, a wave crashed against the sea wall. Moments later it was followed by a second, and then, as if tiring, a third.

Wake of a ship. But what ship? Whither bound, and with what unspeakable cargo, what pale, unsmiling crew? Out there, in the featureless dark, some ship was sailing to the end of the world, and now, long after it had gone by, its wake had come to bury itself among the shale skirts and granite foundations of this humble, sea-considering town…

I thought – thinking about my own situation – that there was no such thing as a woman without roots; that every woman was herself a root. But perhaps there might exist, under the guise of women, a small band of child-spirits whose fate it was to wander the world, possessing randomly, never themselves possessed, until, chaste and self-delighting to the last, they became at last the elusive agents of the ecstatic mind, images of its own orphaned loveliness… Who was it that said that in heartbreak alone wisdom might enter the world?

'And now,' said the Lady in White Terylene, 'Now I have to go.' And she rose and looked, suddenly scared, about her.

Where was she staying?

At his family's.

Could I walk her there?

I could not.

Would I see her again?

She looked at me with an odd mix of consternation, tenderness – and something else. 'Maybe. Thanks for sitting with me.' Her hand, when I shook it, was dry and cold.

I watched as she turned, her dress yielding its white shining to the incarnadine haze – and walked swiftly away; out of the darkroom of history, and into my mind.

THE MAKE-UP GIRL

Call her Sharon. She was Jamaican. More brown than high-brown, she'd be in her early forties now; and she belonged to that generation of the Jamaican lower middle-class which was swept into status and material visibility by the 'fifties boom in that country. Her parents were divorced, but the settlement had been generous – her mother lived in one house and was landlady of another – and Sharon, when I first knew her, though still an undergraduate at Mona, had her own car: a snorting green MGB, battered but running, which she drove, I remember, stylishly and fast with the hood back and her pressed brown hair flying, in black leather gloves with cutouts for the fingers.

The car was one of the things Sharon had going for her. Another was a frank and pleasant face, with just enough of a hint of smudginess around the mouth and eyes to make the itinerant Don Juan look again, sniffing a pushover (I'm talking frankly, you understand; youth is cruel). And all this is also another way of saying that one of the things Sharon didn't have going for her was a body. By this I don't mean she was ethereal – far from it – or shapelessly skinny, or fat. But Sharon's was the kind of body that had to grow on you, for it wasn't your classic 'sixties body. Slender and scalloped, Sharon's body was not, it remembered its peasant origins too closely; and though it was a good enough body, not without shapeliness despite the too-much flesh, it was what condemned Sharon, I suspect, to a depressing series of supporting roles in the sultry season of melodramas and farces which constituted young love in those days, and which, for all I know, constitute it still.

In a roundabout way, her body probably also accounted for Sharon landing herself a reputation, in due course, as a terrific help behind the scenes of plays, modelling shows and the like; and as a make-up girl.

I don't think this was her original plan. Far as I can remember, there was a brief spell when Sharon fared forth onto the ramp herself. But the memory is fuzzy, an image dimly swimming; and where it clarifies and takes on depth is with Sharon settling down, apparently without angst, and becoming a terrific help behind the scenes. She moved with that crowd and, as I said, she was okay enough to look at; and from time to time, through most of her undergraduate years, you would see her in this or that ad – not as The Girl On The Beach Towel, you understand, not as the Lilithian vision of loveliness and languor to whom the dashing young sport, emerging from the surf, ceremoniously presents the treasurable beverage; but as one of the gang in another shot, swilling the stuff in between cheering lustily for some racehorse or cyclist or boat. And maybe this eased the transition for Sharon; I don't know.

Come to think of it, I never really know her well, except briefly. Mostly, after that, I knew her as we all did: which is to say, as a good sport. And you have to get a lot older than twenty-two before you can comprehend the untellable grief that, in a girl's heart, can go into the forging of that fiction, 'a good sport'. How many Good Sports and Terrific Helps (how many fumy feminists nowadays, for that matter) would not throw away a lifetime of that stuff for one hour of being worshipped, as the poet Lowell puts it, by a man 'silent, absorbed and on his knees/ As men adore God at the altar, as I love you'?

How many make-up girls ever lived who would not have swopped the cosmetic genius of the Orient for one session in front of the reflectors, moving this way and that defiantly, in white light, in floating cotton or falling chiffon or sliding silk, stalked by the camera sucking its teeth, *shuck-tuck*, inserting itself into the interstices of her every pause and, *shuck-tuck, shuck-tuck*, turn and comeback, all Meaning concentrated, *shuck-tuck*, in her body, motion, gesture, expression…?

But Sharon was a good make-up girl, and, as the years passed, and with them her youth, I'm told she became a great 'stylist'. Certainly, I have this picture of her, working on a young model in a teeming pavilion overlooking Doctor's Cave Beach, with rain gusting on the milky green water and blowing in onto the traffic-green benches and tables and onto the sand-strewn concrete floor, the sand flies suddenly biting, the producer gnashing his teeth, and the model (a high-brown prima donna whose long legs, long back and flawless skin, it was thought, would greatly assist the sales of the wretched cocoa butter or whatever suntan lotion it was) only kept from sulking past the point of tears by her awareness of the effect she was having on the cameraman, an upwardly-mobile Kingston rake in his own right; and the memory is of a sacred, churning stillness.

There is the squall, passing by on the water. There are the other occupants of the pavilion, tourists, bathers and picnickers, coming and going or pausing curiously to watch. There are the half-dozen men and women involved in the ad standing or sitting around, the producer chain-smoking, the cameraman lounging, arms folded, frowning slightly, just at the edge of the model's vision, making a great show of studying her face from an aesthetic and professional point of view. And at the centre of this loose group, in a great stillness of mutual absorption, sit the bikinied model with the towel around her shoulders, her face tilted back, eyes watchful and unmoving upon Sharon's face, the tense line of the lips severe; and – facing her directly, so close that their knees are interlocking; negligently dressed in Bermuda shorts and a T-shirt; staring in turn intently and unmoving into the model's face from all of nine inches away, her own cheeks drawn with concentration, lips pursed, her brush hand poised – Sharon, the make-up girl.

A young man without sisters, I confess I hadn't thought overmuch about this business of girls making-up themselves. But what I saw Sharon achieve with the modelling kid that squally morning – that, to a young writer's symbolising imagination, was an education I have never forgotten.

When we'd met her earlier, the modelling kid had been attractive enough, in that kiln-fired, Jamaican high-brown way: nice skin, good figure, long back, long legs – if not the swan's neck and prepubescent torso Twiggy was even then decreeing for models – with a pretty, sensual, innocent face, and semi-curly, glossy black hair. At seventeen or eighteen she was really still a child, and new to the work as well, it turned out; and she gave off an ingenuous gaiety that had to do, not only with the prospect of the shoot, but also, it was impossible not to see, with the effect her effect on the cameraman was having on her.

Sharon soon fell pensive, glancing at them; and I recalled that back on campus a couple months ago she had reputedly endured some definitive heartbreak at the hands of a shady character in Econ.

There was a flurry of consultations, and the session began.

While the camera crew descended on the beach to choose a spot and start setting up their paraphernalia, Sharon went to work on the kid; and by the time she was finished it seemed to me, glancing curiously at her handiwork, that what she had done was to sharpen the kid's features and highlight the planes of her face, imposing a sort of sculpted immobility upon the innocence and snubbed look of youth.

The ad's hook was simple (this, remember, was still the amateurish sixties): to associate the suntan lotion with the desirability of its user and with the legendary glamour of Doctor's Cave Beach. The script called for the camera, starting in close-up on the supine girl's face, gradually, lingeringly to pull away, while heraldic music rose, until the whole girl was revealed, and then the beach – the latter with its prostrate population of Caucasian North Americans: a major subliminal prod for the product. ('Subliminal' was a new and exciting word in those days.)

And that was all; the other parts would be shot, or had already been shot, in the studio.

An innocent in the advertising field, I was startled when, immediately prior to being ceremoniously laid out on the beach mat, the child's body was anointed, not with the lotion being advertised, but with plain common-or-garden baby oil: a counterfeit which nonetheless had the desired effect of setting her tawny torso a-gleaming like a weapon. Then, though, there was some last minute fidgeting by the camera people because the light was changing, the sun was coming and going – and, next, the aforementioned squall swept down on us. The camera people ran with their equipment, the prop person ran with his props; and though Sharon and the model ran-walked for shelter with Sharon selflessly holding a towel over the girl's head, the latter ended up, back in the pavilion, distinctly bedraggled and close to petulant tears (the producer was cursing and threatening to abandon the shoot).

And then Sharon sent the modelling kid off to wash her face clean, and – what the script hadn't called for – to soak her hair and plaster it back along her head; and when she came back Sharon began to work on her again, with a curious intensity; without a word.

I've already told about that part: about the teeming pavilion, the passing squall, the chain-smoking producer and hovering cameraman, and about the great stillness of absorption that quickly developed between Sharon and the bikinied kid with the towel around her shoulders, her face tilted back, eyes watchful and unmoving upon the stylist's face. That stillness drew my attention – and not only mine: more and more passers-by, sensing something special was happening, were pausing to watch – and I saw that she, Sharon, had forgotten herself, and was putting her whole being into recreating the kid's face; and I saw that she was doing something quite different, this time around, and that she was applying to those still unformed features what I can only describe as a kind of drenched and half-blind look.

And it was stunning, the difference!

The first time, the kid's face had wound up sharply-etched, iconographic; now it reflected, instead, a rubbed-smooth psyche elemental as marble. Then it had been almost aquiline, recalling if anything ancient Egypt, desert sands. Now it mirrored an amphibian sensuality and slow passion. It was as though, at the first session, Sharon had thought to marry the kid to the sandy beach itself, and now (in what impulse of sudden self-abandonment herself?) had decided to let her stand, instead, for the susurrus of life without loneliness or pain: for the carnal genius of the sea.

Next, I thought that Sharon (staring appraisingly at the model's face, like a painter at a canvas, her own cheeks drawn from concentrating, brush hand poised) was enduring inwardly herself a kind of dying, except it was a dying-into-life, into another's life,

125

or a dream of loveliness; and, thinking that, I suddenly understood that Sharon's art was akin to the writer's art – that it involved the immersion of selfhood in the creation of another world, and in the peopling of that world with various fictions. And I had an intimation, then, that the respective costs of our art – the costs in good citizenry and domestic solidity and all the other staunch and stolid consolations of what the peanut-crunching crowd calls 'life' – might in the long run be about the same for us both.

In this way the image of Sharon got mixed in dimly with my idea of my career, and her art became in my mind a material metaphor for my writer's art. And like that, with an obscure stab of woe, I have thought of her from time to time over the years.

And that's all, really. Sharon never married, so far as I know, nor had any kids; and, last I heard, she was greatly in demand as a stylist, but still living alone with her aged mother, in an old house in Stony Hill. And I only write this now because, out of the blue, I dreamed of Sharon for some reason the other night.

In my dream she was much older than when last I'd seen her, which was close on twenty years ago, and had suffered much in the intervening years: all that, I could tell from her back, some-how, in my dream. Her back was to me in my dream, and she was bending forward like one preoccupied – hunched over in the act of recreating, I supposed, some just-out-of-focus, young girl's face. But it must have been a happy dream, after all was said and done, in the end. Because a point came where Sharon turned, and I saw that she was gently smiling, and that what I had taken for a model was in fact – or had become, now – a baby in her arms.

A PLACE TO LEAVE

A weekday morning, one day last week. Bright blue sky. Small white clouds like a map of the Antilles, though the celestial geography's wrong (there's Cuba between Tobago and Dominica). The south-easterly's blowing diligently and hard, keeping the landscape in motion all around us; and we're walking, me and this guy, old pardner, up and down the road outside my house.

Why we're walking instead of sitting on the windy verandah in the shade of the bougainvillea I don't quite know. Except, I've been sick and housebound for two weeks, and glad to be out in the sun; either that, or we unconsciously let ourselves be inveigled road-ward by the young Doberman, Twice. Twice loves to go for walks. Everything about her pricks up, head, ears, and she trots like an alert thoroughbred. Looks like a girl in her prime already, the ol' Twice. You'd hardly know she's really only a puppy, eight months old.

My house is in the V-turn of a crescent, steep uphill, steep downhill, level bit at the top, and we're walking there, me and Neville, in a high suburban silence broken only by birdsong and the wind in the trees – and, each time we pass it, coming and going, by the house of Alsatians. Five of them. They hurl themselves at the gate, and the ol' Twice hurls herself at it from the other side, and a kind of sharks' feeding frenzy ensues, until the Twice breaks it off and comes trotting after us, tongue lolling, excited and happy. Five big Alsatians. They'd kill her in an instant but for that gate.

Anyway. We're walking slowly, Neville and I, like priests saying their breviaries, along the level top of the crescent, and Neville is saying: '...every day. Every day! You have any idea what's going on in this country?'

Neville's a burly character, fortyish, no grey yet, with the slightly abrasive manner and rumpled look of a man with no real woman in his life. No one to smooth out the edges, to say sternly as he's preparing to go out: 'Neville, where you going in that shirt? You don't see that shirt needs ironing, and besides, is the wrong shirt to go with that pants? Go and change it, put on so-and-so,' etc. The usual things a man needs a woman to tell him. Neville was married, oh, for years – I knew his wife well, she was a Thackorie, from Point – but then it ended when nobody knew a thing, five, maybe six years ago, and now Neville says he's 'done with that for good'. Since then I've seen him with this girl once or twice. She's quite good-looking, in a breakable, non-long-lasting way, but she's the mousey sort that hardly ever talks when you're around, and I don't think she would tell the ol' Neville to go change his shirt. Maybe I'm wrong. Anyway.

What Neville's doing at my house, bright and early on a weekday morning is, partly he's visiting a convalescent ('Hadda feeling you were sick when I didn't see your columns'). But mainly he's come to say goodbye, since, as it turns out, he, Neville, is migrating.

This is news to me. Neville's migrating to Canada; it's settled, he himself is leaving next week (this week!) and this is the first I'm hearing of it. I say helplessly, 'Neville, what a helluva thing!'

'You think is only me?' he adds defensively; and that's where he launches into his spiel.

What's happening in this country every day, according to Neville, is: dozens and dozens of people are leaving. 'You should have seen the scene at the Canadian High Commission,' he says, when he was there fixing up his 'papers'. And over at Marli Street, he says, it's just as bad. 'They nearly had a riot there the other day, you know that?'

I shake my head uncertainly. Face it – the image of people *rioting* to get out of this country *is* sort of hard to credit. Since when has Trinidad been the kind of country people riot to get out of?

'It can't be as bad as that.'

I say this vaguely. Having been sick makes you vague.

Neville laughs: a short, harsh laugh. What do I think – he wants to know – the real unemployment figures in this country are today? What do they mean in terms of crime, in terms of worse-than-crime? What do I think the recent Bail Bill was really all about? Do I know the price of 'crack' these days? Do I have any idea where the dollar's going to have to fall to, in reality? What do I think…?

An elate eruption of the morning stillness into cacophony cuts him off – we're passing the house of Alsatians again – and after it's over, the need to conserve his breath on this, the steep uphill part, keeps him tight-lipped for some minutes more.

We plod to the top in silence, and stand there, panting a little for a while. The ol' Neville starts up again, more soberly this time, but I'm not really listening to him. I'm looking out over the plain to where the Central Range is blue and clear in the morning sunlight, and I'm thinking: Maybe it's true; the rains will be coming soon.

The Twice goes over and sniffs at a crawling something in the dry drain under the razor grass, but it's obviously below her dignity to mangle it – too small, too slow, too uninteresting – and she comes back and stands around flat-footed, tongue lolling, with that air of listening out of the corner of her eye which Dobermans sometimes have.

I look at Neville and I say: 'So you really going, huh?'

Meeting my gaze, he looks guilt-stricken – but only for the briefest of moments. Then he's off again. 'You know what it really is, Wayne?' he confides desperately. 'You know what's really the frightening part?' I say the frightening part must be all the things he's just finished telling me put together; but Neville says no. The frightening part, Neville says, the really frightening part, is that the Government is going crazy.

'You been watching the Ministers lately on Panorama?'

I say: no. Nowadays I turn on Panorama strictly to catch the sports news. Lalonde-Stewart, the Epsom Derby, the First Test, the French Open. One of the privileges of being sick, I tell Neville: giving the Ministers and their 'functions' a miss.

He gives that laugh again. Then he says that X (a Government Minister, Neville names him) is talking high-pitched all the time nowadays; that Y (another Minister) nearly had a break-down the other night ('his face was all twisting up'); that Z, ditto,

129

I should have seen how his eyes were bulging half-out of his head. Minister after Minister, Neville diagnoses incipient insanity.

'As for A and B, well from the beginning, neither of them was what you would normally call sane, eh?' No – from where he stands, the ol' Neville has sussed them out. Alladem going crazy – alladem!

All of them?

All but three, actually: Neville amends himself. 'You know who those three are?' I hazard an uncertain guess. Turns out I get only one right; Neville proceeds to name the three sane men.

'You know what that is, boy? Three sane men in a whole government? And you know why that is! Because those three have fallback positions! That's the only thing saving them. That if this Government goes through they ent going through with it. Check it out.'

Down the hill again. The Twice trotting heavily down the steep slope, shoulder blades alternately thrusting, flanks swinging like a horse's flanks – and Neville still extolling on his theme of Ministerial madness.

And I'm thinking: It's no use. I've lived in three countries, and I tell you flat: when you see a man get that gotta-go look in his eyes, it's no use arguing with him. (Worse, actually, when a woman gets that look. Believe me, I lived in Jamaica, I've seen these things!) And I'm about to say something else, but he beats me to it. Shaking his forefinger at me – we've reached the bottom, and turned – Neville delivers his sober conclusion and parting warning, the Last Words of Wisdom of Neville W:

'Never let a bunch of guys without fallback positions get into power in your country.'

Makes sense, I suppose. But what really knocks me out is that 'your'. It isn't, I realise suddenly, a way of talking. Trinidad is my country, not his, anymore. He, Neville, has another country now. Canada.

Neville, the Canadian?

Wow.

Some things I'll never understand, long as I live.

Back up the hill. At the top I stop and say, 'So what's going to happen about the kids?' Meaning his two kids, boy and girl, living with his ex-wife, Joselyn, down in Point.

A look of woe crosses Neville's face, but it passes. Speaking for himself, Neville says staunchly, he knows he's going to make a go of Toronto. Once he's properly set up, two, maybe three years, he's pretty sure Joselyn will agree to him bringing the kids over for schooling – look what's happened to education in this country. Who knows, by that time she might be ready to leave herself. Who knows, the way this country is going?

'Face it, Wayne,' the ol' Neville says now. 'Trinidad has become a place to leave.'

I look down the slope and decide: no more. I know this will deprive the Twice of the incredible ecstasy of passing the house of Alsatians again; but that's how I feel. No more today. Another day, puppy-dog!

We turn into my drive, me, Neville and the Twice, and my visitor is suddenly anxious. He's not coming in, he has a million things to do, you know how it is when you're leaving a place, he just dropped in to say, well, so long. We shake hands, promise to stay in touch, each know we won't; and he gets into the car; not his car, a white Mazda. The ol' Neville sold the Bluebird three weeks ago. PAS something, I think it was.

I say hopelessly, 'Well, Neville, what can I tell you. We'll miss you. Good luck in Canada.'

Don't ask me who that 'we' is, but it gets to him, because he gives a little stiff salute. Starting the Mazda, he pokes his head out the window and calls earnestly in parting: 'Listen! You should get out too! They don't have anything here for people like you anymore, you know! You'll find out!' I smile wryly and wave, and he pulls away, and goes protestingly in 'first' up the short slope, with the Twice cantering alongside like an escort, just in case; and on out of sight around the bend; and now the Twice comes trotting fast back. I'm still standing by the gate, looking vaguely around at the garden, and it strikes me I really ought to get it done before the rains start coming down in earnest. The Twice misconstrues my absorption for indecision and hangs around panting, thinking perhaps we're about to head out on another walk. But she soon gives it up – I'm not going anywhere – and then gets another bright idea and goes over to her water bowl and begins ravenously to drink, wolfing it down.

Slurp-slurp-slurp-slurp! You know what beats me about that dog?

Eating, she's a lady, she picks daintily at her food, but when it comes to drinking, this is it:

Slurp-slurp-slurp-slurp! Water all over the place.

THE FLIGHT NORTH

Leaving Trinidad the flight was late, and by the time we stopped over in Barbados it was evening: the sheer island-light mellowing in a depthless sky, the dying gong of the struck horizon all around. In so many Caribbean islands the approach to the airport gives the scale: you come in on a finger or small plaque of land, surrounded on three sides by sea. You disembark thinking, 'How lovely', or else with a disorienting sense of having arrived nowhere. The one's narcissism, the other exhaustion; but the sensation holds.

My companion for the ride, it's turned out, is a young woman I can hardly bear to look at: one of those carnal apparitions, not quite human, that elicit the carnivore's epithet 'luscious'. Great red gash of a mouth, fleshy neck, plucked and pencilled eyebrows, black, staring eyes. From Arima, she'd said she was, the red mouth widening for the middle vowel – though those disquieting, staring eyes never changed. But when I suggest her racial background's 'Spanish' or Carib, or likelier some mix of the two, she says triumphantly: No, dougla. Straight dougla.

'My father is Indian. And my mother? She's a full Negro, but fair.'

The look with which she imparts this news (and I am too stunned by her – *nearness* – to query the 'full, fair Negro' part) imbues it with a mysterious and personal significance. It is some time before I understand that her attentiveness to me, which in another mood I might have mistaken – and which, even in my present sleepless spaced-out state, has felt impersonally flattering – her attention is solely intellectual.

(Well, maybe not solely. There'd been a moment early on, after an initial, brisk trade in information had flared up and then died down, and I'd leaned back and into a semi-doze – the kind in which the drone of the plane is taken into the inner ear and becomes there the incurious, but quite comprehensible, if only one chose to decipher it, mumbling of one's spectral Other – when, in obedience to her wordless command, I opened my eyes and saw that, for some reason, she'd unclasped the gold chain bracelet I'd first noticed on her farside wrist and draped it over the one lying limply on the armrest between us, and that she was now directing me, by glances alone (from my face to her wrist, and back) to reclasp it there for her. But sometimes you can be so tired that your body hurts; she was of that ilk whose black stare a man must either shy away from or be prepared to fall forward into; and it was frowningly, wordlessly, in my turn (glasses pushed back, leaning half over into her seat, my own elbow perforce indenting her stomach) that I accomplished the ticklish transaction. Finished, I said 'Okay?' and her eyes went blank, and I leaned back, irritable and relieved. Soon after that – I think in retrospect – she decided to make ours a pedagogical affair: trying out her lines, gauging my reactions, seeing what needed fine-tuning, and so on.)

Somewhere north of Barbados I enquire her age. I'd been thinking twenty-four-ish, but she says, 'I'm, ah, twenty,' and from her hesitation I realise: nineteen!

And that is all I think – 'Nineteen? Nineteen!' – as she explains, in a tone I find hard to decipher (somewhere between coy and grim) that she's just left Trinidad for good.

Then she launches into her spiel.

'I woulda left long ago, but I get pregnant; so I stay home and make the baby. Then last year I went up for six months. I travel everywhere, checking out the place, deciding where I would like to live. New York, New Jersey, Washington D.C., Philadelphia, Pee Eh – '

I interrupt, because I cannot stand it anymore – cannot stand, less than a foot from my face, the great gash of a mouth and black staring eyes – 'Yes? You went to Pennsylvania?'

The eyes go momentarily blank. Then I see her opt for an answer, and press on.

'No, not Pennsylvania; Philadelphia Pee Eh. But I really like New Jersey. Is there I going.'

I nod speechlessly. She searches my face, concludes she's doing okay, resumes.

'Yes, so I check it out, deciding where I would like to live and so on; and I decide, New Jersey. So I come home, and I make up my mind to come back up and do geriatrics. Because that is what I really like: geriatrics. And America ain't like Trinidad, you know. In Trinidad they does drag everything out, a course like that might take two years – even, say, three. But in New Jersey you could do geriatrics in three months, and after that they give you a paper, and you could more or less, well, help yourself, so to speak...'

And the baby, the baby's father? Seeing as how she's leaving home for good...?

The baby was with her mother in Arima. 'She really more the baby mother than me, eh.' (This is said without a smile either rueful or wry: with only the black eyes staring.) As for the baby's father:

'Well, I have to say, he wasn't too happy at first. But I explain. A girl like me...'

(...and she *says* that, 'A girl like me', black eyes staring into my face from a foot away!...)

'...I married so young, I don't just want to end up a housewife or so. Because if in ten years, say, he decide, well, this or that, what is my position then? So I explain, I have to take my chances, and this is my chance, and I goin' to have to take it. Because, you never know, it might turn out good for the both of us one day – right? So I make him see that. He still not too happy; he want to know, well, what if – '

...and here I am aware of her braceletted wrist on the armrest, the hand hanging over into my seat...

'...and so on and so forth. I suppose is only natural: two young people. But I tell him, *life* is a chance. So he understand. When two people have good communication...'

Nineteen!

She frightens me.

I see her for the last time around eleven that night, outside the arrival hall at Kennedy. She's talking up to a tall young black man who's come to meet her, and who now is standing directly in front of her, hands on hips, smiling; and to me, watching from a certain distance while she talks up into his face (pausing often to glance, without curiosity, at the goings-on around her) she seems for the first time in context.

She is a young Trinidadian, hardly more than a child, yet already quite clear-minded, no-nonsense, stern. She is a fugitive from an impoverished island, who saw that she could sink and pulled herself clear, hacking away whatever held her, 'taking [her] chance'; a nineteen-year-old from Arima, with no knowledge of the world, yet not without resources in the wide world of men, not so long as, from all that lushness, indulgent Time averts its gaze...

And thinking that, I think wryly: she'll go far.

Then, though, I look around me at the airport hustle, with its irritable cab honkings and clank of baggage carts, the spit and hiss of bus brakes, the lamplit shapes hurrying to and fro in a New York night that is black, raining and cold, with, ahead of us, the inconceivable press and milling of unseen souls, New York, city of dreams, or so it still sells itself, though for most who walk its canyoned streets it is where the dream died, leaving them in graffitied apartments with bad heating and dark stairwells, riding the treadmill of two part-time jobs, or even three, the unending, mean struggle for survival...

Standing, hands in pockets, just out of the rain, on the wet-black pavement outside Kennedy, guarding my bags and awaiting my ride, I think of all that, and I wonder...

When I look for her again, she is gone.

GOODBYE WASHINGTON

Okay – so there's this girl on the bus. Smallish, thirty, thirty-five, hard to tell – these women age faster than our women – with darkblond careless hair and a face you'd like. It's a face that's lived, that says things haven't always been easy, that it's known its fair share of men and grief, but that it's come up each time smiling.

It's a nice face and its owner is sitting there, in corduroy jeans and a black corduroy jacket and a silk scarf, and I'm thinking she's hard to place. Brazilian maybe, but not typical, or French, but not typical French. But then we get to talking and it turns out she's Italian, and her name is Cinzio. She has a gaze that attends to you while you're talking, and her voice is like that, friendly, steady, and she talks with an accent, only not so's you'd notice it; not unless you were attentive to such things.

I'm in Washington for a week en route to a convocation of writers in, of all places, Iowa. She is a student of film, or so I gather, and here for some seminar on the art of movie-making. Cinzio. Cinzio something. She told me her last name but I forget it.

Anyway, we hit it off, and soon we're laughing and joshing the driver all the way in from the airport, because the bus is nearly empty, and because it's a windy, sunny late-summer afternoon, and because there's a fine spaciousness and serenity about Washington – which isn't strictly speaking a city, but the administrative capital of The Greatest Nation on Earth – and because we're both here on vacation from our lives and feeling already ten years younger – or at least I am.

We're driving north towards Constitution, past the pristine white phallus of the Washington Monument standing by itself in a faultless blue sky, with on the right, past the Smithsonian, the grassy slopes rolling up Capitol Hill, wide open, as if this could be country, the wind banging on the panes of the bus; and there's something quite ingenuous, yet truly impressive about the Federal architecture. Graeco-Colonial, I'd call it, if that made any sense, because behind it you can feel this phenomenal placid self-confidence, yet also this little air of surprise; and it's all splendidly proportionate yet somehow light-hearted; self-confident, whimsical and fine. There are places in this country where, if it ever reached them, the idea of America has been lost; in its daily doings, Washington may be one of them; but the men who built Washington never doubted for one moment the grandeur and insouciance of the idea.

Something French here: a feeling of boulevards. The wind smells of the sea. Up close the White House looks less formidable, looks like somewhere you could conceivably live. I do not see Mr Reagan. Neither, reports Cinzio, does she. 'What a shame,' I say and, 'What a shame!' she echoes, and the driver chuckles: 'You guys'll jes' have t'cum beck!' For her benefit, mainly, I bet him he doesn't remember Brando's great line in *On the Waterfront*. He glances at me amusedly. 'You mean – ' and he says it in a wry drawl: 'Charlie, Charlie, Charlie! Ah coulda bin a cun*ten*dah! Ah coulda bin sambaady!' I say, 'Awriiight!' and slap him on the shoulder, and Cinzio is looking out of the window, smiling, she knows the line too, you can tell, as we hang a right on Pennsylvania and then another right, and now the city closes in a little.

I disembark at the Du Pont; she's going on. We shake hands, and I wish her a happy life and a great career and a dozen Italianate babies, and mostly that she should behave herself while in Washington, which is the administrative capital of Quote Unquote; and I leave it at that and follow the porter inside, because sometimes you have to leave it at that, sometimes you have to take what the moment gives and not get greedy and push – and a half-minute later, I'm checking in, this guy I'd hardly noticed on the bus comes in and say that Chinzy says to tell me she's staying at Hotel X; and he goes back out to the bus.

This is nice, but so strange (I mean, who's that guy?) that I neglect to write down the name of her hotel, and up in my room I discover I've forgotten it. I try hard, but it's gone. I think, 'Fool!', knowing now I'll never see her again – and two days later, whaddya know, me and Chinzio, we run into each other in a stand-up eatery in a mall.

So we're talking, standing there, not eating, till it's nearly time to go; and then she says they're showing her film at the Kennedy Center tomorrow night, and would I come to it and to the party afterwards. I say 'Sure', and she turns to this guy, who materialises out of nowhere once again, and tells him (*who* is this guy?) that Mr Brown will be coming to her showing, and he pulls out a pocket book and obediently writes this down.

But the funny thing is, I wasn't going! I said 'Sure', but I just wasn't – don't ask me why. And even if I'd been maybe going when I said it, by the next day I definitely wasn't, because by then I'd come down with the airport flu and was feeling self-cherishing and petulant; and how I ended up going was: I had this *other* engagement I couldn't duck out of. It was a formal do hosted by the Institute of International Education, and I felt I had to go, flu or no; so I suited up and went over to the place.

And it was one of those horrible, glitzy, dead affairs, where five hundred people each talk to you for seventeen seconds exactly and you end up feeling lonely as hell, and to cap it all somebody wrote out a name tag and said smilingly that I should wear it. 'Wayne Brown, Trinidad', it said.

Now, I have to tell you: you ever want to get rid of me in a hurry, give me a name tag to wear. I don't know why, but wearing a name tag makes me feel the way a racehorse looks that definitely doesn't want to race, stutter-stepping down to the starting gates with its neck lathered, its head swung sideways and the whites of its eyes showing. I mean, it's that bad. Name tags blow my mind, like the promise of immortality suddenly rescinded. I hid it under an hors d'oeuvre but it was no use, everybody else was wearing theirs, and the lady who'd written mine out caught up with me and said, Naughty boy, you've lost it; and wrote me out another one.

So I had to get out of there. I thought of Chinzy, and thought, 'an appointment at the Kennedy Center' might sound like a grand enough excuse; and so I made the rounds of my hosts, making it. My hosts shook their heads and made clicking noises which sounded like disapproval feigning disappointment, but I was out.

I dropped my second name tag in a plant pot, and lit a cigarette, and took a cab back to the hotel; and then got bogged down in the idea of going to the Kennedy Center, after all. Because Chinzy was *nice*, and we'd gotten on so well, and she probably wanted moral support while her little documentary ran before the critical eyes of two dozen fellow-seminarians, who would pick it to shreds, artistically-speaking, at their next seminar, and besides – yeah – who could say what the ensuing party might bring?

The evening had gotten cool, and by now I was sick, *sick*; so I changed and put on a sweatshirt, and a jacket over that, and then I hailed a cab and went over to the Kennedy Center – and got lost. I got lost in the Kennedy Center, and couldn't find Chinzy's theater, and not one but two extremely unpleasant middle-aged ladies asked me at different times, with extreme nastiness, kindly to put out that cigarette, smoking having become the newest apparition of Evil to American Puritanism, and smokers being pursued here nowadays every bit as humourlessly as the flower children once stoned with petals returning Vietnam vets. And I was about to give up and go back to the hotel and take a dozen aspirins and get into bed when the elevator doors opened – not by my hand – and I looked full-face into the reception lobby of Chinzy's film.

And it was a big thing!

I mean, the place was full, the guys all had on tuxedos, the ladies all had on like, gowns, there were chandeliers; there was even a reception line! I looked at the reception line and thought: Cinzio? I looked at the reception line and thought: I am the only sweatshirt-wearing person in a roomful of tuxedo-wearing persons. I looked at the reception line and thought: I am too dam' sick to even *think* about all this, and anyway they said this was America; and like that I went down the reception line, being introduced as a writer from Jamaica – and, when I corrected this, as a writer from Treeneedad, Jamaica – and a friend of Cinzio's, and met the Deputy Chairman of, I think, MGM, guy called Rosenthal, who graciously offered me a ride to the party afterwards in his limousine (he said that: limousine); and I mean, these people had class! Not one of them glanced at my sweatshirt. Not one of them betrayed anything other than cordial welcome. Can you imagine if this had been, say, the Royal Albert Hall?

And so I came out at the other end of the reception line for the premiere of the full-length feature film, *Hotel Colonial*, starring John Savage and Robert Duval and directed by my little Cinzio – and stood around dazed and discovering to my dismay that when I said my name in this country, Wayne, everybody replied uncertainly, 'William? Wyn?' ('Say Waaayne!' said a friend, weeks later. 'You have to draw it out.' But I never could bring myself to do that, not to my own name, for Chrissakes, and so it must be goodbye America, because how can you abide in a country where they can't even pronounce your name?) and in due course was introduced to John Savage.

He looked a nice enough kid, manly, clean, no foppery, none of that; but 'Chinzy's friend' is a phrase, the more it's said, the more meaningful it starts to sound; and it wasn't long before I registered that his conversation had the not-so-covert goal of discovering how well – how well, *exactly* – I happened to know his director. Which is the wrong tack to take with a Treeneedadian-Jamaican who's feeling sick and sorry for himself, and who's already had about as much drama as he's willing to take in one night. I essayed what felt at least like an evil smile, and then looked around and said I hadn't seen his co-star, and learned from him that Duval was off in France filming; and then an admirer pounced and led him away, and someone else was standing in front of me saying, 'Hi, I'm X. I gather you're a friend of Cinzio's?'

And Cinzio was late. Cinzio was so late that everybody gave up standing around and went and sat down in the theatre; and the ol' Savage was just taking one last shot at me, twisting around to inquire across several intervening rows of seats whether I had Chinzy's hotel room number on me, when she arrived, with – bless her cheerful heart – the darkblond careless hair still so, and dressed in the corduroy jacket and jeans and the scarf, but looking distinctly unfocused as she glided in, gently propelled by a tuxedoed gentleman. Everybody clapped and clapped, and Savage rose and went over to sit with her in the front row, and the guy Rosenthal made a short speech in which he talked about 'the privilege' of having Cinzio present in person for the premiere; and then they killed the lights and the movie began.

And, O my people, *Hotel Colonial* was bad! That movie was so bad!

Savage has a strong face, good bones, strong lines, and every time he appeared on screen the camera made love to it. ('Ah-ha!' I thought, suddenly thinking I understood.) But for the rest she had overreached herself, had tried to make a humdrum thriller about the Colombian cocaine trade into some kind of Statement and failed; failed in that awful overreaching way that mashes up everything: the timing gone wrong, the pace of the movie shot to hell, the dialogue sounding portentous-absurd, the plot not artfully staccato, just incomprehensible – and I sat in the dark shivering with fever, and because American public buildings, the grander they're supposed to be, the higher they turn up the air-conditioning, and thought with pain for her, *O Jesus, Cinzio*, because at the end the lights would come on and she'd be there, helpless before five hundred pairs of eyes, with her frank-level gaze, and the careless hair, and the corduroy outfit with the scarf.

And then, I don't know, but, somehow, the fever and the shivering and the pain for her got mixed up with the glitz of the occasion, but also with the true civility of it, and then with the badness of what we were watching – and all of it swirled together and started draining away like water through the black hole of a sink when you pull the plug, and I knew I was losing Washington, which I'd only just found, and all I could think was: I want to go home.

And then it's over, and the lights come on. There's a moment's silence, then everybody starts clapping, and I'm watching Savage sitting there, slowly shaking his head, the *bastard*, with Cinzio sitting unmoving next to him and looking straight ahead.

The guy Rosenthal makes a short speech thanking everybody and reminding them of the party at his place, and we all rise, talking, and start filing out. I know by now I'm not going to any party, I'm going *home*, but it occurs to me I may be the only person there who can tell her what she needs to hear, which is 'Okay, so you blew it. Forget it. It happens to everybody sometime. Go back to Italy and start again.' And I'm thinking, I'll tell her that, and maybe after all this is over and done she'll be okay; or at least, she and I, we'll have been okay.

But I must be either sicker or a bigger heel than I thought, because I come up to her and I say – nothing. Not a word. She is standing there stoned with pain, and as I come up she glances at me, but without hope; and what I do is, I kiss her, gravely, precisely, on the cheek. She murmurs, 'You're going?' and I look at her and nod, doing everything now with a somnambulist's precision and gravity, and she looks away. Then I'm leaving, hearing some yuppie starting to tell her how *interesting* he'd found *Hotel Colonial*, and knowing this time I'll not see her again; and I go on out, not looking back, and go down the corridor, walking with a somnambulist's glide and not saying anything to anybody, and get into the elevator.

In the elevator there's this young guy and this bejewelled matron, and they're strangers to each other, but they're talking. She's connected with the production some way, and he's a journalist with a Washington newspaper. Going down, she asks him what he thought of *Hotel Colonial*, and, 'I thought it was terrible,' he tells her flatly. There is a silence while she considers him expressionlessly; and then she asks him his name. He gives it, and I think to myself, 'This kid's editor had better stand by him,' because in her voice and look now is a certain steel that says, 'There's a billion dollars behind me that's going to string you up like a scarecrow, young man.' And then I'm out of the Kennedy Center and crossing over to the bus stop, feeling the Washington night less cold than her theatre had been, and fumbling for a cigarette.

Okay. So in the bus stop, waiting, there's this girl. Angular, high yella, amused eyes, bony hands. We get to talking and turns out she's Jamaican, over from California where she lives, to vacation with a girlfriend in Washington. 'I used to live in Jamaica,' I tell her, and as I say it it sounds to my ears like a phenomenally portentous piece of information. She asks, and I say I'm a writer, but she thinks, I think, I'm giving her a line, and in that lovely Jamaican woman's drawl, centuries of bored amusement and disbelief behind it, inquires the name of the book I've written: any book.

I look at her and want to smile, despite everything – despite how sick I'm feeling, and the pain of Cinzio and *her* pain, and despite how bad I'd let her down, and how bad her film had been; despite, even, how I'd gone and lost Washington, which I'd only just found – and I'm smiling, I can't help it, because in her gaze, and in the sceptical dry amusement of her voice, is a place that feels to me like home. I say, 'A biography: *Edna Manley; The Private Years*', and, '*Rah-tid!*' she says.

ANOTHER TIME, ANOTHER PLACE

She was born in 1960, the eldest of three girls and a boy, in a wooden house on concrete stumps with the paint peeling, but with a fair-sized yard, a few miles off the main road in Lower Santa Cruz. Her father was a mechanic and kept ducks; her mother took in ironing and was something as well with the local Pentecostals, something that kept her busy and often left her weary – she was always coming and going, but I don't think she minded it. The father was part many races and looked it; the mother was black, or what passes for black in this country; and none of the children that I knew looked like either of them – or like each other, for that matter.

Call her – anything. Call her Lillian. She was the dark one, the one with the glossy skin and the cheekbones, the good body and the straight, pulled-back hair. She was also apparently the studious one: she had attended San Juan Government Secondary, I think, and come away with three 'Os', including English, which was a matter of much pride to the parents, I gathered, in those serious, pre-CXC days.

I say I think because I didn't know them then. It was only in '84 that I met her father, courtesy the old Hunter, which was going through a bad phase at the time. That was when I first saw her; and that is also why I never knew her youngest sister.

Lillian's youngest sister – whose memory we shall not slander with a *nom de plume* – had been killed a couple years earlier when the taxi she was travelling in got involved with a truck on the Main Road, not five miles from her parents' home. She'd been ten or eleven, I think. Her mother told me the story once, telling it casually but looking at me in a watchful way as she spoke; and that was the only time I heard her mentioned. Neither Lillian nor her father nor her surviving siblings ever referred in my presence to their dead darling.

But her dying, I deduce, changed them all. It was why the father when I met him was a taciturn man, who no longer showed pleasure or displeasure, but worked in your engine or under the car with the uninflected air of someone doing what needed to be done. It was why the mother never complained, though the church work was demanding, and in the hot sun sometimes with her varicose veins she could hardly walk by the time she got home. It was why Lillian's younger sister, the pretty pale one with her hair forever in curlers, spent her life in front of the mirror, so far as I could see; and her brother who, I gradually realised, was really a serious and responsible young man underneath, came across as don't-carish and semi-wild.

And it was also why Lillian, when I met her, seemed older than her twenty-four years, with something of her father's air of no-hope and no-more-expectations already beginning to mute the native cheerfulness that goes with young womanhood, and with looking good, and knowing it.

But all this I deduce, I may be wrong; and in any case I've got ahead of this story and must go back.

So there they were, long before I knew them: back in '72, say. A family of six: father, mother and four children, three girls and a boy, ranging from Lillian, twelve, to the dead one, who would have been a babe in arms then: living in a wooden house with a biggish yard, out in Lower Santa Cruz. The father working as mechanic with a Main Road garage, the mother taking in ironing – no Church work in those days, no varicose veins – and all in all the family getting by, though only just, we may assume: those were hard years.

Then, in '74, the oil boom. This is the story of their lives since then, as best I can reconstruct it – chiefly from listening to the mother talk from time to time over the past seven years.

In '75 the father quit his job with the garage and opened his own place, to one side of the house.

In '76 he launched into his peculiar sideline, half-hobby, half 'business venture': keeping ducks.

In '77 the mother stopped taking in ironing and got involved, in her new spare time, in doing church work on a voluntary basis.

In '78 Lillian left school with her three 'Os' and got a job, virtually at once, as a clerk with the Water Authority, down in Port of Spain.

In '79 the father converted – much of it with his own hands – the front two-thirds of the house into a concrete structure, with stuccoed walls and terrazzo tiles and glass-louvred windows with drapes, and several large framed prints: Jesus and Mary, a seascape with dunes, a white horse at gaze in a meadow. The new money didn't stretch to converting the service rooms at the back, and the kitchen and bathroom remained as they had been. But it was a fine two-thirds of a house, and in later years, after I'd become a familiar, Lillian's mother, or sometimes Lillian, would invite me in and keep me going with a tall frosted glass of Kool Aid, while out in the yard the father performed the necessary on the old Hunter.

Then in '80 the mother's varicose veins began.

In '81 Lillian's sister, the pretty pale one, moved out and shacked up with a taxi-driver from El Dorado, and for the first and quite possibly the last time in his life Lillian's father went berserk, threatened, raged, wept, till something older or deeper than even the drug of young sex called to his prodigal daughter in her damp bed, in the upstairs room of the Caura Road house, and she picked a row with her new paramour, and got a good beating, and that same night ended up back home, while her mother, who had blamed the devil, thanked the Lord.

In '82 the young one was killed.

In '83 the father's garage failed, and he was lucky to find work with a Morvant gas station, though he still went on fixing cars at home in his own time; and the mother resumed taking in ironing; and the son got some fortnights' employment with the Government road works programme.

And that was how things were with them when, one afternoon in '84, following directions given me by an acquaintance, I first nursed the hurting Hunter into their yard. They were a family of five now, and things were once again getting very hard. But for the moment they were holding. And, as it had been for the past six years, there was Lillian, arriving home from work on the last day of every month and handing her mother thirteen hundred-and-something dollars, regular as clockwork.

'Regular as clockwork,' Lillian's mother repeated to me, years later, her strong voice mellowing with retrospective pride and love.

Regular: that was Lillian, in her life, as in handing over her pay cheques to her mother. Lillian's mother did the household arithmetic and gave Lillian back what she could. It was never much, and as time passed it grew less. In '84 they had a scare when Lillian's father missed an instalment on their Home Improvement Loan and the bank called him in and spoke to him very sternly, and Lillian's mother, after an interlude of great agitation and desperate prayer (she was not the crying type) pulled herself together and resumed taking in ironing (recall the varicose veins now, and the church work).

After that, Lillian's allowance never exceeded $200 a month, which included her fare to work; but she didn't complain. Each morning, she rose with her father in the pre-dawn stillness – he made their 'tea', she made their sandwiches for lunch – and together they departed the silent house where Lillian's mother and brother and the pretty pale one still slept, carefully closing the garden gate behind them: a gesture tender rather than precautionary, since the driveway had no gate. They would travel together to the Croisee and take a taxi, Lillian's father getting off at Morvant Junction, while his firstborn – his great and secret solace, grown up now – dark Lillian of the glossy skin and the cheekbones, went on to Independence Square.

From there she walked the mile and a half to the WASA office, down on Wrightson Road; and thither, after work, she walked back. One assumes she endured the usual mix of compliments and catcalls – the good body, the pulled-back hair – in her straight skirt and medium black heels. And one assumes she responded to them with the usual mix of mortification, anger, or secret pleasure, depending on the tone and intent of the voices signalling to her from that indistinct world of men, as from some premonitory twilight. But the young woman who alighted at the garden gate in Lower Santa Cruz around 5.30 each weekday evening seemed

148

– to my casual glance, at least – oddly untouched by the enervations of the workaday world. Except, sometimes, for a faint air of weariness.

'Hi, Mr B!' she would call to me with impersonal cheerfulness, taking off her shoes with relief, climbing the concrete steps. Then in a different tone (less cheerful, more caring): 'Hi, Pa.' Her father would extract himself from the bonnet of the Hunter and say gruffly, something like, 'It have a Julie mango on top the fridge,' or, 'Your mother say to say she left the peas soaking,' or – straightening up, wiping his hands, looking at her seriously – 'You see Bolts [Lillian's brother] down by the Main Road?'

Lillian: 'Bolts? No. What he doin' there?'

And, like that, she would go on into the house, closing the front door behind her; and that was all.

Work, home, household chores, bed; work, home, household chores, bed: that was my chief impression of Lillian in those years, and it superimposed a faint query upon my preoccupation with my car. Why should a young woman who looked as Lillian looked content herself with a life that was no life; year after year, content to abide so, while unrepeatable young womanhood lengthened out towards its span? Even the death of the little one, when I learnt of it, seemed insufficient explanation; even the fact that she was her father's favourite, and he hers. She was twenty-four, then twenty-five, twenty-six – where were the men in attendance, the one man she would not be able to evade? How was it she never went out?

These questions were not half so clear in my mind at the time as I have made them sound; and for a time in late '84 and early '85 I was at least half-wrong. For in that period, which lasted several months, whenever I happened to be at her father's, Lillian would arrive home from work, not in a taxi, but in an old white Datsun 180B driven by an Indianish guy of maybe forty. She would not immediately alight. They would sit in the car talking for ten, sometimes twenty minutes; and then Lillian would emerge, slamming the door (the high spirits of youth showing, after all, in that gratuitous slam!) and there would be a swing in her stride as she came up the path, waving to him over her shoulder, not looking back, while the 180B pulled away from the verge; and her greetings to her father and me would be so cheerful as to seem somehow like dismissals.

Much later, Lillian's mother told me that the Indianish guy hadn't given up easily, and that many a night he would come to visit, sitting with Lillian on the couch in the brightly lit living room with Jesus and Mary, the seascape and the white horse looking down on them, and with the rest of the family, oblivious, coming and going. But Lillian, though glad to see him, declined for some reason to go out with him; and after several months, as I said, the 180B ceased to appear.

She was getting older, in mind if not in body – even I, a casual visitor, could see that. Her greetings became more perfunctory, her expression less mobile, and the occasional faint weariness I had seen in her from the start now began to appear habitual. The thought occurred to me that, inexplicably, she was headed for spinsterhood.

But I have forgotten the business of chronology, and must resume it. In '85 Lillian's sister, the pretty pale one, got married and moved – without parental protest this time – with her new husband to Valencia and had a baby. The husband, I gather, grew produce, or something. Lillian's mother spoke of him at first with dubious hopefulness as 'a good boy'; then something happened and she stopped speaking of him.

In '86 there were general elections, and a new regime priding itself on its modernity (its members wore grey suits and metal-rimmed glasses and talked about deregulation and 'trimming the bureaucracy') came to power. In '86 also, Lillian's brother, Bolts, slipped from the wilting payroll of the Road Works Programme and sat around the house all day reading comics.

In '87 Bolts left home; I never learnt whither bound, or to what.

'What happen to Bolts?' I asked Lillian's father, when I realised he was no longer around. His reply was unenlightening. 'Bolts is a big man, he gone about his business.' More than a year later, Lillian's mother took me inside and showed me with pride the new gas range which Bolts, she said, had sent her; so in important ways I guess he turned out all right.

Then, also in '87, the Water Authority, with whom Lillian had worked for nine years, instructed her to take her accumulated leave forthwith.

She had ten weeks; she went to Brooklyn, to relatives of her next-door neighbour's there. It was the first time she had gone beyond Barbados, the first time she experienced winter; and winter seemed to please and amuse her.

'How was the trip?' I said one afternoon soon after her return, when she leaned out the window to offer us something to drink.

'Boy, it was cold!' she said with pleasure. 'I never knew it could be so cold! But New York is something else, eh? All those tall-tall buildings, O my God...'

This last was said almost thoughtfully, as her animation trailed off. In a sleeveless housecoat with the top buttons undone, her hair not pulled back for once but falling, slightly dishevelled, around her face, she looked different.

In fact it couldn't have been that great a vacation. Lillian phoned home, her mother told me later, twice a week and, towards the end, almost every night: but the letter she was fearing hadn't come. (Owing to some clerical or postal default, it never came. It was only after Lillian returned from Brooklyn and made enquiries that she was able to confirm her suspicion: that, after nine years, she had been retrenched.)

She spent six months back in Trinidad, trying with equal unsuccess to collect her severance pay and find a job. Then she flew back to Brooklyn.

'Don't tell Ma I told you,' she said, the last time I saw her. 'But I thinking of goin' back to the States. It ent have nothing for me here anymore.'

In our long but casual acquaintance, it was the first time she had unburdened herself to me of anything resembling a confidence; and it took me aback. I said, with that creole mix of chauvinism and bonhomie: 'I feel it have some man waiting for you in Brooklyn, you know!' And saw, in her confusion and dismay, how cruelly I had slighted them all: Lillian, Lillian's parents, and their predicament.

She said, somehow ashamed: 'Is not that; is not that at all. But things really really hard for us here now, you know? And Pa, you could see for yourself – Pa not getting any younger. At least from over there I could try...'

We talked a while longer. I said the usual things, about winter and cities, about an illegal immigrant's life not being easy: the usual, useless things. But I really wanted to get away, to hate myself in peace for a spell; so I was relieved when she prepared to go in.

'Well, goodbye,' she said smiling, almost gay.

I wished her good luck. We shook hands.

She was twenty-eight. She got a job as a live-in maid with a white family with three small children, somewhere out in Long Island. The pay amounted to almost nothing – board, lodging, a little pocket money – but there was the promise that, after two years, the husband would sponsor her and Lillian would get her 'papers'. And this was what Lillian's mother increasingly spoke of when I turned up at their yard in Santa Cruz: Lillian's papers. Did I know anyone at the American Embassy who could help Lillian get her papers?

I did not; but Lillian's mother averred confidence. She was praying day and night, she said, and she was sure that for Lillian, for them all, things were going to turn out all right. 'Only trust in Almighty God an' all will be well. Listen to me! You hear what I sayin'? Have trust in Almighty God! Say your prayers!' She said this looking at me fiercely. As if I were the one fighting bereavement, panic.

As for the father, he only referred to Lillian once, and that was when, some months after she'd left the second time, I asked: 'So how's Lillian getting on?'

He paused and seemed to consider the question. Then: 'Lillian up dere in Long Island,' he allowed. 'She putting up a good fight.' He paused again and thought of what he'd said. Then he looked at me and nodded.

A good fight.

I saw less of Lillian's parents after that; for I had been one of the lucky ones. In the same year Lillian lost her job I landed a second one, and so was able to change the Hunter for a Mazda 626, which meant that my monthly visits to Lillian's father's garage now dropped to three or four a year.

In between two such visits, without warning, Lillian's father turned old.

It happened just like that, and it was extraordinary. In the space of four months Lillian's father's hair turned white, and he lost maybe fifteen pounds, and began to walk with the deliberate, slow gait of one newly conscious of the malignant subterfuges of gravity. Lillian's mother said he had been sick; but illness alone could not explain his faraway air, nor the fact that his gaze – never animated, but always clear – now seldom seemed to focus. Whenever he wasn't actually doing something, Lillian's father looked off now into the middle distance, with an expression which said that he knew exactly what he was seeing there, and neither liked nor disliked it; and now, whenever I spoke to him, it was with the sensation of having to call him back.

This was mid-'89, and Lillian's father could not yet have been sixty. Yet I saw the change in him at once; and next I saw that Lillian's mother had seen it too, and was all caught up – so suddenly! – in making the fight of her life for her man. Where before she would not mention him, except on occasion, and then casually, now, over Kool Aid in the living room (still watched by Jesus and Mary, by the tossing seascape and the white horse) her every other sentence included his name. Where before Lillian's father and I, out in the yard, had hardly been aware of her, now she appeared at the window half-a-dozen times in half-an-hour to ask his opinion about this, pass on some gossip about that, even once, heartily – and how painfully! – cracking a joke, at which she herself laughed loud and long: all this in a futile effort to get him to turn to her with other than a stranger's incomprehension and small resentment. She, too, I saw, was trying to call him back, calling to him as to fully one-half of herself; calling from the depth of her being, the depopulated terrain of what all along had been *their* life; and in the mixed desperation and despair with which she harangued him now there was something both of a wolf calling to its mate and of a wolf, scenting loss in the valley below, giving forth with its inconsolable loneliness to the silhouetted pines and the moon.

It was soon over, that terrible struggle. When next I returned to Santa Cruz and Lillian's mother leaned out the window, she did not address him, only invited me in for a drink; and in the living room she once again turned to the subject of Lillian and her papers. There was no more mention of Lillian's father.

By mid-'89, the house in Lower Santa Cruz that seven years earlier had been home to a family of six was nearly empty. The youngest one had gone first; and three years later Lillian's other sister, the pretty pale one, had married and moved to Valencia.

(I only saw her once after that, one evening in late '89, when our visits coincided. She had two small children in tow, and a third looked to be preparing inside her; and though, allowing for the vague thickening of figure and feature that accompanies pregnancy, she seemed physically unchanged, her manner now was altogether different: not quite insolent but somehow boldfaced, even crude. Still: arriving that afternoon I'd found Lillian's father sitting on the step with the toddler on his knee, and for once not looking off into the middle distance but speaking softly to the uncomprehending child: so there was that.)

In '86 Lillian's brother, Bolts, had gone: I have the impression, though I cannot say why, that he either migrated illegally to Venezuela or else got a job on a ship. But I knew he was no longer in Trinidad and had all but lost touch with Lillian's parents, though on occasion he still sent them things: a second-hand compressor, a new gas range, a fancy Bible for Lillian's mother, with the pages bearing Genesis Chapters 7 to 9 marked by a brown envelope containing US$100.

It was Lillian's mother who insisted on the significance of the 'marked' pages.

'What Bolts ever know about de Bible?' she said to me triumphantly that evening. 'You don't see is Almighty God that guide his hand to mark dat exact place?' And reopening the gilt-edged tome she read, in a voice rich with emotion: '*Then God said to Noah and to his sons with him, "I will establish my covenant with you, and with your descendants after you; and with every living creature that is with you, the birds..."*' – here I thought with irreverent irrelevance of Lillian's father and his ducks, diminished from a sleek pen of maybe thirty to the half-a-dozen bedraggled survivors wandering about nowadays in the mulch and wild grass of the backyard – ' *"...never again shall all flesh be destroyed... never again... I will set my bow in the clouds... I will remember my covenant."* '

And, closing the book, Lillian's mother said to me, with such fierce triumph that, startled, I imagined I heard in it almost a note of hatred: 'Almighty God has set His bow in the clouds! An' dere is nothing new under the sun! For in wisdom dere is sorrow an' in knowledge dere is grief – lissen to me! *An' all else is vanity, saith the Lord!*'

It was not a lesson I was averse to. I nodded, and she saw I was not merely being polite, and her passion abated somewhat. 'Look how de Lord put a hand with Bolts, eh, boy?' she repeated, but softly, fondly. 'You don't see the only thing is to trust in Him?'

By then that trust was about all she had. For by then Lillian too had left and was working as a maid in Long Island; *putting up a good fight*, as the father had said, but in reality working for nothing, or rather for the day when she would get her 'papers' and be free to find a real job; and, in her absence, one fine day, Lillian's father had abruptly relaxed his grip upon the world. The world with its engagements and griefs, challenges and disappointments, small solaces and abiding hurts – he had let it go, all at once, and was now no longer the proprietor but like a boarder in his own house; no longer a husband but his indomitable wife's thankless charge.

So by mid-'89 the house at Lower Santa Cruz was nearly empty; and, in its desultoriness, the house itself now began to seem schizoid. Once, alive with inhabitants, its two-stage construction – the modernised living area to the front, the rickety wooden service rooms to the back – had seemed natural: part of a process, involving the whole country, from its impoverished past to the tenable present. But now, with its air of desertion, of having lost its function and ceased to grow, it seemed like a house divided against itself. As though the stuccoed walls and terrazzo floors now sought, ashamed, to hide the rickety kitchen, while the rickety kitchen for its part stood sardonic, mocking the other's pretensions and futility. So strange, that sense of a house no longer straddling past and present, but where past and present, withdrawn into their separate assumptions, stood apart and loathed each other, while all around them, in the untended yard outside, their common future, the bush, gained ground.

Through those rooms the father drifted, an unseemly ghost, taking stock of nothing any longer – the stain of damp on the ceiling, the woodlice in the sill, the loose or broken tiles; and among them, moving heavily because of her varicose veins, the mother – yes, even the mother, with her passionate piety and lioness's heart – seemed alternately lost and like someone cuffing at air. Lillian and Lillian's 'papers': these were now her lone preoccupation and last hope; and behind them both, she prayed, stood God. Sometimes – often – she would flare up with some homily in my presence, a fierce exhortation to faith. Other times, worn out, she would sit, apparently lost in thought, until she would remember her manners, and say, something like: 'So how the university treating you these days?'

It was in the latter, pensive mood that, one afternoon, Lillian's mother said: 'Eh-eh, I nearly forget. We get a letter from Lillian today.' Then she surprised me by adding: 'You want to see it?'

So I sat there (beneath Jesus and Mary, the seascape with dunes, and a large pale oblong on the wall where the white horse had stood at gaze for a decade) and, under the mother's watchful eye, read Lillian's letter. And as I read, my fear of invading a privacy faded: Lillian's letter was impersonally, casually cheerful. I recognised it as the kind of letter that, young, most of us would have written to our parents at one time or other, when, in distress or trouble, we nonetheless wished to protect them from worrying. Lillian's letter was like that; she gave of herself by withholding herself.

It wasn't long, two airmail pages, the handwriting large and rounded, in an upright, careful hand. Lillian's handwriting, it struck me, was like her life; in its painstaking rectitude it recalled the 'studious' girl. And, like her life, I could not connect the handwriting to the physical Lillian: the young woman with the dark eyes and the cheekbones, the good body and the pulled-back hair. It was easier to visualise her while reading her words than when contemplating their lettering; for Lillian's letter, as I said, was full of forced cheer and creole elidings.

For her room at the back of the house of the family in Long

Island she had just been given her own thermostat. They had also lent her a TV; and from the local library she'd begun borrowing books on accounting. The husband was, she thought, a good man; the wife was usually quite nice, though sometimes she had her moods; the children were a little bit spoilt but basically sweet. All in all they were treating her well, she couldn't complain; and whenever she began feeling lonely, on her days off she would visit with their Trinidad neighbour's relatives, over in Brooklyn. The weather was turning cold, but fall was something else; sometimes on evenings she'd walk to the park just to take in the trees. There was nothing to report, really: she was looking forward to the day, now just nine months away, when she could get her you-know-what (carefully, Lillian had refrained from writing 'Green Card') and things would start looking up for them all.

The rest of the letter concerned the family. How was Ma's varicose veins, when last had they heard from Bolts, was Pa still having his night-sweats? She'd been reading up on night-sweats in a medical dictionary, but they could be related, it seemed, to all kinds of things. Could Pa be persuaded to go to the doctor, for once? How was Trinidad, the economy, things in general?

'Give my love to everybody,' Lillian ended. 'I think of the both of you always. Your loving daughter.'

Lillian's mother had waited while I read. Handing it back, I said – because I had to say something – 'She sounds okay.'

Lillian's mother glanced at me, then looked away out of the window.

'She's a good child,' she said. 'She doin' her best. Me, I only crossin' my fingers an' prayin'.'

That was October '89.

After that I had a good spell with the Mazda, and it was not until July '90 that I took the car back for a routine servicing to Lillian's father's place. To my surprise, the house was shut up and seemed abandoned; the grass was unkempt in the yard. What had happened in my absence, I learnt sketchily from the next-door neighbour, and in rather more detail from Lillian's mother later on.

One evening in the second week of May, Lillian had phoned her mother in hysterics.

('Cry?' Lillian's mother told me later. 'In all my born days I never hear that child cry so! Not even when' – she named the youngest one – 'get kill', Lillian never cry like dat! True to God! Because everybody know Lillian was not a child to ever cry. Hear nuh man! Even when she was small *so* – Lillian, cry? Never!' And so on.)

It seems that back in March the couple for whom Lillian worked had separated; the wife left, taking the children with her; and while at the time the husband somewhat distractedly reassured Lillian that her job and future would not be affected, he'd returned from work that afternoon in May to tell her gravely what he'd just, he said, discovered: which was that, being now effectively childless, he'd lost the grounds on which he'd intended to sponsor her with the US Immigration Department. Moreover, he added, apparently not unkindly, while he would never force Lillian to leave, his changed situation made her presence in his house something of a social liability, Lillian being young, single, attractive, etc; and he would be much obliged if in due course she would find alternative employment for herself. Not that there was any hurry.

And so on.

Lillian's mother told Lillian to come home. ('Jesus, Mary an' Joseph! Is not like the child din' try! Two years she up dere workin' for nutting! Bed an' board! Bed, board, an' a lil bus money – you t'ink dat is any way for Lillian to live? I tell she, "Come home, darlin', your fadder missin' you" – Lord God, if you know how dat man missin' Lillian – "You try a t'ing an' you loss; it ent have no shame in dat! To hell wid America! Nobody could ever say you din try!" ' Telling this, Lillian's mother was herself overcome by weeping.)

Lillian's mother thought that by the end of the call Lillian was a little calmer. She also thought she had persuaded her daughter to come home. But Lillian did not come home. When, a week later, Lillian's mother, to ease her mind – or perhaps she'd had a premonition – phoned Lillian to discuss her return, she was told by the abandoned husband that Lillian had moved out; and her immediate, next phone call, to Brooklyn, elicited only bewilderment. Brooklyn hadn't heard from Lillian in months. Wasn't she still working with that nice couple over in Long Island?

There followed, for Lillian's mother, a nightmarish fortnight of futile pilgrimages: to the US Consular Office on Marli Street, the Trinidad and Tobago Ministry of External Affairs, Police Headquarters in St Vincent Street, even, for some reason, to the offices of the Red Cross. It ended with the mercy of a short note from Lillian, telling, what the mother already knew, that she had moved out of the Long Island husband's employ and home, and adding that she, Lillian, had decided not to return empty-handed, after all, but to 'make my own way from now on as best I could'. She would phone again, she ended, when she was 'settled'.

For Lillian's mother, however, this was only a respite. More weeks passed and Lillian's phone call did not come.

Lillian's mother decided to fly to Brooklyn. Her married daughter, the pretty pale one, expostulated that Lillian was thirty years old and could take care of herself, and that Lillian's mother would be no better placed in Brooklyn to trace the whereabouts of her prodigal daughter than she would be in Lower Santa Cruz.

(Lillian's mother: 'So what? I mus' siddong here and twiddle my toes while Almighty God alone know what happenin' to Lillian up dere in America? When I t'ink... *Lord* Jesus!' Lillian's mother wept briefly.)

Unexpectedly, it was Lillian's father who stopped the quarrel. 'Let she go,' he told the pretty pale one. 'Your mudder only doin' what she have to do.' With a ghost of the old authority, he went on: 'Dat is de onliest t'ing it have in dis world. Everybody do what dey have to do. *You* know dat.'

This would have been mid-June.

Another frenzied fortnight ensued. Unbearable days were wasted trying to contact Lillian's brother Bolts, who alone, it was thought, could raise Lillian's mother's air fare – till one morning the pretty pale one turned up at Lower Santa Cruz and, in between scolding one or other of her three children, counted out 15 hundred-dollar bills onto the dining table, saying to her mother: 'Here, look the fare, go. Since you so mulish to go, go!'

(Lillian's mother, surprised and angry: 'Whey you get dat money?' The pretty pale one: 'Look, Ma, don't get me vex here today! Jes' take de dam' money an' go. I done tell you you wastin' your time.' And the mother: 'Chile, have some respec', you hear? You don't ever talk to me like dat!' And so on.)

But that was the easy part. Lillian's mother had sought help from the US Embassy to locate her disappeared daughter, and the Consular Section now very nearly denied her a visa. It took a late-night trek by Lillian's parents to the home of a high Government man whose cars Lillian's mechanic father had once maintained before the treasurable visa was released.

Finally, there was an unexpected hitch. Lillian's mother refused to go and leave Lillian's father at home alone. For some reason, the pretty pale one could not leave her husband to come and stay with her father; and Lillian's father refused point blank to budge.

'What happen,' he demanded. 'I's a child? I cyar mind mihself for a few weeks? I tell you you ent have me to study, woman, is Lillian you suppose' to be studyin'! I good right here; I ent goin' nowhere!'

Lillian's mother remonstrated, wept; demanded piteously of no-one how 'dis man' could force her to park herself in Santa Cruz while his daughter, his own flesh and blood, was lost in America, a prey for wolves. But it was no use. Lillian's father, having said his piece, lapsed back into an old man's resentful silence; and Lillian's mother had already unpacked her bags, shouting that, between them, Lillian and Lillian's father were killing her, when the pretty pale one, in turn, intervened.

'Pa, you know Ma. If she say she ent goin' an' leavin' you here alone, she ent goin'. But you self say she have to go; so let her go! Come stay with us. Come help me mind your grandchildren for a few weeks. You know perfectly well that is what you suppose' to do.'

Father and daughter eyed each other; then the father rose. 'Wha' bout de ducks?' he demanded.

The pretty pale one lost her temper. The next-door neighbour could mind the blasted ducks.

And so, on July 18th, Lillian's mother flew to Brooklyn. She had never flown before and was in a terrible state (the pretty pale one: 'Ma, is just like takin' a bus!' Lillian's mother: 'Eh-heh? *You* say dat! If Almighty God had meant for man to fly he'd a' give him

160

wings. Quite up dere! Oh Jesus, look at my cross…'). But she got on the plane (first blocking the doorway to Immigration to repeat to her daughter many last-minute instructions concerning the care of her father) and flew to New York. And so she was in Brooklyn when Lillian phoned Santa Cruz, and, getting no answer, phoned the next-door neighbour, and, by this roundabout route, finally got hold of her mother.

Later, Lillian's mother could not bring herself to repeat their conversation – not, at least, to me. All I gleaned was that it lasted a long time; and that Lillian refused to say where she was calling from. It could have been Queens or the Bronx. It could have been Detroit or Philadelphia, it could have been L.A. or Denver or Houston or New Orleans. By the time it ended Lillian's mother understood – what the pretty pale one had told her from the start – that America was vast, impenetrable, and as alien to her as the moon.

She did the only thing she could think of: she went to see the Long Island husband with whom Lillian had worked for two years. But her timing was unpropitious, the husband had company ('If you see the little vixen! Is *she* make de man get rid of Lillian! So help me God! As soon as I see she, I know. Dat scum!') and in any case there was little he could tell her, except that in the days immediately prior to moving out Lillian had made several phone calls to D.C. Her heart pounding, Lillian's mother copied down the number; but the bleary male voice on the D.C. end of the line had never heard, it claimed, of any Lillian. So that was that.

Lillian's mother flew home. She booked first to return on July 29th, but in Trinidad an attempted coup was underway against the government, the airport was closed, and she didn't get a flight back until August 6th.

I next saw them, father and mother, in late September (that was when I learnt the story I told above). Lillian had phoned again, but with the same ground rules – asking after everyone, assuring that she herself was well, but refusing to say where she was or what she was doing – and, when I saw her, Lillian's mother seemed stunned by exhaustion and disbelief.

'Who'd a' t'ink it could ever come to dis, eh?' she said, almost cooingly. 'When I t'ink back to jes' a few years ago…' Then: 'Is dat blasted Government of yours. Those dawgs! Take 'way de chile work from she after nine years, jes' like dat!'

The brakes of the Mazda were giving trouble; I was back at Santa Cruz in October. And on that visit I learnt – what not even Lillian's father had been told – that in the intervening weeks Lillian's mother had received an envelope, by an unknown courier, and found in it a brief note: 'All for now. Will send more when I am able. Your loving daughter.' And found, in the folded notepaper, twenty US$100 bills.

At which Lillian's mother sat and stared dawningly and long, as a man fallen overboard in mid-ocean on a calm night stares at the receding lights that he knows will not return; or as Lillian's father, not long after his daughter's departure, had taken to staring for hours on end at whatever it was he discerned awaiting his pleasure on the smoky horizon.

'Whey Lillian get dat kinda money?' Lillian's mother asked me softly, in a voice so richly woven of contradictory emotions I could hardly separate them out.

The money had panicked her. And she was glad, she told me later, that Lillian's father was not at home when it came, for she would have rushed to him with it as with a burning brand – and that would have been the end of Lillian's father. But Almighty God, for all His wrath, could yet be merciful; and Almighty God in His mercy had given her time to catch herself, and the chance to protect the only man she ever loved from the meaning of that envelope's contents.

'Whey Lillian get dat kinda money?'

And, given her tone, Lillian's mother might equally have been asking, 'How could Lillian succumb to Satan?' or, 'What greater love – ?' But behind both of these there was something else: something womanly and knowing, triumphant and hating. And, underlying it all, I thought I heard a kind of crooning grieving, as if Lillian's mother had said, with Perse: 'The beauty of the world hath made me sad.' I shall not soon forget that voice.

I said truthfully that I didn't know. Then I added - hastily, because I feared her laugh – 'But I know she loves you all a lot.'

The small, sad, bitter, ironic smile stayed on Lillian's mother's face. She looked at me as woman to man: a distancing look. I wondered, but dared not ask, what she would do with the money. I said: 'You're a strong woman, Mrs —.'

And, driving away, I thought that I should not return; that I had just been privy to a tragedy which had taken me beyond my depth; that I should find a new mechanic. But a few months ago, driving up the highway, the Mazda abruptly began emitting a startling knocking; and since it was a Sunday afternoon, all garages closed, and since I am a mechanical moron and could not tell whether the noise signified a minor rubber ruptured or the engine about to drop out, I turned left through El Socorro and crossed the Croisee, and made it into Lower Santa Cruz.

Silence. Heat. Lillian's father tinkering – myopically and ineptly, as an old man tinkers, misplacing every washer or plug as soon as he put it down – with someone's disembodied engine under the shed. Lillian's mother sitting alone in the living room, fanning herself, the television screen on, the volume off. The Mazda's ailment was serious, it turned out, but not urgent. I don't know why I didn't excuse myself and leave when Lillian's mother at the window said: 'It ent have no Kool-Aid, you will take a Sprite?' But I didn't, I stayed awhile. And so I saw the change in Lillian's mother.

I saw that Lillian's mother was now alone, and that she had grown massive with solitude, her gait and gestures a kind of freewheeling lumbering through nowhere that could ever be home. I saw what I had not expected: that in this new scheme of things, Lillian's father had become her mother's mother; that it was he now who fussed over her, humble and ineffectual, appearing often in the living room to ask, '—, you want dis?' or 'You want me to turn off dat?' (Flickeringly on the TV screen tiny horses were streaming around a bend.)

But chiefly, as we spoke, without fluency now on either side, I saw that Lillian's mother had entered into a new relationship with her God: a relationship at once more intimate and ambiguous.

'Almighty God is something else, eh boy?' she said to me once.

And, later: *For thy God is a wrathful God.* But let Him do His worst! He will not find His servant wanting. Me? Huh!'

163

I felt that He was her only reality; that she was all concentrated now upon wrestling Him down into the dust with her; that they would go down together to the end, she and her God. In vain I asked about Bolts, about the pretty pale one: her responses were noncommittal, inanimate. Bolts was 'out dey somewhey'. The pretty pale one had her life.

And Lillian?

Lillian's mother looked at me stonefaced. 'Lillian? Lillian okay. Me an' she fadder, we does hear from her all de time.'

So that was that.

Unwittingly, as I was leaving, I put my foot in it. I made some casual remark about the political scene, beginning blasedly, 'So I see your Government – .'

Lillian's mother's response sobered me. I had not thought her capable of such hatred.

This was in March '91, and I haven't seen them since. I don't know what happened to Lillian, and, knowing something of big cities and winter, and of the wolfish hearts of men therein – and recalling those cheekbones and the glossy dark skin, the good body and the pulled-back hair – I don't really want to know.

But when I think of the other Lillian, the 'studious' girl, who left school and went and worked with the Water Authority for nine years, and all that time lived at home, warding off suitors and handing her mother her pay cheque at the end of each month, until one day she was casually retrenched – and *then* migrated illegally, and worked as a maid in Long Island for two more years, until her hope of a Green Card fell through – when I think of that Lillian now, I find there are many things I no longer want to hear.

I don't want to hear how black people are lazy. I don't want to hear how public servants only want to take, take, all the time, and never give. In fact, there are so many things I don't want to hear that there's a whole range of verandahs I no longer visit. And most nights I manage to miss the ebullient parade of blown-dry Cabinet Ministers which passes for news in my country, in our time.

But Lillian – she is thirty-one now – Lillian isn't her real name, you know? When I began telling her story I called her that, meaning to protect her and her family's anonymity. But now I think: protect them from what? She is gone beyond the pale, she will not return; and, as for her parents, they have already lost more than any decent man or woman has a right to expect to lose, even in this brave new entrepreneurial world of ours. So what the hell. Learn her real name. Her real name is June.

June.

She existed, she exists, she will always exist:

June. A young woman with three 'O' levels, including English. From Lower Santa Cruz, Trinidad, West Indies.

IN A TROPICAL PARADISE

I: *The Ladies of the Day*

It was the week before carnival, the foreign yachts were in; and down in the west, from Bayshore to Chaguaramas, from the Yacht Club to Peake's Marine, the ladies of the day – kissing cousins to the ladies of the night – were disembarking from route taxis and maxi taxis and buses and even, I saw once, the dented tray of an old pickup driven by her – brother? pimp of a paramour? casual village oaf? entrepreneurial spouse?

Now that's an overstatement, they weren't exactly flooding in; they came rather in a steady but innocuous trickle; and unless you were in the habit of driving the length of the western peninsula several times a week you probably wouldn't even have noticed them. Even I, who like to think myself observant, missed the meaning of their sudden, quiet descent upon the place, until, crossing the water one early, bright blue morning, I was bemused by the sight of a pink-shorted, white-bra'd, fleshy child from Central, padding barefooted along the deck of a spanking white ketch to clasp from behind the bare chest of a denim'd, stubble-bearded and sunbaked Hun (who said something to her without turning).

Anyway, here they came, in the week before Carnival, looking freshly scrubbed, and cool and bright as cool, clean water, in the dusty mid-morning heat – and that was how you'd first notice them, if you noticed them at all: how cool and bright and freshly-scrubbed they looked, on a workday morning otherwise given over to the usual weekday hassle and heat – disembarking from their various transports in high heels and crotch-cramping jeans and frilly-edged blouses, or else (and these, I surmise, were the 'better class' ones) in Roman sandals and pleated shorts and brand new T-shirts neatly 'bloused' at the waist.

It was interesting to see how some hadn't yet put on their faces, and looked merely preoccupied, or even to be purposefully stalking; while others (more experienced? innocent? romantic?) were already deep in their impending roles, and walked towards the gates of this or that boating establishment as though mysteriously infused with light, the dark eyes already shining as if with wonder (at what, whom, themselves?) the rouged lips precociously parted, with that air which only certain Liliths, still in the full, the roaring after-bloom of puberty, can achieve, and which says to the world: 'Here I am, your Valentine, your impossible dream, your miracle!' – and how, at the sight of these, the passing traffic would slow down and the drivers would peer.

I might have added – because this too was interesting – that ninety percent of them were Indian, but fear attracting to myself the curt attention of Hulsie X or the Maha Sabha's answering crash of rage. So let's say instead that ninety percent had glossy-black hair, with, in their complexions, that hint of sallow recessiveness beneath the brown, which, in beauties of their type, can make them look positively burnished (as opposed to the best of their African sisters, who under the skin are immortal rose!) and plump underlips which, by contrast with their straight thin siblings, can bring thoughts inappropriate to Lent; and I wondered, not without wryness, whether the preponderance of their 'type' reflected their greater ambition (and what a fecund pearl of thought, that 'ambition', to drop into the middle mulch of this vegetable sentence!) or represented the visiting yachties' preference, or both.

Now, at heart I am a nationalist, I confess to that corruption, and I am told I am reputed (wrongly, but beyond redemption) an unreconstructed chauvinist. So I might as well go whole hog and confess that while the sight of the plainer of these disembarking Janes – the coarse-faced or too thick-necked or really stick-legged ones – never mind that the latter often looked as though they'd grown, not donned, their jeans – left me as unmoved as some bored anthropologist making by rote his cursory jottings, the sight of their luckier, variously luscious counterparts, and the knowledge of their destination, stirred in me a vague, dog-in-the-manger pang.

In *Othello*, a prattling fop drives Brabantio mad with the news that his fair daughter Desdemona has run, from the ineffectual blandishments of her own kind, to 'the gross clasps of a lascivious Moor'. Cata-corner, in Chaguaramas I find I am depressed by the image of one of the flowers of my tribe (the tribe of Trinidad, I hasten to add, defiantly but no doubt anachronistically, writing this in post-Indian Arrival Day week, in these ethnically-jumpy times) wriggling in the gross clasps of a bearded meat-eater from beyond the waves, while her sweat on the plastic-covered bunk mattress makes her slide and flail for purchase – aiee! – wherever she can, and her pleasurable cries (and I don't care if they're faked) echo in the low-roofed cabin with its brass barometer gleaming and its faded orange life-jackets hanging on the wall.

(As for that peculiar epithet, 'meat-eater' – it represents two different references, garbled into one by your columnist in his distress: the Aztecs' complaint that the unwashed conquistadors stank, and one Eurocentric historian's attributing of this, not to the fact that Spaniards in those days never bathed – the Aztecs did, every day, though fat lot of good it did them, in the end – but to the fact that they ate meat: which diet allegedly gave them their pungent b.o. in the nostrils of the Americans, who ate fish.

Of course, that's merely a jealous slander: most yachties – as anyone knows who's ever lined up behind one at the TTYA for a shower – most yachties, whenever they get the chance, bathe and bathe. And bathe.)

Now, I think I need to dissociate myself from either the clarity or the stridency (you choose) of the views expressed in 'Married Prostitutes' by another columnist last Sunday. Call this fond foolishness if you like, but I find it hard to equate the full-bodied (w-e-l-l) engagements of the Ladies of the Day with the brisk transactions of their nocturnal counterparts; and I don't even like the word 'counterparts'. The business of the latter, so far as I know, is specifically missilic; and it's virtually always over in 'a short time'. Not a lot of laughter, emotion, or shared adventure – other than the putatively orgasmic, that is – adheres to it.

By contrast, your Lady of the Day is off to partake in the life of her live-aboard yachtsman. And whether it turns out to be for a weekend, a fortnight, a month, or even – and this is of course her moistest dream, and has been known on occasion to come true – till death do them part, she will never forget 'her' yachtie. In best-case scenarios she will get to take him home, to amaze the village or scandalise the suburb (and do God-knows-what to her folks); and his small framed photo will probably adorn her mantelpiece thereafter, and her girlfriends will grow sick of hearing her reminisce about him. For years thereafter, there's a fair chance she and he will exchange letters; and if, before they cease, his battered prow noses back into her Boca's oily swells, odds are she will know of this festive occasion in advance, and – having first donated a celebrant's 'blues' to her most trusted beautician – will gaily go down to the waterfront to meet him when the time comes, even as in Nantucket the wives of whalers would pace and peer from their widow's-walks, or as in the Aegean patient Penelope once awaited her wandering Odysseus.

If her motive is profit, it's seldom the flat cash transaction that transpires between your laconic Lady of the Night and her moronic clients. And even if she sets out with the ol' dollar sign in mind (and we live in an age, after all, when – as in 'The Price is Right' – phonebooths, supermarkets, or whole amphitheatres full of perfectly normal-looking men and women, can be reduced to screaming by the mere thought of that sinuously pulsing sign) she soon surrenders this narrow focus and relaxes into the pleasures and bruises of live-aboard yachting, and the peculiar new adventure of Him.

You have only to watch her – she who, by every right conferred by shared soil and syntax, should be *yours* – shriek and grab hold of the guy, in real terror or fake excitement (or fake terror, or real excitement) as their outboard-powered inflatable skids about on the chop, to know she is *living*, not merely 'transacting'. All of which, of course, just makes it worse.

Don't get me wrong.

Most 'yachties' come married or in quasi-paradisal pairs, not as lone sea-wolves nosing out a promising port. Most aren't that young but in the prime of their lives, thirty-five to fifty-five, say. And most are respectable, perfectly normal men and women (except, of course, that they're American) whose sea-keeping duties and flexible timetables usually make them the best sort of small-island tourist: easy-going, interested, already tanned, and in general free of fuss.

If they often top up their crew lists with what, in the Personals, are referred to as SWMs – footloose young bachelors out for a tropic lark, or else their recently-divorced semi-elders, not averse to fleeing the scene of the nuptial crash till the emotional and financial dust settles – what's wrong with that? And if, at the thought of these latter, the lights come on in the eyes, not of panthers in the peaceable kingdom, but of ochre Indra in Arima, or nubile Nisha in Newtown, or swart Phyllis in Penal, what's wrong with that? Which sailor doesn't deserve to root again in Earth, after so long in the limbo of such a small boat, on a wide and tossing ocean, under the merciless stars, whipped day and night by the salt aphrodisiac of the air?

And what's different here to the sixty thousand or so Russian SWFs, all crazily filling out forms as you read this (in small and graceless rooms where pale oblongs on the dirty walls mark the place where Lenin's portrait was yanked) in the shameless hope – because, child, may you never know it, but desperation, real desperation, is shameless – of selling themselves to an American, any American, be he the most lumbering oaf of a shotgun-toting, beer-swilling redneck from somewhere like Gainesville or Oklahoma, while the queues lengthen in Red Square, and Muslims to the south draw straws for the next kamikaze mission, and from the wings Virinovsky watches in hopeless dog-in-the-manger rage – watches and grits his teeth, like your columnist? (Except, of course, Virinovsky would *kill* them, kill them both, thin Katya and sturdy Stu alike; while your columnist – a wimp, alas, even in his dreams – probably wouldn't go quite so far.)

When in all of human history have females of a threatened or vassal tribe not run for cover, protection or cash, to the beds or bunks or throw-rugs of their conquerors, though they often take advantage of the soft fool there, and wind up giving it to him good? I thought – because I'd been reading much ancient literature of late, and what's literature for, if not for consolation at stressful times like this? – I thought:

Delilah was a frontier daughter, a Philistine child, at a time when the Philistines were just beginning to expand into the

Hebrew-dominated Judah mountains. Which was why, no doubt, she contrived to twist her ankle just as a muscle-bound young denizen of the home tribe was lumbering by. The rest is history: in no time, the surging Philistines had occupied the foothills in force: whereupon, the hitherto-melting, tall wench (because the Philistines were *tall*) brusquely pulled the plug on her hirsute hunk.

I thought: Ahab, Israel's king, niftily thrashed the Aramaeans; but that only had the fateful consequence of making Jezebel – daughter of the king of a really, *really* weak Canaanite tribe, the now terrifically-imperilled Zidonians – flee preemptively to his powerful arms. (OK, maybe she was sent.) Except that by the time the abominable but resourceful child was finished with him, ol' Ahab could only totter forth to battle, to have his once-impressive army decimated, and himself unpunctually killed, by the same Aramaeans he'd once lustily scattered.

I thought: Sheba swooned for Solomon (if in fact she did) because there was no other way for her kingdom's exports to reach their trans-Israel markets. Cleopatra ruled a colonised Egypt, a vassal state of Rome, when she lured the conquering Anthony to 'exchange (his) empire for her beads of sweat' (Walcott) – though a fat lot of good it did either of them when the remaining Roman legions, no especial sentimentalists, came a-knocking on their humid boudoir.

Almost every striking spade in Sam Selvon's London (we are skipping around a little, you see) sooner or later takes refuge from the cold and rice-and-peas-less dark in the pale gleam of indigenous arms: in the heated basement flat of some Ladbroke Grove 'number' or 'craft' or 'thing', with its creaky single bed or tatty divan. Which just goes to show – though too late, I guess – it isn't a gender thing, this fleeing to the winning side.

And *what's wrong with that?* I ask you.

The answer is, of course: nothing.

The nations, the races – at heart they are one; we are all of us Milton's 'Blind mouths' under the skin. And just as the cosmos sings with binary systems, two stars that in their solitary hurtling passed close enough for Newton's Cupid to grab and twin them, so men and women passing each other too near will always swerve inward, and wind up perhaps making the music of the spheres, what you in your lingo call 'sweet music'. The LAPD (as Simpson Trial aficionados will have noticed) may have recently changed its tune, and now refer to a black man or a white woman as a 'male black' or a 'female white', trenchantly swapping around epithet and noun. But that's just because America's all shot to hell. Gender was always more pivotal (yeah!) than race.

And yet.

And yet, compatriot satyr, look me in the eye and tell me you don't have to beat back the small irrational lunge of a grudge whenever you see one of 'our' women with one of 'them' – tell me that lunge, sexist slob, isn't loud or whispery in direct proportion to the lady's lusciousness or lack of it – and I will tell you, with sonorous, sympathetic sorrow, that, sir, you lie, you lie!

So it was that when your columnist, one morning in carnival week, passing too close in his rented pirogue to one moored and stately cutter, from the cool shade of whose blue-canopied deck, 'she' –

– she who had to be th'essential flower of Chaguanas, never before seen, and now never to be forgotten, reclining, with her cheekbones and her sloe-eyes, like Cleopatra in the lap of some lout, in her white shorts and lime green boob tube, while the morning breeze teased the glossy glory of her hair on the dimples of her temples, her dimpled shoulders, her naked throat –

– when *she*, I say, incautiously let her dark gaze fall distantly on your columnist's sudden glare, and rest dreamily there (while my passing pirogue roared and went on roaring) all the while reflexively stroking the horrible blond arms clasped from behind around her naked tummy, with its little slouch-bulge –

– I have to tell you:

When that terrible, epiphanic moment was over, and, with a little private smile – a small homage bestowed, not on me, alas, but on the familiar, dim wonder of her own beauty, and of its power – the dark cat's-eyes slipped sideways from mine, to contemplate without pity the spreading wound of my damned boat's stygian wake –

– your columnist felt –

– depressed.

I don't as a rule stop for tourists, but the squall that abruptly clattered like hailstones on the Crown Point airport roof had caught them out in the open. The man was an Englishman in his sixties, paunchy, avuncular and balding. 'Kind of you,' he said as he got in beside me. 'Whew! These showers come so suddenly here!'

I asked where they were heading.

'Anywhere!' cried the girl in the back. In the mirror I caught her tense gaiety. She was a sallow Trinidadian Indian. Head inclined, she was wringing out her hair. In the rain she'd looked to be in her early twenties. Now I saw she was older than that.

The man laughed obligingly. 'Actually, we're going back to Turtle Beach,' he said. 'It was such a fine morning we thought we'd walk part of the way' – and I registered with scepticism that 'we' – 'but wherever's most convenient…'

I hesitated. The squall had already passed Bon Accord and the black road was steaming in the sun. I hadn't planned on the beach. But I'd just come from seeing off a beloved woman at the airport, and the day ahead felt shapeless, desultory. 'Well, I'll take you there,' I said.

And soon I was glad, for the man – call him Charles – turned out to be a retired cameraman from one of the big British television stations and had been most everywhere in his time. Korea, Vietnam, Rhodesia. Northern Ireland, Beirut. He'd even followed the British bobbies ashore in Anguilla.

'That must have been funny,' I said.

'Actually, it was very embarrassing.' He grimaced. 'The chaps, you see, nothing in their training or experience had prepared them for that sort of mission. The Anguillans didn't want them to leave, you know. They kept begging them to stay, hanging on to their arms. Oh, they were very ill at ease! So of course they took it out on us.'

In the back seat the girl was huddled in the corner, looking out of the window with a kind of resistant waiting. With her reddish-brown hair and pallor (which the sun had burnt to yellow brass), with her broad face and small hooked nose and leonine eyes, she wasn't a typical-looking Indian; but she was striking. When I asked, she said she was from Couva, 'originally': which I took to mean she didn't want to talk about it. In the brief silence that ensued after Charles and I swapped names I glanced at her, but she declined to donate her own name, and Charles either forgot or chose not to introduce her.

'I often thought,' he said soberly instead, 'it was the beating the Government took over Anguilla that began them thinking along the lines that led to the Falklands' Policy.'

The Falklands' Policy was a new military policy of pooling and controlling the movements of journalists in war zones. Designed to make them into virtual propagandists for the war effort, it has been fairly successful – as the US proved in the Gulf. Trinidadian journalists don't go to war zones, and I hadn't thought overmuch about 'pooling'. But listening to Charles, I realised the Falklands' Policy signified to him a professional debacle of Orwellian proportions. He had retired, he said wryly, 'at just about the right time'.

In the back seat the girl laughed abruptly. 'Look how they spell portugal!' she said, directing our gaze to a roadside sign which read: 'YES! Apples! Grapes! Portigals!' Charles didn't comment. I murmured obligingly, 'Potty gals'; but failed, I saw, to preempt her sulk. It was Charles's interest she'd been seeking, Charles she'd been trying to call back to her from his incomprehensible, boring, small talk.

At Turtle Beach I stayed behind to change (I had a swimsuit in the car but no towel). Then I wandered onto the beach, in such a way as to make it easy for them not to see me – in the circumstances, it was Charles's call. He made it, waving from the partial shade of a thatched umbrella as if to say 'Here!' I went over.

He was putting the finishing touches to the girl's back while she lay on a lounger with her bra undone. 'There you are,' he told her. 'Sunny side up!' And he slapped her bottom affectionately. The girl started and pushed his hand away. 'Your hand have oil on it!' she protested. Squeezing her bra with one arm she peered over her shoulder, trying to see what he had spoilt.

'Sorry, darling,' Charles said. He said it as if he meant it, but not terribly.

'And what field are *you* in?' This, conversationally, to me. I told him.

The girl was suddenly alert. 'Which paper?'

When I answered she looked disappointed, then decided to pursue her query anyway. Did I know X, from the *Bomb?* I said, only by name. She looked at me hard, concluded there was nothing more of interest there, and replaced her cheeks on her hands, facing Charles.

'That's wonderful,' Charles said. 'I've always wished I could write.'

I'd sat on the free beach chair where it was. This was on the far side of the girl. For perhaps half an hour, while she fidgeted occasionally, we chatted across her oiled back. It was a constant magnet in the silences. Each time, you had to dredge your next thought up from it.

Beirut had been his scariest assignment – 'You got in there and couldn't wait to get out' – but an earlier crisis had been worse. 'We'd all been taught at school, you know, to sing "Britannia" and salute the Union Jack. And then suddenly, everywhere you went your first thought was to get the hell away from the flag! Because wherever the flag was, if it was for example painted on the side of a van, that's where the shells and bombs would be coming. And that was very strange – finding out that this flag you'd been taught to be so proud of was so hated everywhere else in the world, you always had to run from it. Don't salute it, run from it!'

In Northern Ireland in the late '80s he'd finally 'got his': shrapnel from a bomb, which landed him in hospital for a long time and resulted in his taking early retirement. Northern Ireland in some ways had been worse than Beirut. There'd been no way of telling who was who.

The talk turned to Tobago. He'd been here for five days, loved it, wished he could have persuaded his wife to join him. But his wife, she loved Montserrat, and had chosen to stay behind with friends there. Tomorrow he'd be flying back there. To Montserrat. To rejoin his wife.

This account of his timetable was punctuated as follows. At Charles's first mention of his wife the girl lifted her head and looked at him, and Charles placed his hand placatingly on her head and went on talking, quite casually, without looking at her, and by the time he'd finished she'd had no recourse but to return her cheek to her hands and make a show of closing her eyes again. And it was all quite silent, casual, and devastating.

The curious thing was how those small gestures – the mention of the wife, the girl's bluff, the casual hand on her head – made Charles's life seem real to me. If you'd spent forty years coming under fire all over the globe, I surmised, there had to be many things you no longer bothered with. A man of the world, I thought him now. And it was with unusual candour (for me) that I went on to tell him about Trinidad.

When I'd finished, Charles shook his head. 'It's quite amazing,' he said. 'You come to a little island, you think it's paradise, and then you discover it's just a sort of mini-England. Do you know, all the problems you've described – we're having exactly the same problems back home? Amazing!'

Here the girl – whose stillness, of late, had had nothing of quietude in it – abruptly fastened her bra and rose. To Charles – or rather, at him – she said: 'I goin' in the sea.'

'We'll join you soon,' Charles told her, and with a toss of her head she went. Long brown hair, long gleaming back, bikinied bottom kinked back. Long pale stride which, swinging her arms, leaning forward and rotating slightly on the balls of her feet, she turned into an angry swagger.

She didn't go directly into the sea, after all. A beach boy intercepted her, cutting off her angle, and – perhaps to punish Charles, perhaps to begin amending her own timetable – she acquiesced and stood talking to him for a long time, standing very close and talking intently into his face.

To Charles I said wryly: 'Paradise, huh?'

He glanced in amusement from me to the girl. Then he smiled, shaking his head.

'Ah, she's a lovely child,' he said.

III: *And None of It for Love*

The menus at the *Coyaba*, at Grande Anse, Grenada, are printed in English and German; but on a weekday morning last month, on the bright beach beyond the hotel lawn, the sun-worshippers were all French. No doubt there was a charter, I thought without much pleasure, lugging my lounger out from the line of almond trees, looking in vain for a place to be alone in what might have been the middle of Marseilles.

There was the pretty brown-haired girl, freckled and tanned, sitting in the shade in bikini top and wrap, having her hair corn-rowed by a taciturn male stylist, lifting her eyes (without moving her head) to attend to something her hovering escort was saying to her.

There was the dark-haired young man in black briefs, propped on his elbows with knees drawn up and soles spread wide on the sand, presenting his bulge to all-comers and the sun with a tight little, unpleasant little smile.

There were the aged couples, the women potato-thighed, the men with their sagging bud-breasts and knobby knees, wandering in and out of the sea, smiling. (For some reason, they were the only ones bathing.)

There was the pluperfect brunette, oval-faced, narrow-nosed, straight-lipped, and as flawlessly tanned and manicured as a mannequin, reclining, reading a paperback, in a rainbow bikini, in a lounger, in the sun, but doing so with such an air of transfixed immobility (as if she might shatter at any moment) that I silently took my hat off to the unknown author who could so imperil such perfection by prose alone.

And then there was The Blonde in the Thong – she and her escort, a long-haired, black-haired guy with a goatee, wearing wraparounds and wielding a camera.

I had freshly flown in from Trinidad, checked in, and made straight for what is rightly reputed one of the great natural beaches of the world. In general I endure aeroplanes, but now I wished the flight had been longer. Half an hour from Piarco to Point Saline, another half-hour from Point Saline to this... *brilliancy... brilliancy!* There hadn't been nearly enough time to shed the shadow, the mottled moral penumbra, of Trinidad. Dole Chadee, Abu Bakr, Ramesh Lawrence Maharaj; and now, suddenly – this!

I wrapped my watch and glasses in my T-shirt, strode down the beach and threw myself into the crystalline turquoise. The coolness and translucence were like undeserved acclaim. I swam out beyond the geriatric waders to where the seabed shelved away to blue, and there, like a languorous seal, disported for an indefinite interlude, diving and rolling, swimming and floating... and when I emerged and regained the lounger (towelling my head and re-donning the photogreys) there was The Blonde in the black thong, and the guy with the goatee in the wraparounds.

The Blonde might have been twenty-one, twenty-two, or twenty-eight, twenty-nine: for some reason, it was hard to tell. She was passably attractive – this despite a facial expression which hardly changed, and which I first thought 'frank' but later amended to 'lobotomised'. Her hair fell in golden wavelets halfway down her back. She was as stacked and hourglassed, and with the same mere hint of muscle definition, of steel beneath the silk, as the girls you see swooning over the elephantoid biceps of some pathological materialist on the glossy cover of *Bodybuilder* or *Mr. America*.

The other striking thing about her – which I only saw when she stood up – was this. In the course of her Caribbean sojourn (urged on, no doubt, by Goatee-'n-Wraparounds) she had progressed from Alpine modesty to tropical nudity by definite stages of shrinking swimwear; and the tireless sun, attending to each new twin-wing of flesh as it appeared, had left there a record of her increasing brazenness as conscientious as a tree trunk's rings. Seen from behind, her bottom, reading inward, looked like a Sissons' paint chart (and its mirror image) in the range of Teak to Blush. She must have cost him a small fortune in swimwear. But perhaps, I thought wryly, it was worth it.

Certainly it was worth it, judging from the irritable intensity with which he was now photographing her – and photographing her. From every conceivable angle. In every conceivable pose.

Sitting in the yoga position, palms turned inward on thighs. Leaning back with her weight on her hands (imperiously tossing the blonde mane). Lying on her belly; on her back; on her side, with golden haunch outlined against the blue. Walking towards him; walking away from him, looking back. Wading in to stand groin-deep in the rustling water.

The curious thing was, she seemed neither pleased nor put upon by his inconsolable camera-feasting upon her. She followed his stage directions obediently: without petulance, but without any discernible pleasure either. It might almost have been a professional arrangement. And they might have been alone; quite alone.

And the little string-thing, I saw, obsessed her; with every motion she paused to adjust it. She stood up, cupped the bra-bits, jiggled; then stood and looked at the camera 'frankly'. She lay down, pulled the strings above her hipbones, craned to check the effect; then lay back and looked at him 'frankly'. She rolled over, dusted her bottom, inserted a finger to adjust the thong, craned back over her shoulder to check – then laid her cheek on her crossed arms on the sand and looked at him (try to visualise this) 'frankly'.

At first I'd thought him predatory: he, like a bouncing, squatting ape with his insatiable instrument. But now it occurred to me that they were in this together, and that in a sense she, too, was engaged in feasting on her body.

That body, which for most of her life had to have been private, yet unremarkable as grass, to her: he with his camera and cajolings had given her a new way to look at it. It had been her Caribbean discovery: that her body could be naked in public. Yet, didn't naked have to mean impersonal, here, where there were other people, none naked, looking on?

So. Something that had been part of who she was had become something she had and could deploy. And so she had joined him in this conspiracy of predation: she and he together 'exploring' her body.

The thought felt tendentious and overblown. In any case, it was not what I wanted. I rose and availed myself of a Sailfish, and beam-reached the mile or so to St George's, hardening up around the headland and tacking to go on in between a docked tourist liner and the Nutmeg, doing this partly as a Pavlovian reflex (I cannot remember ever entering St George's from the land) and partly for the sinful pleasure of being out on the water in the middle of a working day. The latter sensation didn't last. Semi-surrounded by vans, trucks and pedestrians in work clothes, I soon began feeling guilty, and a fool. Why is it so hard to remember that, past a certain age, you can't be a tourist in your own islands? I cracked the sheet and slunk away downwind, pulling the centreboard, watching the water fountaining up through the slot each time a gust arrived...

I must have been gone half an hour, but they were still at it when I got back: Goatee-'n-Wraparounds and the Thong Blonde. Only, now they had found an extra: the same taciturn stylist (bare back, gold chain, jeans) who'd earlier corn-rowed the pretty brown-haired girl. He was lifting her up in his arms as I dragged the Sailfish up; and she, with an arm around his neck, was looking as frankly as ever at the moving, teeth-sucking thing.

After that, directed by gestures by Goatee, he crouched to take her on his shoulder. She steadied herself with a hand on his head; cupped the bra-bits, jiggled; looked at the camera.

The next idea was for her to stand on his shoulders. But she didn't quite make it, and came down astraddle his neck. And there adjusted herself, strings to hipbones, bra bits jiggled, and then looked expressionlessly at the camera – while her macho moron wrapped his arms around her legs and glowered for the camera, as though he were some barebacked Darth Vader with a hostage...

Listen. This is not a Black Power column. And I know how intricate and intimate and sad is the bond between beachboy and tourist in these islands. But I have to tell you. Loosened up by the sailing, yet newly angry, I wanted to ask him afterwards (though I am sure he would not have understood me): 'Hey, pardner; tell me something. How does it feel to hold that in your arms; to take its weight on your shoulder; to have it *clamped around your neck* – and none of it for love?'

IV: *By a Winterish Sea*

It didn't happen overnight, the displacement of Store Bay's summer idyll by a winterish sea. For most of October the weather had kept changing and changing back; but now the wind had settled in the north, and day after day the wind-driven seas ran down the west coast and piled up in the bay, changing the sand's contours, washing at the steps, roiling the inshore water to a sandy brown and cutting the width of the beach by almost half.

And perhaps it had something to do with that uneasily moving water, inchoate and grey after the treacherous months of stilly-dreaming azure, but Store Bay one day last week felt almost spooky.

Or perhaps it was my mood, not the water's. Or the weird set of people who materialised at Store Bay that day.

At any rate, no sooner had I arrived, spread my towel and opened a book – then put it away, to sit and stare moodily at the desolate ocean – than a very large young black woman in a blue beachcap – a fond dispenser, it turned out, of that horrible Black-British accent in preemptive flight from which my wife and I, long ago, had snatched up our two pre-speech toddlers and sallied south from that dismal isle – waded through the air in my definite direction, fixing me, while still some distance away, with a glutinous smile, to stand at last between me and the sun and proffer encouragingly:

'Ott, ain-nit?'

Glumly I allowed her veracity on that point.

'Noice dye, though,' she ventured next. 'Laffly hweathah!'

Increasingly glumly I allowed her veracity on that point as well, and then on a whole series of points, while her accent edged my teeth like fingernails on a blackboard, until finally, disappointed, she waddled away and went down into the water, coyly parting it with hands held palms-forward for the benefit of a pair of elephantine thighs.

Behind me, in the stingy shade of a coral outcrop, two grey-skinned young men of around thirty, mid-European or Arab, sat with their minds holding hands (?). Not far from them, a leathery Diana with orange hair, and fifty years' headstart over her swimsuit's daring cut, sat up suddenly, sucking on a cigarette and glancing around like an amused and aging hawk.

Have you ever been in one of those moods where you feel slightly crazy – when, for no reason you can locate, everybody around you seems somehow spastic: disjointed, incoherent, weird?

Often it's a small thing that sets it off, and once you know what it is, it passes. But at Store Bay last week I couldn't find the key (perhaps it was the winterish water) and so everybody went on looking weird, and stuck in my mind afterwards like Fellini grotesqueries; and so I write this now out of that most ignoble of Art's ancient impulses: to dump them on you, dear reader.

But they *were* weird! Wothehell.

Like the pretty Spanishy-Indian Trinidadian girl at the blue trestle-table, who on inspection turned out to have full lips, curly brown hair, a pert button of a nose – and four hands with which, respectively, she held a black umbrella over her head, manipulated a spare rib between competing pairs of molars, pinned down a writing pad (which refused to accept its fate and kept making sudden, fluttery, doomed bids for freedom), and cheerfully wrote on it.

Or like the buxom young woman, whom I cannot prove was Tobagonian – a self-defensive reflex, that careful clause, against the acrid lady in the leafy lounge, who turned out to be a veritable patriot, and who on learning my name advised me (in what felt afterwards like a sustained swamping by a single, long, tensed sentence) that in writing about Tobago I should try not to be sensational, try not just to write for the sake of writing, try not to be so hot and hasty, she didn't have anything against me, but perhaps I should keep my trap shut till I'd been here at least a year, and try not to write just to sell papers, try next time to think about the effect of what I wrote on the morale of Tobago, on the tourist industry of Tobago, try not to show off, try not to... where was I?

Yes. Or the buxom young woman, whom I cannot prove was Tobagonian (perhaps she just had a Tobagonian accent) but who, acting in obedience to God knows what hoary electrical prod in the reptilian recesses of her brain, suddenly stood up, spread her legs, bent over backwards until her spine was an inverted U and her tensed fingers felt the sand, and, in this position – eyes under and forward, knees wide apart and strainedly slow-pumping, pioneering crotch pullulating terrifyingly – crabwalked across the beach and right up into the face of a balding white Brit who watched her and It advance on him with a huge grin which held, I am sorry to report, neither irony nor horror.

Or like the thin black balding Tobagonian, Leonard Lewis minus the glasses and plus a stubble-beard, whom at one point I glanced up and caught looking at me with a gaze of indescribable hatred (has that ever happened to you? Have you ever looked up from some private preoccupation in a public place and found yourself the mysterious object of mere murder in some complete stranger's eyes?) and whom a little later I overheard explaining disgustedly to a middle-aged black American: 'Africans bill de pyramids, buh white people doh war' t'accep' dat. Dey sayin' people from outaspace billit. When Satan come... look at Martinlooterking...' And, later again: 'From de time yuh see dey overpowered dey smilin'. Well, dey always smilin', tryin' to fool you.'

Or this exchange, conducted across fifty feet of glary air, between a terribly emaciated, knobby-kneed old black American with a big head, and his countervailingly ample custodian or wife:

'Hey, *Leee*-o! You kaint swim with that haddorn!'

'Yes I kain.'

'You gorn pud yer 'ead wid dat haddorn unner warder?'

'Ah doan *pud* mah 'ead unner warder!'

A baffled pause. Then:

'Hey, **Leee**-o! You warn sunbloc?'

'Uh-uh.'

Triumphantly: 'You gorn git *burrrrn!*'

Here one of the flat-bottomed reef boats came in, its sound box pulsating resonantly with the voice of the lead singer of some Trinidadian dance band whose name I really should be able to tell you. 'Huh-huh! Huh-huh! Huh-huh!' the singer was saying excitedly. Whereupon, as if that simian agitation were some newspeak version of 'Ah-ooo-ah!', Tarzan came striding from left to right along the water's edge, leaning forward eagerly from the waist, his knees lifting purposefully, his head sailing levelly, as though it were a separate thing, a look of angelic anticipation on his face (the parted lips, the dead-ahead eyes!) – dangling a pair of goggles and crossing paths en route with *another* Tarzan, this one of the post-reef (and pre-Weismuller) generation, who also dangled mask, fins, snorkel, as he painfully hobbled hotel-ward across the burning sands, with the truculent *Huh-huh! Huh-huh!* of the Trinidadian singer falling like a whip across his retreating, bent back...

...and I looked up and saw it was now squalling in two places in the western ocean, two thick squat trunks of misty lace – pewter dead ahead and mauve to the left, where Trinidad just recently had been – bridging the gap between cloud and horizon; while, nearer, the leathery lady with the orange hair stood up suddenly, sucking in her stomach and feeling her flanks...

...and the crabwalking young woman with the Tobago accent lay down and rolled in the sand, and stood back up with every square millimetre of her body covered in sand – ears, hair, eyeballs, all covered in sand...

...and the four-handed girl put two away, snapped shut her umbrella, looked up at the sky and seemed pleased...

...and the black American who'd got the lecture on the pyramids, paroled at last, slid his backside along the bench and picked back up his copy of *Beloved*, sitting next to his wife who, with bent head, was also reading – my God! – her own, identical copy of *Beloved*!...

...it was weird...

IN THE GRENADINES

1

The security guard at the kiosk is maybe thirty. He's tall, with alert eyes and regular features, except for the nose, which is too big, and he has a good body: the belly flat, the back substantial, the biceps tightening the cuffs of the regulation blue and white T-shirt of the Union Island Anchorage Marina. It's the body of someone who used to lift weights and has kept in shape and he's proud of it: you can tell by the way he stands there looking around him at the world and lightly patting his flanks with the flat of his hands, a gesture both self-approving and irritable.

The security guard's job is to keep an eye on the charter yachts that come in to the pier to take on guests and supplies. The fresh water there is metered, like a gas station pump, and part of his job is to run the hose to the boats, read off the price and take their money. But his manner suggests he's engaged in much more than that. There's this impression he gives, of being somehow kept back by his chores, of being involved in something weightier than what you see, so that the job, the actual job, is to him merely a source of impatience. When, coming ashore this morning, I laid eyes on him, he was busy threatening a little local boy of maybe twelve who was edging along the pier, evidently in a ruse to get past the kiosk and within begging distance of the occupants of the yachts.

'Get off mih jetty.'

'I ent doin' nutten,' the boy said, aggrieved.

'Uh say to get off de fockin' jetty!'

'Oh gor'!' The boy protested. 'I ent doin' nutten; gi'a man a chance, nuh, man!'

The security guard picked up a club and rushed at the boy, who fled for perhaps a dozen yards – then stopped and turned.

The security guard also stopped. With the air of someone intolerably provoked he bellowed at the boy, to the effect that, so help him God, he wouldn't be responsible for his actions if the boy should make the mistake of setting foot on 'his' jetty again that day.

'Ah, you is on'y talk,' the boy said sadly. Then, in case he had gone too far, he quickly turned and walked away, glancing back twice: first precautiously, then, a few steps later, with resentment.

On his way back to the kiosk the security guard caught my eye, but he didn't say anything. He'd had trouble placing me at first, I knew – wrong colour for a yacht owner, wrong manner for a black man like himself – but he's seen me come ashore in a sawn-off Mirror with a Seagull, not a hard-bottomed inflatable with steering wheel and two 45s; he knows I buy water in five-gallon containers and don't, as the big yachts do, come alongside and run the hose directly into the tank and take 700 gallons at a go; and he's more or less concluded – rightly, from where he stands – that I'm nobody. So now he doesn't deign to address me, merely sends my way, in passing, a triumphant glance which says: 'If you didn't know I was a bad mother-fucker, you know it now!' I look at him expressionlessly.

That, as I say, was this morning, and this now is approaching noon. I'm back on the pier, and I'm sitting next to the iron ring where the dinghy's tied off, waiting for a kid to bring me shrimps, and this girl comes down the pier. She has long blonde hair in a careless ponytail, and a lovely open convex face that bespeaks Holland, I think, and she's barefooted and palpably braless in a scoop-necked pink cotton blouse that doesn't quite reach to her waist, and a pair of green soccer shorts with gold-lined slits at the sides. You can tell by the way she's walking, and by her tan, which is even and 'set', and by the negligible way she's wearing the few items she's wearing, that she's crew on a charter yacht and used to living on the water, and not some one-shot vacationer or paying guest. The guy at the kiosk says to her brightly, 'So how you doon, dis fine mawnin?' and she laughs and with only a slight accent says Fine, and how are *you* today?

'Waal, yuh know how it is,' he tells her, patting his flanks, and she laughs again obligingly, and takes hold of the pulpit of a big steel ketch whose bowsprit is jutting over the pier and pulls herself up.

The security guard glances at me scornfully, then looks away. The Dutch girl pads aft and goes below. A few minutes later, she re-emerges with a bucket on a rope and a scrubbing brush and some cleaner, and – life aboard a yacht not being the glamorous business most people think it is – gets down on her hands and knees and starts scrubbing the deck, just aft of the mainmast shrouds. The security guard starts pacing the pier and glancing at her; he looks to be in two minds as to whether to try to resume the conversation, but eventually he gives up the thought and retreats to the kiosk and leans out over the counter, looking disaffected and bored.

This, then, is the triangle – me sitting on the pier, arms folded on knees, waiting for shrimp, the Dutch girl down on hands and knees scrubbing the deck, and the guard with the bodybuilder's body, the alert eyes and big nose, leaning out of his kiosk looking irritable – when a vagrant comes swaggering down the pier.

'Wappnin' dere, Southey?' He demands of me in passing (that's what they call Trinidadians up the islands, Southies) – which surprises me, until I realise my T-shirt says 'Trinidad & Tobago'. Ignoring the security guard (who in his kiosk is no more than six feet away from him) he wraps his arms around the bowsprit of the steel ketch and calls to the girl: 'O dahlin', you so beautiful, I lahve you!'

I glance at the security guard. The security guard appears to have seen and heard nothing. Suddenly he's studying a ledger which he's opened on the counter in front of him, frowning down at it as if trying to decipher somebody else's handwriting.

The Dutch girl throws her ponytail over her shoulder with one hand and looks up, sitting back on her heels. 'You talking to me?' She calls uncertainly.

'Who else, dahlin'?' the vagrant says. 'You are so beautiful! I *lahve* you!'

The girl laughs, as if the vagrant has said something funny. Not funny-contemptible, but funny-engaging. 'You love me?' She says. 'That's nice!' And she waves at him and makes as if to resume scrubbing the deck.

The vagrant is your standard vagrant: barebacked, in long torn blackish shorts, wild-eyed, emaciated, hair matted. Now, hugging the bowsprit, he sags his body out over the water and calls to the girl, 'Dahlin'? Sweetheart? Gimme a coke? Gimme a coke an' I *kiss* you!'

I look at the security guard. The security guard is absorbed in his ledger. Seeing no evil, hearing no evil. I look back at the Dutch girl.

The Dutch girl is undecided. Then I see her make up her mind – it's only a split second, really – and she rises and goes below, and comes back up with an open bottle of coke. 'Here you are,' she says pleasantly. 'One coke.'

Handing it down to the vagrant, she has to lean out over the pulpit. Given her bralessness and the cut of her blouse, she might as well be topless. The vagrant says: 'Oh dahlin', I lahve you! I kiss your breasts!'

'Oh no, you don't,' the Dutch girl laughs, trying with one hand to close the top of her blouse, while adding by way of distraction: 'What would your girlfriend say?'

But the vagrant has got hold of her other hand, the hand holding the coke, and is kissing it furiously and loudly. 'Mmm! Mmm! I kiss your hand – mmm! You are so beautiful! You are my dahlin' sweetheart honey! Mmm!'

The Dutch girl is hanging over the pulpit, saying laughingly (but a little out of breath), 'Such flattery!' and trying to retrieve her hand. I stare hard at the security guard. The security guard is absorbed in his ledger. I get up, dusting my bottom, and start towards the bowsprit of the ketch. I'm no Walter Mitty, so I'm greatly relieved when the vagrant chooses this moment to let go of the Dutch girl's hand and take a great swig of the coke.

The Dutch girl steps back out of range. To the vagrant she says: 'Sorry, but I have to go now; I have work to do. You have a good day, okay?' And she pads away down the side deck, as leisurely as you please (but leaving the bucket and brush where they're lying) and goes below.

From maybe six feet away, the vagrant belches in my face.

Then his attention is caught by a burly American who's just come alongside in a Boston whaler, tied up and clambered onto the pier. The vagrant catches up with him. 'Hey, dude!' he cries. 'I borrow yer dinghy, take a message out to dat red boat dere, arright?'

'Get lost,' the American says.

The vagrant stops and stares after him. Then he remembers the coke. He turns to look for the Dutch girl, but the Dutch girl is out of sight below. The vagrant takes another long swig. Tossing the bottle into the sea, he abruptly swaggers away, chanting the words of some Jamaican-sounding dub, stamping out the rhythm with his heels on the slatted pier.

I stare hard at the security guard, and he looks up. This time he condescends to speak.

'Some people could be animals, yuh know dat? Reel animals, man!'

He says this shaking his head.

I say nothing, but something in my gaze gets him angry, and he stamps out of the kiosk. A few minutes later he's down at the end of the pier, directing the Vincentian crew of a big charter cat that's coming in stern-to, and cursing each of them, foully and indiscriminately, as if the whole docking operation's something, he can't help it, just gets him into a rage, every time.

2

I'd seen him there some years ago: a honey-coloured, well-built youth, with an expression of Latin insolence and curly copper locks, like an aborigine's. He was always barefooted, in old football shorts and a sleeveless T-shirt which oftener than not he wore around his neck like a towel, and he walked with a bounce in his stride and a definite air of purposefulness: the hips slung forward, the wrists flexed, the gaze slightly lowered as if in thought – in purposeful thought. He would come along the sea wall from the direction of the town, skirting the shark pond and the lobster pen. He would turn right, onto the pier; and soon he'd be in serious conversation with one of the French or American or British yacht-charter skippers.

Talking to them, he wasn't like your average Union Island hustler. He didn't laugh a lot and slap his respondent on the shoulder and say things like 'Leave it to me', or 'No problem!' So far as I remember, he never once raised his voice in counterfeit bonhomie or hearty ostentation. There wasn't anything obsequious about him that you could see.

They would slowly, thoughtfully pace the pier, skipper and youth, conversing seriously the while; and if I had to imagine the conversation suggested by their manner, it might have gone something like this:

Skipper: 'The diesel's acting up again; could be time for a rings job.'

Youth: 'Okay. I'll take a look at it.'

Skipper: 'We have a Martinique run coming up next week. Any chance you'll be able to make it?'

Youth: 'Gosh, I don't know. I'm pretty tied up here as it is. But I tell you what: see what I can do. Maybe I could pass on most of the stuff.'

Skipper: 'I'd really like that.'

Youth: 'Catch you later.'

That was how I thought of him: as a young man in demand, a responsible and valued resource. It was what I took from his manner; and even the fact that none of the regular Anchorage staff ever seemed to speak to him could be slotted into that scenario. I supposed him, to be precise, his own boss: a freelancer whose occasional crewing with the charter yachts was rather in the nature of taking a break from other, more onerous preoccupations. I even remember thinking casually, with that West Indian penchant for explaining everything by reference to race, that his honey skin and mestizo good looks had given him an unfair advantage over the other islanders in the competition for places in the white world of the charter yachts: million-dollar machines, many of them, with their laidback but not uncalculating skippers, and those female guests with their easy laughter and bikini lines, and their appraising glances.

And, having said all this, let me confess that most of it is hindsight, and that at the time I paid him far less mind than the above might suggest. It is the people we cannot place who arrest our attention; those we size up, or think we have sized up, we easily forget. And so, back now on Union after an absence of nearly three years, I was startled to see him coming along the sea wall, in the dirty football shorts and the sleeveless top; and it was then that I began to examine my earlier assumptions about him.

He came along the sea wall by the shark pond from the direction of the town, in the old manner: hips slung, wrists flexed, gaze lowered as if in thought. He was if anything more muscular than I remembered him, and the bounce in his stride was as pronounced as ever. In fact, it might have been yesterday that I had last seen him, coming along the sea wall like that; and the dismaying thought occurred to me that, for him, time had stood still these past three years.

Then, as he drew nearer, I saw the change. He was indeed three years older; still young; but not as young as he had been. Time hadn't stood still for him. In the interim, too, he had grown a moustache and an untidy goatee of a beard; and I saw that the old insolence, though not gone from his face, was under siege there now by altogether another expression: an expression sullen and strained.

He approached, in the old manner, a French skipper, disembarked from a Beneteau 48 near the end of the pier. The Frenchman was heading ashore, and though he responded evenly enough to the youth's query he did so without breaking his stride, so that the young man was forced to turn on his heels and quicken his pace to keep up with him. They walked side by side for perhaps a dozen paces, conversing; and then the youth, his overture declined, stopped short and looked after the Frenchman with an expression that went (I saw with shock) beyond disappointment to sorrow, and beyond sorrow to something like despair.

After that morning, I didn't particularly feel like setting eyes on him, and in consequence saw him everywhere. He was always accosting some Frenchman or American or Englishman and being more or less cursorily shrugged off. The marina people, the yacht charter people, they had got their acts together in the intervening years, they didn't need him for anything anymore. And he, the young Union Islander with the build, the honey skin and the mestizo good looks, was having trouble understanding that. He was having trouble understanding that he had been trapped, trapped in his life – after all the promise that those silver shining machines had seemed to hold out to him! – trapped, like Mr Biswas, 'in the hole'.

Towards the end of my stay on Union, he did something he'd never dreamt of doing before. He approached me.

I had bought ice, two 10-pound bags, at a shop on the other side of the little airstrip, and I was toting them back to the jetty and my tethered dinghy when I saw him pause on the path ahead and look at me; and I saw the thought take shape – against what resistance! – in his mind.

I knew he was going to speak to me. I half-paused obligingly as I came up to him, and he said:

'Boss – carry your ice? Pay anyt'ing.'

3

'Mih radder tek a man dan t'clean up sha-a-ate!'

I looked around, startled. I was standing leaning against the wall in the 'Ladies' section of the public facilities of the Anchorage Hotel...

I can see this could turn out to be a long story.

Anyway.

If you've a boat like mine that's just too small to accommodate a shower below deck, there are four ways you can bathe while living aboard. One is to bathe on deck with a bucket during the day in your swimsuit – which achieves the practical end of having a bath but not its cathartic effect. Another is to go ashore and bathe there, crouching nude between a derelict pirogue and the spare parts' shed – which is better, but only slightly. A third is to wait until dark and then bathe naked on the foredeck – which is fine if you haven't planned to be on shore by dusk, or if there isn't a moaning 20-knot wind trying to freeze your future off. And the fourth is to go ashore, pay your EC$6, and use the facilities of the Anchorage Hotel.

On this occasion I'd chosen the last – only to discover the men's shower was out of order. Back at the desk, the girl said placidly: 'It's okay, you can use the ladies.'

But the ladies was occupied: from the passageway, just inside the door, I could hear the shower running.

Further in, a cleaning woman was mopping out the toilets.

It was getting on 6 p.m. With razor, comb, deodorant, soap, shampoo, clean shirt, underwear and shorts all rolled up in a beach towel, I leaned against the wall and waited.

After perhaps five minutes:

'Uh wonder what whoever-in-dey doin' wid deyself,' the cleaning woman said. She glanced with irritation at the shower cubicle door. 'Dey better hurry up! Six o'clock come, I goin' home!'

The cleaning woman was maybe fifty-five. She had a dried-out face with a flat wide forehead and a disfiguring wart on one side of her chin. Now, following up on her thought, she went over and tried the shower door (it was locked) then knocked on it. 'Excuse mih,' she called, putting her ear near to the door. 'Could you hurry up in dere?'

Not waiting for a response – nor getting any – she added sadly, 'T'ank you,' slitted her eyes at me meaningfully, and returned to the toilets.

From behind the locked door, the hiss of the shower continued unabated.

After perhaps a further five minutes – 'Excuse mih,' a new voice said.

It was one of the local staff of the hotel: a young woman whom I'd noticed more than once carrying broad and shallow plastic buckets filled with laundry along the back of the hotel. She was tall and boldfaced, with a good figure on the big-boned side, but with something else about her that was striking, and that made you want to look at her again.

I was blocking the corridor; she wanted to pass, to exchange words with the cleaning woman. I shifted and she went in, glancing at the shut shower door.

She and the cleaning woman conversed briefly. I gathered that she had signed off for the day and was going home, and wanted to borrow the cleaning woman's hair dryer for the benefit of a rendezvous she was having later that night with one itinerant 'Charlie': saying the name, she worked her arms and twisted her waist with graphic good humour, like an old-time dancer doing the ska.

The cleaning woman said bad-temperedly she couldn't come yet, indicating the shut shower door. 'An' den it have de mister' – me – 'waitin' to bade.'

The young woman glanced at me, then looked away. Being thwarted, I could see, wasn't improving her frame of mind. To the cleaning woman she said disapprovingly: 'So, what you doin'?' Although it was obvious what the cleaning woman was doing.

The cleaning woman reminded her that the steelband from St Vincent had played at the hotel the previous night. 'Every time dem fellas come here is de same t'ing. De toilets an' dem all clog up, everyt'ing in a mess.'

The young woman wrinkled her nose. 'Mih radder tek a man dan t'clean up shate,' she drawled scornfully; and I looked at her startled and saw her insolent certitude in her womanness and youth and in their power; and saw too her contempt for men who would pay. And for the cleaning woman, which was like the other side of that coin.

I followed her outside. 'What's your name?' I said.

She looked me up and down. 'Judy.'

I told her my name, but: 'Mih know,' she said.

'You know my name? How?'

'Mih hear dem call you dat.' Meaning, I suppose, the members of my crew.

I looked at her. Abruptly she looked as if she wanted to laugh.

'Later den, Wayne!' she said singsong, glancing at me sidelong, moving away.

Back in the Ladies, the cleaning woman had gone berserk. 'Get de fock outta dere!' She was shouting, kicking on the bathroom door. 'What de fock you doin' in dere all dis time? People hadda go home, doh make mih fockin' break down dis door here today!'

But the shower ran obliviously on.

THE MUSE IN THEIR MIDST

Irina Khan was a pale and statuesque Indian beauty whom repeated near-slayings on the field of love had rendered distinctly odd. My ex-partner Keith first became aware of her some years ago, when she turned up without warning one morning at Blackman & Renny and was inserted into the cosy cubicle captioned 'Secretary, Senior Partner', adjoining the expansive office of the roguishly handsome Mr Blackman, directly above Keith's own office. There her ashen presence, striking appearance and startling mannerisms – the wide, staring almond eyes and fine nostrils which, on occasion, tossing her head like a terrible Judith, she would flare; her brittle gaiety and volatile expressions of emotion; her inexplicable disappearances and reappearances; most of all, her abrupt descents about the ears of this or that sedentary employee, heralded at the last moment by the swift clicking of imperious heels as, fine hips swinging, long back straight, the flamey coruscations of her leonine brown hair tossing from side to side, she zeroed in on his desk – so that, however inconsequential the administrative directives she conveyed, they invariably left their recipients feeling as though they'd just been subjected to the disorienting, sudden breath of a sirocco – all these quickly mated with the alarm engendered by Irina Khan's mysterious materialisation outside the boss's door – as well as, at other times (this was taken for granted) in his potent arms – to galvanise fully four-fifths of the mainly black staff of Blackman & Renny to a pleasant pitch of racial excitement, and set the more intrepid souls among them to strenuous sleuthing.

The latter returned, by and by, with a composite (and quite possibly apocryphal) biography, which had the peerless Irina – a McGill graduate, flightily fluent in three languages – already preparing for her wedding (the guest list had been composed, the dress designed) to a 'real' Indian doctor from Bombay, when the perverse medic changed his plans and essayed a lone flight out of Piarco to Austin, Texas; whereupon – or rather, after a couple years, for which no evidence could be unearthed – the vivacious but now doomed maiden re-emerged and settled into the role that was to see her safely through the first half of her thirties, those dicey years: that of the tempestuous mistress of Sy Mohammed, the El Socorro car parts' magnate.

How much longer their affair might have endured cannot be estimated: one rainy night Sy Mohammed was killed in what the press called 'an altercation', and for the second time Irina Khan's life-signal all but disappeared from the grapevine's wavelength, leaving behind a kind of orphaned static.

Thence, however, had come occasional, weak signals, and these the intrepid investigators decoded variously as Sudden Flight To India, Suicide Attempt, and (most popular of all) Whoring Interlude – as a high-class hostess at a discreet dive catering exclusively to expatriate businessmen – leading fairly peremptorily to Patriarchal Disownment and Suicide Attempt, again (though perhaps this was being confused with the first attempt).

Theodore Blackman had met Irina Khan at a Law Association Conference where she had been engaged as interpreter-escort for one of the guest speakers, an ageing German jurist named Kant; and the rest – as the returning sleuths grimly summarised it – the rest was History.

Stodgy Keith (and you would have liked him; I did) had taken no part in this high-spirited prying, nor particularly relished its plums. Unfortunately for him, there existed also a Mrs Blackman; and it appears that at some point Irina Khan, putting anachronistic faith in the power of certain charms which Nature had merely lent, not given, her, and which that dispassionate creditor had already begun surreptitiously repossessing, 'took a chance', as the office put it, and 'went too far'; with the result that when, one otherwise unremarkable morning, my preoccupied ex-partner was expelled as per usual by the sighing machine at the third floor, he found that he had been brusquely gifted with a secretary of his own.

What made this particularly trying for Keith was the creature's grief. This reached such a pitch of distraction that one evening, when the heavyset attorney and his willowy new helpmate happened to be leaving work at the same time, she abruptly danced towards Keith in the elevator and, crying gaily, 'Missa McDonald, you should get Miz McDonald to give you a trim!', fluttered her fingers through the salt-and-pepper curls at the back of his fleshy neck. The sensation this gave Keith so unnerved him that when, some time later, having dutifully notified Blackman & Renny that he was leaving them to open his own small practice, he was confronted in his office by a distraught Miss Khan stormily beseeching him to 'take me with you', he recalled that moment and nearly told her no.

But in the meantime he had come to depend on her (for Irina Khan, for all her unpredictability, was an infallible typist, and had lately turned into a veritable virtuoso of the filing cabinets as well); he was strangely and strongly moved (as well as appalled) by the sight of the ravishing supplicant on her knees on the fawn carpet beside his chair; and, all in all, he had grown so used to her turbulent presence, that he found himself gruffly acquiescing – then having to ward off her hot dry lips when they sought his hand, and, next, the quizzical gulf that abruptly yawned in his mind when, from waist height (for the tear-streaked maiden had sunk back onto her heels) Irina Khan averred that she would do anything for him, repeating with dreaming, soft and quite mad ardour: 'Anything.'

He was a compassionate man, the old Keith, and a creature of habit: two mules that often tug in tandem to convey the unsuspecting burgher through the modest portals of horrible grief, with their sighing, self-locking doors – as you and I, reader, both know...

No remotest premonition of this, however, was in Keith's mind on the morning when, bestirring himself from his brown study, he got on the intercom and summoned Miss Khan.

('Shall I bring my pad? *Very* well, Missa McDonald, I'll be *right* in!')

It was minutes to twelve, the Port of Spain traffic was about to rehearse the Gordian knot it practised three times a day, and the restaurant where he had arranged to meet Mrs McDonald for lunch was on the edge of town, too far to walk. It would have succoured him not at all to remind himself that his wife (whom, I have to say, I also liked, if only by a process of osmosis from liking K) was not the type to start consulting her watch within five minutes or so of his nonappearance. To be punctual was to Keith neither more nor less than to take one's admittedly minor place in the chorus line of some grand, propitious rhythm, through which alone the scheme of things might pacify its irritable Author; and on the rare occasion that, for whatever reason, he wound up defaulting on that score, my taciturn ex-friend suffered.

So now, as Irina Khan (beige chonsang, red stiletto heels) swept ashily towards him, he reached over and sprung a cassette and handed it to her, saying huskily:

'Here, let me have a transcript, by p.m. tomorrow if you can. Seal this and file it with that; and here, take these. File them together under "Maillard, L." That's M, a, i – the name's on the envelope. On second thought, better put them in the safe. What's today, Tuesday? Remind me I want you to take a letter. Leave the NGP file on my desk before you go to lunch. And tell Sanderson when he gets back, whenever that is, he's to turn right around and go see Smart. That matter's been advanced to Friday. I don't suppose – what is it, Miss Khan?'

Irina Khan – great almond eyes distended, fine nostrils flaring, tossing halo of leonine hair flaming agitatedly – was practically hopping from foot to foot, making frightened, placatory little gestures.

'So many instructions!' she cried. 'So many, *many* instructions! Shame on you, Missa McDonald! Naughty boy, you should have let me bring my pad!'

At which point, I am sorry to report, there occurred without warning the staggering epiphany (doubly staggering, if you knew Keith) which led, by a slow but inexorable goose-step of events, to my old friend's loss of his wife, his home, half his clients, his sobriety, his reputation, and finally (for so these things go) Irina Khan herself – whom I hear is currently working with the Tourist Board, and whom I saw the other night, descending the ornate staircase of The Globe arm in arm with the third secretary of the British High Commission (a simpering prig), in a tent-like white mini and Roman sandals: Irina Khan, still, at forty, all long legs and wide-eyed starings and tossing leonine hair, as ashen and flamey as ever.

THE MIND OF MR BAUGH.

One Old Year's day in New York City, a certain Mr Baugh, a resident of Albany, Georgia, walked into a secondhand bookstore and bought (for $1.00, 39 cents, and 59 cents respectively) copies of the first American editions of James Baldwin's *Notes of a Native Son*, Sam Selvon's *Turn Again Tiger*, and George Lamming's *In the Castle of My Skin*, with an introduction by Richard Wright. That was in '59. The US civil rights movement, and the white Southern backlash to it, were between them coming to a head, and Mr Baugh, a middle-aged white Southerner, evidently wished to discover for himself what all the fuss was about. It seems he never got around to reading the West Indians – not unless he used as bookmarks the dated receipts I found last week in his copies of their novels. But the Baldwin he read and pondered, judging from the faded newspaper clippings he left inserted among its pages. (They included the first publication of Baldwin's famous essay, 'The Discovery Of What It Means To Be An American', and three rancorously racist letters-to-the-editor by white Atlanta readers.)

What he made of the whole brouhaha is hard to say; although, from the tenor of the letters he cut out (and meticulously dated in pen) I suspect he found at least some of it funny. (One representative letter, for example, read in part: 'Sir... Herewith is my library card. I will take mine straight with no mixing. The city fathers should hang their heads in shame for opening the library to coloureds.')

But this is speculation; in fact, there's very little I can tell you with certainty about Mr Baugh. I only ever met him once, and that was casually, two years ago. And I very much doubt I shall meet him again, since as I write this Mr Baugh, now ninety-one, lies dying in a nursing home somewhere in the American South.

Yet after last week I shall never forget him. No: however urgently I essay now the old ploy of dumping his memory on *you*, dear reader, I think I shall not forget Mr Baugh.

I met him in his hometown in Georgia while I was teaching there a couple years ago. Mr Baugh, already of a great age, and having never married, was living alone in shabby gentility in a big decaying house in what had long ceased to be an upmarket residential part of the town. He had loaned two of his downstairs rooms as a studio to a Georgia painter named Steve Schatz, who had persuaded the Dark Lady to sit for him. And one day while she and I were at Schatz's studio, the owner of the house – a small, bald, sad-eyed, old man in dressing gown and slippers – shuffled in.

After the introductions were over, he hung around, and it was clear that he intended to engage me, the odd man out, in conversation. With the condescension of the un-old, I braced myself for a polite and boring chat... and so, four hours later, was startled to find that the time had flown, while we discussed, Mr Baugh and I, with great seriousness and intellectual effort, the ramifications of black holes and other natural phenomena for man's comprehension of the nature of Time.

'That old guy's amazing,' I told Schatz as the Dark Lady and I were leaving. 'He has a mind like a knife.'

'Doesn't he?' said Schatz. 'You know, he used to be a friend of Edmund Wilson's.'

But that was all.

My Fulbright year ended, I left the States; and Mr Baugh – already shrinking in memory to a quizzical presence in a big old decaying house – soon faded altogether from my mind. Last week, however, I was back in Georgia, giving a reading at a different campus, when my hosts said conversationally, 'You want some books?' – and I heard again the name of Mr Baugh.

Mr Baugh, it transpired, had abided in good health until, earlier this year, in the manner of the very old, he'd suddenly gone into decline. Now he was bedridden and sinking fast. A distant relative had been located by Schatz, who by now was just about the old man's only remaining human contact, and he had come and taken Mr Baugh away to a nursing home in Florida. He was not expected to live out the year.

In the meantime, Mr Baugh had charged Schatz with the task of giving away his books. They, my hosts, had already gone to the old house and returned home with two large boxes full.

I got in touch with Schatz.

'Most of them are already gone,' Schatz said. 'But you're welcome to have a look, see if you find anything you want.'

In my rented car, at the appointed time, I drove out to the decaying house.

The distant relative – a nondescript, pleasant man, a small-town salesman or small contractor, perhaps – was there. So were his wife, Schatz himself, another guy, and another woman, in their thirties and forties. They'd been packing the house, moving out the old furniture and appliances, and their greetings were cordial and casual. None save Schatz had actually known Mr Baugh; none made any pretence of reverence or grief. As for the place itself, the decaying house, it exhibited now the disorderly, soulless, 'warehouse' air of a home in the process of being abandoned.

Inside, I glanced around. There was a bookcase, half-empty, in the corridor, and in two of the rooms leading off it were other bookcases, similarly semi-denuded, and small stacks of books on the floor.

'As I said, there's only about a fifth of what there was,' Schatz said apologetically. 'But perhaps you should start here.' And he led me to another door.

I made to enter – then stood in the doorway appalled.

The room was a medium-sized room, fourteen by fourteen, say – and it was chest-high in boxes and stacks and spilled piles of books, and fallen junk-heaps or burial mounds of books. There were bookcases on three walls, packed solid, there were books stacked under the bed, there were boxes of books piled high on the bed, there were thousands and thousands of books!

It was almost impossible to enter; one had, like a man in a jungle, to clear a path. Termite droppings lay thick as autumn leaves on every horizontal surface. The electricity had been disconnected, the curtains were half-drawn, and the room was dark and cold.

I thought: This is what happens when a man grows old

without wife or children. When his time comes, he's just – *cleared away*. I thought: This is what happens when you let strangers into your house to rummage through your things before you're even dead: they think about you in the past tense.

But mostly I just stood there staring, while a great wave of woe swept over me at the sight of all that fossilised evidence of what had to have been (I knew at once) one of the richer minds in the world.

Understand: It wasn't books I was seeing in that dark cold morgue of a room. It was the anatomy of a mind: a mind which was being abolished, which was being broken up and parcelled out, its organs and ligaments and bones and blood fed piecemeal willy-nilly to passing strangers. It was a mind which had consigned itself to disintegration and silence: to nullity. And its owner not yet dead!

To Schatz, I said with pain: 'I can't believe this.'

Then, vertigo rising: '*Who was this guy?*'

'Oh, he was a *very* erudite man,' Schatz said. 'You'd be surprised at some of the people who corresponded with him.'

'But what did he do with all that knowledge?' I said. 'Was he a professor? Did he publish anything?'

'No, he was a medical doctor. But, yes! Back in the '40s he contributed several articles to literary journals. Did I tell you he was a friend of Edmund Wilson's?'

Schatz couldn't help but be vague: Mr Baugh's productive years had been long before his time. But his vagueness left me with the difficult thought of a life in literature that had been as inutile as it had been rich. Somehow it increased both the horror and the wonder of what I was seeing.

'Why didn't he just donate them to some university library, get them to come in and take everything away?'

'I think,' Schatz said, 'he thought that way they might just end up in some store room somewhere. This way, he felt if people made the effort to come and choose particular books it meant they were probably going to read them.'

This piece of intelligence I found comforting; Mr Baugh, it seems, had kept his faith in books to the end. My feeling of sacrilege at what I was about to do retreated a little. I opened the nearest box (the termite balls fell in a quiet shower), inclining my head in the half-light to squint at the spines...

Yet in the end I didn't stay long in Mr Baugh's decaying house. It was too cold, too dark, and what I was doing still felt too blasphemous. If the owner of those books had been dead I might have felt differently. But the knowledge that he was still alive in a nursing home somewhere – and quite conscious most of the time, Schatz said – made me feel like someone taking part in a lobotomy. Within half an hour I'd lost the will to persevere. I found an empty carton, transferred to it the books I'd stacked in the corridor, said my goodbyes to Schatz and the pleasant folk packing the house, and left. More than a little relieved to be driving once more in the inflectionless sunshine of a cool fall Georgia afternoon.

I had taken some three dozen books. They represented perhaps a tenth of those I'd glanced at, which represented perhaps a tenth of the books in that room, which represented in turn, according to Schatz, a fifth of what there'd originally been. They can hardly be representative, 36 of 18,000, and I have no idea what treasures mutely waited – and perhaps still wait – in the boxes and stacks and piles and shelves I left without examining. But here are some of the authors:

Melville, Murdoch, von Kleist, Tibellus, Graves, Tennessee Williams, Lowell, Lévi-Strauss, Chekov, Auden, Wells, Shakespeare, Narayan, Powell, Quasimodo, Kazantzakis, Pushkin, Lichtenberg, Dumas, Wagner, Steinbeck, Saroyan, Huxley, Fitzgerald, Tolstoy, Wouk, de Maupassant, Wright.

In the week since my return to Trinidad I've been leafing through them – initially for the pleasure of the books themselves, but increasingly for clues to the life of the mind of the man who read them before me. There were, I found, more than a few – though one was only incidental to Mr Baugh.

(On the 17th October 1942 – that is, in the middle of the Battle of Stalingrad – Edmund Wilson sent from Moscow to Mr Baugh – who kept the envelope, perhaps for the stamps – a fine edition of essays on Pushkin as well as a copy of Wilson's own essay, 'Evgeni Onegin', torn rather than cut out from *The New Republic*

– the latter presumably part of Wilson's throat-clearing for his famous quarrel with Nabokov some years later over Nabokov's translation of the Russian epic.)

Mr Baugh was a meticulous reader, and often marked words and phrases as he read, sometimes underlining them, sometimes drawing around them neat rectangular boxes (which however became spidery in the '80s). If he made notes he must have done so separately, in a notepad; yet it is usually possible to infer the intent of his markings. Several drew attention to typos or misprints, or to bad editing by the books' editors. On occasion Mr Baugh would change or insert a word or phrase in pen, connecting the correction by an arrow to its justification.

In Harvard University Press's 1954 edition of Arnold, eg, Mr Baugh added an ess to 'toward' in the phrase, 'thy look strays toward me,' referring it to its rhyme two lines later: 'this stranger regards me.' In his copy of Hemingway's *The Garden of Eden*, I saw with pleasure that – though, by then, he was eighty-two – Mr Baugh's copious markings resonated silently with the derisive anger I'd felt and expressed at that trumped-up, money-grubbing, posthumous travesty of the deathless Hemingway prose. And I wish I could list all of Mr Baugh's markings, and tell you what he meant by them, and so pass on to you the mind of Mr Baugh, or that part of it which has come down to me. In that way you might have made a posthumous friend, and I – I might have expiated a remorse.

But that would take a month of Sundays; so here are just two more. They are the only instances in the books I have in which Mr Baugh wrote more than a word or two at a time. They were made 30 years apart.

1. In the mid-'50s, in the back of his Arnold, Mr Baugh copied out these lines of the poet's: 'Eyes too expressive to be blue,/ Too lovely to be grey.' Their apparent critical inutility suggests – a pleasant thought – that it was some private significance, not impersonal scholarship, which led a lovestruck Mr Baugh to note them.

2. In the mid-'80s, in a theological tome, Mr Baugh placed an asterisk beside the following sentence: '...from our vantage point, God's world seems arbitrary and without design, like the

underside of a carpet.' At the bottom of the page, he wrote: 'Their stories are like the underside of a carpet – nothing but the stringy grain of the tissue – a muddle of figures without shape and flowers without colour. (H. James, *Watch and Ward*, Ch. 7).'

Mr Baugh had caught a plagiarism on the wing. In his meticulous way, he had tethered it to its source.

In the cold dark room in the big decaying house whose solitary tenant had been taken away to die, I must have looked at the titles, authors and publication dates of three or four hundred books. They weren't nearly enough to do justice to the scope of the mind which had supposedly read (and *absorbed*?) perhaps fifty times that number. But perhaps they were enough to suggest the evolving interests of that mind.

In the '30s and '40s (both the century's and his own) Mr Baugh had read predominantly fiction and poetry; but by the late '40s he was turning to scholarship and the classics. (A Get Well card from 'Myron and Francis Blumenthal' left inserted in a 1949 book on Shakespeare's sonnets, read: 'I know your non-tendency toward fiction but am running out of ideas – your taste is too exacting – if you think of something you do want, will get it for you.')

To these, in the '60s, he added (rather than displacing them by) an interest in contemporary history and mythology. His exploration of the former was apparently cursory. His interest in the latter persisted and grew.

By the '70s he had all but ceased reading poetry and fiction and was pursuing a curious combination of mythology, ancient history, and the natural sciences. The last were represented by a number of no-nonsense scientific texts on biology and physics such as I, for one, could not have comprehended.

In the early '80s, Mr Baugh's scientific inquiry apparently ceased altogether. So did the scholarly tomes, the mythology and the ancient history. In their place there appeared a large number of philosophical and theological works.

And Mr Baugh resumed reading fiction.

But my time is up, and I see I have given you very little of the substantial man. I don't have his photograph, only a photograph of a painting of him done by someone else. I don't have his words, only the words of others which he meticulously copied out. I can't even say whether, as I conclude this, the corporeal Mr Baugh – that mild-mannered, lonely, stern-minded man, of such erudition, yet so few words – survives. Perhaps he has already left us. Perhaps he is even now leaving us.

But it strikes me now that this incorporeality, all these refractions – and the ultimate silence of them – may be apposite. Perhaps they are what Mr Baugh, the lifelong solitary, essentially was.

At any rate, they are what Mind is: that ravening hoverer, promiscuous yet quite impersonal, trailing its sails in the evening light – the refracted, golden light! – over the far slopes of our longing, the earthbound griefs, the inchoate rain forest of this world.

THE NAVEL OF THE WORLD

Navel:... 2. The central point of something. ['The hero as the incarnation of God is himself the navel of the world, the umbilical point through which the energies of eternity break into time.' – Joseph Campbell.]
(Webster's Third New International Dictionary)

1

Her name was Jackie. She was dark, tallish, long-necked, curly-headed (the last by dint of art, I know now); she had the lit look and brazen sheen you sometimes see in certain childless women drifting fecklessly along the approach ramp of the years toward the merciless illumination of 'forty'; and the whisper of androgyny in her cheerful name – a whisper you might think amplified by the slight swagger of her walk, by a glance at once gay and corroding, and by the hipster trousers and men's shirts knotted under the ribs in which she habitually faced and faced down the world – that whisper was bemusingly nullified by something else I never stopped to interrogate (fact is, I hardly knew her), but which I saw the other day, unforgettably, in her eyes when, for the first time, without preamble, I held her head – too tightly – in my hands.

I first became aware of her existence in the late '70s, those Gatsbyesque years, when everybody had more money than they'd ever had before, and my generation – just about the age then that she was now – was about to take over running the world and knew it. They were free and slapdash years, the last years of the era BC (Before Coke, Before Crime, before crime and cocaine arrived and roiled this little country under) and they had about them the light-loined, postcoital ease of some fundamental inkling of

Unmeaning after the grim ideological orgies of the '60s. Today I remember them by a claque of unlikely conjunctions: ABBA and Ray Charles; *Apocalypse Now* and *Saturday Night Fever*; Kung Fu breaking out in the schoolyards of the nation just as money was proclaimed to be No Problem; Jimmy Carter pronouncing America free of the fear of Communism even while Cuban infantry romped through the Angolan bush.

And for us here, abruptly – or so in memory it seems – the immemorial weight of Eric Williams slipping from our shoulders (because he died to us, to my generation, a full three years or so before he died), lubricated thence, no doubt, in part by the scotch which flowed like water at house parties from Valsayn to Petit Valley, until we each of us felt secretly, in the unremarked interstices of the psyche, like Atlas coming upright at last, at last, squaring his shoulders and experimentally turning his wrists, while from his back the world slipped...

– not that we knew that was what we were feeling.

I first encountered her at one such party in '79. She would have been nineteen or twenty: hardly more than a kid, in my eyes – because a twenty-year-old girl can seem younger to a man of thirty-five than to a man of forty-five, or even fifty-five – and I doubt I'd have noticed her if I hadn't been drinking, and if she hadn't been there with a guy nearly as old as I am today. And if it hadn't been for The Navel.

The couplings of young girls and older men – there're different ways of looking at them, and it's odd how each disqualifies the others. Your friend may claim to be happier than he has ever been, and you look at him and see he's on his mettle, and may even be *man-alive* as you've never seen him before, and you concede he's telling the truth. Yet *in the same moment* he seems undignified and ridiculous, 'a big man making a fool of himself' over some young thing.

As for the Young Thing, ditto. You know that by now your friend has wrecked his perfectly viable marriage, lost the home he spent his best years paying for, and is being put through hell by his teenage children, the eldest just a few years younger than the Young Thing herself. So you look at her covertly with salacious awe, having seen the destructive reach of her power, and being chauvinistically, pornographically sure of its source, and that it's her fault. Yet, next moment, you know the Young Thing to be negligible and imperilled: as easily discardable by him in a certain light as she'd feared herself to be at the beginning, in the scary-happy opening act of this, her first affair. And hard on the heels of such knowledge comes the obscene fiction – which nonetheless arrives in the chaste and grudging garb of a vegetable certitude – that you could have her too, anytime, if you wanted.

Thus is every encounter between young girls and older men – that most private and primordial call-&-response of old wounds to new wonder, of affirmation to absurdity, of fantasy to fucking, of lechery to light – made foul in the eyes of the world.

But I digress.

Midnight. The soaring porch of a cliffhanging Cascade house, weakly illumined yet festive by comparison with the packed and blacked-out living room behind it. The floor shaking, even out here, from the stamping of a hundred feet within. (*Can they really be playing the Bee Gees?* What a thing!) In my peripheral vision, the prone black bulk of Chancellor Hill, doggedly enduring under the different festivity of stars I'd never thought 'indifferent' – not until now.

Streetlights only, in the black valley below.

It's a night in '79, a year that stands out in my mind because in the course of it I turned thirty-five; and that, for some reason, struck me at the time as somehow important.

My immediate companion on the yellow porch cantilevered over the dark valley is a stranger: a taciturn, burly man of maybe fifty. When he first came out and, with a trenchant sigh, lowered himself into the chair next to mine, we'd exchanged a few words, neither of us paying more than sketchy homage to the hearty party mood inside. Since then we haven't spoken, but it's okay, because I am danced-out and rum-&-coked-out and thirty-five, and want mainly to go on sitting there; and I suspect that, like me, for the time being, he too is content to be alone.

Only, now this tallish, dark girl comes out (knotted white shirt, off-white denims) and sits on his thigh and puts an arm around his neck and says something to him. And because of the way the chairs are, her navel is more or less in my face.

So I consider it.

It's one of those emphatic navels which would be carnal if Absence could be carnal: a little hourglass inversion, a little Black Hole, which from the fleshy centre of the belly-bulge of its material host – gleaming with sweat and still palpably rising and falling, courtesy the Bee Gees – abruptly sucks inward with no end in sight. Elbow on chair's arm, cheekbone on forefinger, I study this apparition, which seems to have been thrust into my face for that purpose – because that's what happens after thirty-five, you know: the things of the world, which used to leave you so robustly alone, now start presenting themselves dumbly for your inspection, one by one – and it seems to me that I can see it silently and ceaselessly taking to itself the edges of the moistly shining surfeit of flesh around it. So much so that I become absorbed next in trying to decipher whether the vertical ant-trek of short black hairs below it (horizontally truncated by concave denim) represents a desperate flight down from the brow of that Nullity or an anaesthetised and sacrificial ascent up into It.

I look up speculatively, meaning to see if I can ascertain which by the expression on the face of its still-slightly-panting propri-etress or – a new and disturbing thought – *prey*, and am startled out of my dreaming metaphysics by a corporeal girl hardly more than half my age (shock of black curls, long neck, pendant silver earrings, smudged lower lip) looking down at me – at what had to have been, till now, the top of my head – with a ghastly smile.

2

Past fifty, a man thinks of the future and talks of the past. This shouldn't be surprising, for love – as distinct from being-in-love, that simultaneous concentration and mushrooming-outward of the Moment, over the wild waves of past and future – is most itself in recollection – at dusk, in a garden, with a whirling dervish of gnats inscribing their fury in disappearing dashes under the mango tree – while the future, being merely an hypothesis, is unspeakable in more ways than one. Disconnected and denatured seems the future, whenever we try truly to imagine it. And the curious thing about Jackie, now that I have come to write about her, is that in my memory she appears as forever vanishing, like those dashes, or else like some statuesque but incomplete bronze, the vigorous gesture of an impatient artist, abandoned with the tag, 'Study for a Woman'.

In short, I see her as hazed in gauze: wrapped in the disembodied, discontinuous air one rather associates with images of the hypothetical future than with recollections of the palpable past. And though the reasons for this may be circumstantial and no one's fault, it's wearying to know that merely for me to write about Jackie now is to distort her.

Indeed, there has already been distortion, for I have called her Jackie, and when I first encountered her – or rather, her navel – on that soaring yellow porch I didn't know her name.

That was in '79; and when, soon afterwards, I left Trinidad for a three-year sojourn abroad, I still didn't know her name.

Not long after my return, I exchanged glances in a mall one day with a tallish, dark, curly-headed girl. Her glance was knowing and somehow scornful; it seemed to say, with no pleasure, *So, you write* (I was writing this column by then). Yet, though she looked vaguely familiar, I am sure I would not have recognised her if I hadn't registered her midriff. Her midriff was bare.

It wasn't a pleasant sensation, recalling her; and when I asked myself I realised why. She had dawned on me, had first intruded on my reverie, not as a young woman, alive, free and whole in her own right, but as the oppressed proprietress or prey of a little Black Hole at the centre of her being. And in my spaced-out mood I had seen us, her and me, as near-conspirators: joint witnesses to the invisible but insatiable designs of that infernal, third – *thing*.

So now, in the mall, even after the lapse of years, I saw her as somehow damaged: as carrying around a secret imperilment. As for her insistence on baring It publicly, what was that – defiance? A Lazarean showing of one's sores? The O-gape of a silent, small howl for help?

All this is freaky and morbid, I know. But first impressions are sometimes irretrievable; and for a long time they were, in her

211

case. With hindsight, it's clear I should have accosted her, should have elicited words from her – angry or scornful, it wouldn't have mattered – should have elicited, even, her name. If I had, she would have become Jackie X, a human being with a history, a winsome young woman with imaginings, needs and moods, and the fetish at her centre would have faded. But you must understand: I didn't know her; she meant nothing to me. I didn't expect to see her again.

But I did: perhaps half-a-dozen times, casually, over the next two years: on a pavement, at a party, and in other places which I could itemise but won't, because to do so would be to make our chance encounters seem significant. To begin with, our exchange of glances repeated the old story, of faint scorn on her part and a leftover queasiness on mine. But in due course these gave way to something like indifference. Recognition. No emotion. The years were passing.

Once, at an Old Year's party, we found ourselves on the floor at the same time. Slow-swaying temple to temple with her partner (whose face I couldn't see), she opened her eyes and gave me a glance which said, *I'm being happy, don't look at me*, and lowered her gaze again; and that was all. She was in her late twenties by then, and she looked, I thought, like someone well on the way to becoming whomever or whatever it was – the woman, the wistfulness, the wound – she was supposed to become; and I remember, I thought she looked *fine*. It is only now that it occurs to me that that was just one of those truncated impressions I was always having of her. Fine! What does that mean – fine?

That was in '86, the first, heraldic Old Year's night of the NAR. A few years later the heraldry was gone, and the air of Trinidad was filling up with poison when, one sunny morning, I saw her in the mall (boob tube, pleated slacks, long neck, shock of curly black hair), strolling with a grim-faced, crew-cut, blond guy, older than me – I was forty-four – who looked to be from somewhere like Oklahoma or Arkansas. I remember that encounter vividly, because she gave me in passing, for the first and only time, a look of perfect familiarity and candour. It was a look that said: *I don't exist, I am absolutely His, I am Trapped and Happy and Scared and Trapped and His*. So much so that I flared a look of resentment at the guy, which he instantly returned in spades; our auras bumped roughly in passing.

Later, the memory of her with him got mixed up in my mind with grim socioeconomic thoughts about liberalisation and divestment. So I was surprised to see her next with a bunch of Trinis, in a packed Pelican, one night in the shell-shocked aftermath of 'the coup'. I'd assumed she'd flown the coop with the Oklahoman. I know it's the only time I ever saw her so happy.

Soon after that I learnt her name, courtesy somebody's passing reference to her father, a paunchy, sour-faced red guy whom I'd seen around from time to time. (He was about as much older than me as she was younger, and sold heavy machinery, as his own boss during the boom years, and later, when the crash came – or, perhaps, after he'd retired – on a commission basis for some firm). And so we settled down, Jackie X and me, as part of the largely unexamined bric-a-brac in the neglected storerooms of each other's lives...

And all I have written here is a distortion.

How could it be otherwise? How, unless what I have written, however purposefully vague and desultory, had appeared interspersed amid the chronology of a ten-volume story about Trinidad and its people, one spanning the past seventeen years? Only then would it have been proportionate to her actual presence in my life and thought in those years. For as I say I hardly knew her: she was someone I saw around from time to time. And the hapless retroactive significance I give, merely by writing about them, to what were occasional, brief and wordless encounters – that significance falsifies everything.

Understand this, or you will scant my bewilderment when, a few weeks ago, a woman purporting on the phone to be Jackie's mother (a woman 'of the people', judging by her speech) got in touch and agitatedly made me to know that Jackie had killed herself, or tried to kill herself – for dilatory discretion or garbling grief debarred the distracted woman from clarifying that vital ambiguity – and that my presence at the sickbed or death-house was requested.

The townhouse in the Valley was unexpectedly hard to find: with misplaced economy, a single signpost had been erected at a non-judgmental angle to three streets. I reached the end of the first, wrong one (cul-de-sac, culvert, slight bush) and turned back.

'Mr Brown? This is Jackie's mother.'

Who?

'Jackie —. I am Mistress —. Jackie is my daughter.'

Who?

Silence. Then: 'Is this the Wayne Brown from the *Guardian*?'

Only as in the Latin 'ex', ma'am. Meaning in this case not 'from' but 'out of'. Out of the *Guardian*. As in Out of Africa.

'Excuse mih. I hope I am speaking to the gentleman who write the Book – ?'

No, that was Matthew-Mark-and-Luke, that crowd. But God bless your article, ma'am.

In the end, the block of townhouses was tall, squat and dirty. It stood at the top of a short steep drive, crammed against the base of a mountain which had been brusquely mutilated to accommodate it. Since then, the mountain's inconsolable revenge had been presumably its ceaseless, silent shedding: those bauxite-discoloured walls.

' – ever since the father died. You din' know? I say you know! It was in all the papers. Yes, my husband, Jackie's father, died in March! He went in the Caroni river with the Bluebird. PAP Thirteen Ten. He love that car. I say you know!... Well, t'ank you, so-so, yes! I have to try. Almighty God in His wisdom...'

Jackie's mother, when she opened the door, was like her voice on the phone: too apologetic and anxiety-ridden to smile. A plump, dark, otherwise nondescript woman, she yet looked younger than she had to be if she were Jackie's mother. She looked about my age, in fact; and Jackie by now had to be in her late thirties. Maybe the sour-faced, paunchy red father had liked them young.

'Sssh! She restin'. Wait here. I will tell her you here.'

I tried by my expression not to show I'd thought her daughter might be dead, and she left me and went stolidly up the stairs.

The sadness of certain interiors, with their finical and worth-less bric-a-brac! That conch shell, for example, its once-roseate inward blush long faded to a neglected pastel. Those little framed photos on sideboard and whatnot, still glossily, determinedly gay, though the child is long grown, the husband dead, the Yankee paramour gone! That calendar with its Alpine cascade frozen! That effete and radiant blue-eyed Christ, his heart all ablaze on the outside of his chest! And all of it like a little counterfeit of arrested Time, or like Love protesting, *We exist, we matter, we were here*, while outside, on all sides, above, around, below, through the unspeakable immensities of eternal night, the great, oblivious universe thunders on...

'She say to come, so you could go up. I will wait here. She was the father daughter, you know. I hope you will have a good effect.'

I have had enough of other people's griefs, I thought, as in turn I ascended the stairs. *A good effect.* Jesus. Why are you breaking our seventeen-year silence, lady? And what am I doing here?

I had been imagining all along the slight swagger, the smudged, *I'm-a-pushover* lower lip, the contradictory glance, at once gay and corroding, the long neck, the shock of black curls. I had been imagining the perennially bare waist with its twenty-year-old's baby fat gone, and a different ripeness beginning there of late. So now, entering her room (upstairs and back, with a raw red cliff soaring claustrophobically not six feet outside the window) I had for a moment to take it on trust that the propped, recumbent woman on top of the sheets in a yellow housecoat (aren't they hot in those things?) with her un-made-up face and short stiff hair pulled back in a bauble was her.

She looked in that moment like a stranger whom, nonetheless, I had always known. In her unexpected *thereness* and naked-facedness and immobility, she looked – how shall I put this? – she looked like Trinidad.

Yeah. Kill me for that. She looked like *Trinidad*.

On her bedside table, among flowers and philtres, I glimpsed a familiar orange book jacket, its lithe and black-maned chocolate girl elatedly soaring amid blue-and-yellow swirls and eddies. *What are you doing here?* I enquired en passant of *The Child of the Sea* (the book, not the girl, for she is dead). And got in return a worried, *I-am-blameless* look.

To the woman on the bed I said, with horrible banality: 'So we meet at last.' And here my gaze fell on her wrists. Her wrists were bandaged; both of them.

She'd followed my glance. She lifted them limply. 'See what a mess I made?' she said wryly. 'God, I made such a mess of it!'

'They say,' I said conversationally, 'the trick is to choose one wrist and stay with it.'

She giggled. 'Stay with it? Oh, that's priceless!' She giggled again. 'Yes, I suppose I should have' – here she almost choked on a rising, truncated yelp of a laugh – 'stayed with it! Oh my God, that's so funny! *I should have stayed with it!*'

Abruptly she went into hysterics, throwing her head from side to side, the laughter coming from her in high-pitched shrieks and gasps –

– Hey, take it easy, I was joking –

– banging her head against the bed-head and laughing, until I grabbed it in both hands, her head, I mean (while behind me the door swung open in alarm) and held it, so tightly that the corners of her eyes pulled, and felt her spasms, like the beating of a great fish, subsiding, while her gasping shrieks subsided in tandem, to a frail, falsetto wail. Then that, too, stopped, and there was silence.

Take it easy, okay? Take it easy!

With her head in my hands, I looked into her eyes.

And saw.

Gentlemen. You may adore a woman; you may be obsessed by her. You may thrust in her arms as though by such hammer blows your flesh and hers might meld. You may root in her flesh as though Immortal Life lay always just one millimetre further up inside her.

And she may come to you, your impossible beloved, in all manner of shapes and forms. As a mermaid, a Lilith, a terrible happiness. A terrible hunger. A limp-wristed smile. And she may come to you, your ineffable fiction, in dreams, in fever, in distraction.

Perhaps she will come to you on your deathbed. Perhaps she

216

will bring you there flowers, or fire, or songs, or a red roaring. She may even, in her mercy, taking your hand, show you the unfolding wings of flame.

Yet none of it matters, not ultimately – no, because at the last she is a door through which you cannot pass. The skull is a space helmet, says Nabokov. We go on from this world alone.

And yet that was the door which now swung open, in the eyes of this woman I had never, and had always, known, when – with her throbbings having subsided, and her frail wail having ceased – she went silent and still in my hands. (They pulled the skin tight over her cheekbones, my hands, they elongated the corners of her eyes!) It swung open as though in obedience, that door – because that was the tenor of it, obedience – and I saw the perfect consideration, the kindly, suppliant nullity, with which she held it open, while I stared…

…and I let go of her head and stood up, turning wildly away (here Mrs —, who had been standing behind me, backed out of the room as though I were an assassin, hurriedly shutting the door); and when I returned to the bed she was lying limp, her head turned to one side on the pillow, panting a little and perspiring, while on her left wrist a brand new red rose bloomed, like Jesus' heart in the picture downstairs, through the burnt sienna Elastoplast.

4

'You wrote a column once' – Jackie X said to me – 'about a phrase, *The horror, the horror!* I think you were quoting somebody.'

'Conrad,' I said. '*Heart of Darkness*.'

'I was trying to find it.'

I glanced at *The Child of the Sea* on her bedside table, obscurely elate among the roses, toiletries, pills.

'It's not in that book.'

'Oh.'

'But I could find it for you if you want.'

'Yes.'

After a pause:

'So,' I said.

I sat in a morris chair, a safe distance from her bed, not so much exhausted as rendered quite purposeless: as utterly without function as she – she told me by and by, all her saved life spilling out, running down now like an old clock – had known herself to be, that morning more than twenty-five years ago when she'd stopped abruptly in a doorway and watched in silence while, on an old couch in the garage, her father curtly butt-fucked their Scottish neighbours' red-haired, prepubescent and quite naked daughter.

'Imagine that,' Jackie said. 'With my friend, in my house. My mother's house.'

She'd been twelve: the same age as the thin white child uttering frightened squeaks beneath the thrusting, huge... *thing!*... which instantly became to her, impossibly! both her Absolute Idol and Horror Incarnate.

('It's not even that it, or he, took turns being one and then the other. He was both at the same time, my God and my Hell. I know it's hard to imagine. But he was.')

She'd stood in the doorway transfixed, waiting for the world to end: because *nothing*, she knew instantly, could survive the vision she was being granted. At some point her father would turn and see her – 'because April, you know, she saw me at once; she just sort of half-knelt there with her cheek on the cushion and looked at me' – and the world would end. She would look into his eyes and be extinguished.

She couldn't say how long she stood there, because 'time just kept stretching out'. But her father didn't turn, and a moment came when it occurred to her that she might as well go on up to her room. She couldn't think why; but she couldn't think, either, why she should go on standing there. After all, she had seen what 'they' had wanted her to see. She let her bare feet turn and lead her inside.

I understood the purposelessness in the last part of what she'd said, the perfect equipoise of *why-do-anything?* and *why-not?* Moments earlier, I had thought to leave, then thought to stay, and neither had made any sense. I said, because it seemed to be required (one's always reading about such things these days): 'Are you trying to tell me your father and you – ?'

'Oh, no.' Jackie said. 'Oh, no. No, I was probably too dark.'

She pronounced it parodically, *dawk*, and half-smiled, so that I glanced to see if the hysterics were coming back; but they weren't. It occurred to me to tell her that in seventeen years this was the first time she'd looked beautiful to me. But the words presented themselves as estranged, faraway counters: as though I'd have to swim the breadth of some shoreless Gulf to get to where I could say them. I said instead:

'The Bluebird in the Caroni. Your father killed himself.'

She nodded quickly.

'Your mother thinks it was an accident.'

'Well, it's what she wants think. I let her.'

Silence.

The drip-drip of a water tank somewhere outside. Jackie inspecting, with no real curiosity, the darkening red rose on her wrist.

'I know what you're thinking. You're thinking that because he did, I tried. Well, maybe. Or maybe not. But that's only part of it. The thing is, my father had this thing with cars. Like, the morning with April in the garage, I can tell you what car we had. It was an old, grey Vauxhall Victor with a floor shift: PH something. It was supposed to be a brand new Chevvy.'

I lifted my eyebrows: her last remark had not made sense.

'I didn't tell you. After he died, I found this book.'

The book was a diary her father had written in, back in '49, when he was a boy just leaving school. It comprised a list of resolutions, like planned stepping stones, leading ineffably up to a great and fulfilling life. Only, her father had conceived that life entirely in terms of the cars he would own: what make, how old, by when.

Thus:

1950: Second-hand Morris Minor.

1955: Second-hand Austin Cambridge.

1960: Nearly-new Vauxhall.

1965: Nearly-new Mercury.

The list soon became absurd, of course, for the morose, determined boy (who would later – with what vengeance? – plant his bitter seed in the womb of 'a woman of the people') had the

219

typical teenager's complacent idea of time as a definite canal (instead of the diaphanous shimmer you and I know it to be) and several of the cars he predicted for himself soon stopped being made, and other makes began appearing.

The thing is, his hideously damaged daughter said. *The thing is.*

The thing was, her father never quite managed to get abreast of the cars he'd promised himself. Indeed, as he grew older he increasingly fell behind.

'I mean, the Renault Station Wagon, which we got in '78: that was to have been a Humber.'

The Renault was the closest Jackie's father ever came to overtaking the young man's crassly glinting dream. He only got that near to it courtesy the oil boom; and the boom was already peaking. In '84 he made a last despairing all-sinew-counting lunge and acquired the Bluebird, PAP 1310. But that was it; that was his swan song. The Bluebird was where it stopped.

'And a new Bluebird isn't a "Jaguar Convertible", you know?'

1990 had been scheduled for 'a Rolls'...

'...but I'm sure,' Jackie said. 'I'm sure by then he knew...'

'What?'

'That life is meaningless.'

Silence.

I said: 'Well. I can see how you could get from the diary to – .' I lifted my chin towards her wrists. 'But you know, of course, the April thing had nothing to do with you?'

'Well, it did. Because I saw it. And I was twelve.'

Silence.

The thing is, Jackie said, lying propped-up in bed and looking up at the ceiling. 'I read his stupid little dream about the cars, and I couldn't help putting them against the cars we really owned, as far back as I could remember. And it just came over me – what you wrote about. *The horror! The horror!* You know? It just came in on me, all of a sudden, and I couldn't stop it. So I went and – frightened the hell out of mummy. Oh God.' She said this last wearily.

I said: 'I remember passing you in the mall once – I think it was in 1990. You were with this crewcut guy from, like, Oklahoma, a good bit older than you. I thought you looked really happy...'

'Is that what you thought: Oklahoma?'

She smiled, remembering. 'He wasn't Oklahoman, he was German. He still writes me about once a year.'

I said, making a huge effort: 'I have to say that, even that day, you didn't look half as beautiful as you looked a little while ago.'

I said that, or I think I said it. At least, I intended to say it. But maybe I didn't, because she went on with her thought, exactly as though I hadn't spoken. '…and it wasn't 1990, it was '89. I know, because in '89 daddy suddenly caught a vaps and started telling us he was going to buy a Laurel. Maybe some bonds or something came in, I don't know. But he really meant it, I know that, or we wouldn't have believed him; and we did. I mean, think of it: a Laurel!

'But then something happened, and he didn't. Or maybe he was never really going to; I don't know, anymore. Maybe it was the first time he had a premonition he was going to have to end it, and he just started fantasising instead, in sort of fright. But that was the last time he ever talked to us about buying another car. I remember; we were happy, then.'

DON JUAN'S STORY

I'd never seen her before; never saw her again; never even learnt her name. I'm still not sure how it happened. This was at Buccoo Reef.

We were half-drifting, half-wading, masks in the water, over the fairyland below. There was a current and it eased us together, and away from the others, I think. It kept bumping us together, the current: arms, shoulders, thighs. At one point I grabbed her wrist to show her some fire coral we'd have to skirt. At another she stumbled; I held her. Like that, somehow, it occurred.

She kept her eyes lowered throughout. Her sneakered heels abraded the backs of my knees. When I let her go afterwards she couldn't touch. That's how fast the tide was coming in. My eyes burned from the sun on the ripply water and the salt.

This was strictly speaking my first time but I never counted it. Somehow it's different in the water, when nobody says anything and you don't even know their name.

In the boat, going back, she sat with friends. They passed a Bermudez tin with cheese-paste sandwiches among themselves. When it reached her, she twisted around and with a shy look held it out to me. Taking one, I felt as if some sentry, who had been standing watch inside me for as long as I could remember, had suddenly gone off duty. Gratitude flooded through me – gratitude and relief. Till then I hadn't realised how lonely I'd been, for how long.

Phyllis was compact and pretty and, the fellas said, experienced. On our first date I bought her a corsage. I was seventeen, she, a year older. When I went to pick her up it was raining. In the passenger seat of my father's car, Phyllis said with awe: 'I don't believe it. He bought me a corsage!' At dinner she said it again. All

222

through dinner she kept stopping to look down and finger the sprig. Then she'd look up and smile.

Later, in the damp night by the water's edge, Phyllis unpinned the corsage and placed it on the dashboard. 'Whatever happens,' she said firmly, 'This is not getting crushed.' Below us, the small waves came leisurely in, one long white scroll after another. They came in with a shushing rustling all the way up the beach. Each paused at the end, turned to gleaming silver, and withdrew. The beach went from pale to black to pale as clouds passed over the moon.

In the car, when things reached a certain pitch, I broke away and said, 'Come in the back.' My heart leapt when Phyllis, dishevelled, nodded.

The corsage lay on the dashboard in the moonlight. At first I was scared. Then I wasn't scared anymore.

Driving back to town was all exaltation. I thought, 'I've done it! I've really done it!' Not counting the time in the sea, the time with the sandwiches and the no words spoken. On the radio, Roy Orbison was singing 'Only the Lonely'. Beside me, gone pensive and faraway, Phyllis smoothed out the sprig of the corsage, over and over.

In Jamaica, at the campus in the bowl of the mountains, I turned a corner and came face to face with Sonya. Sonya had almond eyes, sunken cheeks, wavy hair, a teetering walk, and a way of looking at your mouth when you spoke. She was the most beautiful girl I'd ever seen. I was twenty-one, and it hit me in the stomach – suddenly to have the shape of the rest of your life revealed to you like that. But what could I do? I knew at once that Sonya was the one.

Knowing this made me so happy that for a week, two weeks, I made no move towards Sonya. Some days I would catch sight of her, alone or with others, passing by in the distance or near at hand. Other days I didn't see her, and those days too were fine. I walked about her campus all in all. Wrapped in, alive with happiness.

It was so powerful this happiness it created its real-life image in the world. One morning Sonya fainted in front of me on the stairs going up to Soc. Sci., and it fell to me to carry her down and across the lawn to a worried lecturer's car. I carried Sonya in my arms in the morning sun as Tristan carried Iseult.

The week Sonya spent resting at her parents' home up in Irish Town was the happiest week of my life. I would look up at the hills and picture her there. When, shortly after her descent, I overheard a conversation in the cafeteria, and in this way learned that Sonya had *gone back to sleeping* with a Greek guy called Mikali, over in Chem – when I learned that *even after the abortion* she was still apparently hoping he would marry her – I lost for a time the faculty of thought. For weeks after that, at odd times, my pulse raced, my vision blurred, and I perspired from the soles of my feet.

After this phase passed I took stock of my life and saw it was not going to be perfect. It might turn out okay, it might even turn out pretty well. But I saw it would not now be perfect. That it was time to put away that dream.

In retrospect I think it would be fair to say that Sonya broke my heart.

After that, there was Fran. Fran had a soulful look, and a build, and shiny black hair that fell either side of her face from a part down the middle. She was the first one I went with that had brains.

She also had a terror of getting pregnant. Half the time we spent together, me and Fran, we spent trying to make sure Fran wouldn't get pregnant. It took the cake when one morning, at a lecture on Shelley, Fran passed me this note over my shoulder: 'After you left last night I found traces of you-know-what under my fingernails. I keep trying to remember where I put my hand but I can't. What chance I might have got myself pregnant?'

Irritated, I scribbled on my pad, 'About the same as another immaculate conception,' and held it up. I got a hard shove in the back.

The lecturer looked at us with rage. For some reason he'd been explaining how in the different seasons the prevailing winds blew in Europe.

When I told Fran we had to part she went inert, sitting there like a sack of potatoes on my lap. Her arms hung heavily from my neck, and that too was her expression: heavy. I thought: now I know what a dead body feels like; and, sure enough, Fran died the following year of an embolism. Brought on, they said, by The Pill.

Fran was twenty-one. She was the first girl I ever knew that way that died.

I heard the news of Fran's death in Dominica, Roseau. I sat on the seawall and looked at the lights of the *Federal Palm*, anchored offshore. The *Federal Palm* was taking some of us students from Jamaica south for the summer. Later that night, in the ship's lounge, Liz, a young Irish Pre-Med who was doing the Caribbean, agreed to go back with me to my cabin. Liz was plump and blonde, and wept a little each time she came. She was the first one I met that didn't try to wrap herself around you, but lay there uttering little cries while her fingers fluttered like birds' wings along your flanks.

It wasn't that great, actually, what with the double-bunk setup and the saggy springs. But I kept her going all night, because of Fran.

After that she became a leech.

Sometimes you get lonely, you know?

When I was twenty-two, I developed this line: 'You love me?'

You have to say it like a challenge, not a bleat. It doesn't sound like much, I know. But for some reason it freaked them out. If they were really young, seventeen or eighteen, they'd blush and drop their eyes, and maybe even whisper, you know: 'Yes!' If they were more your age they might say, like, 'What do you think?', grinning grimly but saying it humidly and cuffing you on the shoulder, and you'd know what they meant was yes. Some might even say moonily, 'How could I not love you?' if they were older, twenty-four, twenty-five, getting on in years. That last was terrible. It really was.

On occasion you'd run into one who'd be impervious. She'd say something like: 'Whatever gave you that idea?', not smiling when she said it, and you'd know you were wasting your time and to desist. But those were the exceptions. A simple 'You love me?', said like a challenge: nine out of ten, it pushed them over the edge.

Another line was to break into whatever they were saying, saying: 'Keep talking like that and you'll never get me into bed.' You had to be more careful with this line: when you used it, who you used it with. Sometimes you'd run headfirst into a withering retort. Other times, though, it would get you a shocked or delighted laugh, and it'd be easy to see where you stood.

Or else they'd fall silent beside you in the car, and you'd hear their little minds going *click click click*.

Those were good lines, and I never understood why, using them, I sometimes wound up disliking myself. Prior to that, the only other line I'd had was when I was sixteen. This was to point at a star and say: 'That's Venus. See it there? Now you have to make a wish and seal it with a kiss.' It wasn't Venus, I never thought it was, and one day I found out it was part of Orion. But that was still okay. I never disliked myself using that line, the way I disliked myself sometimes with those other, later lines.

Sometimes you get lonely, doesn't matter what you do. You try keeping to yourself; for a few days it's fine; then you start getting lonely. Or you try sticking with one on a regular basis but she soon gets predictable, and you're bored. So you play the field, free as a bird, except that half the time you're disliking yourself or being lonely. Sometimes it seems to me, men, we were born to be lonely.

I still think of Sonya from time to time. I never forgot the way she made me feel. Mikali didn't marry her in the end, and she married a Jamaican businessman ten years older than her and they'd moved to Miami, last I heard. But I don't think about her too often. There's no place in my life for the feelings that come when I catch myself thinking of Sonya.

Jeannine, now, was dark, with an Afro, a round forehead and a splendiferous smile. She didn't so much kiss as lick you all over: nipples, eyelids, balls. She was the happiest one I ever knew. Come a point and Jeannine's straining would give way to laughing and you'd know she'd felt herself beginning to come. We lasted almost three months, me and Jeannine.

One Sunday in her apartment, while we were lying naked and sweaty on the living room floor, Jeannine put her mouth to my ear and said, 'I love you', and I knew it had to end. I didn't say anything, and, after a while, Jeannine got up and went into the bathroom, and stayed there till I left, and a year later married this guy from her office and had three children with him.

I still run into Jeannine from time to time, and it's a funny thing: of all the ones I ever went with and ran into later, she's one of the few I never suggested to – you know. A lot of the time, their reaction would surprise you. But I never tried that with Jeannine; don't ask me why.

Not that it would've worked, anyway. One New Year's Eve when I was home alone, I sat down and penned a note to Jeannine. 'You were the best of them,' I wrote, 'and I should have married you. We would have had a life.'

A few days later my note came back. On it, Jeannine had written: 'I'm really sorry you're unhappy, but I'm married now. Please don't do this again.'

So that was that.

Where was I?

After Jeannine there was Dit-Dit. Dit-Dit was small and wiry and played hockey. I liked her okay to begin with. Then as time passed I liked her less.

Dit-Dit was the only one I ever met who really preferred taking men in her mouth. Other women, they mostly do that part as a duty, never mind they pretend doing it drives them wild. But not Dit-Dit. At a given moment, Dit-Dit's chatter would cease, Dit-Dit's animation would fade and be replaced by something else, something faraway and dim, and next moment Dit-Dit's fingers would be at my fly, and Dit-Dit's head would sink into my lap. At first, at such times she would let me touch her. Later on she pushed my hand away.

To begin with, her sincerity impressed me. But I soon began to have my doubts. Seemed to me, as time passed, Dit-Dit was more interested in that part of me than me.

It ended really badly, that one. One night, driving home from the beach, Dit-Dit got up to her usual tricks in the car, and I thought to myself, Enough; and then I said it. She wouldn't listen and I had to push her away. Her head hit the dashboard and she came back crying and clawing, and I had to stop the car and slap her up.

After that, for the rest of the ride, nobody spoke. I remember the miles and miles of darkness flying by, the forest fleeing past like tall black walls...

Joyce, now, was red, nasal and nervy, and liked it a way you never knew. Rebecca had a swan's neck and vague grey eyes, but she soon went away to study. Miriam had the greatest breasts you ever saw, but in bed she was all tight and whimpery, and the guys said she was frigid, and I had to tell them they were right. Around this time, too, there was Grace.

Grace was brown on brown – hair, skin – tall and lanky, with impregnable green eyes. She was twenty-nine to my twenty-five, but I liked her laconic ways, so I gave her a look-up from time to time. One night Grace turned up at my door late, with tears in her eyes and nothing on under her tartan shift. I didn't ask – I never ask – half the time they're just waiting for you to ask – and Grace, give her that, never explained. Three days later, in a swank society wedding, Cathedral to Country Club, Grace married a high politician. I thought: Heh-heh, Mr Politician; bet you don't know, etc... But later, on reflection, I got scared. I'd been out of my depth without knowing it all along.

I saw Grace a year or two after her marriage. I said, smiling bitterly: 'So you dropped me.'

A flash: the green eyes; the laconic smile. Then: 'You're not dropped, mister, you never were. Not unless you want to be, that is.'

This was at a party at the Chinese Club.

I said, 'You're probably putting me on, but if you're not –,' and I named a hotel restaurant, a date and a time. I half-didn't expect her, but sure enough, when the time came there was Grace, sitting alone at a corner table, in a green trousers suit and dark lipstick and with her hair piled up, sipping something from a wineglass and smoking. 'Good afternoon, sir,' she said in her laconic way; but upstairs she was different: hungrier, somehow. At one point she said, 'Oh God, you so sweet!' and that really set me back. The old Grace would've never said that.

I didn't see her again, not that way. But that afternoon, I realised later, Grace opened up for me a whole new world. It's a world of lunchtime assignations and hotel rooms, of hunger and pliability on their part such as you wouldn't believe – of even, sometimes when it's over, such gratitude, it's pathetic. There's a great fraternity out there of famished expectations. Walking sorrows. Other men's wives.

Me, I'm thirty this year. Which always surprises me when I think of it. Feels as if I've been around a lot longer. When I look ahead sometimes and see how long life can be, I quail. How do people get through such long lives?

'Ah, life's just a dream,' my partner Walter says. He says it dismissively, smugly, because he's married, and doing well at work, and he thinks he has it made. Sometimes I want to tell him what his wife has to say on the subject. People like Walter, they're contemptible, really, Grinning at you from inside their little bubbles of illusion, like foetuses in a fat land.

Walter's wife, by the way, is the aforementioned Joyce: they got married a couple years ago. Joyce still gives me a lookup on occasion – driven into my path, I suppose, by some futile petty quarrel with hubby or the wild light of her personal moon. At such times, soon as I'm lodged in her forbidden place – forbidden to Walter, that is – Joyce commences a groaning such as you never heard. As if the earth itself groaned.

Fit that song into your dream life, Walter!

Me, I hardly dream anymore. Sometimes, when I'm sick, with the flu, say, I have bits and snatches of dreams. But they don't mean anything, they're not connected to anything; and most of the time they're more like nightmares. Fran underwater with her lank black hair fanned out, frantically trying to ward off a little fish that keeps darting for shelter in the mossy grotto between her legs. Miriam gasping, 'I can't breathe, I can't breathe!' and me trying to tell her I'm the one who can't breathe, but her breast is pressing against my face and I'm smothering. Or, one time, there's this pleasurable sensation, but accompanied by a faraway howling, as if a great storm were approaching. I look down and Dit-Dit's head is between my legs, and I see with shock I've turned into a banana there and Dit-Dit is eating it, piece by piece. The storm explodes in my head and I realise: it's me who's howling.

I wonder if any of those qualifies as the dream Walter says life is.

One time though, sir, not long before I started telling you all this – I know, my hour's nearly up – I had a different kind of dream. A real dream.

What happened was, I'd been sanding furniture and inhaled sawdust, and come down with a lung infection (this is not the dream). It was really bad, they had me on oxygen for two nights and a day, a lot of the time I thought I was dying, and perhaps I was. But it was sometime during that time – and I cannot say when – that I had this dream. Or call it a vision, because I wasn't asleep at the time. Or at least I don't think I was…

There was this pine forest on a mountainside, and I was walking uphill in the early morning through the cool of the pines carrying Sonya in my arms. She was asleep in my arms, with her head on my chest, and the scent of her hair filled my nostrils, and it was like the scent of morning. I'd been walking a long time but it was no problem, because she, Sonya, was light as air; and so, come to think of it, was I. Overhead the sky was blue, sunlight freckled the pine floor, and whenever a light breeze stirred it was cool.

From time to time, early on, we passed the naked bodies of girls, asleep or dead, some of them in grotesque postures, among the pines. Some of them I recognised, others I didn't, but it didn't matter, they had nothing to do with us. They were like part of the forest, they had always been there: glistening sculptures with which some unhappy artist had strewn this part of the hillside in another life, long ago, when Time was.

Now there was no Time, only my darling's heart beating quietly against my chest, or mine on hers. When we started uphill there'd been the sounds of the forest: lizards scurrying among the pine needles, the distant moo of a cow, bird chatter, breeze in the trees. That was in the time of the bodies, but as we climbed the forest, noises petered out. We ascended into silence, my sleeping heart and I, through cool shade and freckled light and the eternal fragrant morning of her hair.

Then we came out of the pines, and in the brilliant sunlight, for the first time, I saw where we were heading. It was an old wooden cottage with a little verandah, perched on a grassy height up ahead, with a guava tree half-blocking the windows on one side and an old citrus grove sloping away on the other.

It doesn't sound like much, I know. Then, how can I explain – I know, my time is up – but how can I describe the happiness that burst like a sun in me then, as, understanding where we were heading – at last, at last! – I stepped out of the pines and into that blaze of light, with my darling, my whole life, asleep in my arms, her heart beating steadily in my heart, or mine in hers – and all around us the fragrance of eternal morning, the towering blue columnar vault of the sky, and a silence like the Silence that must have been before the world was made?

I carried Sonya in my arms in the morning sun as Tristan carried Iseult.

THE VAGRANT AT THE GATE

Bad news: the 626 abruptly decelerating, all power gone, in a stressed and disappointed silence. But then, good news: an acquaintance in a white Galante had been behind me all along and now obligingly stopped too. ('Pull the hood.') His brief and hesitant self-insertion therein proved – as we'd both expected, though I still hoped – infertile. He left to go in search of his mechanic, 'an electrics guy' from upper St James.

I'd pulled over to the curb facing south on X, two or three car lengths above Y. (X: a north-south residential Woodbrook street. Y: one of the main roads crossing it.) It was not yet nine, but already there was only one viable pool of shade left on the pavement. It came from the dormer-window protrusion of an old, 'forties Woodbrook house which had been expensively and hideously 'modernised'. I retired into to it to wait.

Almost at once, the vagrant materialised. I glanced at him irritably.

He was your standard vagrant: matted hair, too-bright eyes, red skin upon which the passionate sun had laid a light gloss of washed black, like an old jou'vert greasing. Baggy trousers, still recognisably khaki, curling outward at the waist like the lip of a vase, from which rose the stem of his tucked-in torso, with its furious navel.

'Eh, uncle, uh beggin' you,' etc.

The way he said it, it sounded rehearsed: not quite your true-blue vagrant's heartfelt expression of illimitable desperation. And the light in his eyes was not quite ownerless, I saw: not quite the unsigned light of lunacy. But what to do. My pocketful of coins changed hands ('T'ank you, boss!') and he was turning away when the oblong bulge in my shirt pocket caught his attention. He ducked and peered at it, making a vagrant's urgent mime – two forked fingers tensely pumping from his lips – and I gave him the Benson and lit it for him, doing this with a look which told him we both knew he was pushing the envelope.

For a moment, inhaling, he was all concentration. Then: 'Heh-heh-heh,' he said sheepishly into his chest, turning away. He didn't go very far. There was an electricity pole not far from the corner, a car length or so south of the 626, and he went and leaned on it in the immemorial posture of a whore: hand cupping elbow, cigarette at the ready, one bare sole cocked against the pole.

And, five years ago, I might have rounded on him ('Haul y'ass! What the fock more you want? G'won, move!'). But I discovered I didn't have that part anymore – or at least, didn't have it that morning – and so I lit one myself, and paced irritably back and forth in the little pen of shade by the 626's boot, and presently fell to considering the house across the street, to which my attention had been drawn by the sound of a car engine being laboriously tumbled… and then wailingly revved… until, with a few last, precautionary, throat-clearing revs, the car itself was modestly induced to demit its driveway – or so I deduced, since both were out of sight on the far side of the house.

On my side there wasn't much to see. Chain link between unpainted concrete pillars, backed by a tall, untidy hedge and bisected by a padlocked garden gate, BRC on steel pipe, from which a flagging flagstone path led almost at once to four or five concrete steps with, at their summit, an empty, small verandah and a door through whose half-height panes of glass the morning sun irradiated confusedly. The place had a neglected, impoverished look. The galvanised zinc roof was rusting badly.

From twenty feet away: 'Watch dis,' the vagrant said. He might have been speaking to himself.

In the house behind me, the 'modernised' house, a glass sliding door opened, then closed, and a big, paunchy, Portugee man in perhaps his late forties came down the steps and out onto the pavement. He was evidently dressed for work: white short-sleeved shirt (pulling tight at the waist) with an undervest showing; dark trousers. Big forearms, the hair on them long and black; the hair on his head, too, suspiciously black. He crossed behind

233

the 626, close enough that a passing nod at its owner would have been natural. But he merely glanced angrily from the car to my face, and went on over. At the padlocked gate he looked up and down the street, then banged the metal saddle three times.

'Um bad!' the vagrant wailed softly (the Michael Jackson song). 'Um ba-ad!' And he pinched the stub of the cigarette, inhaled mightily, and blew the smoke up, straight up, to the bright blue morning sky.

In the house across the street the glass-paned door opened, and a woman – a youngish, brown-skinned woman in a housecoat of fading flowers with her hair in curlers – emerged and came down the steps to the garden gate. She might have been in her mid-thirties, or she might have been younger, for her face had the graven, naked-sad look of one not long come from sleep, and her gaze when she glanced across the street (at me, then at the vagrant) was appraising rather than disapproving. She and the Portugee man stood at the gate talking.

How is it that one can unerringly tell from forty feet away when a man and woman are talking about 'doing it'?

Maybe it's just that they stand too close – even when separated by a BRC gate. Or maybe it's the way they take turns glancing around, though not as if expecting to see anyone. Or the sense you get, though out of earshot, that they are talking softly yet urgently...

At any rate, the woman seemed of a mind to demur (perhaps, I thought, because of the presence of two witnesses across the street). But the Portugee man's broad, white-shirted back gave off the uncompromising, 'planted' air of someone who was not about to move; and abruptly the woman broke away and went up the steps into the house and returned with a bunch of keys and opened the gate.

Locking it after him, she glanced a last time at the vagrant –and I saw that the vagrant had gone perfectly still. Then she turned and went up and in, closing the door behind her.

'Um baaad,' the vagrant crooned softly, as though to himself. 'Um ba-ad!'

Abruptly he sang it out, harsh and loud: 'Um baad! Um ba-aaad!' – and I turned, then said angrily: 'Hey!'

The vagrant had slipped his hand into his trousers-front, and – staring hard at the house – was vigorously agitating himself there.

'Hey, *you!*' I shouted enraged, and the vagrant swung away, interposing his shoulder between me and what he was doing, and went on doing it.

I said, *'Jesus Christ!'* and swung away myself, and started walking – and in this way found myself abreast of the driveway of the 'modernised' house from which the Portugee man had come. There was a car parked in it, some way in, near where the back steps would be. It was a silver shining Mercedes 300 SL: PBA something or the other.

And, writing this now, I cannot explain it, but I looked at that car and knew – *knew* – that what was taking place in the house across the street, the house with the once-more-locked garden gate, was not at all what I'd assumed it to be – not a solitary man's heat and hunger calling into some stifled night of marital loneliness (though I understood that the wailing, revving car, laboriously leaving from the far side of the house, had been the signal the Portugee man had been listening for); not a free negotiation between loins and heart, impassioned, urgent, yet free; not male want calling to female bewilderment – but the brute operation of money upon moneylessness (those broken flagstones, that neglected verandah, that badly rusting roof!), the adamantine imposition of power upon powerlessness and need.

Behind my back: 'Um baad!' bellowed the vagrant suddenly. 'Um ba-ad!' And I turned and saw that – hand out of sight, trousers-front shaking violently – he was glaring at the shut, glass-paned door of the shabby old 'forties Woodbrook house across the street – glaring at it as if he could kill it.

2

It was minutes past nine, and though the street where the 626, without warning, had crossed over from life into death (and now lay by the curb, embalmed in silence) was a quiet, residential Woodbrook street, cars still came down it, one by one. I stared at each briefly but hungrily – for who wants to stand in the burning sun not fifty feet away from a violently masturbating vagrant? – but none was a white Galante that might be bearing my acquaintance and his 'electrics guy'. So, gloomily, I watched each car come, decelerating as it passed, and then of necessity – just as it came abreast of the engrossed vagrant – braking for the major road ahead.

('Um baaad!' bellowed the vagrant at sporadic intervals, glaring at the glass-paned door across the street, one hand working wildly in his trouser-front.)

Like that, there came down the road:

1) A dark blue Sonata driven by a young Syrian woman who, when she saw what she was pulling up next to, accelerated so desperately that she swung onto the major road barely ahead of a thundering garbage truck, which repaid her by shattering the quiet morning with a three-second blast of its horn.

2) A brown PAY Laser, piloted by a young creole tess who shook his head when he saw what he saw, bending over in such exaggerated disbelief or misapplied mirth that his forehead bumped his horn and made him jump.

3) A pastel Laurel, the padded cell of a well-dressed, middle-aged, red-skinned lady, who must have suffered terribly – or so the back of her head seemed to say – while she waited for a gap to open in the main road traffic, and who was full of hatred by the time it did, judging by the vengefully accelerating swerve with which she put behind her forever (except, perhaps, in her dreams) the lit and dreadful apparition suffusing her peripheral vision for a petrified Eternity.

None of these fazed the vagrant in the least.

('Um baad!' bellowed the vagrant at the house with the two unseen occupants and the locked garden gate. 'Um baaaad!!!')

On the other hand, not even he could have ignored the battered pickup with three Indian guys wedged in front and a fourth with a power mower in the tray.

'Yuh crazy nigger!'

'Yuh nasty bitch!'

'Stay right dey, we bringin' de police for yuh mod-ah cont!'

The vagrant's hand stayed in his trousers but stopped moving. The guy in the tray jumped up and with an oath flung a cardboard box at him. (It missed.) Reflexively the vagrant picked it up, looked inside, then tossed it away into the gutter. With a chorus of obscenities the pickup turned onto the main road and was gone.

The vagrant looked dismayed. He glanced around him (including at me) disappointedly. And I was just judging it safe to return to my pool of shade, two car lengths or so from where he stood, when his gaze fell again on the glass-paned door, and I saw it strengthen there, and grip, and his hand slipped back into his trouser-front; and I said to myself with feeling, 'Oh, *fuck!*' and for the *nth* time looked up the street in vain for the Galante.

(And if some amateur psychologist wishes to explain to me at this point that my reluctance to stand near the vagrant in that state was due to latent homosexual tendencies on my part, fine. I only know there's a certain, irrefragable distance from a masturbating man within which I am not prepared to stand; and the only pool of shade on the pavement lay well within it.)

'Um bad,' the vagrant said pensively; and I saw that with him the trouser-front business was now meditative rather than frenetic.

Here a black PBB Corolla with dark-tinted windows came down the street, pulled up for the major road; and stopped. There was a lull in the main road traffic, but the Corolla didn't move… a stream of cars passed by, then another lull… still the Corolla didn't move. And I had just amazed myself with a surge of fury, which for a moment actually had me looking around for a stone to pelt at it, when the vagrant threw himself upon it, screaming, 'Uh go kill you! Uh go kill you!', kicking and banging on the fender and boot, and the black car leapt away like a startled animal, out onto the main road and was gone.

'Uh go kill him!' the vagrant screamed, and his eyes were terrible. 'Uh go kill him!'

Our eyes met. I nodded, and the vagrant saw, and his wildness abated slightly.

'Uh go kill him,' he shouted at me a third time, as if making sure I'd heard him right. And I said, quite loudly (returning to my patch of shade at last), 'Yeah, kill him. Kill his ass!'

'Uh go kill his mo-dah'ss,' the vagrant said with desolate

satisfaction. And he leaned on the telegraph pole and folded his arms and resumed watching the glass-paned door across the street, but without frenzy now.

And so we stood there, me and the interrupted vagrant, and watched the silent house across the street (in which, for some reason – though I claim a robust imagination and am no especial prude – I could only imagine what was taking place in there as occurring in the (foully-named!) 'missionary position', with the brown-skinned young woman almost out of sight and struggling to breathe beneath a great pale threshing bulk.)

And, sure enough, presently the glass-paned door opened and the Portugee man came out, dressed for work just as before, with behind him the young woman, barefooted now and wearing only an old, thigh-length white T-shirt, imprinted with some fading festive scene.

She was in the process of taking the last curler out of her hair (and that, for some reason, depressed me even more. To think he hadn't minded her keeping the curlers in!). She deposited it on the verandah sill and came down the steps and unlocked the garden gate and let him out.

'Uh-go-kill-his-mo-dah'ss,' the vagrant said.

But he said it experimentally, in the tone of one rehearsing a phone number; and I knew that nothing was going to happen.

The Portugee man never looked at him. As he had done earlier, he glanced from my car to me (but without anger, now) and went on down his driveway and got straight into the Mercedes and started it and backed out and drove off, stopping for the major road, then going on. And I marvelled at his doing all that as if nothing at all had just happened: as if he were just a normal guy, driving off to work on a normal weekday morning.

The young woman in the T-shirt had stayed at the garden gate: presumably, I thought sourly, to wave goodbye to her gruff ex-smotherer and philanthropic paramour. But now she lingered a moment longer, fingers lightly gripping the BRC at breast-height; and I saw that she was looking at the vagrant... looking at him with a sort of tutelary patience... and that the vagrant was looking back at her, with an expression I couldn't quite name.

I glanced from one to the other – from bare feet to bare feet, from matted locks to ex-curlered, untidy curls – and realised, startled, that, across the width of that quiet Woodbrook street, dishevelment was considering dishevelment.

Then the woman locked the gate and went in, picking up the plastic thing from the sill in passing, closing the glass-paned door behind her. And the vagrant turned and walked away without a parting glance at me, walking now not with a vagrant's swagger but as any man would walk, going unhurriedly about his business, on a normal weekday morning – and *that*, I suddenly understood, had been the expression on the vagrant's face which I'd be unable to name.

From behind her garden gate, she had turned to him her unmade-up, naked-sad face: looking at him, not as one man's housewife, nor another man's whore, but as a woman: just a woman. And from the pitiless glare of a shadeless pavement, he, the vagrant, had looked back at her, not with the bright eyes of his kind, nor with anything even remotely resembling a lecher's leer, but levelly, steadily, as a man considers a woman who means something to him. As a man. Just a man.

They were sobering, somehow wondrous, realisations. And, left alone on that empty Woodbrook street with the occasional car coming down it, I stood there for a long time, in my shrinking pool of shade (until, as he'd promised, my good Samaritan returned in the white Galante, with his 'electrics guy') musing over all that I had seen.

BRING ON THE TRUMPETERS

To begin with, the setting's wrong, even granted that its essentials are here dutifully assembled: the little cemetery enisled by the great park which manages, in addition, to support the twin ovals of race track (thin nibbed, white) and exercise track (ochre swathe), the fact remains, someone's been tampering with the details, and, in this business, a miss can be as good as a mile. Who added these peripheral skyscrapers? That vista of palms? These crawling cars which are not our cars but their elongated American relations, named for wild horses and weapons? Worst of all, some unauthorised author, some wry or rebellious soul, has gone and abolished the grandstand, that old green barracky refuge, in favour of this cream monstrosity, which from here could pass for a giantess's handbag left lying on its side, its black mouth fixedly yawning – and which you and I both know belongs far away, in stony Santa Rosa. And now – now it's too late. Already a clock tolls and goes on tolling, a dozen exhausted bongs, and here come the untidy crowds – among them two boys, one tall, the other short, upon whom we shall concentrate – here come the snow-cone carts, the peanut vendors, the mounted policemen, the ambulance; here in earnest now comes the ant-queue of strange cars. Not to worry, not to worry: we shall work with what we have. Bring on the trumpeters! (Wait)

'Bet on The Wrag then,' the short one, Rupert to you, was saying. 'Bet on anything.' He got up from the depopulated bank halfway along the backstretch and looked around him vaguely. Then, either because there was nothing to see or because the physical act had absorbed its emotional imperative, he promptly saw down again. 'Bet on The Wrag then,' he muttered.

The taller boy – henceforth Jonathan – drew inward his brows, perhaps to deflect the other's words (for verbal anger finds its mark, like a sharpshooter's bullet, right between the eyes) but did not otherwise respond. Instead, he plucked a spear of grass from the vicinity of his hip and tore it carefully lengthwise along the spine before losing interest and letting the halves drop. They lay where they fell. Rupert tried again.

'Look,' he said exasperatedly. 'Stargazer never lose yet. Nine outa nine he beat them.'

'Nine outa nine!' he repeated, one clawed and uplifted hand alerting the sombre heavens to bear witness. 'But now' – *sotto voce*, slant-eyed – 'suddenly you say he cyar win.'

'I never say he cyar win. I say I don't *think* he could win.'

Rupert looked uncertain. Then: 'Words,' he concluded bitterly. 'Just words.' He squinted up at the sky and the other boy might be excused for thinking he was about to comment on the weather; but sad Rupert only crossed his elbows between his thighs and, jackknifing slowly forward, applied his shining forehead to his knees.

Out of sight of the track, discrete but near, like a parent – and, like a parent, never wholly to be ignored – lies the Allotment: a rhomboid of ruined pastureland across whose weedy surface generations of beeline walkers have impressed a pattern of dirt tracks like spokes. Mysteriously, it has escaped development, and the mystery is heightened by the fact that it has never been far from the minds of an alert populace, members of whom have, over the years, periodically written into the press suggesting how it should be put to use. Concerned Patriach ('an enduring eyesore') invited the Government to remember the tourists; Pedagogue begged leave to postulate for it a regional conference centre; and Housewife suggested, timidly, a park, 'with statues and fountains and trees.' NASP demanded a national stadium, Comrades in Christ, a shrine. Committees arose, recommended, and subsided. There was even an ode by an old and much read poet which began 'Thou alone, O desert hoar/ Shalt the sands of Time deride,' and for which the opening rhymes were 'gnaw' and 'pride'. The Chamber of Commerce ('a gross waste of resources') asked the Government for a statement of intent; whereupon the Children of Africa warned 'the people's Government not to let the Chamber of Commerce get its' – here followed a tantalising trickle of dots, the handiwork no doubt of a prudent but scrupulous subeditor – 'hands on it.' When word spread that an American hotelier, one Ludendorf (a shady character) had approached the Government to buy it, everyone wrote at once, and the odewriter, swept off his metrical steed by the reverberations of the fray, added a scalding cascade of vers libre. But nothing was ever actually done. Beneath the crossfire of recommendation and report the Allotment, dourly oblivious, remained what by default it had long become: a playground for the children of the poor.

But today it was a car park for the race meeting, and when, a couple hours ago, our young friends walked past it on their way to the track it had already been filled. 'Boy,' quipped lanky Jonathan (a compulsive quipper). 'Look at the desert whore today!' 'More like a tank factory to me,' retorted stubby, stubble-bearded Rupert. And in truth there was a sinister air about the cars – as though, standing shoulder to shoulder, rank on rank, they concealed a collective and malignant will of their own, all the more potent for their having been left unattended. (Some of their windshields blazed in the sun.)

In the distance now a loudspeaker said something which ended in a brief scream, and Jonathan, looking up from the bank, saw that the betting booths had set up a mild magnetic field and were drawing people gently towards them from all along the homestretch rail. The betting booths were low green-painted structures built predominantly of corrugated zinc. They had been created a month ago, they would be abolished in a month's time, but now they squatted, tremulous in the afternoon heat, looking passably like a pair of poorly camouflaged pillboxes (grim Rupert's remark) facing the stands, with the winning post showing between them. Jonathan eased his binoculars from their case and focused them to the offside of the betting booths where the parade ring would be and, yes, was. There was nothing happening there and he lowered the glasses, telling himself that there was still plenty of time. He reversed the binoculars-extracting process (left cap, right cap, fold the wings, slide, change hands, buckle the case) and, having deposited that precious possession tenderly, flat on the grass, glanced warily at his companion.

Rupert sat with his back to the stands, glaring at the innocuous mountains. It was hotter now that the sun had gone in and the mountains, blue and vague, gave off a directionless haze. Above them the sky was high and silvery, like the light which announces the sea. Looking at it hurt the eyes. Jonathan, returning his gaze to his friend's immobile face, with its slightly bulging eyes, thought: The boy could be a statue, or dead. 'Boy,' he attempted. 'You sitting there like a statue. Wapnin Einstein?'

The statue of Einstein blinked. 'I just want to know,' it said gloomily, 'how you could be so mulish. Every tipster in town say Stargazer but you there with the kiss-me-ass Wrag. I just don't understand you, daz all.'

Arguments like this one, when indulged in by the young, are apt to ramble on into the dusk, since the young are both more adamant and more generous than us, their brittle-spirited elders. What follows is therefore a ruthlessly telescoped version of the ensuing conversation. (Also, my trumpeters, grown restless, have fallen to running the scales: an insane ascension of blasts, repeated over and over. You knew!)

Stargazer, like most local horses, had been bred to sprint (Jonathan), though he'd won a mile race (Rupert). That had been a slowly run mile (J) and Stargazer had been pushed to win it (J), but these were both big lies (R). The race today was two furlongs longer (J), which hadn't seemed to worry the tipsters (R), who were merely being sentimental (J) like everyone else (J) though 'everyone' obviously did not include him, J (R, scathingly). A man had to know what he knew (J) and a man had to know what he felt (R) though feelings couldn't change facts (J) and J knew every thing, right? (R).

'Awright!' declared violently irritated Jonathan, 'Tell me this. When last, WHEN LAST, a creole win the Governor's Cup?'

'President's Cup,' corrected Rupert acidly. 'Try to remember: the name change.'

'Same race,' muttered Jonathan.

'Well,' said Rupert bitterly, 'I glad you say it.' Hugging his knees he had begun to rock back and forth.

'Say what?'

'What you just say. That a local horse could never beat a

English horse. That a English horse mus' always beat a local horse. I glad you put it like that. At leas' now we know where you stand.'

A petrified instant fled by before Jonathan understood what the other boy was saying. 'We?' he demanded threateningly. 'Who "we"?'

'We, the people of this country.'

A mirror-multiplication of petrified Instances marched stiffly out of sight. Jonathan stared wide-eyed at Rupert.

'Look, you!' he yelled suddenly. 'Just go to hell, you hear?' Rupert stiffened but did not reply. Abruptly he got up, dusting his trousers, and set off in the direction of the betting booths.

'Where you going?' called Jonathan.

'Hell.'

Jonathan sat and watched until the other boy, grown anonymously small, disappeared into the crowd around the betting booths. Then he got up, shouldered the binoculars, stuck his hands into his pockets, and set off miserably in that direction himself.

Now, Jonathan loved horse racing. It was a true love in that it lifted him out of himself, and it might have saved him (indeed, may yet have done so, for who is to say that in some simultaneous, purified universe – all essence, so to speak, not, like ours, hopelessly mired in dross – some reincarnation of that melancholic boy is not at this very moment sitting in eternal animation at the right hand of the Track Steward?). Many mornings, rising early, he would cycle up to the track to watch the horses exercise before getting back on his bicycle to pedal the rest of the way to school. And in this way he had learnt many things. He knew the tipsters by their first names now, and the man who rode the snow-cone cart across the park on his way into the city, appearing promptly every weekday morning at six-fifty around the edge of the foothills. He had come to look forward to seeing the mountains change, altering from black to grey, from grey to blue, from blue to green and black as the sun climbed; to the smell and creak of leather, and the stable boys' cries, which carried emptily, without resonance, across the early-morning fields; and to hearing the

horses' hooves thud when it was dry and plash when it had rained.
He could recreate at will the scent of wet grass, the great beams
of light which the sun threw across the sky, like the headlamps of
a conquering army, in the minutes before it cleared the mountain, and its sudden warmth on his face when it did. You could tell
the time, he knew, by the way in which the cars trickled, and then
poured, into sight around the bend from which earlier the snow-
cone man had come; and if the Indian coconut vendor had done
well the night before, you knew by the amount of chippings
swept beneath the bench near the spot where he parked his cart
each evening. Kaiser, the newspaper tipster, had a habit of en-
thusing when a horse he was sure would not win put in a good
gallop, as such horses sometimes did – and of falling furtively
silent whenever one went by which he did think would do well;
so you knew that too, and you watched him, and hoped besides
that one day you would know as much about racehorses as was
contained behind that bucolic expression, with its slack mouth
and chronically bleary eyes. Likewise, you watched the trainers:
tall black austere Tom Charles, and the others, like red-faced,
foul-mouthed De Vere and his polar opposite, Chin Yen; or you
tried to edge near enough to overhear what little, quick-talking
Boodoo had to say to his trainer when he came back on Morgan's
Folly from a mile run which began cunningly at the four-furlong
post and ended abruptly in the backstretch, leaving you with your
stopwatch foolishly ticking on; and, in between all this, you
watched the girls. You watched with frank interest the daughters
of the owners, standing around in jeans and boys' shirts and
chatting, like girls who are not being watched; and you watched,
with sixteen-year-old shyness, the wives: handsome, mature,
brown-skinned women for whom a husband seemed always at
hand when needed for something, such as to explain the significance of a gallop, or help with the adjusting of a shooting stick, or
confirm what their stopwatches said.

But mostly you watched the horses: stocky, barrel-chested
bays that swished their tails and bowed, and felt the ground often
with their forehooves, until released into a gallop; long-legged
chestnuts, matt or gloss, cantering like dogs with their heads
down; long-striding, mottle-silk-coated greys; the occasional

high-stepping black – month in, month out you watched them, learning their habits and matching proportions to names until you could tell a horse at a distance, and which had acquired or shed bandages since when, who had the leg up on whom in whose place, and which would go left better than right. Then, in your first free period at school, you wrote it all down in a red-covered notebook, shielding what you wrote with your left hand and glancing up often at the presiding priest; and in the evening, sitting in the lounge with the TV on, or in the pencil-biting silence of your sister's room, you tried to work out what it all meant.

'Jonny, what's an egotist?'

'Ummm?'

'An egotist. What's an egotist?'

'Someone who thinks he's the boss.'

'It says here, Toussaint L'Overture was an egotist.'

'Ummm.'

'Is that what it means?'

'Ummm.'

'You're not listening!'

'I am listening.'

'No you're not, you're writing.'

'No I'm not, I'm listening.'

'Tell me about Toussaint L'Overture.'

'He was a slave. Ex-slave. He freed he slaves…'

'Stupidy! I know that already. I mean, like what kind of man he was.'

'An egotist.'

'Besides that.'

'I don't know, man, Lydia. Ask Dad.'

'I asked him. He doesn't know.'

'What you want to know for?'

'We have an essay to write about Toussaint. Not less than five hundred words.'

'What's the book say?'

'Just that he was an egotist who freed the slaves.'

'Some book! I don't see how they could expect you to write an essay about somebody who's not even in the book, only barely.'

'Mr Borde says we must Use Our Resources. He's always saying that. It means, go check in the library. But the library's so far, man, oh gosh! I wish you'd hurry up and get your licence. Then if Daddy lent us the car we could go, I don't know, places. We could just get up and go to the beach.'

'But, Lydia you don't like the beach!'

'No, but you do. And I wouldn't mind. Not if we had the car.'

'He wouldn't lend it. Lydia…'

'What?'

'You ever thought of going abroad?'

'Not really. Why?'

'I been thinking about it. Listen – why don't we go abroad for a bit?'

'You mean, just like that? Go where?'

'Anywhere. Canada, Mexico, Spain. Let's just get up and go.'

'Man, Jonathan, you're a joker. You go.'

'Maybe I will.'

'You serious?'

'Yeh.'

'How would you live?'

'Work, nuh!'

'I don't know… it might be fun for a while.'

'You'd come?'

'Jonny, I couldn't!'

'Oh shit!'

'Look, I have thirty-eight dollars.'

'Keep it.'

'It's yours.'

'Just keep it!'

'Okay. But I won't spend it.'

'Spend it!'

Jonathan's depression deepened. He paused, sighted the betting booths off to his right, and adjusted his course accordingly. The drone of the crowd clarified itself as he walked, and as he walked, hands in his pockets, head down, kicking at the paper cups which appeared increasingly now, and which to his mournful mind seemed to have been placed there wilfully to obstruct his path, the weak shadow of a crow idled across the grass in front of him – and a mere minute later fell indiscriminately upon a gaggle of schoolgirls (among them Lydia of the dark cheek and grave gaze) riskily crossing a boulevard, coming, more or less, this way – an outworn narrative device, but let it pass. (My lead trumpeter has just caught my eye and, respectfully but firmly raising his arm and tapping the wristwatch thereon, reminded me that their bus leaves town in just over an hour from now.)

When he reached the spot where Rupert had disappeared all he could see was chaos. The queues to the betting booths had broken down, and it was a shapeless, heaving sea of people that, shouting and swaying, dollar bills held high, fought for a place at the tellers' windows. He could not see the windows in the corrugated wall, but he knew that they were small and finely grilled. In the airless gloom behind them the tellers would be sweating and irritable.

He stood on tiptoe at the edge of the crowd and tried to locate Rupert. Perhaps he's by the other one, he thought; and, glancing over his shoulder, he saw where the tote board said that Stargazer was odds-on to win. Next to him in the betting was Helen's Armour, and that was away down at sevens. The Wrag was at fifteen to one.

He did not wait any more. Folding the binoculars' case against his chest he picked a place at the edge of the crowd, dipped his right shoulder and pushed. Noise and the sour-sweet stench of bodies closed around him. Someone, driven back, stepped hard on his foot. An elbow was needling his ribs. Increasingly sharply he pushed them away. Soon he was flailing and grunting like everyone else.

A woman screamed suddenly, 'I stifling! Oh God!' and he turned his head; but just then there was a tidal surge from the crowd and Jonathan felt himself being carried along, still hugging the binoculars, until he came up hard against the flared, red-merinoed back of a man in a thin-brimmed straw hat with a handkerchief tied around his neck. The man thrust casually back with his elbow and Jonathan felt the pain. But he was nearly there now.

'Five on the nose,' the man boomed.

Jonathan could just hear the woman's reply. 'Number eleven?'

'What else, darlin'?'

Number eleven was Stargazer.

There was a pause while tickets and money changd hands, and then the man turned, and looked back over the sea of faces, and Jonathan saw him grin. Then, without warning, the man hurled himself into the crowd. There was an abortive rush and cries of 'Aieee!' as they tried to fall back for him; a woman (the same one?) screamed again; and Jonathan found himself at the grill with a big bosomed woman gazing patiently at him from the gloom of the cage.

'Two to win,' he began, raising one shoulder to fish flat-palmed in the pocket of his jeans.

'Eleven?'

'Eh?'

'Number eleven?'

'Number five.'

The woman's hand, which had been travelling towards the lever left poised over 'eleven', stopped. She was a handsome, big-boned woman with short, ironed hair. Her red blouse, open at the neck, was darkened by sweat in the usual places.

'Number five,' he repeated. 'Two to win.'

'Number-five-two-win; the woman echoed, enunciating each word separately. She let his money lie on the counter and pushed the tickets towards him with the backs of her fingernails, her face without expression. We, the people of this country. Jonathan took the tickets and turned.

He did not have to fight to get out. Beseeching and waving, the crowd closed around him, thrusting forward with frantic elbows, thrusting him behind them and out.

He pushed his shirttails back into his trousers, adjusted the strap of the binoculars on his shoulder and looked around. There was still no sight of Rupert, and Jonathan stopped next to buy peanuts from a man on a bicycle who had halted, one foot on the ground. He asked for two bags, changed his mind and said 'One.'

'Make up your mind,' the man grumbled. He took the twenty-five cent piece which the boy held out, handed over the bag, and made as if to ride off.

'Hey,' Jonathan said, 'what about the change?'

'Twenty-five cents a pack,' the man mumbled, and moved off.

'Hey!' Jonathan shouted.

The man rode faster. Jonathan stopped and watched him go, weaving crazily through the crowd, until he was out of sight.

A movement on the tote board caught his eye and he turned, in time to see the red ribbon above The Wrag's number rise past ten, and then eight, and still as he watched it was rising. It climbed all the way to four before it stopped, and Jonathan caught his breath in dismay. 'Sonuvabitch,' he muttered again – then heard, rising around him, a roar of astonishment, like a wave withdrawing over shingle, and then at once another roar (same wave returning) which was flat, derisive, enraged. Startled, he looked around – and was instantly, chillingly certain that whoever it was that had just sunk half a fortune on The Wrag was not there at the track, nor in the stands either, but that what he had just seen was an offcourse betting shop laying off some huge bet it had received, probably over the phone.

Who, though?

An image reared up suddenly in Jonathan's mind (so suddenly, Mr Trumpeter, that even I was unable to suppress it: though, mindful of your stricture, I did try!) He saw a lush, wood-panelled office with potted philodendrons in one corner and seascapes on three walls. The fourth wall was a great plateglass window with, beyond it, only sky, and before it a desk, and on that desk, he saw, were many small things littered around like the debris of a lunar landscape. There was a shiny black three-pen penholder with the flags of many nations rising in miniature from its base. There was a pink blotting pad, unstained. There were three telephones, two white, one red. The desk was of dark wood and glass-topped, and on it he saw also an intercom (matt grey), the back of a photograph frame edged in silver, a black, glass-perfect radio – and, among these things (and suddenly dwarfing them, as in a dream) he saw the white freckled backs of a pair of hands which lay on the edge of the desk. The radio was droning indecipherably on, and the hands lay immobile on the glass-topped desk and grew till they were huge, huge! Finally, one ham, or hand, moved. It moved to one of the white and pitifully shrunken phones. It picked up the receiver. With difficulty, it push-buttoned a number. Then, slowly, holding the receiver as a grubby-handed child holds a toothpick, as King Kong held the wriggling girl, as Jehovah (okay, okay, Mr Trumpeter), it rose out of sight. Our young friend saw all this, and thought awedly: But in truth things happen in this world you don't see! Yet he felt no fear, but thought again of that office in the sky and of those white immobile hands. Such a man does not throw away a fortune, he told himself (and here for the first time I feared for you, my Lydia, my vulnerable girl!) and felt a thrill of recognition, as if somehow he had been chosen – and then of gladness, that he was not alone any more. He no longer felt vaguely like a fugitive, and as he walked he looked clearly and with cold interest into the faces around him, so that they looked back at him with quick resentment; and I, in mild alarm, searched for you, and found you, inclining your head to hear something a girlfriend was telling you, your lips parted, your gaze grave, coming across the track by the seven-furlong post in flat shoes and a red-and-yellow sleeveless shift that nearly broke my heart there and then.

He found Rupert sitting, huddled as before, on the bank where they had been. Rupert did not look up as he sat, and Jonathan, glancing at his set, gloomy face, decided to keep his peace. He was feeling strong and free of care, inside, and he did not want to spoil it by arguing with Rupert. They sat in silence for a while. Finally, Rupert spoke.

'You bet on The Wrag?'
'Yeah.'
'How much?'
'Two dollars.'
'To win?'
'Yeah.'
'Good luck' – bitterly.
'I suppose you bet on Stargazer,' Jonathan asked, after a pause.
'Yeah.'
'How much?'
'Same as you.'
'Win or place?'

'Same as you.'

There was nothing to do now but wait. Jonathan looked at the blurred mountains and saw that the sky above them had lost its sheen and was now lustreless and very low. 'One rain coming,' he thought, and wondered whether it would reach before the race. It would be even worse for Rupert's horse if it came before.

'Tough on you,' he thought – and, looking around then, saw his sister strolling across the grass with a small group of schoolfriends, and waved. Unlike some boys he knew, he did not mind coming upon his sister unexpectedly in a public place, and he liked, in a general all-inclusive way, the girls with whom she moved. He liked the languid way they carried themselves, with their toes outward and their hips slung lazily forward, and he liked the quick, slightly circumspect smiles with which they greeted him, Lydia's brother; and how, if he made a joke with one, her eyes would crinkle and she would look at him archly before replying. Sometimes he was puzzled to think what such a gaily chattering flock of schoolgirls could have in common with his sister, who was quiet and had about her a responsible air; but he did not think about it often, and mostly he was cheered to have them around. So now he waved and watched to see what they would do, and when they waved back and changed direction to come towards where he and Rupert were sitting he was pleased and, forgetting, he elbowed Rupert to look.

'Hi, beautiful!' his sister said as she came up, letting fall a hand on his head to ruffle his hair.

In an altogether different voice – 'Hello, Rupert,' she said.

Jonathan heard it, and looked up, and saw, and: *Jesus I never knew!* he thought.

How could I not have known, he asked himself, suddenly scared, yet seeing very vividly the party a weekend ago and understanding many things all at once. Then he was frowning at the grass, unable to think anymore, and Lydia's hand was on his head. He heard Rupert say shortly, 'Hi', and felt the silence grow abruptly dense, and felt Lydia looking in puzzlement from him to the other. 'What's up with you two?' she asked, and he heard – what, by now, I knew he had to hear – the apprehension in your voice; and he knew the other girls were watching now too. Your

252

hand was no longer on his head, but he kept his eyes on the grass, not wanting to look up but waiting now for what was going to happen; and *To hell with them!* he thought suddenly. 'To hell with them!' he repeatedly inwardly, trying in this way to feel something and feeling nothing, but hearing Rupert say tonelessly 'He bet on The Wrag', and hearing, with great clarity, one of the girls gasp. They were looking at him differently now, and he was keeping his eyes on the grass and thinking 'All of you go to hell', and now he heard his sister speak.

'Leave him alone!' she said, so fiercely that Rupert got up suddenly; and Jonathan, looking up then, saw her as he had never seen her before and thought, 'But she's a *woman!*' and knew then, and might have wept for the knowledge, that he himself was still a boy.

Rupert spoke again. 'Sister, the race…' he began, in a voice heavy with doom, but she cut him short, crying, 'I don't give a damn about the race. Is a free country, he could bet on who he want. But look at my cross here today!'

'Lydia,' Jonathan began, but she turned on him too, saying, 'Oh shut up, Jonny, just shut up,' and he thought she was going to cry. She looked from one to the other and he thought again that she would cry, but she held herself in, and when she said only, '*Men!*' holding herself in and looking from one to the other, it was with the bitter knowledge and hard pain of a woman twice her age.

Then she turned on her heels, leaving them staring after her. The other girls, with here and there an uncertain glance back, turned to follow. They closed around you silently, like a flower.

Neither boy spoke for some moments. Then Jonathan said 'Whew' and glanced at Rupert and looked away again.

'Women,' Rupert mumbled. There was sullen admiration in his voice, and Jonathan felt, rising in him, the beginnings of laughter.

'So you and Lydia…?'

Rupert managed with a grin and a shrug to convey both embarrassment and nonchalance.

'But you young people eh?' Jonathan began to laugh shakily. 'To think I never knew!'

Rupert hung his head and grinned.

'Casanova Einstein!'

'Aw Jesus!' Rupert said.

They sat on the bank shelling and eating the peanuts. Rupert ate with concentration, decanting the shelled nuts into one hand and raising his cupped palm to his mouth as if to drink. After several minutes: 'Hey, guess what?' he said.

Jonathan tossed a nut into the air and moved his face about under it so that it fell into his mouth. 'What?'

'Hosang find a next way to get rich.'

'A-gain?'

Hosang was a boy at school they disliked.

'He invent a nonstick icetray.'

Jonathan snorted. 'You tell him about the new frigidaire from America with the automatic ice-maker attach?'

'Is that what I tell him. Exactly! I say, "Hosang, lemme ask you something. It already have fridge with automatic icemaker attach. You ever think of that?" I know because I see one already. Johnson father have one in the den.'

'I seen it, is a damn good den. So, what he say?'

Rupert shrugged. 'What he could say? I catch him there!'

'Hosang is a' ass.'

'Boy, you could say that again.'

There was a short silence. Jonathan squinted up at the skyline, where now the clouds lay heavily piled. It was getting very dark.

'One hell of a rain coming,' he said – and thought at once of Stargazer, and that the race was still to come. I wish to God it would rain like hell, he thought, let them cancel the damn race. But he did not think that would happen, and, looking for some other way out, he wondered next if he might indeed be wrong and Stargazer hang on to win. Then it came back to him, the mile race Stargazer had won, and he felt sure he wasn't wrong.

He remembered that race well. Morales had ridden cleverly and won by a length, but Jonathan had only just bought the binoculars, and he had kept them trained on the big chestnut the whole way, even after they had passed the post, and he had seen, what the tipsters had not, or not wished to, how the horse's ears had gone back in the last strides, and how quickly he had come to a stop, shaking his head and changing down into a loose-jointed, slowing-up trot, while the chasing pack swarmed around and past him; and Jonathan had realised with a thrill of surprise that Stargazer had been dead on his feet.

If only, he thought, old man Dixon had not been so wilful. If only, for the creole's first race among the imported horses, he had sent him in the sprint.

Jonathan could see it: the long bunched driving run up the backstretch with Stargazer outsprinting the best of them; Stargazer laying out on the corner, clear; Stargazer stretching forward his great golden neck and pounding down the homestretch rail... They would have come at him in the straight, to be sure, especially a strong brute like The Wrecker, and probably there would have been Andromeda too, finishing fast and wide under the stands; but Stargazer would have held them, he was certain of it, he would have hit the straight so full of running, and there would have been the roar of the crowd and he would have been one of them, leaping in the air and shouting, like everyone else... Jonathan saw it all, as if it were really happening, saw it from start to finish; and when it was over he found himself grieving for the race that would not be run, and cursing the greed and stupidity of old man Dixon that he should send his great horse out to meet defeat for the first time like this.

'Listen,' he said to Rupert, 'they making a mistake, you know.'

'Who?'

'The Stargazer people.'

Rupert grew wary. 'How come?'

'They shoulda send him in the sprint. He'd a'bound to win that.'

Rupert looked as though any moment he might frown.

'What I don't understand,' persisted Jonathan, 'is why is so important. I mean, okay, so he's a local horse, and it would be nice if he won. But why it should be a matter of life and death – that is what I don't understand.'

'Sometimes,' Rupert muttered, 'I think you don't understand anything.'

'Listen man,' Rupert went on, turning to look squarely at the other boy. 'You don't see what happening here today? You don't see how this horse bring everybody together? Black, white, rich, poor, everybody unite in this horse. When last you see this place like that, everybody laughing and talking with everybody else?'

'Don't know,' admitted Jonathan.

'Not since Independence. Not since Independence! You don't see is not just a race? Everybody feeling this thing! Look around. Everybody have their money on the creole to win. Everybody excepting you.'

'Me and somebody else,' said Jonathan. And he told Rupert about the odds shortening like that on The Wrag and about the image that had come into his mind.

Rupert listened attentively and, when he had finished, nodded.

'Exactly. Exactly! Some white man. Some Yankee executive, come down to bleed the people. You see it yourself. Man, Jonathan, I don't know. Sometimes I just wonder: how you could gang up with a man like that?'

'Is not ganging up.'

'Old man, people have to back up their own! You don't see it?'

'People have to know what they know.'

'Oh shit! You always know what you know. You is God.'

'Well,' said Jonathan surlily, 'This good united feeling you say everybody feeling. I only hope they still feeling it after the race. After Stargazer lose.'

It was happening and he did not want it to happen. A fear, greater, it seemed, than any the occasion could have warranted, was closing on him, and he was afraid, afraid. He said, 'I wonder where they are,' meaning you, Lydia, meaning: I wish you were here; if you were here everything would be okay.

'Probably over by the stands,' Rupert said, sullen, but accepting the offer. He stood up, peering, and Jonathan thought he had seen her and was going to wave. But when Rupert spoke it was only to say, in a voice to which all the deadness had returned: 'The horses out.'

Now the start of a race was something Jonathan tried never to watch. The shattering wail of the bell, the instantly answering roar of the crowd, as if it were some monstrous animal which the bell, a spear, had found out, as the startled horses leapt from their stalls – these were things he shied away from. He too would be pierced by the bell if he watched; he too would want to cry out as in pain.

Nor, he concluded, was there any sense in trying to pick them up too early. They would break from the ten-furlong gates, he knew, only to disappear almost at once into the corridor between the stands and the homestretch crowd, and there would be the baulked, heartbeating seconds with only the caps of the jockeys going along above the crowd as behind a hedge and flickering in and out behind the betting booths and the tote board before they poured into sight at the far end and ran down, in clear view, to the seven-furlong pole and the long banked turn at the bottom end of the course. So now he raised the binoculars and found that marker and worked the cogs to bring it into clearest focus – and when the red light began to flash, when the bell wailed and the crowd answered, when Rupert said softly, once, 'O God!' and a man nearby began immediately to leap in the air and shout 'The Gazer! The Gazer!' in a voice which seemed to start below his collarbone and to rattle with saliva as it erupted, Jonathan raised the binoculars and fixed them on the crowd-free place near the seven-furlong pole and tried to keep his hands from shaking.

They were a long time in coming. The roar of the stands' crowd reached crescendo, passed, and he thought 'They coming now', then, 'Now!' and still they did not appear. Then they came, one horse by itself and then the rest all at once, and he swung the binoculars to find the leading horse again and it was in truth the red and black of Stargazer and he was two lengths clear.

'Who?' demanded Rupert, 'Who?' And when he said, 'Stargazer,' Rupert shouted once, 'The creole!' before demanding 'Who next? Who next?' Jonathan did not answer at once. He was raking the field for the green and gold of The Wrag and not finding him. Then he saw him, lying seventh or eighth on the rails, and Jonathan kept the binoculars on him for several strides until he was sure that Maraj was doing nothing, just crouching over the horse's neck with his hands still, and that The Wrag was neither dawdling nor pulling but running strongly and steadily in

257

his place, and then, answering Rupert, he said, 'Oleander,' and eased the binoculars to the right to find Stargazer again.

'How he look?' asked Rupert, suddenly anxious.

'Okay. He look okay.'

They were streaming around the bottom turn now to come up into the backstretch and Stargazer had gone three lengths clear. He's going too fast, Jonathan thought, but he did not say it, only wondered whether this was old man Dixon's idea of tactics or whether it was just that Morales couldn't hold him, because it was bloody stupid tactics if it was. Maybe he would rest him going up the hill, but it was still bloody stupid – except that Oleander was already being broken, slipping back through the field, and now Great Vulcan had come up and was second. The horses swung into the backstretch, seeming to concertina as they came, and Rupert was shouting again, 'Come on, Stargazer!' and now Jonathan said it.

'He's going too fast.'

'Bullshit!'

'Watch and see.'

'*You* watch and see!'

They were coming up the long slope now, and even with them heading straight for you you could tell Stargazer was in front and running all by himself. In the binoculars he was very near, and Jonathan was struck by a kind of light, a kind of energy that played off him as he raced, and he thought, *But in truth that is some horse!* He could see Morales sitting high and looking grim and pinch-faced behind his goggles, and Jonathan felt a knot starting in his throat and his eyes were beginning to swim. The binoculars were dragging his eyes out and he lowered them against his chest and watched the race coming, the horses spread out across the track but with the chestnut drumming strictly along in front. He could see the depth of his chest now, and the exultation in his swift earth-pounding stride and in the way the horse kept swinging its head from side to side against the restraining of the reins, as if seeking a way to break free of them and into the pure joy of running, and Jonathan felt his insides turn over, and he whispered, 'Christ, but he's beautiful!'

But travelling too fast: the thought came slamming back, as from some iron arctic in his mind, and a great weight of doom passed over him and left him trembling slightly with anger and with fear. 'Such a horse,' he thought angrily, 'should not be doomed. Everything's wrong in this world.' But then, as the horses stormed up to where he stood, as the thunder of their hooves rose up to overwhelm the returning cries of the spectators, the beauty and the doom seemed to fall together within him and mix, his body blazed, the earth shook terribly under his feet, and they were gone, going away, already gone, leaving falling at his feet a brief shower of sods, the lone blast of a trumpet note hanging on the air, a jockey's desolate, cautionary cry, and the tail of the last horse swishing helplessly.

Someone, far off, then nearer, was screaming, over and over, one word he could not grasp.

'Stargazer!' Rupert screamed, 'Stargazer!' He ran stiff-legged a few paces after the receding horses; stopped; ran back; turned. There was a rigid, convulsed quality about all he did and Jonathan, watching him, incomprehension giving way to recognition, came slowly, dismayingly back to himself and looked around.

The crowd had entered ecstasy. Men, their heads back, fists held to the sky, stood rigid as lightning conductors, but roaring; women grabbed each other and screamed; and one man (whom Jonathan recognised as the man who had started bawling 'The Gazer!' from the word go) now abandoned his place on the backstretch rail and ran thundering across the field towards the winning pole, stopping suddenly to peer like a startled animal over at the hurrying horses and to bellow once 'The Gazer!' before dashing off again.

Jonathan remembered the horses. Reluctantly he raised the binoculars. A slow dread was staining through him and he did not want to look at them. But something made him look.

They were streaming around the home turn now and the creole was still three lengths clear. Behind him, Jonathan knew, the jockeys would be shouting and jostling. Those who felt they had a winning chance would be hustling to get into positions to challenge; some, boxed in, would be pleading to be let through. Some, sensing their mounts had had enough, would pull out and drop back, as Great Vulcan was doing now; others, uncertain of their chances, would be sitting stubbornly in their places, riding hard and waiting to see what the homestretch would bring. Jonathan found Stargazer in the glasses and saw that he was running on the bit still, and, startled, thought: *Jesus, suppose...!*

Then, abruptly, as he watched, something gave, some rhythm, some harmony vanished, and there was no longer the effortless onward-sweeping of the horse, no longer the great neck motionlessly sailing, but Stargazer's head was going up and down, Morales' hands were scything on his neck, and the horses were bunching behind him to swing for home. And Jonathan, with the returning sorrow of a man who has laughed himself empty, steadied the binoculars on the chasing pack and waited, knowing that what would happen next would come from there.

They were in the straight now and he saw that The Wrag was through on the rails and going up to close with the leader. Helen's Armour was finding nothing, he could tell, and something in pastel colours, its jockey's whip hand flailing, was coming up fast on the outside, going past horse after horse but with a lot of ground to make up. Jonathan watched only long enough to see The Wrag go clear, and to make sure the pastel-coloured jockey had left it too late, and then he lowered his binoculars. They would be going into the crowd soon, and besides, he would not need them for the rest. You did not need binoculars to tell who that far, toylike figure of a horse was, sinking, as you watched, so quickly through the field, no longer second, nor third, fourth now, no longer fourth, fifth, sixth, out of it; nor to see the pastel colours go a clear second. Nor did you need binoculars to see your friend, Lydia's boyfriend, standing dreamlike with his hands by his sides, slowly opening and closing his fists. A man might curse and throw his tickets away, but you did not need binoculars for that, nor to know that all the shouting had ended, and that people were standing numbly in their places.

Nor to watch Rupert's hands.

Jonathan looked at his friend's hands, obliviously, rhythmically clenching and unclenching, and thought suddenly of those other, white hands, lying immobile on the desk in the sky, and he felt a great surge of pity for the hands before him here, seeing how helpless, how childlike they seemed. Watching them, he forgot everything else. Then Rupert turned and looked at him and he knew that the race was over, and that it was time to speak.

'Boy!' he said, with fraudulent heartiness, 'You was right. That was some horse!'

Rupert looked at him dully.

'They break him,' went on Jonathan, 'but he take a good few of them with him. You saw…' and now he was talking and could not stop himself '…you saw how he break Oleander? Oleander break like a glass bowl. Four furlongs, and he kill off Oleander. Even Great Vulcan, stayer of stayers…' He stopped. Rupert was looking at him with incomprehension.

'Listen,' Jonathan said earnestly, 'forget the finish. He was the best horse in the backstretch. He was the *only* horse.'

'He lost, though.'

'Forget that. FORGET THAT! If you had seen him in the backstretch…'

'I saw him. He was in front.'

'I mean, if you had seen what I saw…'

Abruptly the rain began: big separate drops that stung your face or hissed into the hard earth.

'I wanted him to win,' Jonathan said. 'I wouldn't lie, I wanted him to win.'

The rain began coming down in earnest, and Rupert seemed to come awake with a start and recognise him. 'Yeah?' he demanded harshly, 'I didn't know that. I thought you bet on The Wrag!'

It was true. Jonathan remembered. He had been right all along. Two to win, number five. The tickets nestled in his jeans like a secret diploma of solitary comprehension. He felt a twist of pride, and an immense, liberating self-assurance. He was a man; he knew what he knew. There was nothing he had to fear.

'Traitor!' groaned Rupert. 'Traitor!'

And now it began to happen.

With the rain strengthening upon them, and with people everywhere drifting off, still dazed, to stand to silent attention under the trees; with the tickets snug in his jeans' pocket, and with Rupert's grief-and-rage-contorted face bulbing out of the rain at him, the things that had started to happen to him once before, and had so frightened him then that he had invoked the saving memory of you, Lydia, began now to rise in him again, only this time he thought: Let it come.

Happen nuh, he thought, addressing the thing still hesitant in him, unafraid now and strong in his new-found freedom. And a glass wall thudded down between him and Rupert, and Rupert turned on the instant into a gross and warted insect butting hopelessly against the glass wall.

Jonathan shrugged.

'You are nothing,' he said, a trifle sadly, addressing the hopelessly butting creature that had been Rupert. 'You never were.' And slipping the binoculars beneath his shirt, and holding them there, he turned and began to walk, and then, crouched over the binoculars, to jog towards the shelter of a spreading samaan tree. His back was to the creature that had been Rupert, and he did not see the effect of his last remark. But I, horrified, saw. The creature that had been Rupert began to fade. It paled; it pulsed; after each pulse it was more translucent. The rusted roof of a hillside shanty swam into sight through its head; visible now through its torso, coming and going between pulses, a naked boy, armed with a stick, rolled a bicycle rim through the rain. Then everything vanished – creature, shanty and boy – leaving only, for a moment longer, the impress of strange footprints in the grass; and now, with one motion, a fistful of flung raindrops obliterated these. I expect you're right, Mr Trumpeter. (He says, boys will be boys.)

Jonathan reached the crowded shelter of the tree, and turned. The rain was lacing down so that he could hardly see into it. In the grey light everything looked insubstantial. But he did not care. It was good to be standing there, among, yet separate from, these others, in the shelter of the tree. A raindrop fell on his cheek; he licked it away.

And then there was a shuffling movement among the people standing behind him, and you pushed your way through and took his arm. 'Hi,' you said, and you were smiling, and your forehead and the slope of your shift and your dark dimpled shoulders were wet: 'What a rain!' Then, peering over his shoulder: 'Where's Rupert?'

Jonathan looked startled. He had forgotten Rupert. He had assumed, he supposed, that the creature had merely grown weary of butting against the glass and had wandered off somewhere to sit and rub its forelegs together in the rain. He waved his hand vaguely at the insubstantial fields. 'Out there somewhere,' he said.

'You mean, out there by himself in the rain?'

Jonathan shrugged. There was a swirl of movement at his side, and, before either he or I could prevent you you had gone, running out into the open, calling 'Rupert! Rupert!' as you ran. Soon you too had become insubstantial, your cries obliterated by the rain.

Jonathan swore. He felt a quick hurt at having been abandoned, but it passed. He was feeling alive and strong, standing among the falling roots of the tree, and he told himself that no harm would come to you in the rain. In a little while he forgot you, and began to think instead of Stargazer.

He had been gifted, he knew, with seeing the great creole as no one else present had; and so, when he came to write it down in the red notebook he would have to write it strangely and well. It would have to be, he thought, like a painting with music, a great golden horse against the night sky – and here, seeing the danger he was in, I acted. Lydia, I did try! I elbowed my way through to where he stood; I cupped my mouth and whispered hoarsely, deep into his ear: Remember what you saw! Remember this horse had this defeat in him always, from the very first time they sent him out to run. Remember that, and remember how he carried himself, and won nine races first; and then set out to like this again today. So if you set him there against the night sky you will have to make him very small, and the darkness very big. Make him golden, if you like, and shining – the only light, the only life, besides the darkness. Yes, yes. But tiny! And make the darkness huge, and make the music – for God's sake let me help you, I have musicians here! – the music should be small and whimsical. Lighthearted but with an edge of sadness to it. An edge of silence.

He would not listen. Lydia, *he would not listen!*

So he had time only to project the image of a great golden horse, galloping to martial music ruinously over the roofs of men, scattering light through the nightworld, on a beautiful, swift, apocalyptic run – and then he vanished! I say 'vanished'. He did not fade; he winked out, as though plucked hellward by a lightning-fast hand; and the man who had been standing next to him beneath the tree, a mulatto with a nerve-tic at the corner of his mouth, was mildly surprised to find himself with elbowroom on one side, and, shuffling six inches to his left, folded his arms, planted his feet, and stared in vacancy at the rainswept fields.

The trumpeters have gone. I stood and watched them leave. In silence they packed their burnished instruments; in silence they filed out. From the dark doorway their leader, pausing, threw me an evil look; but that was all. No words passed between us. I accepted the reproach of his silence. There had been a moment or two, earlier on, when it seemed... but by and large I had wasted his time. Perhaps next time...

But you, my Lydia! You who have been the watermark in these otherwise counterfeit pages. You in whose honour – let me say it – I had, at no small cost in effort and time, assembled such a wealth of talent. I believed – let me be explicit – I believed that from the defeat of this horse your Rupert would have learned (and it is the only lesson I have to teach) to cherish the moment and ignore the consequence, since we remain the children of darkness. I dreamed (and I have the right to dream) that, upon such cherishing, the shell of history would have shattered, and your Rupert would have stepped free, unsteadily and perkily as a newborn ruffled chick. I underrated (oh yes, very badly) the power of the Cyclops, Ego; I underrated the fear of the very young, the self-laceration of hatred; I could not save him. It was beyond my knowledge even to know where to begin.

But, even then. Even then I never doubted your brother. Not for a moment! I knew the depth of his knowledge, I understood his melancholy strength. That, wounded, he would think to use his knowledge, his strength, to body forth an image of vengeance, this was something that never crossed my mind; not until it was too late. My trumpeters were waiting in the wings. They were ready to play for you, to herald you. You, escorted into the shining future by your brother and your lover. Given by one to the other.

My poor Lydia, they are gone; they were nothing. Distractions of the sun. Spectres of the insomniac mind.

But you, grave Lydia! Vanished, calling into the rain, child of hyacinths and tears, history's orphan! What shall I do with you, who now will speak for you, twice betrayed girl?

LANDSCAPE WITH HERON

1

The strange thing, it seemed to him when he emerged from the museum, was that nothing appeared to have changed. The park, which had been swept clean of loiterers by rain when he arrived, was silent and empty still; the tyres of passing cars still hissed on the asphalt; and the night seemed neither blacker nor more festive with stars. (There was, it should be added, a new moon, but it had been punctually palmed by a western samaan and he missed it both going in and coming out.)

At the time, he'd had the sensation that everything had paused, before sighingly resuming again. But already he couldn't be sure. If it had, it had been momentary, a mere hesitation, like a bowler stutter-stepping on his way in to bowl. (He liked cricket.) *So this is the one*, he'd thought, standing beside her; thinking it with no especial excitement or elation; with, if anything, a small click of relief. And he later told himself the surprising thing had been that he'd been so unsurprised. He was forty-four and had been waiting, without knowing he was waiting, for the world to discover her to him. For the world to desist at last from its swarming fuzziness, and open pristine petals and yield her up to him.

'So this is the one,' he thought again (or it may merely have been the backwash of the first thought). And in the flatly-lit, white, high-ceilinged room, strollers among the paintings, if they had looked at him at that point – and not at the dark slim girl beside him – might have thought his expression gloomy. He had been habituated to the fuzziness. However momentarily, we all of us haplessly mourn whatever passes.

He had wandered into the exhibition by accident, having set out from home to take in a movie at the cinema across the street.

But on arrival he'd discovered that the show – an Irish romance, replete (he confidently expected) with hazy vistas, sheer cliffs, and sheep on moors – wasn't on, after all (he'd scanned Coming Attractions by mistake). Under the 'Now Showing' sign in the lobby, a flagrant-hued poster depicted a barebacked, beardless Chinese youth vehemently kicking a dismayed mandarin in the face. He had turned away in disappointment, descended the steps… and then noticed, across the wet-black street, lights among trees, and the museum gate open…

Even then he should have been politely turned away: opening night was By Invitation Only. But the feckless custodian of the gate (a ravishing, tall, red-skinned A-level student, the curator's stepdaughter) was at that moment being thoroughly, if pleasantly, disquieted by the ferocious blandishments of an unshaven young clerk from the French Embassy, and she didn't notice him. And so, unchallenged, he wandered in. By such defaults are worlds made and unmade.

She was standing, a slim dark figure in a white high-necked sleeveless shift, in front of a medium-sized pastoral, a programme lightly clasped before her loins. He thought her in her mid-twenties (she was thirty-four) and registered with unconscious pleasure her flat white shoes amid the strapped and stilettoed ebony all around. She was standing with heels together and toes apart. The backs of her calves were round.

Approaching the painting himself, he noted automatically how the skin gleamed on the small bone at the base of her neck, and saw next that the second button there was undone. And he half-lifted his hands to fasten it: a gesture so unlike him, yet so instinctive, so *natural*, that, really, he should have had at least an inkling at that point.

But he didn't. He was forty-four and a bachelor, and vaguely content with his life; and he didn't know that he had been waiting. And so he took up a position at her shoulder, standing closer than he might have, had she been anyone else (but he didn't realise that either), and considered the scene she was considering. Pebbly stream, glistening rocks, soughing bamboo, misty olive mountain in the background. (He would remember that painting vividly for the rest of his life.)

Presently – aware of him, not turning her gaze – 'Can you see the heron?' she murmured.

So this is the one.

Abruptly he coughed; cleared his throat.

'What heron?'

'There's supposed to be a heron. Look.'

She held the programme up, half-turning towards him with the little movement by which he would forever remember her: swift, slight, sure. It had been so *natural*, that little half-turn, he would tell himself, recalling it, time and again, long afterwards. And the wonder of her, which he'd felt no need of in her presence, would come to him then in her stead.

'It's called "Landscape with Heron". But I don't see any heron, do you?'

Obediently, he looked – and saw the heron. Or rather, he saw – quite clearly – the shadow of great, uplifted wings (a trick of the artist's dexterity, of his deployment of light and shade) spanning the entire painting, like an ethereal negative superimposed upon a print of Earth. And he was about to point it out to her when she said in a different voice, 'Oh, hi, Jenny!' to someone on the other side of her, and reflexively moved in that direction.

Going away, she glanced back at him, smiling apology, and for the first and only time he saw her eyes. They were brown but flecked with yellow, like a cat's.

Then she was gone.

Left alone, he thought to himself: 'Yes, like a cat's' – thinking this with mysterious satisfaction, as if (though this was quite untrue) he'd just won some ancient, small bet with himself. And again the image of her undone button came into his mind; and again he was moved to go in search of her to button it. But that, he realised for the second time in two minutes, would almost certainly be construed as inappropriate. And so he stood there, having at forty-four, with no warning, received his life, and fell meditatively to considering the painting again.

'Yes, quite definitely, wings,' he said to himself gravely, aloud – so that a foreign couple standing nearby (the young woman, a straggly blonde with unshaven armpits, palpably braless in a jersey halter top which nonetheless managed to scant both modesty and allure) glanced at him oddly. And this time, bestirring himself, he went in search of her: to bring her back, to show her the heron.

When, quite some time later, he concluded that she must have left, the thought left him nonplussed, yet by no means worried. It didn't occur to him that he might never see her again. Just as the realness and rightness of her had been, in him, too deep for surprise, so now they were deep beyond anxiety. If she had gone, he would find her tomorrow. Or the next day. Or the next. That, he simply, absolutely assumed. For the remainder of his life – long after he could no longer summon up her face but only the texture and tone of her, so to speak – he would recall with perfect clarity her murmurous voice as she inquired of him – casually, intimately, *naturally* – 'Can you see the heron?'

Before leaving the museum himself, he detoured over to the painting once more, to bend and scrutinise – with some difficulty: he owned a pair of bifocals but loathed and never wore them – the signature of the artist. This he did as a precaution, it having occurred to him that, by the time he got around to showing her the wings, the exhibition might be over and he might have to track the painting down.

Out on the pavement, he registered with a small twinge of surprise that the world appeared not to have changed. He located his car (after considerable searching: it had been parked, by an impostor bearing his name, quite a long way away, against the prison wall of a well-known girls' school where the pupils all wore ties) and drove home, his tyres hissing on the road, and then at a certain point ceasing to hiss. In his driveway he fended off as usual the berserk happiness of the bounding creature, let himself in – and saw at once that it wouldn't do. That the curtain-less, carpet-less rooms he had for so many years been content to call home would be hideously cold and bare to her gaze.

'I'll have to fix that,' he thought; and he made a mental note next day to ask Marion at the Ministry for help in dealing with the esoteric matter.

After that, for quite some time, he went from room to room, registering through her eyes the commodious sprawl of things and seeing it for the first time as chaos. He actually began what he conceived of as tidying up – putting things rather aimlessly in cupboards – before the thought occurred to him (fully formed, in words): 'She'll know what she wants where.'

Whereupon (it was now nearly midnight) he retired to bed, and immediately fell into what felt afterwards to him like the deepest dreamless sleep of his life…

2

He didn't find her, of course. He hadn't even inquired her name. You might think that Trinidad is such a small place – but no. He never saw her again.

For three days, he busied himself with brightening and softening his cheerless abode (not that it seemed cheerless to him), doing this with the help of a deeply flushed, but by the third day inexplicably grief-stricken, Marion. ('Moody Marion,' he said to himself, not unfondly, and left it at that.) After that, he stopped; thought; and, next morning, made his way back to the museum. There he introduced himself to the curator, and announced that he had come to find a certain young woman.

The curator, a lanky ingenue, looked at him oddly.

'I don't know her name,' he told her. 'But she had on a white dress; one button was undone. She would have been twenty-five, twenty-six. About my colour, a little darker. Slim. She was looking at the painting called "Landscape with Heron" at one point.'

Hard as it may be to credit, he said all this with an air of complacent certitude.

The curator said: 'I have no idea who you're talking about.'

'She knew somebody called Jenny,' he said, remembering.

The curator waited.

'Can you check your guest list for a Jenny?'

The curator stiffened. 'I'm sorry. We can't do that.'

There was a pause.

'I have to find her,' he said bewilderedly. (He hadn't anticipated this hiatus.)

The curator said, pronouncing each word distinctly, as though on the verge of rage: 'I'm sorry. I wish you the very best of luck in finding this – person. But there's nothing I can do to help you. Now…'

Leaving her office, he returned on the off-chance to the gallery, but of course she wasn't there. A tall, middle-aged white man in a grey suit, arms folded, stood with his back to some sort of fabulous turgidity, receiving the animated conversation of a pretty, dark-skinned – not her. A bickering wave of small school-boys (blue shirts, khaki short pants) surged from room to room, pursued by a scolding, bespectacled Not-her. His feet carried him over to stand before the painting, on the spot where he had stood four nights before. She failed to materialise by his side (as he'd half-expected her to), and for a moment he knew himself, with utter lucidity, to be alone. But then he saw that the shadow of the heron lay over the misty mountain and the bright stream still. He left the museum shaking his head, but undismayed.

After that, for weeks, then months – which in turn lengthened into years – he became a searcher: a looker into the faces of female passers-by, everywhere he went. In this way he became in mid-life a connoisseur of women's faces. They filled up his memory, disconnected, inutile.

And yet, in time, a strange thing happened. The habit of looking became ingrained in him. And – even stranger – in time this habit insensibly widened, until it included everything around him. A landscape, a caterpillar, a little boy playing: they were vivid to him now as they had not been before. The variegated richness of the world, unsought, came to him. He became enamoured of the vivacity in things.

A hundred times, a thousand times, in that first year he saw her – only to discover (often at the end of a lumbering, short trot) that it was not she, after all. But the startled look on the faces of the women he thus accosted, he saw impersonally, made them beautiful. And, as for the tight little smiles, tense or unpleasant or, occasionally, wistful, with which they acknowledged his mumbled, 'Sorry. I thought – ': well, he hardly noticed those.

His life until then had been unremarkable; and so, outwardly, it continued. Only, now there was this richness all around him. And now, by and by, his dreams, too, changed.

There is a species of nightmare in which virtually nothing

happens yet the dreamer is filled with such insupportable horror that he knows (and it's a last, lung-bursting, lunging thing) that he must hurl himself awake or he will die. Likewise, there are dreams in which nothing much happens, yet the dreamer is suffused by such sweetness, such loveliness, such *bliss*, that it bears him up irresistibly into consciousness – there, perhaps, like Caliban to cry to sleep once more.

Such dreams are the closest mortal men and women come on earth to the horror of hell or the radiance of heaven. They occur when, in the dreamer, a limpidly stirring soul or a brimming heart is turned back upon itself by a defaulting mind – so that presentiment is denied its parable, emotion its efflorescence in dream-action – until, excruciatingly intensified, yet unbearably baulked, it is forced to erupt *as itself*.

Such dreams now came to him in his sleep, alternately to destroy and anoint him. (His life, after all, had been given its theme, yet denied that theme's expression in plot.) One dream, in particular, now began recurring. It returned to him, at irregular intervals, perhaps half-a-dozen times during the remainder of his life.

It comprised nothing but a silver, shining wall, which progressively reared above him, turning concave and intensifying in radiance, until it was an impossible and blinding concavity, towering above him, beginning to topple...

...at which point he would awake with the absolute knowledge that she was sleeping beside him (half on her stomach, one knee drawn up: in the darkness he could visualise quite clearly her glossy shoulder and silver, silken haunch) – so much so that he would lie there in stupefied bliss, staring up at the indistinct ceiling, for an indefinite interlude before realising...

Sometimes, after such dreams, lying awake in the dark, he would see again with perfect lucidity the untrammelled solitude of his life. Yet next morning he would be buoyed up by a great sense of wellbeing, and he would rise and go about his business in the world as though he were a whole man, whole and free, knowing afresh that She was in the world, and that that meant the world was good.

One day, somewhere around his fifty-fifth year, he stopped

what he was doing and faced squarely the thought that he would probably never see her again. By now it hardly mattered: she was with and in him all the time. Only, he would have liked her to have known it.

'Ah, you,' he said aloud, with infinite tenderness and regret. And he waited a little longer, as though listening.

Then he shook his head, and resumed what he had been doing.

So, as he grew older, he grew gentler. He laughed less, and smiled more. Those who previously had secretly thought him a nonentity – acquaintances and fellow-workers, mainly, for he had few friends – now saw him as a smiling nonentity. He knew, and didn't mind. All around him as he aged was her silent gift to him: the variety and vivacity in things.

He died unpunctually, though not shockingly so, of prostate cancer, at sixty-four. And though I will not affirm that his issueless life was any less than yours or mine, it seems to me a matter for irrefrangible anger that he died not knowing so many things.

He never learnt her name: it was Catherine; Catherine Marshall, nee Gomez. Her friends called her Cathy, her husband – a hard-drinking, womanising, hearty man – her husband, in the good times, called her Kate.

He never knew that when they met she had already borne her children: three sons, each a year apart. The eldest later astonished them by winning a scholarship. The others she took with her when – finally abandoned by her husband for a young, wasp-waisted Indian thing from the office – she migrated to live with her sister in New Jersey.

One morning, while he was sitting watching a test match in the Oval, an awesome premonition overcame him – so suddenly and so strongly, like a beating of great wings, that he half-turned to look up fearfully. He never knew that he'd turned the wrong way, and that for several moments she had been standing in the aisle just a few rows behind his other shoulder, pointing him out to a female companion, saying, 'You see that man? I have a feeling I know him from somewhere' – then falling pensively to sipping her coke and glancing back as she followed her friend along the aisle and down the steps.

One Sunday afternoon towards the end of his life, while he was sitting, reading, in the whispering shade off to one side of the pebbled garden path, he distinctly heard a voice say, *Can you see the heron?* – and, lifting his head, became aware of a distant drone. The jet on its approach passed so low overhead that its shadow fled across his house and lawn. Yet, as he staggered to his feet, cringing like Saul on the road to Damascus and blocking his ears against the blast that exploded in them, it never occurred to him that it was She that had flickered across his face, returning home for the wedding of her son.

I cannot say whether, as he lay dying, the blinding concavity returned for him. But I am moved to futile anger to think that, in all those years, he – this mild-mannered, time-sunken man – never once made bold to inquire of it its name; which was Happiness.

PART II

THE NAME OF HAPPINESS

1

The light founders. Rain puckers the ocean.
I see a small town, found, then forgotten,
rusting in silence by a sea's edge
where liners no longer come.

Those lines, and the verses quoted below, are from the writer's 'Port Antonio poems'. They were written in the late '60s and early '70s, when to begin with, as a kid at Mona, I discovered and fell in love with that somnolent town, safely south of the real tourist belt on the north coast whither, even then, its small handful of hoteliers looked wistfully.

Portland is the rainiest parish in Jamaica, and Port Antonio, broad-leavedly lush and mountainous, was already then a decaying town (for the price of bananas was down), sustained mainly by 'produce' agriculture, by, nonetheless, its banana exports – and by the hope of a tourist trade that kept on never quite materialising. With its two horseshoe bays (one housing the port) and its narrow alleys (straight and crowded on both sides of the road on the flat, by old-fashioned two-storey commercial buildings, then winding away from them up into the wet, populated and cultivated hills) it reminded me of St George's, Grenada: a rainier, somberer, more 'powerful' St George's, its people less garrulous, more fatalistic, its air sleepier, its hinterland rising in fold after fold to the cloud-obscured peak of the Blue Mountains.

I arrived there by train the first time, what everybody called The Diesel; rented a room for almost nothing in an old, wooden, two-storey guest house (high ceilings, sash windows, big rooms) on the promontory overlooking Navy Island, took what I now

277

remember as 'one look around me' (though from other evidence I know this to be a drastically foreshortened backward view) and fell in love with the town.

Or rather, I fell in love with Her. Which, as Sam Selvon ('My Girl and the City') knew, is the same thing.

Call her —.

But no. We shall not call her anything. Not blaspheme with a feckless alias she who became (at once!) his most secret name for happiness; then (almost at once) for loss; and then, gradually, as the years passed – for in time he discovered that the memory of her (backlit by her Port Antonio, as it were) had sunk deep into the heart of his poems, to remain for all time ineradicable there – his most elate and secret name for happiness again.

Where? When?

Oh, one day, a Sunday, a Saturday, more than thirty years ago...

Blare noon. He looked up, squinting even through gold-rimmed shades, from the blinding white beach of Boston Bay (since tragically destroyed by Hurricane Gilbert) and saw –there is no other phrase – 'the most beautiful girl in the world', standing with some guys (her brother and her brother's friends, it turned out) perhaps thirty yards away.

Dark chocolate gloss of the dougla; white bikini; curves still voluptuous with baby fat. Great matt-black lion's mane, all but shrouding her face. (She never shook it back, tossing her head in the sea wind; she drew it away from her eye with four fingers, like a curtain, and looked out.)

People! He was suddenly aware the beach was full of people. He rose and threaded his way towards her, taking a long time, for even though his throat felt parched, he was shy, and moved towards her only because he had to. Uncertainly, hesitating often and pretending to be otherwise absorbed (how? with what?) he closed the gap between them by indirection.

Even so, he knew (though their eyes never met) the moment when she saw him, and knew he was coming...

You came to me here, bewildered girl,
your body warm and heavy with sleep.

278

Your eyes were calamitous waters.
How grave were your admonitions!

Her father was a Jamaican Indian: a courtly, soft-spoken gentleman. Her mother was the kind of creole-of-the-islands it's easy to love: retiring yet animated, perennially cheerful. (For years he would remember her as bringing to the polished mahogany dining table some steaming dish for Sunday lunch, holding it with two dish towels, saying softly, cheerfully, to all and sundry, 'Come'....)

They lived, she and her brother and their parents, off to one side of the town, in a sprawling old plantation-style house (deep, covered verandahs on three sides, double doors opening onto it from the shady living room) on a large knoll above the sea. Flowerbeds, royal palms, roses (can this be true?). Lawn sloping away down towards the sea...

> Later you spoke to me quietly,
> as at a distance or under rain
> the sea nuzzles its sandspit.

Shy, grave and soft-spoken, or self-amused, blushing and smiling (head inclined, four fingers pulling aside the matt-black mane), or grievous and whispery and soft, dark and warm, the splayed fingers of one hand laid flat on his chest, and her not looking at him, looking at them, at her splayed fingers on his chest, shy, grave...

She was seventeen to his twenty-two, and forever being embarrassed by her own beauty.

And yet in the one photo I have of her (chequered blue-&-white boy's long-sleeved shirt with the cuffs turned back, white shorts) she has half-turned away and is looking back at the camera laughing, one hand hanging limp-wristedly from a forearm held horizontal, in the West Indian schoolgirl's way...

How long for?

A month, six weeks; no more than that; for she was going away, to university in France. She went away, to university in France, and he never saw her again.

You were beautiful and I loved you.
Will you never be home again?

Five years later, when in the early '70s he wrote those lines, she had become his Muse of Loss. Yet, just three years after that, he found she had changed in him, the muse of loss giving way by insensible degrees to the crinkle-eyed mien, as in her photo, of delight.

As though she had never left! As though it were he, not she, who had left her Port Antonio behind him for good.

> Composed as a child, yet earthen-eyed,
> she was the coast
> for which your tossed craft tried.

> Now, as in the lacing rain,
> all unforgetting things –
> this yard, this shack on stilts
> the weather's honed
> to supplicating fingers, that dead tree –
> resurface with the boyhood you once owned,

> her wet mouth blooms
> and vanishes; the wings of her cheekbones
> beat in your face!

Cut.

Cut away half a lifetime, lived by him all over the world, and by her in legendary obscurity, God knows where. Cut to Easter Monday 1998, and your boy (now fifty-three) starting to tell his irascible pardner Chris about her – which is strange, since he's never spoken about her before, except to a couple campus friends at the time – as they drive through Port Antonio, heading east in search of some probably apocryphal Italian restaurant, out by Frenchman's Cove.

He (pointing): 'That's the promontory where they lived.'

Chris: 'Hmmm.'

He: 'I wonder if the house is still there?'

Chris: 'Well, if you're planning to find out, make it snappy; I'm getting hungry.'

He: 'I probably won't even be able to find the driveway leading up to it.'

But he did. Ah, reader, he did.

2

The concrete tyre tracks leading up the unpaved driveway to her house were 'new' (that is, added some time in the past thirty-two years); the garden was now a luxuriant glory; the house sported a small wing at backstage left which it hadn't had before – and her father was sitting on the verandah where I'd left him, thirty-two years earlier…

Five minutes later, driving away, awed and partly disoriented by the calisthenics of Collapsed Time, I passed on his news to my impatient pardner Chris, who'd stayed in the car to underscore the fact that he was hungry.

'She got married and lives in France, has a son. They come out to Jamaica every year. She'd have been here now – imagine that! – but when she heard the Reggae Boys had made it to the finals she decided to stay. She'll probably be out in the summer.'

'The husband is French?'

'Yeah.'

'She still married to him?'

'I don't know. I wanted to ask, but I lost my nerve.'

'How old is she now?'

'She would be – about forty-eight, I guess.'

'Okay, Brown, now listen to me. If you're planning to see her when she comes out, my advice is: Don't. She'll probably be fat as a tank, with droopy breasts. You'll just go and fuck up a great memory. Forget the woman and keep the memory! That's my advice.'

I winced; the image he'd proffered was like a blow. (My pardner Chris, as you've probably realised, is a man of the world.)

But then I thought: Would it really matter?

Not – I concluded (a little sadly) – not as long as she was herself.

But what did that mean, 'herself'? And could she – she who had been at seventeen 'the most beautiful girl in the world' – could she be 'fat as a tank, with droopy breasts' and be herself?

That was hard to imagine.

I said: 'The father was exactly as I remembered him; just older, that's all. Amazing!'

'Did he remember you?'

'No. But I wouldn't expect him to; I only knew them for a short time.'

'Well, Brown, do what you want; you're a romantic. I know if it was me, I wasn't going near that woman. Thirty-two years! Rahtid!' And he chuckled and said something unprintable.

I thought about it some more, then let it go: summer was still months away. But a recent sojourn in Ocho Rios had taught me that, living up in Irish Town, I missed the sea. And so from time to time, in May and early June, I drove out to Port Antonio in search of a modest cottage or room in a guest house to rent on a long-term basis. The World Cup interrupted those excursions; and in fact it was another Proustian irruption (same set, different props, different heroine, later era) that prompted me to resume them.

This time I was lucky. A tip led me to an early-'60s house in the hills (high white-planked ceilings, ceiling fans) with a large, well-kept garden, a wonderful view, and a most unlikely 'landlady': a feisty little blonde German 'thing' of twenty-seven, who contentedly abided there alone, designing and making dresses for a living, and who occasionally took in the odd guest.

From the verandah I could see on the skyline, beyond a low ridge, the stately queue of royal palms that distinguished 'her' promontory. I dumped my stuff and headed into town...

Port Antonio, as you'd expect, has changed over the years, in unhappy lockstep with so many small Third World towns. I don't want to overstate this; it's nothing like, say, San Juan, or even Arima. But it's noisier than it was: dirtier, more crowded, more run down, its lassitudinous air displaced by a muted version of the preoccupied, anxious hustle of a bazaar. Cocaine, vagrants and boomboxes have all taken up residence in Port Antonio, as in so many other ex-paradisal places... (One fluorescent, handpainted sign nailed to a lamppost announced: WILD WALK PROMOTION PRESENT'S [sic] KILLER MAN JARO INC, LONG BAY, PORT-LAND, HEART BEAT LAWN, AUGUST SAT 1ˢᵗ 1998, ADM. $150 B.4 MIDNIGHT. LIVE VIDEO.)

It's still an easy town to walk in, but you wouldn't stroll there for the pure pleasure of it any more.

On a still-modest scale, the pedestrian tourists – German, mainly – are nonetheless more visible than they were; and in thirty-two years a fair sprinkling of hotels, commodious or eccentric or downright shady, has bloomed in the foothills and along the peerless coastline leading east from the town. Easily the most idiosyncratic of these is The Castle: a Gatsbyesque structure of turrets and cones, with a ceremonially wide and balustraded flight of steps, seemingly designed for the trailing trains of brides, but leading – directly down to the water! It was built by a wealthy white Jamaican of Jewish ancestry, in a joint venture with an Austrian baroness – who, after a parting of the ways galvanic enough to set tongues wagging in a soap opera vein, migrated to the other side of the horseshoe bay and vengefully built there an almost-as-sumptuous edifice, which she named (this is not a joke) The Palace.

So, nowadays, whether under the hammered-gold of the midday sun or by the light of the silvery moon, The Castle and The Palace stare stonily at each other across a quartermile of flat inshore water. Both are reportedly nearly always nearly empty…

I had by prearrangement an afternoon assignation. But I was early, and, on a whim (at least that's what he told himself: 'on a whim') I swung off the road, and up the concrete tyre tracks, and at the house disembarked from the Corolla and reintroduced myself to, this time, her mother – who, again, looked exactly as I remembered her, only older.

When was — coming? I enquired pleasantly.

Her mother looked startled. When? Today! She should have landed at Montego Bay already! She should be here by nightfall.

(Today?!!!)

'Well!' I said, with counterfeit heartiness as I was leaving. 'Nice to see you again. Maybe I'll drop around later.'

'That would be nice,' her mother said.

The news ruined his date, of course. He kept up his end of the conversation as best he could, which wasn't very inspiredly; and when, night having just fallen, he precociously slapped the waterfront tabletop and said, 'Well! I gotta go,' her toss at concern ('You okay?') seemed to him to express both scorn and sudden self-doubt in about equal measure.

He dropped her home to her western hill, then headed out east on the coast road, en route to his own place, but having perforce to pass 'her' promontory. And, as he drove, the dialectic between his Self and his Soul went something like this:

'Go in/ Don't go in/ Go in/ Don't go in.' This became, at the appropriate point, 'Slow down/ Don't slow down' – and this, in turn, became at the death, 'Turn/ Don't turn/ Turn!/ Don't turn!' – and he didn't.

He didn't turn; he drove on and returned to his new pad, where the feisty fraulein took the pins out of her mouth and said brightly, 'You're back early!' ('Tired,' he said morosely, 'Tired'; and, saying it, he suddenly did feel very tired.) And he went and made them both coffee, then spent a long time cleaning up the mess (her coffeemaker sort of exploded; he must have done something wrong), then sat and chatted with her for a while, then went out onto the unlit verandah (but there was a moon) and sat for a long time, overlooking the white-walled Palace overlooking the lamplit bay overlooking the black promontory with its dim-lit, turreted Castle overlooking the glinting Caribbean; and he thought:

'And so you will be seventeen forever, my shy sybarite, my undergraduate soul!'

Well: for one last night, anyway. Because, I know him; I know his heart; know that indiscreet, unruly heart. I know that in the morning, dressing to return to Kingston, he will find himself donning the best clean things he has left (black T-shirt, black trousers, black shoes & socks), and will realise at that stage, the shoes-&-socks stage, that this time he's not going to pass her promontory...

And he will turn and ascend the drive, and pull up to the verandah; and she will be there, after thirty-two years, sitting in the shady living room (in cotton house coat? jersey house coat? T-shirt and shorts?); and, after some meaningless eternity of words, words he will not be able to pre-imagine, he will hand her a book with a certain page marked and say, 'I wrote a poem for you that you never saw. Here it is.'

She will read it, sitting with bowed head – and he, standing, will watch her read it – and when she is finished she will look up at him, standing there empty-handed, bewildered and lost, like any man faced at last with the name of his happiness.

And she will smile.

Or weep.

Or blush.

3

It had rained, a short sharp shower, and the coast road was steaming in the sun. Pulling up at their verandah he saw her at once, sitting with her mother in the living room in a flowered housecoat, facing the open double doors. She rose; but standing up out of the air-conditioned car into the hot damp morning his glasses fogged, and it was as a myopic blur, 'the shape of the past', that she came out onto the verandah and then down the steps, saying:

'It's you! I couldn't think who; my father just said a journalist...'

After thirty-two years!

He said, with cavalier inanity: 'Bet you don't remember me.'

'Don't be silly...'

Her face had 'come forward' – that was his first impression – from the tangled black mist in which immemorially he'd remembered it. He said, when eventually she stood back from his embrace: 'You cut your hair.'

A greater inanity, of course: She might with justification have replied drily, 'You mean, some time in the past thirty-two years, did I cut my hair?' But she merely said considerately: 'Well, a woman of a certain age, you know...'

The same! She was the same! A little solider, sure, than the tressed and nubile child in the white bikini; she looked maybe twenty years older, her face had 'come forward'; and he would later discover the staunch little testimony to motherhood of a varicose vein behind one knee. But it was the same face, with its indescribable dark mouth; the same thick matt black hair, now shoulder-length and waved; the same husky, grave voice, the same watchful eyes; the same... 'Her-ness'... of her.

The same, the same, the same, the same, the same!

(Blow 'way, Chris!)

In the living room, from which her mother had tactfully absented herself, they remained standing for some reason, shifting this way and that.

She said: 'I'm here with my son – he's sixteen. You'll like him. He's European, but don't tell him that. He's so Afrocentric!'

And suddenly he saw himself as he had been to her (for thirty-two years!): a young, afro-headed undergraduate of the Black Power '60s, who, one night – his impending loss abruptly turning him impassioned, oratorical and fraudulent – had reduced her to tears in his parked car by berating her for preparing to abandon the Caribbean and 'run off to the white man's country'.

A long time ago, those years, he thought wryly. But then the *her-ness* of her swamped him. Those years were Now.

'Are you still married to his father?'

She laughed without apology. 'Yes.'

It elated him to discover the news made him happier than he'd casually thought the converse would. 'I knew you'd be,' he told her, not entirely truthfully but with undisguised admiration; and she saw it and smiled.

'I remember that day at the beach we met,' she said. 'You were there with your girlfriend, English girl...' Seeing his bewilderment, she stopped.

'That can't be,' he said slowly. 'What English girl?'

'Amanda?' She said helpfully. 'Amanda Perkins?'

My God! Amanda! It had to be quarter of a century since last she'd crossed his mind. Amanda Perkins, twenty, blonde Phys. Ed. teacher, in Roman sandals and a lime green mini-shift! She was a good kid, actually, raw-hearted and passionate and ready for anything. But she'd just embarrassed him by over-dancing at a town fete, and he'd been preparing to drop her.

(In retaliation for which, one Sunday morning soon afterwards, she took a Chinese guy to bed – her room in the guest house was above his, her bedsprings creaked – and he lay in bed reading an Asimov sci-fi story in *Playboy*, 'The Something of Venus', full of diaphanous, gliding life forms and tenuous Intelligences in the murky Venusian atmosphere (he remembered that story well!), listening to the odd, anapaestic rhythm of the creakings taking place above his head and thinking, 'Is that how Chinese guys do it?' and, 'You are pathetic!' – this, addressing her mentally. Though, to tell the truth – we are writing for the record, after all – after ten or fifteen minutes those *cruh-cruh-creeks* got to him, and he grabbed a T-shirt and flipflops and, in a foul mood, got the hell of there (so you won that one in the end, Amanda, girl!) and went down to the water and sat on the broken pier, and was soon lost in the new wonder of 'her': so grave and calamitous, so 'seventeen', so – luscious.)

'My God!' he said. 'Amanda Perkins! You know how long I haven't heard that name?'

'Yes. Well, you were there with her. But we talked, and you promised we'd hook up later that day. But somehow it didn't happen.'

He looked at her startled. 'But we did!'

'Yes. But not that day; the next day.'

He stared at her joyously. So that was the memory, that was the sting she'd taken with her to France and kept for thirty-two years! That she and he having met and 'talked' (and what an inept word, reader, for what happens when a man and woman meet and The Thing happens – instantly! – between them), he hadn't dumped poor Amanda Perkins and come to her the same day, as he'd promised!

He said again, more quietly: 'But we did.'

'Yes. But not that day.'

Leaving, he handed her a book, open at a certain page.

'I wrote a poem for you you never saw,' he told her. 'Here.'

She read it standing by his car in the sun; head bowed, she read it twice. Then, looking up: 'This is… wonderful,' she said slowly. 'Can I keep this?'

'It's yours!' he said, almost with pain. 'Look, I wrote in it.' He showed her. '*To the girl of the blinding beach.*'

Abruptly she kissed him on the mouth, hard, then turned and ran up the steps...

They spent the ensuing days together, sometimes with her teenage son in tow. Between them there resumed at once an intimacy, so fragile, yet so deep, that though on occasion one might say something and the other look briefly dismayed, as though suddenly discovering himself in the company of a stranger, at other times each would know so unerringly what the other was about to say, there'd hardly be any need to talk.

In her late twenties, as a journalist with a French TV station, she'd been sent overseas. She knew the world – Africa, India, South America – in a way he didn't; and her taste in music was far more catholic than his. Yet they'd read the same books (she was presently reading Martin Amis, *The Rachel Papers*); thought about the same things; come to the same conclusions.

A single mood enveloped them. Time and again she gave voice to some observation which, till then, he'd assumed to be his own idiosyncratic, private thought. ('*You* know that?' he'd say incredulously; and she would look at him like a woman and say nothing.)

'It's coming back to me,' she said one day, 'why it was such a big thing at the time. It was because we were so alike. Funny, to remember... the other thing... and forget how alike we were.'

'Are,' he corrected her. 'Makes you wonder if experience counts for anything. I was listening to us talking, last night late, and it occurred to me: Forget France and Trinidad; anybody listening to us would think we'd spent the last thirty-two years in this room!'

The look she gave him made him grin.

Another time, her son came out of the sea at Frenchman's Cove and up to where they were lying on beach loungers. 'You two look like brother and sister,' he blurted out; and the man thought: 'That's not what he means, he doesn't know what he means. But I know what he means...'

One morning –

– But enough.

('Are you going to write about this in your paper?' she'd asked him at one point, late in the first day they were together. 'No.'

And, next day: 'Are you going to write about this?' 'No.' '...about this?' 'No.')

So. No more for you, Unknown Reader.

No more for them, lady. Not until one of these columns is being written one day in, like, 2015, and, like a dark-winged, radiant moth, the memory of this strange interregnum, July '98, beats up into the light, from what by then will doubtless be the cataracting spume of the past...

Our theme has been Memory Triumphant: not Proust's 'temps perdu', after all, but the pathetic collapsibility of totalitarian Time. I always had a hunch, but with you, for the first time, I was sure. And I tell you now, without sentimentality, that all things have signatures, changeless, eternal; and this means that, except in the banal bodily sense, attrition, time is a fiction. And if time is a fiction, so is death.

You are She of the Blinding Beach.

Tell your husband he's a lucky man.

FOR AULD LANG SYNE

I've always been bad at remembering names, specifically, the names of movies and people. The first has the Dark Lady slitting her eyes in disgust at least once a month, when I arrive home with my weekend trove of rented videos. ('But we saw this one already! You don't remember?') And the other has caused me more embarrassment over the years than I care to recall. So, in Jamaica recently to address a function, I walked with dread. I'd lived there once (twice, actually) long ago, and still had many Jamaican friends and acquaintances. And while the friends would not be a problem, I deeply feared running into the acquaintances, as, at the function, I knew I would.

In the end it wasn't too bad. I couldn't begin to remember the name of the Minister of Finance when he familiarly shook my hand 'after all these years' – we'd been undergrads at Mona together – and it took me several minutes' worth of covert glances to decide that Trevor Munroe was Trevor Munroe, and Michael Manley's second wife had to stand in front of me and wail, 'Wayne! It's Thelma!' before I could react. ('You realise,' said Rex Nettleford discomfortingly, 'Not only the literati but the glitterati are here.') But a lot of other faces swam up from the penumbral past with phosphorescent tags snugly in tow.

At one point, a woman approached me smiling. I said uncertainly, 'Beverley?' – because it seemed to me she might somehow be 'Beverley', and because, in Jamaica, if you can't remember a woman's name, Beverley's the best odds you can get – and wasn't over-dismayed when (after 30 years!) she said tolerantly, 'No, Beverley's my sister; I'm Margery.' And I'd begun to think I was home and dry, when this other woman barred my path, hands clasped before her loins, and smiling as only a woman smiles who has known you, *really* known you; or, at least, thinks she has.

I didn't have a clue. I said lamely, '*You* look familiar' – Gad! – but, even given that inanity, her reaction seemed extreme. Her reaction was to crumple visibly and sort of stagger away. I stared after her, half-resentfully.

'Who's that woman?' I asked Rachel Manley. But when she told me, the name, like the face, meant nothing. Call her Joan.

Next morning:

'You know, you really shattered Joan,' Rachel said. 'She phoned me late last night, she couldn't sleep. Apparently you and she had a big thing once – '

'Who, me and she? Nonsense. When?'

'When we were at Mona, Wayne! And you didn't remember her, at all!'

I thought: Something's wrong with this. I forget names, not faces.

'You really don't remember her!'

I shook my head.

'Well, she remembers you, that's for sure. She told me every-thing. How you and she were dancing at a New Year's Eve party and she fell off a cliff – '

' – she fell off a cliff?'

' – and how her son, who was four at the time, his name was also Wayne, so you were Big Wayne and he was Little Wayne – '

' – Big Wayne? Little Wayne?'

' – and I really think it's horrible of you not to remember her – '

' – but I'm telling you I don't know the woman – '

' – you had the poor girl in tears. You men are all alike. I think you should phone her.'

'Me phone her? No way! To say what?'

But here both she and Saffrey, my younger daughter who's currently at Mona, began hectoring me, and in the end she dialled the number herself and handed me the phone. Like that, resistant, disbelieving, I found myself on the line to a putative past, my own, inexplicably as unknown as the future.

'Hi.'

'Oh, hi!'

'I hear I owe you an apology.'

'Oh, that's not necessary...'

'I have to tell you, this has never happened to me.'

'I know! To me, either! I feel like such a fool... It must be strange for you...'

'When did you say we knew each other?'

'Oh, I don't know. Late '67, early '68, I guess...'

'And how long were we... together?'

'Maybe three months. It wasn't long. But I mean, we did everything, we went everywhere! I really thought...'

Her sentences kept trailing off.

'I hear you fell off a cliff.'

'Yes! Don't you remember? You shouted, 'Hang on, I'm coming down!' and I was so shaken up, I called back, 'No, don't come! I'll just sit here for a while!'

'Where was this?'

'At a party in Red Hills.'

'What were we doing dancing on the edge of a cliff?'

'Oh, that! We'd gone outside to take in the view, and then started dancing – because that's the sort of thing we used to do, I mean, we were so young – and I must have had so much to drink by then, I – fell off the cliff! *Don't you remember* – ?'

I didn't.

'How did we meet?'

She told me. It sounded credible. I remembered the girl, though not the party, at whose party she said we'd met.

'Where was I living?'

She told me.

I remembered the house on Hope Road, an old 'forties three-bedroom with its garden gone to weed, and the two Jamaican guys I'd shared it with: Ruel, an insatiable womaniser with a leering laugh, and George – black, bearded, bespectacled, timid George – who used to stand at the kitchen counter for, like, forever, mincing the garlic for the roast lamb into ever tinier pinhead fractions, who would say with a laugh, when I impatiently queried his dedication: 'Oh, I don't mind doing it.' It was from George that I learnt (a) that men could cook, as distinct from throwing together something to eat, and (b) that if you wanted the lamb to taste really good, you just had to *mince that garlic*, boy!

All this I remembered easily enough. But I didn't remember her.

'So. What else did we do?'

She told me.

It sounded pretty interesting, some of it, and not improbable. She even mentioned people we'd hung out with, and they were people I knew. But not a single thing she said we did struck so much as a spark in the kindling of my memory. And neither, still, did she.

'You have any photos of us?'

'No-o-o.'

'Any letters I wrote you?'

'No…'

'Then,' I said, trying to joke, but much too irritated and semi-alarmed to be funny. 'If this were a paternity suit you wouldn't have a single shred of evidence that we'd ever known each other, would you?'

(Here my daughter rounded her eyes and made slashing gestures at her throat.)

'No, that's true, I wouldn't…'

She said it amiably enough, but trailing off.

'Well,' I said. 'Clearly we have to meet. How about a drink this evening?'

I'd offered this, I thought, to make amends: for not having recognised her, for still not having a clue who she was, for the joke not being funny. I'd offered it, I thought, from a position of strength: as a sop to a lady in distress. But in the seconds that lapsed before she replied, I suddenly realised: it was I who was the desperate one. What if now she huffily refused to see me? How could I return to Trinidad leaving three whole months of my sovereign past in the sole custody of a stranger? What does any man own but his past?

Besides. *What the hell was happening here?*

But she agreed, a little uncertainly, so I knew she had been hurt. ('Imagine that,' I said to Rachel Manley when later she arrived in Trinidad to launch her book, *Drumblair*. 'Imagine being hurt by someone not remembering something that happened thirty years ago!'

'Well, it wasn't only her,' Rachel replied. 'Her son phoned me from Florida when he heard. 'What nonsense is this about Wayne

Brown not remembering us,' he wanted to know. 'I remember *him*; and I was four!')

And that evening she picked me up to drive us to the Mona SCR, where I'd arranged to meet someone else a couple hours later: someone I actually knew.

Nearing the university she detoured into Hope Pastures, a modest middle-class Kingston suburb, and stopped the car.

'This is where I was living at the time,' she said. 'This is where you used to come.'

I looked. It might have been any Diamond Vale house. It meant nothing to me.

'That's where we used to sit and watch TV,' she said, pointing at a louvred room fronting the little lawn. 'Till it was time to put Little Wayne to bed.'

Little Wayne.

'There used to be a big tree right there,' she said helpfully, leaning across me to point.

'I don't know...' Her voice trailed off. 'I guess they cut it down...'

Then, abruptly, she laughed.

'Do you know,' she said, 'Just now, just for a moment there, you actually looked scared?'

The Hope Pastures house was mute; and the woman besides me in the car was a stranger. I said, as we drew away from the curb: 'Tell me something: did you know X?' Naming the girl I thought I'd been dating at the time. Still trying to disbelieve.

'Yes,' she said. 'I met her with you once.'

'You know she and I – ?'

'Yes...'

'Then how come – you and me – ?'

'I think you'd had some sort of quarrel. I was your distraction, I suppose...'

She said it levelly enough, but trailing off.

There was nothing to say to this news. In fact, I realised, there might be any number of things this Joan might tell me to which there'd be nothing to say.

'So!' I said savagely (because hopelessness can be savage): 'Tell me more about us.'

'Well,' she said animatedly, not taking my tone. 'My happiest memories of us are in the mountains. You used to take me there to paint. You'd help me get set up, then leave me alone, go for a walk, sit and read, whatever. I'll never forget that.'

'Why?'

'You see, I'd just come out of a marriage, and he was a very jealous man. Jealous of me with other men, jealous of my painting. I was young, and I suppose I assumed all men would be like that. So I couldn't believe my luck, that you didn't mind me painting.'

That such a negligible benignity on my part could have been so memorable to her came like an insight into the mysterious oppressiveness certain lovely women have always complained of with men. I pushed it away. There's no slave like a sympathetic slave; and she – this strange woman, to whom baffling Fate had apparently granted sole custody of three months of my unrepeatable life – she was my captor, after all.

'So. What else?'

She told me.

And then, without warning, as we drove through Mona Heights, her voice – not her, but *her voice* – came back to me, as familiar and vivid as a remembered scent, so that I started violently and stared at her, and saw incredulously that the words were issuing from a stranger's lips… and next moment I was staring at her legs.

How to explain this?

Her speech was distinctive: in pitch, each sentence crested midway through then trailed huskily off, as though concluding, each time, in its own caress; and now her voice, her speech, came back to me, from the hoary black maw of the gluttonous past, coming and going at first like little gusts in a silent white rain, and then coming and *staying* – O triumphal breakthrough! – her voice as intimate and caressing and tender and sweet as a girl's face laid in the hollow of your neck, so that I thought *She really loved him!*, for it was stranger than that, I was not I, but a young man I only imperfectly remembered (how were we different? *Why* were we different?)… and next moment, for some reason, I was staring at her legs…

…until she observed amused, not averting her gaze from the road: 'You're looking at my legs.'

295

'You used to wear shorts a lot?'

'Yes.'

'Short-shorts?'

'Ye-e-s...'

'Green?'

'Oh, I can't remember. Some might have been green.' Then: 'You're not going to tell me you remember my legs!'

Like Jacob I wrestled with the Angel of Oblivion. The image of long brown legs and a young woman's unfallen ass tucked away in green short-shorts – an image which had leapt at me out of nowhere, simultaneously with the breakthrough of the voice – that image failed to connect to anything else.

'I don't know,' I said. 'But I remember your voice.'

'Well, there you are,' she said.

But it was clearly not what she wanted to hear. What corporeal woman wants to be remembered, thirty years later, for her voice?

And yet to me now, as it had been for Gatsby, her voice was a deathless song. And when, over drinks at the SCR, I contrived to keep her talking, it was in large part for the pleasure of basking in her voice: basking, that is, in being him, and so loved.

Her life, as she told it, sounded somehow to have been both eventful and uninteresting. She had inherited money; been in and out of various marriages; lived for many years in Michigan, then Ohio; owned an art gallery in Montego Bay. She was just packing house, in fact, to re-migrate, to Florida. If I'd come a month later we'd have missed each other.

'It's been the story of my life,' she said at one point. 'I get into relationships with men so easily. And then they make it so hard for you to get out.'

'It's the voice,' I told her mildly. Then, remembering, added: 'The voice and the legs. And something else. I imagine.'

Her smile told me I had not been forgiven.

There was one more illumination. She was saying something, she accompanied it by inclining her face towards her shoulder and, with spread fingers, drawing the air towards her throat; and the gesture leapt at me with absolute familiarity out of the long gone past – except that, weirdly, more weirdly than I can describe, it attached itself to the voice, not to the woman sitting beside me.

'Do that again.'

'Do what? Oh, you mean, this?'

Obediently she inclined her face towards me and drew the air towards her. Abruptly I became aware of the laconically chatting barman, the expatriate wife with the bewinged toddlers by the pool, the off-duty academics morosely drinking at the bar.

My daughters were to meet me at the SCR; we were being collected here by a friend for dinner. I was telling her goodbye at her car, and had already spotted them by the light of the streetlamps, two tall fine young women walking together down the road from Irvine Hall, when the thought occurred, and I asked her:

'Why are you going to live in Florida?'

She hesitated. Then she said:

'My son that I told you about? Little Wayne? He's in his thirties now, and, well, he has cancer. He's in a nursing home over there. So I'm going up to be with him.'

So. She had kept the real thing, the only thing, for last. In fact, I thought, she had probably intended to leave it unspoken; and she had nearly succeeded. But pain past a certain point cannot be unspoken. Beyond a certain age we are all of us Ancient Mariners.

I saw at once, of course, that her belated news changed everything. That it just about cancelled out all that had gone before. I said, 'I'm sorry,' meaning it every which way at once. Then: 'Tell Little Wayne hullo for me.'

'I don't know if I will. He'll be very hurt you didn't remember him.'

(As I later learnt, she did, and he was.)

But she waited to meet my daughters, then said goodbye... and late that night, asleep in someone else's flat, I woke to the thudding of horses' hooves on grass, and remembered...

I remembered a short Trinidadian guy, something Joseph (whatever happened to you, Joseph?), and the small bay mare, and the rangy chestnut filly, which he and I respectively had been riding in an illicit madcap race across the playing fields. I remembered the horrible moment of immense doubt, which was the sensation of my saddle beginning to slip – and, next, sitting on a stainless steel table in the UWI Hospital, my T-shirt covered in blood, while Archie Hudson-Phillips, a resident doctor there at the time, withdrew a pair of tweezers from my scalp and held it towards me, saying, 'You want to see a piece of your brain?' (Funny guy, Archie.)

When had that been?

October-November, '67.

Now, twenty-nine years later, in the dark of a Kingston apartment, I tried to remember something, anything, of my life in the months immediately after that fall and found I couldn't. The memories, the normal memories, resumed from the following February. They didn't include her.

I got up, turned on the light, and phoned Joan.

'Did you know,' I said, when she came sleepily on the line. 'I fell off a horse and was concussed, just before we met?'

'No… I didn't know that…'

'Well, I just remembered it,' I said. 'And it explains everything. Don't you see? I can't remember a single specific thing from the next couple months.'

'Well, I'm glad for you. You must have been getting very worried…'

'You can believe that,' I told her. 'The word "senility" kept popping up.'

'Well, I'm glad,' she said again, though not as though she believed me. 'Listen. What time is it?'

So you see, Joan, I had to write this, because you chose to keep the hurt and disbelieve me. It wasn't my fault; you are not forgettable; and at midnight this past New Year's Eve it was to you, the real-life, fifty-something-year-old Joan with the son dying in Florida, and not to that other, intriguing intimation of my own eventual death – the voice without the vocalist, the gesture without the girl – that I drank a cup of kindness, dear. For auld lang syne.

THE SOLITARY DINER

'You have to understand. Men don't love children, dem love *you*.
So once you stop sexing dem, dem stop giving you money.'

Her name was Jean. She was serious, pretty and plump, she
wore her hair in upswept copper braids, she was manageress,
waitress and cashier, all in one, and she was talking about the
vagaries of child support.

He liked her for that 'dem love *you*'. And though the potato
salad was mushy, the stewed pork mostly bone, and the ash tray
– a small, fluted gourd – was crammed after two butts, it was okay.
It was past seven on a weekday night in a decayed and noisy coastal
town, and he was in a mood to be grateful for small mercies. Her
returning to the unlit balcony after bringing his order, to sit at his
table and contemplate him wordlessly, with a look at once
dubious and expectant, was one such. He had expected to be
eating alone.

Behind them, at a corner table in the flatly-lit dining room
(plastic chairs and tablecloths, scuffed tiles, fluorescent ceiling
tubes) a solitary client, a bespectacled, gaunt mulatto in his early
seventies with skin like blemished parchment, was joylessly
reducing, by about a forkful a minute, a plateful of curried
mutton and white rice. On a stand above the formica bar, a pale
and misty television, its volume set much too loud, was crackling
out some spectral sitcom.

'An American writer called John Updike said something like
that about women,' he told Jean. 'He said women live with men
but only really love their children.'

She considered this seriously. Then: 'That's not true,' she said.
'*Me* love men. But men, once you make baby for dem, dem start
to stray. You understand?'

At thirty she had two daughters. The father of the older one
was dead. ('Him was involve in drugs; dem kill him in Miami.')

The father of the five-year-old had 'strayed'. 'Den, now, time pass and dem mebbe want to come back. But dem two men cause me so much grief, me make up me mind; me say, no more.'

'But you are with a man now.'

She drew back and looked at him. 'Why you say that?'

'Because I know.'

'Why you say you know?'

'I just know.'

'Well… yes. But dis one nah give me no trouble.'

'He knows you badder than him, right?'

She threw back her head and laughed. It transformed her. Her round cheeks shone with glee and her eyes (which remained on his) slitted with intelligent delight.

A little later:

'You are alone here?'

'Yes.'

'Married?'

'No.'

'Children?'

'Two. Grown up.'

'What it is you do?'

He had seldom, he reflected, had such a choice of answers. 'I teach,' he said.

She looked at him keenly. 'Den how come you out here in the middle of the week? School not in vacation.'

'No, but university is.'

This was imprecise. But he was getting tired, and he didn't bother to explain.

It lasted only a couple seconds, but he saw when her gaze dropped from his eyes to his chest, and an odd expression – dull, slack, almost arrogant – passed across her face.

A little later:

'Next time you pass a bookstore in Kingston,' she confided, leaning forward now, hugging her elbows on the table, her face close to his. 'I want you to get me a book. It call' – here she extracted a slip of paper from her blue manageress's jacket pocket and read – '"The Power of Positive Thinking". By Norman Vincent Peale.' She pronounced it 'Pele'.

In the Falklands War, the British navy coded its messages by compressing thousands of words into a blip. Like that now, all the pathos of West Indian history seemed abruptly to come to him, encoded in her request.

And yet, he saw, she was likeable; in a certain light, even admirable. And he thought, Why not? Why not – anything? And he made a mental note to get her her book.

'You will be eating here tomorrow?'

'I don't know.' Then: 'Yes, probably. Tomorrow night.'

'Den I will see you den.' But she made no move to rise.

He reached across and lightly hefted the underside of her thigh. She slapped his hand away grinning, as he'd known she would.

So, the next night, I went back. The flat-lit dining room was again empty save for – again – the taciturn old parchment-skinned gentleman. He'd exchanged his drab plaid of the previous evening for a short-sleeved shirt of faded cream, and he was methodically dissecting a slab of baked chicken in a thick red sauce. But he sat at the same corner table, in the same chair against the wall; and the terrifying thought occurred to me that every evening, at the dying of the light, he came here to dine like this. Slowly. In silence. Alone.

Ignored, the misty pale screen above the bar was scratchily declaiming something or the other. I went out onto the shadowy balcony and lit a cigarette.

Jean appeared presently. This time, though, there was some-one with her: another young woman of the town. And she was taller, slimmer, paler and younger than Jean.

Comprehension came swiftly; and with it, something like woe. I rose.

'Me a'bring a friend to meet you,' Jean said. 'This is Carol. Carol, Mr Brown.'

(How it stung, that unexpected, in-all-ways-distancing 'Mr Brown'!)

'Wayne,' I said, looking from one to the other.

Jean's gaze softened.

'Me wasn't sure.' Then, to the girl: 'This is Wayne me was telling you about.'

301

'Hi Wayne!'

I sometimes wonder about women who do what Jean, so misconstruing me, was doing. Produce a surrogate, saying in effect: 'I am taken, but I like you. So here, take this one in my stead.'

What is that, selflessness or self-defence? A kindness, or a dismissal – or a vicarious thing? Something they do with amusement? with pain? as casually as they might shake your hand?

I suppose it depends on how and how much they like you. But what do I know?

Now, though, I had the distinct sensation that Jean – serious, pretty and plump Jean, whom I knew to be likeable, indeed, to be admirable – was saying to me: 'Take this one. And nat to worry. You will see; it will still be me.'

And, thinking that, I seemed to intuit something of the eternal, bewildered patience of women – women beset by men all the days of their childbearing lives, yet still moved, at some level, to accommodate each one, to *take him in* (because, O, the pity of it! that this one too, beating on my door for entry like a moth on a lampshade, he too will be dead one day). And I thought: 'Maybe there is a place where every woman in her time is all the women that have ever lived.'

And then: If that's true, it must mean – but something else in me stopped the thought dead in its tracks – something that said, with finality, 'No', and left me feeling proud and relieved and like myself, and knowing myself to be alone.

True courtesy derives from freedom. And it was from that place – of perfect circumscription, and therefore of perfect freedom – that I took the new one's hand, saying (not too formally): 'Hi, Carol.'

She was long-legged and slimmish and in her mid-twenties, and her face was small and oval, her eyes were bright, and there was enough of what showed above the square cut of her dress to subject the flesh there, whenever she moved even a little, to those syncopated dark-gleaming small undulations, and she asked a lot of questions and said O-*kay*, O-*kay!*, as if in surprised admiration, to pretty much every answer I gave her, and her bright eyes said plainly what Jean's, the night before, had only once (covertly,

302

briefly) allowed. In short, in most any circumstances she could have been a contender – and, precisely for that reason, wasn't. I became aware of the shouted exchanges of the taximen in the little square below; of the sere and damaged disc of an old moon standing vacantly above the black chapel; of the industrial, stale smell of the sea.

I couldn't protect her from the moment of uncertainty, with its initial mix of self-doubt and pique (mercifully for us both, the latter won) when she saw the shape the evening was taking. But that, too, passed. Soon we were merely chatting.

Jean was peeved.

'Me never know sey you was a proud man,' she said, in the flat-lit dining room with its lone client, when I went in to pay and leave.

It was a serious accusation. 'Proud' meant stuck up. It meant to be a smug prisoner of one's class, a moral nonentity.

'I am not proud.'

'Den how come you don't like my friend?'

I cast about with difficulty for something to say.

'Because she isn't you.'

It was a fluke, but the right answer. The shining cheeks, the intelligent, slitted eyes.

The solitary diner placed his fork and knife at twenty-to-four on the white clockface of his plate and stared at us.

I know your pain, I said to him silently. *And I salute your courage.*

With an angry look he deflected my intrusion, as I'd known he would.

THE MIRROR OF THE SOUL

1

How does one write a double-column about a single moment: a look, exchanged by two women in a church, that lasted no more than three seconds?

I suppose that, like Michael Holding, one takes a long run-up. Therefore:

The American poet Robert Lowell once went through a phase of composing sonnets by editing and delineating letters written to him by his middle-aged ex-wife and his young mistress. And, many years ago, coming out of the tail-end of a soulful tryst with a calamitous young mother of two, I tried doing likewise with her 'goodbye' letter.

I still have the latter, but I lost the poem – it was written on the back of a programme, in a racketing, swaying train, with outside the passing panorama of England's green and pleasant land and an endless queue of telegraph poles running up to my window to bowl – and all I can remember of it today are three lines:

'...I cleaned the house, both floors, then baked a cake,
Then sat and blew my mind out with Pink Floyd,
The Dark Side of the Moon...'

Even those lines I hadn't recalled for at least a decade. But they came back to me a couple months ago, in the humid gloom of a Kingston church, where I found myself one weekday afternoon, some time after 3:00 p.m.: a funeral.

I was late (torrential rain, traffic backed up on a streaming road) and in the doorway I hesitated twice over: first upon discovering I was the only male present sans jacket and tie (Jamaicans take their funerals seriously!), and then because the little church was full. It took me several seconds to locate an empty seat, up near the front: just two rows behind the widow, it turned out. I took a deep breath and advanced purposefully up the aisle.

At the place, the sedentary, dark-clad bodies looked up, then obligingly shuffled over. I genuflected, slid apologetically into the aisle-end of the pew and sat.

Now I confess I am not an aficionado of churches. Occasionally, I can be persuaded to attend midnight mass for the sake of auld lang syne; but that's all. Except, of course, for weddings and funerals. And there're quite a few of those, for I am of an age where the stubbornly longer-lived parents of friends are still tardily dying out, and the children of friends, like the field in a Grand National, are thundering towards and over the water-jump of marriage. And that's fine. I mean, what else is there to commemorate in this traffic-jammed, rained-out world? Weddings and funerals, love and death: the bright and dark sides of her Pink Floyd's moon.

Anyway.

The man whose shucked-off mortal coil presumably lay in the wreath-adorned coffin (mercifully, it was closed) had been a colleague of sorts. He had died, rather precociously in this day and age, of some obscure ailment at sixty-two; and about his widow, a tall and handsome brown-skinned woman a few years younger than him, there was now a sort of graven immobility. She sat in the front row, one from the aisle, flanked rather than consoled – for that was the impression the back of her head and shoulders gave, of a sort of granite solitude – by (I supposed) a son and his wife, or maybe a daughter and her husband, while sundry other children and children's spouses (late twenties, early thirties) and pre-teen grandchildren (the younger ones fidgeting, the older ones subdued) filled out the rest of the pew.

As may be deduced from the above, I hardly knew the widow, except as a colleague's wife, to say hello to at various functions from time to time. Yet from those brief encounters I'd come away with the impression of a formidable woman, whose life, for some reason, had been hard, and who in consequence was not inclined to suffer fools gladly – if indeed she would suffer them at all. At maybe fifty-eight, as I said, she was still easy on the eye: better than easy, in fact, for beyond a pleasing symmetry of feature and form, there was more than a hint of a stern fire. But it wouldn't have occurred to me to mess with her.

As for the dead man's mistress – a divorced mother of two, a lovely, grievous 'browning' in her late thirties, whom I was startled to discover sitting directly across the aisle from me – I'd known her, also casually, before I knew she was with him. But even then she'd had that air of being someone's woman.

(How do they *do* that, these unmarried-but-taken women – post those invisible 'Unavailable' signs, I mean? My partner Chris, who's more than halfway down the road to being a misogynist, says you can always tell a woman who's being well-fucked; but I don't think it's just that. I mean, there're well-fucked women who give the impression that they wouldn't mind being even more well-fucked, you know? No – I like to think it has to do with love: with that sense of a woman abiding contentedly in the harbour of some man's heart, and he in hers.)

Now, I admit 'contented' isn't a word you'd normally associate with a mistress, and it certainly wasn't a word I'd have used of this one now. If the widow gave off an air of impregnable solitude, the younger woman sitting across from me, by contrast, might have been a lightning conductor for all the free-floating grief adrift in the gloaming of that church. In fact, what shone in her lovely face, I thought (glancing covertly at her), wasn't even grief; it was anguish. And pondering the difference, I realised it was also defiance.

She, too, was alone in that packed and humid place; much more alone, come to think of it, than the widow. For, however motionlessly the latter sat, encased in her inscrutable privacy, the empire of the church was hers. It was her and her dead husband's children and grandchildren who flanked her now, it was their friends and acquaintances who filled the pews, while the mistress (why did I only see this now?) had most certainly to know herself in enemy territory.

I had the impression she might not be by herself, that the pleasantly round-faced, miniskirted and chubby-thighed woman sitting beyond her might be a friend, come along to give moral support. But even so.

'Mistress'. What a word. To champions of the heart, what drama inheres in it; to the salacious, what prurience!

If every wife is in a sense an empress, the empire of a mistress consists solely of someone else's husband's loins and (if she is lucky) his heart.

If there are wives who have everything, yet 'at the end of the day' have nothing, a mistress has nothing, yet at the end of the day – everything!

Wives, like the sun, preside over their husbands' worlds.

Mistresses, like the moon, preside over their souls.

And each envies the other, wanting what the other has: what she herself can never have.

What a thing.

Anyway.

Like that, they sat now: the wife in severe black, two rows in front of me, immobile and quite alone (though flanked by the fruit of their loins, the living proofs of a long, shared life), and the mistress (also in black, but of some filmier material that fell in pleats, though only to her knees, and left her shoulders bare) shining with anguish and defiance, and hideously alone, never mind the friend: an exiled empress now the man was dead.

The presiding priest, a young American (too young, I thought, to know anything worth knowing about death), was saying something.

The decline of Roman Catholicism into Humanism in our time has been marked by the oratorical shift, on occasions like this, from projecting the dead man's putatively glorious future to celebrating his putatively exemplary past; and the young consolation-giver had just finished remarking how much 'justifiable pride' the dead man had taken in his children, when, for the first time, the widow glanced around her, and her impassive gaze encountered the shining eyes of the mistress – and for perhaps three seconds they looked at each other: the handsome brown woman of fifty-eight and the grievous-lovely 'browning' twenty years her junior.

And then a single tear started down the mistress's cheek, and the widow turned away and sat face forward again.

Everybody must have seen it, I thought: the look exchanged between the dead man's widow and mistress: the air in the hot, damp little church seemed to crackle with more than static electricity.

'…Ronnie and Yvonne,' the young American priest was saying, calling by name the offspring of the marriage.

And because I had flinched from their mutual stare, feeling myself a gross intruder upon a too-private moment, I tried to turn my mind from what I had seen and concentrate on the objects of his attention. But whether the thirty-five-ish couple flanking the widow were Ronnie and his wife or Yvonne and her husband, I couldn't tell (far less which of the little children were whose); so they remained uninteresting to me, the sibling inheritors, and I found myself thinking about the dead man instead: he whose unremarkable-seeming life was now being dramatised in death by the presence of the two women.

He had been a colleague of sorts, as I say, and I hadn't really known him. A tall, bespectacled, dark-skinned man on the cusp of retirement, he was quiet; the sort of man whose grin, if you stopped him in the corridor to give him a joke, would be rueful-abashed and accompanied by downcast eyes, as if having to smile in public made him shy. When, enquiring of my partner Chris about the lovely, anguished 'browning' now sitting across the aisle from me, I learnt that (a) she was somebody's woman, and (b) that the somebody was he, I thought in surprise, 'Well, well…!'

But the salacious reflex didn't hold. My casual sense of him was of a man whose private muse was Order; he didn't fit the mould of the hearty, middle-aged adulterers of this city. And when I overheard, literally (albeit at third-hand), something he'd reportedly said once, I thought, Now that makes sense. 'Her smile kills me,' the dead man had confessed of his wife to a male confidante, whose own wife was now in turn – over jerk chicken and pasta in Sovereign Deli, of all places – in the process of indignantly passing on that little piece of intelligence to her female companion. Overhearing this, I remember, I tried and failed to imagine the widow's 'brave smile'… Yet none of it made him quite real to me – there was no need for him to be, after all. And it was only now, now when it had ceased to matter, that I looked at the wreath-adorned coffin and imagined the man whose remains it secreted, and imagined the rich agony of his final however-many years. Maybe that's what killed him, I thought.

Like that, I knew he had loved his wife; for their children were grown and had their lives, and yet he'd stayed. And that meant in turn that this one across the aisle (I glanced at her) must have been like ultimate life to him; for in her name, in her arms, he had cruelly hurt, and gone right on hurting – cruelly, cruelly, for how many years? – the wife he had esteemed too much to leave.

Thinking this returned me to the stare they'd exchanged: the impassive gaze of the good-looking, fifty-eight-year-old, stern brown woman, and the shining anguish (issuing at last in a tear) of the grievous-lovely, lighter-skinned woman twenty years her junior. What had passed between them, I knew, was something too ambiguous, electric and fluid to be reduced to words. But words are my business; so now I rehearsed the way it seemed to me it had gone.

You have been my grief for X years (the widow's gaze said.)
And you, mine.
You shame me being here.
You shame me being 'her'.
Why couldn't you leave him alone?
Why couldn't you let him go?
What do you have now?
What did you have then?
I had his children, our lives, the years.
I had his hands on me.
I am getting old.
I am alone, I have nothing.
I'm so sorry for you.
I'm sorry, too. But you have his children.
You had his hands on you.
Yes. And now he's dead!
Yes. My husband is dead.

And I have nothing anymore! (A tear starting.)

And I am getting old, and cannot help you. (The widow turning away.)

From this imagined call-&-response – so urgent, yet so ancient! – from this circular mantra, I was rescued by a small commotion. We were on our feet, and singing.

'…Let me hide my face in Thee…!'

I sang along, *sotto voce*, gravel-voiced. Sang along while thinking, with sudden blasphemous anger: There'd better not be a God. Because if there is, when my time comes I shall tell Him: 'I never once wanted to hide my face in Thee. Only ever in Her, Thy creation. So don't let me in here – not unless here's where She's heading. Otherwise, send me wherever She'll be. I abide with Her, not Thee.'

Which, I admit, would be a pretty silly thing to say, for more reasons than one. Better all around that He should just not be.

More busyness… new things happening. The beardless young priest and his ageing black acolyte were down in the aisle, the latter frowningly adjusting his censer's chain. The pallbearers had taken their places (which was Ronnie, and which, Yvonne's husband?). The coffin and its carcass started on their journey to the fire.

'Rock of Ages…'

Shattered but impervious, erect in austere black, glancing neither right nor left, the widow passed by me in a haze of incense so strong it was like the sting of the tears she declined to weep. And as she came, and went on, I had the sudden sensation that we – yes, even the mistress – were all her acolytes. And I was proud – this woman I hardly knew made me proud, to be alive and a West Indian: proud! – and I thought, 'I know now why he couldn't leave you.'

And the odd thing was, I did know, though not in any way I can now explain.

The pews were peeling away, two and two, into the aisle; almost at once, it was my pew's turn. I put a foot out at the same time the mistress did, and stopped.

She gave me a look I shall never forget (though I know it was not meant for me)... as if 'aliveness' were but a synonym for pain, and all the world's aliveness were shining now in her face... and, flinching back, appalled and illumined, I nonetheless managed a little, courteous gesture, turning my wrist, meaning, 'Go'.

Then she was gone, launched on her own pilgrimage through the fire, walking the gauntlet of two hundred pairs of eyes.

The dignity of the widow!

The nakedness of the mistress!

Following her out into the aisle, her companion (miniskirted, chubby-thighed) gave me a look of bewildering intimacy. But I let her go, I let half her pew go, before initiating my own side's exodus. I couldn't bear to be near so much... light.

Dignity, nakedness.

They were like ships in the night, really, the older woman and the younger one; they'd had nothing in common but their womanhood and a man. And what they stood for in my mind was so different, I thought it should be possible to withhold judgement evenhandedly from each.

I thought, to be explicit, that without the widow, civilisation would fall, and we'd be negligible creatures, you and I, beasts of the field. And that, without the mistress, there'd be nothing sacred about life, nothing deserving of civilisation, in the first place.

And yet they'd married each other, *through* him. And had found their fates, their variegated doom, in being the bright and dark sides of his moon.

Issuing at length from that sweaty cave into a bright blue late-afternoon, I didn't want to think anymore. Above all, I didn't want to have to choose between them. Yet, obscurely, I felt I would have to, sooner or later. And the odd thought occurred to me that the shape of the rest of my life would depend on whose side, widow's or mistress's, I came down on.

In the churchyard, a sudden breeze shook a heavy shower of raindrops from a branch beneath which I was walking to my car. I ran a hand across my splashed face and hair. Then, tentatively, I tasted the water. It was brackish.

HER OLD ALBUMS

I only ever knew her as an old lady, so leafing through her albums was a banal surprise. In all but a few of the photos she is younger than me; in many, she is less than half my age.

Well! 'Old'. She must have been thirty-five, still a young woman – and inexplicably still unmarried – when I was five. But to a five-year-old, of course, thirty-five is ancient: as ancient, as permanent, as Earth.

Ten years later, to this teenager, she was merely there: 'Auntie Shelagh', an unremarkable spinster in her mid-forties, sitting on the verandah, smiling pleasantly at the camera from a morris chair on whose arm she would absently drum with the fingernails of her left hand: still ageless, aka 'old'.

In the same way, sixty to thirty was old; eighty to fifty (eighty to anything!) was old. We went through life in lockstep, me and Auntie Shelagh. Auntie Shelagh was always old.

And old she remained in the earliest photo I have of her: a little girl of three, staring expressionlessly at the camera with its no doubt hooded photographer from her sedentary mother's lap (someone must have toted that rocking chair out into the garden specifically for the shoot), mother and daughter surrounded by stone-faced adults. For that wasn't, of course, Auntie Shelagh. A three-year-old is but the premise of a person, and one accepts her as that. So there was no tension in the thought that this was Auntie Shelagh. This was merely genealogy.

But who was that indistinct, brown girl of thirteen or fourteen in the sepia print, her hair still in plaits, smiling shyly at the camera from the thwart of an old rowing boat adrift on the flat water of Staubles Bay, surrounded again by, this time, beaming grownups?

Who was that girl guide, suddenly flesh-and-blood, already at sixteen with the figure of a young woman, standing with chin tilted and an inexplicably proud smile, shoulders back, hands clasped behind her, in the courtyard of 'Convent', her definite attractiveness highlighted by her unfortunate companion: a square-set, pale child with a wavy 'madonna' hairstyle whose presumably blameless gaze some lapse on the film developer's part, or else some trick of the light, has turned into a glare?

Who, above all, was that ravishing young woman of twenty-three or twenty-four, long-necked and short-haired, full-lipped and filmy-eyed, with a face that should have launched a thousand men (tapering in due course to the One) – a face that had bedrooms and babies, marriages and mortgages, PTAs and boredom and lunchtime assignations, and other men's divorces, and maybe in time her own, written all over it?

What happened, Auntie Shelagh? What went wrong?

The question is rhetorical, for she is dead, and so are those of her contemporaries who could have told me.

So I riffled her albums for clues, discovering myself oddly bitter on her behalf to find that, by the time she and her world burst into festive technicolour therein, Auntie Shelagh was in her fifties: still pleasant-faced, but now with that middle-aged spread, quite definitely solid, 'past it'.

There were a bewildering number of locations. The on-the-lawn shots, the verandah shots, the school shots: I had no problem with those. Nor with the hack weekend locales of old Trinidad: the bushy, rocky aspect of down-the-islands; the mandatory light-&-shade of the Botanical Gardens; the shady porch and fretworked eaves of some cocoa-plantation home in the foothills of the Northern Range; the lacy surf and arty-looking driftwood of Mayaro with its fallen coconut trunks, astraddle of one of which some brown-skinned, mustachioed Rudolf Valentino was strumming a cuatro for the benefit of three young women, arms interlinked, laughing at the camera – all of them, including the balladeer, in those vest-top, square-thighed one-piece bathing suits people used to wear in the 1930s. (And maybe this is hindsight, but something about the difference between Auntie Shelagh's laughing mouth and circumspect eyes – and perhaps, too, because she's so strikingly the rose between the thorns – I mean, she's clearly a beauty, and the other girls, they just look like good sports, you know? – makes her seem the odd-one-out: as though somehow she shouldn't be there, and isn't, really.)

But then there were all those interiors I couldn't place – including a bedroom with a big old four-poster double-bed sans canopy, on which Auntie Shelagh, Bermuda-shorted, big-calved (a distortion of perspective) is half-reclining, looking languorously and with faint amusement at the camera. (This was circa 1950. Auntie Shelagh would have been in her mid-thirties by then. There is something quite disturbing about that shot.)

There was one of a woollen-capped, overcoated and scarved Auntie Shelagh, still only in her late twenties, smiling brightly at the camera from the jovial embrace of a black-frocked, old white priest (although – I have to say it – she is too lovely, and he is too old, for either nationalism or prurience to forgive him that fulsome hug) on a dramatic promontory with a little stone church. (Auntie Shelagh went to Ireland?)

There was one in a gondola (Auntie Shelagh went to Venice?!!) with a tall, angular, and passably distinguished-looking white gentleman in perhaps his late forties. He is sitting with rolled-up shirtsleeves, smoking a pipe and clearly striking a pose, and Auntie Shelagh, by now pushing forty, is looking at him with amusement, and not without tenderness; though I somehow doubt he was The One – except perhaps on that trip.

Nor was the cuatro-playing Valentino the one, I think, never mind he turns up quite often – though always in group photos – in this young phase of Auntie Shelagh's mysteriously obscure life.

Even the handsome, always serious, chocolate-brown young man gracing several of the photos of Auntie Shelagh in her prime – the long neck, the short hair, the luscious mouth, the misty eyes! – even he, I don't think, was The One. And this despite the shot an inexperienced eye might well see as the smoking gun: he and Auntie Shelagh standing – he, suited up and serious, she in a tight-waisted, straight-skirted floral print and a stylish large black hat, her wrist in the crook of his arm, her expression that of a young woman who *feels* beautiful – at the foot of the steps of that church in Santa Cruz, at which some wedding or funeral would appear to have just taken place, though the shot yields neither bride nor hearse.

Maybe he was 'captain of the Second Eleven'; maybe he was very nearly the one. Maybe, even, she loved him, but he was just Too Dark in her parents' eyes; for Auntie Shelagh was nearer to octoroon than black. Maybe.

But me, I think it was someone else: a stocky, square-faced, Portuguese-looking guy, whose unsmiling image turns up only once in Auntie Shelagh's albums: in a passport photo on an otherwise empty page.

That empty page! Its ripples of nothingness, its shockwaves of silence, spreading outward from the exclamation mark of his ill-tempered stare! Somehow, I don't even think he gave Auntie Shelagh that photo. Somehow I think she filched it from him.

At any rate – and all those who could have proven me wrong are dead – I think he messed her up good and proper, ol' Stone Face. I think she entered the tunnel of 'him' all lovely and delicious and life-ready and moist, and came out the other end as… Auntie Shelagh. Auntie Shelagh, the precinct now of hoary Irish priests and pipe-smoking gentlemen in gondolas, though for many years she would be beautiful still.

And I think: You should have fought off your parents, Auntie Shelagh, and married the too-dark, good-looking, serious young man.

But she didn't – maybe she didn't love him; maybe she just liked him a lot – and so, left unbraced, lovely and vulnerable, running the gauntlet of her perilous twenties, she fell into the arms of the Portuguese felon…

…and, after that, it was just a matter of Auntie Shelagh getting through the years.

But I don't know. The Mermaid says I'm too harsh. Maybe we should leave Auntie Shelagh's life as the *tabula rasa* it was always heading to become.

So, okay. Scrap this little memoir.

IN MIAMI IMMIGRATION

[*Though for stylistic reasons this piece is written in the third person – 'the man' – it is of course autobiographical. I have 'the Argentinian's' permission to excerpt here from her own diary account of that evening.* WB.]

In the harbour that May afternoon the wind was up, and the yacht hissed downwind under mainsail alone on the crinkled flat water off Palisadoes. The woman steering it – for the first time – was in her mid-forties. She was a fair-skinned Jamaican, and the strong following wind blew her black-maned-lion's hair around her face, so that the man thought of her (ungrammatically) as The Argentinian. She sat, body taut, chin tilted, the hand holding the tiller extended out sideways, correcting course with little jerks this way and that. Watching her, the man thought: *What's beauty but aliveness?*

Now, one month later, as the night of June 23rd wore on in one of the interrogation rooms of the Immigration Department of Miami International Airport, that image – of her, the hissing yacht, the windy afternoon and blue sky – kept returning to the man as he sat in a low chair and watched, at eye level, Mr Olmsted's thick, discoloured fingers hitting the keyboard on the desk between them inexpertly but hard.

'Height?'

'Six-one.'

Mr Olmsted typed laboriously. There had been no introductions, but his navy blue Homeland Security uniform bore a metal breast-tag, 'Olmsted', and so the man thought of him as Mr Olmsted.

'Weight?'

'Two-ten.'

Mr Olmsted typed.

When that particular computerised form was finished, he printed the pages and added them to the neat and growing sheaf of papers beside the keyboard. Then he rose, saying, 'Come with me.'

Mr Olmsted was a big, square-shouldered man, sixtyish, whose Nordic features had been tanned and hardened by life in America, or the sun, or something else. Watching him type, the man thought he had never seen such thick and dirt-discoloured fingers; and he wondered what Mr Olmsted had done for a living – been a farmer in Iowa? Dug foxholes with his hands in Vietnam? – before finding himself in this room, at this desk, in hot, Hispanic Miami, with pension and insurance plans being routinely slashed by the Bush administration and his own retirement looming.

In the corridor, a group of Hispanic Homeland Security personnel were chatting heartily. 'Jamaican guy,' one said, of a man in another room. 'When I asked him about all that cash, he said it was to buy jewellery for his girlfriend.'

The others laughed.

'In here,' Mr Olmsted said.

The room was little more than a cubicle; it held a fingerprinting machine and digitised camera, both hooked up to a computer screen.

'Give me your right thumb,' Mr Olmsted instructed. He produced a cloth, wiped the pad of the man's thumb, wiped a small illuminated square on the machine, then pressed one down on the other. The man's thumbprint came up on the monitor, hugely magnified.

'Now, your right index finger,' Mr Olmsted said. Again he wiped the pad of the man's finger, wiped the illuminated square, pressed one down on the other. Mr Olmsted did this, one by one, with all ten of the man's fingers.

'Now look at the camera there.'

The man looked. His face came up on the monitor.

Mr Olmsted cast around him. Not finding what he was looking for, he said, 'Wait here,' and went out and returned with a letter-sized beige card, which he inserted in a printer. It

317

emerged with ten fingerprints and a photo. The man looked at the latter and didn't recognise himself.

'Sign here,' Mr Olmsted said.

The man looked at the form. It was headed: 'Criminal'.

'I'm not signing that,' the man said.

'Say again?'

'I'm not signing a form headed "Criminal".'

'It's the procedure,' Mr Olmsted said. 'These are the forms they give us.'

The man looked at Mr Olmsted and shook his head. 'No.'

Mr Olmsted's jaw tightened, his pupils grew small, and it occurred to the man that this was someone who would not hesitate to hurt him if his superiors ordered him to, or if he thought it were for the national security of the United States; and who could say that, in Mr Olmsted's mind, the two were not the same?

'Wait here,' Mr Olmsted said again.

There was nowhere to sit. The man stood in the windowless cubicle and waited.

In the harbour that afternoon the wind was blowing, and the yacht hissed downwind on the flat, crinkled water... The wind blew her black-maned-lion's hair around her face...

He waited for perhaps fifteen minutes before Mr Olmsted reappeared. But in fact he had been waiting for four hours – ever since, at five that afternoon, he'd presented his passport at the Immigration counter, had watched the officer stare at the screen for longer than seemed appropriate, then rise, telling him, 'Wait here,' and go inside.

When he returned, there was a colleague with him.

'You may want this,' the man told them, and presented a letter to US Immigration from the Head of the MFA Creative Writing Program of Lesley University, Cambridge, Mass, that explained he had been invited to teach a nine-day residency of creative writing workshops there. It ended: 'Please don't hesitate to contact me personally if you have any questions,' and it gave the Head's phone numbers (including his cell).

The man had travelled to Cambridge twice before with the same visa and papers on the same programme and had had no problems. But now the first officer pounced on the letter.

318

'You're coming here to *work*?' He demanded, with strange incredulity and rage; and the man thought: Not again. Two years earlier, en route to giving a reading at the Miami Book Fair, he'd been pulled from the line and interviewed before having his passport returned to him and being allowed to proceed.

'Wait right here,' the immigration officer said now; and soon a female airport officer came and escorted him to the same holding room he'd been in two years before. There were about twenty-five people there, sitting in plastic chairs fastened to each other and the floor: mainly Hispanics, with a few European youths and working-class West Indians (including women with babies and small children), and one unkempt Asiatic man who might have been Korean.

The man handed his passport as instructed to a uniformed woman standing behind one of a bank of computer screens. She typed briefly, looked from screen to passport, then told him: 'Oh! I know why you're here.' But at that point the officer next to her said something to her and she didn't elaborate.

'Take a seat,' that officer said. 'Your name will be called.'

That was around 5:15.

The Argentinian had flown up from Jamaica to be with him in Cambridge, and on their flight too had been a mutual friend, a mild-mannered, middle-aged Jamaican schoolteacher, 'D', likewise travelling to Boston. Landing in Miami, they knew they'd have to hurry to make the connection; and the man was just thinking that, when he failed to appear in the baggage hall, they wouldn't know what to do, when the mild-mannered schoolteacher was ushered into the room and came over and sat next to him.

'They told me to come in here and wait. They took away my passport,' she said.

The man thought with horror of the Argentinian – who'd been ahead of them at the Immigration counter and been passed through – waiting for them in the baggage hall, and them not appearing... not appearing...

[*From the Argentinian's diary:*
I can't remember what the guy at the Immigration counter looked like now. Pleasant-voiced, he stamps my documents, giving me until

September to stay in the US. One casual glance over my shoulder to see
W and D now behind a couple of French girls who had been rewriting
papers. Oh, well. I'll wait for them in the Baggage Hall. It's now after
5 and our flight is 6:15, so we have time…
…What's keeping them? I find a seat at the bottom of an escalator
with a clear view of the second escalator… Come on, you guys, we'll
miss the flight…!]
…and for the first time that evening the man felt the depth of
the wrongness of what was being done, not only to him but more
so to the two women who'd travelled up with him.

'They only brought you in here because they saw you talking
to me,' he told the gentle and now pale schoolteacher. 'You'll be
out soon.'

She gave a little, shocked laugh. 'They asked me if I was your
wife,' she said. 'I said no.'

The man said nothing for a while. Then he said: 'The Argentinian's alone.'

[*I watch as travellers descend into freedom from immigration. I look*
for shiny black loafers. It's like checking lotto numbers. Black shoes: 1st
number. Now check for black trousers (2nd number), topped by yellow
polo shirt (3rd number). I only get to the second number twice. Most men
are favouring sneakers as travel wear, or those topsiders with leather
laces. What about D? Black shoes, jeans. I have more luck with this
ticket. But still no jackpot. Still no familiar, calm, smiling face. If I
crane my neck to the right I can see the shoulders of the descending
travellers on the escalator directly above me. A yellow shirt… YES!…
I jump up. But it is not W's face coming down to me. The shoes and
legs and torsos of strangers have never held my attention for so long.]

Now, at 9:15, Mr Olmsted returned to the cubicle where the
man had been standing waiting. His expression was purposeful,
his manner brisk. 'You're being returned to Jamaica on the first
flight tomorrow morning. Till then they're going to hold you
here. Come with me.'

The man thought: '*They*'? *They!*' The terrible, monolithic,
faceless They.

Back in the interrogation room, Mr Olmsted started on another computerised form. The first one, the man deduced, had
been designed to prove he was travelling on the wrong visa, on the

basis of which, he assumed, he'd just been told he was being refused entry to the US.

'You say,' Mr Olmsted said now, 'the university told you it was the right visa, and you entered the US on it for the same purpose twice before?'

'That's correct,' the man said, adding: 'Without any problem.' Though by now he had ceased to hope.

Mr Olmsted typed.

'And did you file tax returns here on income received on those visits?'

'I wasn't paid for those visits. I was paid later when I was back in Jamaica, for follow-up work I did by correspondence there.'

'Whatever. Did you file tax returns in this country on that income?'

'Yes.'

Mr Olmsted looked up from his typing. 'Can you prove that?'

'If you mean, did I walk with copies of my tax returns, no.'

'Never mind,' Mr Olmsted said. 'We can check that easily enough. Take a seat outside.'

The man rose and went back to what he thought of as the holding pen. It was now 9:30 and the number of unfortunates still lolling there had shrunk to maybe a dozen.

Four hours earlier, he had sat there with D, the mild-mannered Jamaican schoolteacher also pulled from the Immigration queue. He'd been angry on her behalf – she was pale with shock – but also relieved. Through her, he'd be able to get a message to the Argentinian, waiting by herself in the baggage hall, in the grip, he imagined, of the far greater horror of not knowing what had happened to them.

[By 5:45 I am talking to everyone in uniform who has a hand-held radio. 'Excuse me, my friends are in immigration and I don't know what's holding them up.' I repeat this over and over, until I hear the futility of my words.

'Sit and wait.'

'There's nothing you can do but wait.'

'Ask them to find out if they're being held for questioning.' This last from a large young woman pushing a laden baggage trolley.

I can't get anyone to even do that. They look through me while I

321

hover, trying to look suitably humble, patient, grateful and persistent all at the same time. I am frightened and hungry and afraid to go to the bathroom and miss my companions. My insides are in spasm. My mind whirls.]

'Listen,' the man told D. 'You'll be out of here long before me. When they let you go, you and the Argentinian go and book in at the nearest Marriott. If it's full, go to Red Roof Inn. Then phone the administrator of the Lesley MFA programme; tell him what's happened, and not to meet our plane at Logan. I'll call the Marriott as soon as I can. If you don't hear from me by morning, tell the Argentinian to either go to her family in Florida or fly back to Jamaica. You go on up to Boston.'

He registered the glazed look the schoolteacher gave him and said again: 'Listen, this is important. Wait; I'll write it down.'

But, writing, his heart sank. The Argentinian, he suspected, would refuse to leave the airport without him.

'Tell her,' he told D, 'she *has* to go and book into the Marriott. Tell her it's the only way I'll know how to find her.'

[*This is not happening. This is a nightmare. What am I doing here? Now I have to do something to help and I have no way of helping.*

I'll call my brother [in Miami]. *I have a few quarters. My hand shakes as I try to locate my change. The phone needs four quarters to make a call. I have two. I am alone in a strange place where no-one cares what happens to me and for the sake of fifty cents I am unsafe. There are no machines to buy a phone card. They say I can go outside, but then I can't come back in and I won't go any further away from W and D. I am already a lifetime away from them. Where are they? Is W okay? What are they doing to him?*]

Presently: 'I'm hungry,' D said.

The man rose, picked out a not-unattractive, young, blue-uniformed African-American and went over to her.

'My friend there,' he told her, 'hasn't eaten since breakfast. Is it possible to get her something to eat?'

'I'll see about it,' the young woman said. She left the holding pen, and did not return.

[*The shoes and legs and bodies of men and women keep coming down into the hall. They step off the escalator so carelessly, not realising how lucky they are. I am sitting on a slatted wooden bench. I stack my red bag, D's black bag and my carry-on around me. This island of possessions is my world...*

I am cold. I fumble to open my bag to extract a jacket. Everything is taking me so long. I am trembling. I haven't eaten since around 7 a.m. so convince myself that it's low blood sugar making me shaky...]

When the man returns, D has taken out a paperback and is trying to read. The man glances across and sees it's Roethke. Over her shoulder, he reads: 'The lost self changes,/ Turning towards the sea...'

The great, melancholy American poet!

In the harbour that blue afternoon... the yacht hissing downwind... the Argentinian on the tiller looking straight ahead, chin tilted, the wind blowing her black-maned-lion's hair around her face...

'Put that away,' the man says. 'This isn't a place for poetry.'

D giggles, then closes the book.

[*A young Frenchman shares my spot at the bottom of the stairs. We are castaways on the island of uncertainty. It connects us. It makes me brave. 'Excuse me, do you speak English?' I have forgotten whatever French I know.*

'Little bit,' he smiles.

I do not hesitate. He has a cell phone. 'Please, would you let me borrow your phone? I will pay for the call...'

'Please...' He hands me the phone.

I feel choked up, the way you do at a sudden kindness.

I get through to W's friend's house in Jamaica and have to leave a message with his young daughter. 'Tell daddy right away,' I emphasise.

She reads the message back to me. 'Uncle W is in Miami Immigration and having problems.' She pauses. 'What would you like my daddy to do?' She asks intelligently.

I want to scream: 'I DON'T KNOW! Go to Guantanamo maybe, call the Prime Minister, oh, and a lawyer too, and a cardiologist, just in case...'

Instead I say calmly, 'He'll know what to do, sweetheart.' I am trying to be normal, but the endearment sounds out of place in this sterile hall. I feel as if I'm in solitary confinement with no idea of how long my sentence is.]

In the holding pen, a young officer raises his voice. He calls the name of the gentle schoolteacher and she starts up, then turns and gives the man a stricken look.

'I'm okay,' he tells her. 'Go! Remember: you all go to the Marriott! I'll call you as soon as I can.'

[*I am staring so hard at the shoes descending that I don't see D appear. I hear her voice and it pulls me back from my nightmare. I think I embrace her, but I can't really remember. I only know that I have an ally in this strange land of US Law.*

W has written instructions for us to follow. I listen carefully but D has to repeat the message several times. If my face is as shocked as hers I understand why. His writing is neat and organised, so his mind must be too. Don't let them rattle you, W... don't stun them with vocabulary they can't understand. Don't piss them off, please...]

That is around 7:30. Around 8:00 the man hears his name called, and he rises and follows the big Scandinavian-American whose name tag says 'Olmsted' into the interrogation room...

Now, at minutes to 10:00, Mr Olmsted summons the man a second time from the holding-pen. There is no more talk about tax returns; the man assumes his were checked, and checked out. This now is a third form. The information overlaps with that he's already given.

'Nationality?'

'Trinidadian.'

'But you reside in Jamaica?'

'Yes.' From his low chair, the man watches Mr Olmsted's thick, discoloured fingers hitting the keyboard inexpertly but hard.

'Would you fear for your safety if deported to Jamaica?'

The man is startled, but he says shortly: 'No.'

'And if deported to Trinidad?'

To the man, this is a new thought. Perhaps, he thinks, startled again, he'll get to see his Trinidad-based daughter! It occurs to him to reply: *The only place I fear for my safety is in the hands of you goons.* But he says again simply: 'No.'

Mr Olmsted types: 'No.' 'No.'

At 10:20, an AA employee appears and stands in the door of the interrogation room. 'His wife wants to know,' she says to Mr Olmsted, 'if he's still here.'

The man thinks: *She took a chance with that 'wife'.*

324

Then he thinks: *I knew she wouldn't leave.*

Mr Olmsted looks from the man to the AA employee.

'Please tell my wife,' the man tells her, not glancing at Mr Olmsted and speaking fast in case he tries to cut him off, 'to go *now* and check in at the Marriott. Tell her I'll call her at the Marriott. Please.'

The AA woman looks from the man to Mr Olmsted. Mr Olmsted says nothing. The AA woman leaves.

[D and I leave the arrival hall without incident. No-one asks us anything or stops us. My heart is pounding as we walk away from the gate. We are beside the area where AA checks bags for the ongoing flights. The activity looks so unreal. We go to the airline counter and persuade them to check us on to Boston on the early morning flight. They are not keen to check W. The agent, Gina, confides: 'When they keep you longer than five hours, they're not letting you go. I'll have the list of deportees in the morning.' She sees the horror in our faces.

'Deportee!' This word is not in our world.

Am loathe to leave but it is 10:30 and I am faint and dizzy. We leave the airport and the outside world is running smoothly. I comfort myself with the knowledge that I will have a phone in the room and W will find us...]

'Now is there anything you want to say?' Mr Olmsted says.

'Anything like what?' the man asks him.

'Any comments. Questions.'

The man looks away and thinks.

'This had no right to happen to me,' he says distinctly; and he waits while Mr Olmsted types. Then (pausing every few words): 'I'm here on the visa the university told me was appropriate, the same visa on which I've come here twice before, to perform the same function, without any problem. So I'm interested to know why this time it's the wrong visa. I'm also concerned about the disruption of Lesley University's MFA programme. I don't know they'll be able to replace me on a day's notice.'

Mr Olmsted types and types. Then he prints it out, hands the man two pages and says: 'Your visa is being cancelled. If you tick the "Withdrawal of Application for Visa" box and sign at the bottom, it means you're not automatically blocked from applying for another visa for five years.'

The man reads through the form, including his comments. Then he ticks the 'Withdrawal' box and signs it.

'Wait outside.'

[*The hotel room is sheer luxury. I pounce on the phone. D stretches on the bed nearest the door. I try to call W's friend in Jamaica, leave a message. Next, my brother. He wants to come for me at once. I tell him I will call him in the morning.*

Room service takes half an hour. We eat at midnight, sitting on the soft beds. I force the food past the lump in my throat. For two hungry people we take a long time to eat this meal. W has had no food for hours. I feel guilty that I am safe and comfortable. I can't turn off my imagination.]

Sometime after midnight, Mr Olmsted reappears in the holding pen and summons the man. 'We'll be taking your bags now. They'll be tagged for the first flight back to Jamaica. Do you need anything in them?'

'My medication,' the man says. 'And a book.'

'Medication for what condition?'

'Bypass surgery.'

This alerts Mr Olmsted. He goes back into the computer, finds another form, begins typing. 'You had that when?'

'Four years ago,' the man says. Then he asks: 'Is there a toilet in this... room... where I'll be spending the night?'

'There're toilet facilities,' Mr Olmsted says. Then he confides, 'It's not a very edifying environment.'

The man thinks: *Well, look at that. He just managed to couch a threat as a confidence.* And again he looks at Mr Olmsted's fingers, the thickest, most dirt-discoloured fingers he's ever seen, and wonders what Mr Olmsted has done for a living, down the years.

'Any other medical condition?'

'Look,' the man says suddenly. 'Nothing matters to me now except that my wife should hear my voice.' Saying this, he hopes desperately that D and the Argentinian have left the airport and booked in at the Marriott.

'Don't worry,' Mr Olmsted says. 'We'll get a message to her soon. Let's just finish this form.'

'Listen,' the man tells him. 'You look like a family man. Imagine you're travelling with your wife on some perfectly normal trip and suddenly you disappear and she has no idea what's happened to you, and eight hours pass. She won't want a message from the people who are holding you. She'll want to hear your voice.'

'We'll come to that,' Mr Olmsted says. 'Now: any other medical condition?'

The man carefully repeats himself. 'Nothing matters to me now except that my wife should hear my voice.'

Mr Olmsted pushes back and looks at him. Then he rises, saying: 'There's no phone in this room; come with me. We'll use the phone next door.'

The man follows Mr Olmsted into a room where a young Hispanic officer is interrogating the Korean-looking guy. This officer looks up, sees the man, and demands angrily of Mr Olmsted: 'What's he doing in here?' Then, shouting: *'Get him out of here!'*

'Sorry,' Mr Olmsted says; and he leads the man back to their room. 'Tell you what,' he says there. 'We'll call her on my cell.'

He finds the number. 'This is Inspector Olmsted of Miami Immigration,' he tells the Marriott.

('So that's his designation,' the man thinks. 'Inspector'.)

'Can you put me through to —?'

Be there, the man is thinking. *Be there.*

Mr Olmsted hands him the phone.

[*At 1:00 a.m. there's a male voice with a call from WB. I am numb. 'Thank you, thank you,' I mumble. I am pathetically grateful.*]

'Hi,' the man says to the Argentinian. 'You okay?'

'What's happening? How are you?'

'I'm okay. Did you all call [the Lesley administrator] and tell him not to meet our plane?'

'Yes. He was horrified. He wanted to know who I was… What are they doing to you?'

'Nothing, I'm okay,' the man tells her. 'But they say I'm on the wrong visa. They're sending me back to Jamaica on the first flight tomorrow morning… this morning. Till then, I'm to be a guest of the US Government.'

'O God.'

'No, it's okay. Now, listen. Go to the airport early and book in on the same flight. You won't see me at the airport – '

' – O God! – '

' – but I'll be on the plane. Let's just go home and pick up one of the cars and go to Sandals. Right now, all I want to do is go to the beach.'

A pause. Then: 'Okay.' She says it suddenly, like an automaton. Then: 'What should I do with the rum?'

It takes the man a moment to remember: at Norman Manley Airport, in what now feels to him like another life, he'd bought one of those overpriced gift cases of four pint-sized bottles of premium Appleton. The Argentinian had been carrying it when they were separated. He's thinking, 'Women! Imagine thinking about the rum at a time like this,' when he realises the importance of the rum. The rum is all she's had of him for the past eight hours.

'Bring it with you,' he tells her. 'We'll drink it.'

'Okay.'

'Anyway, listen,' the man says. 'I have to go. They' – looking at Mr Olmsted – 'they interrupted the fingernails torture to let me make this call.'

'Stop that,' the Argentinian says brokenly; and the man knows she's all in. But he thinks it was the only way to make her believe he's alright. He hopes he's right.

Handing the phone back to Mr Olmsted, the man thinks: 'I owe you one' (a debt he later repays when, writing about that night, he leaves out certain things he thinks Mr Olmsted would rather he left out).

'Well, that's about it,' Mr Olmsted tells him. 'You have your medication? Good. Now wait outside. They'll call you when they're ready.'

[*Now at least we know.*]

Half-an-hour later, Mr Olmsted appears in the holding-pen, where now there's only the man, the unkempt Korean guy, and one other detainee whose appearance the man doesn't register.

'Hi, Wayne?' Mr Olmsted calls.

The man thinks with incredulity: *He thinks we're friends.*

'There's just one more form. I don't know how I forgot it.'

The man thinks: *Someone keeps sending him back to keep this thing going.*

He is too tired to wonder who or why. He rises and returns to the interrogation room…

'Hey, Olmsted, are you capped?' This from a blue-uniformed Homeland Security officer appearing at the door.

'No, I'm not capped,' Mr Olmsted tells him.

Ten minutes later, there's another officer in the doorway. 'Olmsted, you sure you not capped?'

'No, I'm not capped.'

To the man he confides: 'I know I'm not capped because this is the first time I'm working overtime for the month.'

The man deduces that capped means reached his overtime limit. That these others want some of that overtime for themselves. In his by now semi-surreal frame of mind, the man thinks of them as scavengers on the African veldt, trying to drive Mr Olmsted away from his profitable carcass and take his place at it…

Nearing 2:00, a big, brown-haired Hispanic officer, fortyish, entered the room and went and stood behind Mr Olmsted, looking over his shoulder at the computer monitor. 'What's going on?' he asked.

Mr Olmsted told him.

'How long was he coming for?'

'Nine days,' Mr Olmsted said.

'Nine days!' the big Hispanic guy exclaimed. He stormed out of the room, then reappeared in the doorway and bellowed at Mr Olmsted, '*Nine days!!!*' – and the man knew it was over.

This whole thing was a set-up, he thought. But he didn't know that. And looking at Mr Olmsted, he thought next: *If it was, he didn't know it either.*

Mr Olmsted's face wore the tight, pained look of someone being upbraided who knows better than to try to defend himself.

'Who's that guy,' the man asked Mr Olmsted, after the big, brown-haired Homeland Security man with the Hispanic accent had left the room. 'Some sort of supervisor?'

'More than that,' Mr Olmsted said. 'He's the supervisor of supervisors.' His tone was difficult to decipher.

There was a silence.

So now we're both waiting, the man thought; and he suddenly felt very tired. He glanced around the small windowless room. He'd been awake for twenty-one hours, some twenty of them spent sitting – at his computer in Kingston, in the car to the airport, in the airport, the plane to Miami, the holding pen, this small featureless room – and he wanted very much now to either walk or sleep.

They didn't wait long. The big Hispanic guy returned and went around to Mr Olmsted's side of the desk and tapped him on the shoulder, and Mr Olmsted promptly rose and stood aside, yielding him his seat. For a few minutes (while the silence lengthened out) the Hispanic guy attended to the monitor: reading, changing the screen, reading again. Then he said to the man: 'Tell me again why you're here.'

The man told him.

'So this nine-day residency is like a getting-to-know-you session with the students?'

'Yes, with some readings and workshops.'

'And you're not paid for them?'

'No.'

'You're not paid while you're in this country?'

'No.'

'I hope you're telling the truth.'

The man stared at him and said nothing.

'Well!' the Hispanic guy said, pushing back. 'I still think there're sufficient grounds to refuse you entry. But I don't want to disrupt your university's program, so I'm going to admit you. But check with your lawyer, is my advice.'

Now you're covering yourself, the man thought. 'So what, in your view,' he asked him, 'would be the right visa?'

The Hispanic guy went back into the computer, reading and occasionally murmuring, as if to himself: 'This one? No, not this... Maybe this one... No... No.'

Finally he said: 'I don't know. And it may well be I'm wrong. But check with your university's lawyer, is my advice.'

[Both the university and the US Embassy's consular section in Trinidad later reaffirmed that the man had been on the appropriate visa.]

'Well!' The Hispanic guy rose, offering his hand, and the man rose and took it. 'Good luck,' the Hispanic guy said. 'I hope you get some sleep; you look tired.' And at this point an odd thing happened. The man felt his own gaze harden and saw the Hispanic guy's eyes instantly harden in return, so that as suddenly as the crash and backwash of a wave there was something in the air between them – not hatred, not fury, but like a blind clashing of wills. In the corner of his eye the man saw the Hispanic guy turn in the doorway and look back at him, but he was already resuming his seat.

'So,' he said to Mr Olmsted. 'I assume my visa has been cancelled?'

'Oh, no,' Mr Olmsted said.

'Then why aren't you destroying those forms?'

'Oh, you don't have to worry about these, they're filed quite separately.'

Mr Olmsted was typing again.

'Here' – he turned the monitor around so the man could read it – 'This is what they'll see in Immigration next time you come.'

The man read (something like): 'Entered to work in the US on a B1/B2 visa. He was interviewed and admitted on the authority of – ': the man read the name of the big brown-haired Hispanic guy, the 'supervisor of supervisors' at Miami Immigration, and immediately forgot it.

'How far do you think I'll get,' he asked Mr Olmsted, 'with a visa with "Cancelled" handwritten on it and then crossed out?'

'Don't worry!' Mr Olmsted said. 'Look, I'll put a stamp in it. There: "Admitted", and today's date. So they'll see you were admitted.'

The man said nothing. Then: 'So can I go now?'

'Yessir,' Mr Olmsted said. 'You're free to go.'

There were no more words between them. The man went around to Mr Olmsted's side of the desk, retrieved his roll-on and shoulder bag, and walked with them out of the room and out through the holding pen (where two seeming indigents were still lolling, along with two Homeland Security officers who looked up but said nothing as he left). He rode the escalator down to the big empty baggage hall and walked through it, the roll-on's wheels whirring behind him in the silence, and through the empty customs hall where a lone black customs officer waved

331

him on as he approached; and he walked out through the automatic glass doors and into America.

At that hour of the morning – it was 2:20 – there was a solitary cab parked outside, its driver a middle-aged, blowsy-looking Hispanic woman. He rode it through empty streets to the Marriott, over-tipped the woman rather than wait for his change, and walked with roll-on and shoulder bag across the empty hotel lobby to where two young men were chatting behind the front desk.

[*I fall into a fitful sleep, only to be roused at 2:30 a.m. It can't be D's wake-up call already... Then W's voice, clearing the mist of sleep. 'I'm downstairs. Tell these people to let me come up.'*]

She was standing in the door, beside two room-service trays bearing the remains of a bowl of soup and a barely-touched fruit platter. 'I'm guessing this one is yours,' he said, picking up the fruit platter in passing –

' – Yes – '

– and he was already popping the melon chunks when they embraced.

'D' had been asleep in the other bed. She lifted her head and listened while the man gave a brief account of his final hour in Immigration. Then she said, with unexpected vehemence, 'They set you up!' and went back to sleep.

The man had a sudden, acute attack of claustrophobia.

'I don't want to be in this room,' he told the Argentinian. 'I don't want to be in a building at all. Come outside.'

They went down in the elevator and back out through the wide, empty lobby, she, barefoot, in pyjamas, he still in the T-shirt and trousers he'd left Kingston in (the young men at the front desk stopped chatting to watch them go), and went and sat together on the pavement of a little pathway between the hotel's ornamental plants, him talking in sporadic bursts, incredulous or contemptuous, she hugging his arm and responding urgently and grievously, still shell-shocked herself but giving him everything she had... until, by degrees, they surrendered to an exhaustion that was like a great, stunned calm.

At 3:00 in the morning, Miami was quiet. From time to time, the sound of a car came and went, speeding by somewhere not far away. A light, balmy breeze stirred the tops of the ornamental plants where they sat; and, looking up, the man saw that the south Florida sky was soft and clear. There was even Venus twinkling there.

Postscript:
When he awoke later that morning, 'D' had gone – taken the early flight up to Boston, the Argentinian told him. He made a few phone calls, and then they dressed and went down to breakfast. Then they checked out and took a cab to the airport.

There, at the security screen, the Argentinian was pulled out of the line and subjected to a 'special search' – that offensive procedure in which selected airline passengers are made to place their bare feet on sole-prints on the ground and raise their arms into the 'crucifix' position while strangers pat them all over their bodies, in full view of the passing parade – and when she finally rejoined the waiting man, she walked in silent fury so fast that the man told her to go on ahead, he'd meet her at the gate.

On the Boston flight, the movie was some harmless comedy with Dennis Quaid. In the middle of it, the Argentinian burst into tears. 'I want to go home!' she sobbed. 'I don't feel safe in this country anymore!'

It took a lot of comforting – it took a visit to the Kennedy Museum, and the laidback, strolling air of Harvard Square, and several of the man's university cohorts coming up to stand stiffly before them and say, with dignity and pain, 'I apologise for the behaviour of my Government' – to calm her down.

Back in their hotel room the afternoon after their arrival, the man was going over his writing workshop notes for the next day when the Argentinian said, half to herself: 'What should I do now?'

'Get naked and go in the bed?'

'Get naked and go in the bed! Then that's like, what, my Mission Statement?' Laughing: 'I was hoping for something rather more uplifting!'

Like that, the real world returned to them.

But their hold on it was not half as sure as it had been. That Sunday evening, the man gave what he was sure was the worst reading of his life, quite devoid of nervous energy and beset even as he read by the thought, *What am I doing on this stage reading fiction, to these kindly, intelligent, irrelevant people?* And when, a week after their arrival, the Argentinian left to return to Jamaica and had once again to change planes in Miami, she was seized by an irrational certitude in the Miami departure lounge (as she told him on the phone from Kingston that night) that every pair of blue-shirted officers she saw was coming to get her, to lead her away to some barred, unimaginable fate forever. And this terror grew to such an intensity that when she boarded the flight, and the jet taxied down the runway, and the wheels left the ground, the Argentinian broke down and cried.

She was safe at last. She was out of America.

SAD HALLOWEEN

It's catching on in Trinidad, so many things are; but my daughters were in their mid-teens by the time it began, too old to play 'Trick or Treat', and so I never took much notice of Halloween. To this day I don't know what it's about, really – something to do with witches? And to this day I don't really care.

So when, arrived in Georgia to teach college for a year, I saw signs of Halloween approaching, I let them go. The pumpkins piling up outside of supermarkets, the pumpkin-masks appearing on porches, more and more of the channels of cable TV showing movies like *Friday the 13th* and *The Exorcist* and *Nightmare on Elm Street*: somehow I managed to ignore them all. When something means nothing to you, you blank it out. And when finally a colleague at Albany State said in passing, 'I hope you realise today is Halloween,' I didn't know what he meant. 'What do you mean?' I said.

'I mean,' he said significantly, 'you're going to have hordes of children coming by ringing your doorbell tonight, and you'd better have lots of candy ready for them. Especially in that neighbourhood where you live; there're a lot of children. Lots and *lots* of candy.'

I looked at him in alarm. Candy isn't something I normally buy.

So here I was, Halloween day, 3 p.m., tied up on campus for the next couple hours, and unlikely to get back to my candy-less home more than a few minutes ahead of the first of the trick-or-treaters. I said, 'Jesus, thanks for the warning,' and hurried off down the corridor in search of Tina.

Tina's an undergrad who's been making pocketmoney doing some after-hours typing for me on my new IBM. She's snub-nosed and vague-eyed and never appears in public, so far as I can tell, except in jeans and a floppy hat with the front brim turned up – which makes her look like a character from Lil Abner. She's black but American, which means she doesn't share my insular terror of this infernal machine; and while she isn't the most accurate typist you ever met, she's straight: I have no problem giving her the key to the house when I'm not going to be there.

Tina's also laconic, to the point of silence: she almost never speaks unless she has to. One time I inveigled her into baking a chicken for me ('It'll just cook itself while you type') and midway through she appeared in the living room doorway, saying vaguely, 'Do you have a – ?' and then pausing, lost for the word. I could tell from the gesture she was making with her fingers that she meant a syringe, but by then I was so enamoured of hearing her speak – that laconic, metallic, black Southern woman's drawl – that I feigned incomprehension, till finally she came out with: 'Do you have somethin' I kin use to squirt juice on the bird?' She knocks me out.

This Halloween afternoon, Tina's scheduled to go to the house and type, so I hurry down the corridor and find her and explain my predicament, and ask her to pick up some candy on her way there. 'How much should I get?' I ask Tina.

'Aw. Five dollars.'

I give her ten.

'Hey!' I call as an afterthought. 'How much should I give each of them?'

'You kin give them one stick of candy. And one gum.' (She pronounces it 'gurm'.)

So that evening I arrive home to find that Tina has stocked the place with ten dollars' worth of candy and bubblegum. It seems like an awful lot, two large baking pans filled to overflowing; but I think, 'Better safe than sorry,' and go and bathe. Then I settle down to mark essays (forgetting again, you understand). But a few minutes later the doorbell rings and I think 'Oh, that must be the trick-or-treaters,' and I get up and go to the door. It's 6.30 on the dot, and outside it's getting dark.

I should add that I was living at the time on a quiet street perched tenuously between *the 'hood* and what you might call Television America. If you drove out of my street and turned left,

336

you came at once into Albany's version of the ghetto: the houses wretched, the lawns like junkyards (often with trashfires burning), the brothers hanging about or coming and going in those big old American cars, the women sitting outside on straightbacked chairs, the children playing rowdily in the yards. There at night it was very dark, for there were no streetlamps (how come?), and thence at night, three or four times a week, there'd come the sound of gunshots and police sirens. (One night I heard, startlingly, not the usual single shot or rapid burst of gunfire, but six measured explosions from what was clearly a heavy-gauge weapon, that came at, like, five-second intervals – Boom! (Pause.) Boom! (Pause) – and sounded like some demonic execution of an entire household. Then, five minutes later, the police sirens.)

Life in *the hood*.

That was if you came out of my street and turned left.

If on the other hand you turned right, you came – also at once – into the world of what we in the Caribbean think of as modern America: a world of four- and six-lane city streets and leafy boulevards, of the big fast food and department chains, Kentucky, Hardee's, K-Mart, Sears, of pretty houses and manicured lawns in quiet streets, brightly lit at night: a world of spaciousness, order, greenery, light.

My own street, as I say, marked the narrow divide between these harsh versions of Dante's *Inferno* and *Paradise*; and it shared characteristics of both. There were the children out of doors, but not the brothers; a few streetlights, but not many; the yards were neither particularly well-kept nor trashy; oaks and pecan trees punctuated the lawns, but no shrubbery; and so on. This was the ambiance in which I rose from my desk, at 6.30 on the dot on Halloween evening, and went to answer the doorbell. I'd braced for an exuberant 'Trick or Treat!' Instead, encountering only silence, I felt like someone momentarily falling forward into emptiness.

Half-a-dozen black children, boys and girls, ranging from about eight to fourteen, stood silently outside my door. In the deepening dusk they looked at me expressionlessly. None wore anything that might have passed for a costume. In their hands, I saw, were plastic supermarket shopping bags.

I said encouragingly, 'Trick or treat?' looking from one to another for a reply, or at least some gleam or glint of recognition: an answering nod, a confirming smile.

Nothing. Expressionless stares.

Then the smallest one, a boy, opened the mouth of his bag and made a small thrusting gesture with it towards me. I said brightly, 'Tell you what: you come in' – pointing at him – 'but you have to share what I give you with your friends here, okay?'

He nodded uncertainly. But I had not been understood: as I ushered him in there was a muted surge and the others followed.

In the living room they clustered at once around the dining table with its overflowing baking pans and silently opened their bags. I dropped into each what Tina had told me ('One stick of candy. And one gurm.') while they followed my hand with their eyes, each making sure apparently that no one was getting more than he or she got. When I'd finished, they turned away and, in silence, without a backward glance, walked out.

'Enjoy yourselves!' I called inanely.

But it was as if they hadn't heard.

Shaken, I returned to my desk.

Minutes later, the doorbell rang again.

Same silence, same scenario, except that this time, standing beyond the little group was a woman, their mother or shepherdess. I said to her, 'Trick or Treat?' asking this not as an encouragement now but as a mere question. She nodded curtly.

While I let them in and they, like those before, surrounded the table and in silence opened their shopping bags, she stood a few feet away, watchful, presiding.

'Well,' I said as they were leaving, addressing them but looking at her, 'I hope you have a nice Halloween.' She did not reply. But I imagined her expression softened slightly.

To the children I had already ceased to exist. I stood in the doorway and watched them leave, silent shadows moving away across the dark lawn, and get into their mother's car and drive off. Then I returned to my desk.

After that I didn't feel like answering the door anymore, but the doorbell, once having begun, now went on ringing. Each visitation was the same, and after a few more tries I found I didn't have the heart to assail their numbed silence with words of either greeting or farewell – words that had somehow begun to sound blasphemous. In silence I opened the door. In silence they entered and surrounded the dining table. In silence I distributed the candy and gum. And then I stood in the doorway, like one benumbed himself, and watched their silent shadows drifting away back into the darkness whence they'd come.

In one group there was someone different: a toddler, a little girl of two, too young yet to understand certain things. She grinned at me in anticipation, and I bent down and pinched her cheek, and she looked up at her sister, who was holding her hand, as if she'd just done something clever. Another time, there was the opposite: a group which included a boy who looked to be nineteen or twenty, a young man, really. Partly in tease, but mainly for the relief of saying something, I said to him accusingly, as a Trinidadian would: 'A big man like you?'

He didn't take my tone. 'Sir?'

'You're too old to be playing Trick or Treat,' I told him.

A pause. Then, understanding: 'That's not true!' he said indignantly. 'Look!' And he thrust at me his open shopping bag, showing it to be already quarter full. As though that proved me wrong.

The next day, a female colleague told me kids from neighbour-hoods like theirs, on Halloween night, are often sent out by their mothers to collect what they can. Which she, the mother, later sells back to the neighbourhood shop or hawks herself.

So. What to the kids of television America was a night of fun, of adventure, of wonder, even – to children such as these was merely a kind of begging (at their mother's behest): a once-a-year, after-hours' chore.

The sadness of the South!

Nearing eight o'clock I saw a crisis approaching. Because the pain, and somehow the guilt, of those expressionlessly staring faces had soon become too much to bear, I'd long ceased ration-ing the candy and gum and begun doling them out by the handful; and now one of the baking pans was empty and the bottom of the other one was already showing through. In consternation I phoned an acquaintance. 'What should I do?' I asked him. 'I think I'm running out of candy.'

He laughed heartily, as if I'd said something funny. 'Well, my friend,' he said. 'I know what I'd do. I'd get the hell out of there; go see a movie or something.'

It was an outlandish idea; yet, hanging up, I knew I would take his advice. Life, which has taught me many things, had not taught me to open the door to those expressionless eyes and say, 'Sorry, there's no candy'; and next, looking up and down my street, I saw what I hadn't noticed before: that all the houses were in darkness. I hurried into a tracksuit and sneakers and, locking the door behind me, drove out into the city.

The last thing I felt like doing was going to a movie, and there was nowhere else to go. I drove around aimlessly for a while. Then, finding myself in a white residential neighbourhood – and following a newspaper man's instincts – I turned into a quiet street (brightly lit, neat houses, pretty lawns) and parked.

This wasn't, it soon struck me, a great idea. How would I explain what I was doing if some cruising cop's car should nose alongside mine and stop? What if the law-abiding denizens of this quiet place should turn out to be members of the Klan? ('Oh, Albany's full of them,' a black professor had told me, early on.) What if, even as I sat there thinking, curtains were being surreptitiously parted, and a shotgun – perhaps the same shotgun I'd heard, startlingly, being advertised some weeks ago – was being balefully aimed?

(Overheard on the car radio, in the announcer's too-hearty voice: 'Shop at X between now and October 15 and win yourself – a 12-gauge shotgun!')

The things I do for you, dear reader.

Sitting there, though, the night was quiet and cool, and I didn't have long to wait. At nearly 8.30 the trick-or-treating posses had thinned out, but there was a small group still crisscrossing the street up ahead. I waited, and in due course they came my way, not pausing anymore but walking with the air of it being over, of going home. They were evidently siblings, two girls and a boy, between maybe five and twelve, and they passed on the grass verge right next to my car.

The eldest was dressed as Batman, but carried a devil's fork; the elder girl looked like some sort of fairy, until you saw her painted face; and the littlest one, a curly-headed child, was dressed in what seemed a polka-dotted clown's costume, with a witch's steepled hat. Perhaps having outstayed their parents' permission, they were walking fast, and the little one was having intermittently to run to keep up. As they passed my car, she was complaining breathlessly about that, and the older ones were laughing and pretending to snatch away her bag.

I waited another minute, till the sound of their animated children's voices had quite faded on the quiet night air.

Then I started the Mercury, made a three-point turn, and drove home.

THE SCENT OF THE PAST

Perhaps because it's twice as expensive as Port Antonio's other beaches – Frenchman's, Blue Lagoon, Dragon Bay – San San is also usually the emptiest. Fact, on weekdays there's hardly ever anyone there except the staff: the apologetic guardian of the gate (he knows they charge too much), the chef setting the tables in the windy cafeteria – a morning ritual which he performs with a mysterious flourish, given that no one's likely to come – and a bareback guy raking the jetsam into piles to cart away and burn, the pyre contemplated by the sedentary cleaning lady down from Goblin Hill.

I go to San San for the solitude – that, and the wide vista. The other places are horseshoe coves, 'little Edens', but too shut-in for a certain mood; and at San San the eye's unfettered. The shallow water between the island and the white facades of the still-pretty '60s villas of Millionaire's Row is variously turquoise, emerald, muffled brown; and west of the island is the cobalt of the open sea, sometimes with little white rushes all the way to the horizon, just below which lies Cuba. You can't see Cuba; but like a blind man you know it's there.

At San San the sun goes over your right temple and declines behind your left ear; and the water is always moving slightly...

On this morning, however, I was not the only pilgrim to San San. It was early, minutes past ten, and the light was still silvery with the rain's regret: the early-morning rain that always falls in Port Antonio, to the full Wagnerian accompaniment of thunderheads billowing seaward from the dark hills, the whole sky darkening, and then squall after squall of hard, blowing rain, the wind tightening to gooseflesh the flat water in the bay, before abruptly – a diurnal miracle – it clears...

But this morning there were, already, a young man and

woman in the sea, and – sitting on rather than in an aluminium deck chair on the narrow beach – an old white gentleman in dark glasses and a wide-brimmed straw hat.

Not the glasses so much as the way he held his head, perfectly still and looking straight ahead, told me he was blind. (For the sighted are never still: even sitting doing nothing in particular, our gazes flick with hardly a pause from this to that, our heads turn slightly, our shoulders shift, we're always readjusting, renewing our relationship to our surroundings. But at rest the blind have no 'surroundings', nothing to adjust to. Which is why a blind man seated alone can give the impression he's been sitting there since the beginning of Time.)

I assumed he was the charge of the couple in the sea, one or the other's aged father, whom with filial affection or conscientiousness they'd brought along to sit and listen to the wavelets and smell the sea.

The dutiful jetsam-harvester recognised me. He downed his rake, brought over a lounger, took my ticket in return, mumbled pleasantly something like 'Irie' or 'Yeah man,' and went back to increasing the little brown pile glistening on white sand fifty metres away. I spread my towel, doffed my T-shirt, fished in the scandal bag for Nabokov's *Ada*, and found my page at once (by a sort of mental zeroing in, for I hadn't marked it). I read:

'His own passion for her Van found even harder to analyse. What was it that raised the animal act to a level higher than even that of the most exact arts or the wildest flights of pure science? It would not be sufficient to say that in his lovemaking with Ada he discovered the agony of supreme 'reality.' Reality, better say, lost the quotes it wore like claws. For one spasm or two he was safe…'

Off to my right, the old man seemed lost in thought (well, how else can the blind sitting alone seem?). I wondered whether he knew I was here.

It was somehow a horrifying thought. I turned from it to contemplate the couple in the sea. They were out in the chest-deep water just inside the mossy buoyed rope: he in his early thirties, hirsute, tanned, prematurely balding, she, some years younger, with glistening white shoulders and short black hair.

They were face to face, forehead to forehead, hardly moving... and presently I realised with wry amusement what they were doing. (Why do such types assume that, just because the beached gazer can't see their bodies underwater, they don't know how they're disposed there?)

Of course, until my arrival there'd been no one to see them; the guy with the rake was some distance away, and the blind man didn't count. (Or did he? They were within earshot. Surely their prolonged silence and the absence of swimmers' splashings would have alerted him...?)

I glanced at him – and at that moment a gust of wind took his hat. He made a belated grab, then – pathetically! – briefly kept feeling for it while it was already pinwheeling away across the sand.

I looked around. The guy with the rake hadn't seen, and pale Aphrodite and dark Triton were hardly about to disentwine themselves to retrieve it. So I did. (At the last moment it made a doomed effort to escape me, but I pinned it.) I had no wish to intrude upon his solitude, but you cannot hand a blind man his hat without saying something, so, while still a few feet away, I said: 'Good morning.'

He half-turned and inclined his face – so that, sighted, he would have been staring not at me but directly into the sun – and I saw his sudden animation. When we interrupt a blind man's silence, I thought, we animate him; in some sense, we bring him to life.

'I have your hat,' I said carefully. 'Here it is.' I touched its straw brim to his uncertain palm.

'How kind of you!'

The words were heartier than I'd expected, yet dry. He was American. He turned the hat in his hands, then pushed it down securely on his head. I couldn't think of anything else to say.

'Well, I'll see you,' I said.

'Not if I see you first!'

The joke – so unexpected, so rude, somehow – stopped me; but again I could think of nothing to say. Presently:

'You are not Jamaican,' he said, conversationally enough.

(So he'd known I was still there.)

'No,' I said. 'From Trinidad.'

In the sea it was over. The man turned away with a languid lunge, surfacing on his back a little way off, and the girl leaned back, letting the water stream-comb her short black hair. The gesture briefly exposed her white breasts. She was topless.

'Ah, Trinidad!'

The blind man spoke as before, heartily, yet somehow drily. Just as if he hadn't heard the sudden splashing – though he'd paused at them.

2

He must have been in his mid-seventies; yet it would be misleading to call him old. In his presence, and in his voice – that harsh, dry voice! – there was nothing of infirmity or diminution. His knees were knobby, the shinbones prominent; when his straw hat blew, the wispy hair was white; and melanoma freckled his hands, as you see with so many white people past a certain age in these parts these days. But as he sat there, on rather than in his deck chair, in shorts and shirt, white socks and brown loafers, he seemed obscurely like a force at rest or a natural object; and the young man and woman in the sea – he, thirtyish, balding, Arab perhaps;, she, younger, and white as the moon – now appeared to subsist at his pleasure, and not the other way around, as I'd first thought.

'Ah, Trinidad!' The blind man said now, having paused (I was sure) to register the sudden splash in the water as the postcoital lovers broke apart. 'That's where Mr Naipaul is from, isn't it?'

It was an unexpected question, coming from him.

'Yes,' I said. Then: 'You've read Naipaul?'

'Indeed I have. Long ago, I read a book called *Miguel Street*. Very funny. I read it right here in Port Antonio.'

'The past is deep,' I said.

This was a line from 'B Wordsworth', one of the stories in that book. But he mistook the quote for a quip about his own life, and cocked his head. The ensuing silence seemed to await significance.

'I'm Beck,' he said abruptly. 'Matthew Beck.' And he held out his hand, in that soft slack uncertain way blind men do.

Taking it, I told him my name. We exchanged the usual pleasantries.

'Yes, indeed,' he said, resuming. 'Forty years ago this week. I read parts of it right here on this beach. Of course it's all changed now, I gather.' (He meant the beach, not the book.)

I glanced around at the open cafeteria, the asphalted driveway, the three parked cars, all Japanese, all white – three, not two: why hadn't I wondered at that before? – and the low wall with its four steps down to the sand.

'Well,' I said. 'I guess the sea is the same.'

'Yes, there's that,' he said. 'Some things never change.'

As he said it, I remembered a certain feckless water-haunter telling me, not long ago, that in her childhood there'd been a reef here. But it was curious, the complicated, embattled air the blind man imparted to that imprecise platitude.

In the water, the moon-white topless girl folded her arms and looked at us without pleasure. Her mate, I saw, was now some distance away.

I hadn't heard *Miguel Street* had been published in Braille.

'Oh, I wouldn't know about that,' he said when I asked him. 'No: I have friends back in Connecticut who read to me. But *Miguel Street* I read myself. Yes, I wasn't always blind. In fact, aside from newspapers and magazines, your Mr Naipaul has the honour of being the last author I was able to read with my own eyes. That's why I was interested to hear you're from Trinidad. How old are you, Mr Brown?'

I told him. I'd been standing arms akimbo a little to his right, shuffling my feet and looking around from time to time. Now I sat on the sand, wrists crossed on knee, and considered Mr Matthew Beck. It felt vaguely insolent to gaze at someone who couldn't gaze back, but fifteen years in journalism have pretty much inured me to certain common-or-garden virtues. Too often, meeting someone for the first time, I find myself interviewing him or her and unable to stop.

Beck, however, was no hapless interviewee. The story I elicited from him during the next fifteen minutes was at times taciturnly, but not grudgingly, told. To the contrary, he seemed ready enough to tell it... though I had the impression it wasn't

346

always easy for him; that he was impelled to it less by the lure of immersing himself in the soothing susurrus of the past than by some present, active pain; that at times he seemed not to be swimming with the tide of memory but somehow, angrily, against it. My inquirings were not chronological, nor were his responses; but I set them down so, here...

The younger of two sons, Matthew Beck was a child of money. His grandfather, an Austrian immigrant in the latter half of the 19th Century, had felicitously bought substantial real estate in the northwest territory – lands through which, with renewed, post-Civil War zeal, the Federal Government was soon laying train lines; and next, Beck's father, a debonair, indeed apparently an operatic character, had managed the nifty trick of eliding past the Great Depression, benefiting quite pleasantly from certain opportunities presented by Prohibition without getting bogged down in the hardcore felonious stuff.

As for Beck –

Gifted with a robust constitution, but with no vocation he could think of, and no need to earn a living (the scion of the family, Beck's big brother, 'took care of the money'), the twenty-four-year-old did what in the dawn of the Cold War not a few like him were doing: he joined the CIA. ('Chiefly for the adventure, you understand,' the blind man said. 'Though I suppose a certain amount of youthful idealism shouldn't be gainsaid.')

He sat out the Korean War at a desk in Washington. But Beck's mother was Puerto Rican – Beck spoke Spanish; and, partly for this reason, in the mid-Eisenhower years he found himself posted to Batista's Cuba.

At the Havana mission there was a German-American girl with a blond bun, a pristine, stillettoed walk, and slow appraising grey eyes. (He told me her name, but I've forgotten it.) 'One thing led to another,' and in due course they were engaged. Americans in the diplomatic service require permission to marry, the request triggers renewed security checks of both parties, and the process can take some time; luckily for Beck, as it turned out. The wheels of American Intelligence were still grinding away into the hinter-land of the lady's faultless background when, in the traffic-clogged streets of Havana, Beck fell upon an immense and novel doubt.

The very rich are not like you and me. At any rate, those who have inherited wealth are usually free spirits; they have a certain naïve and calm openness to experience, and no especial herd instinct; and Beck found himself disliking the Caribbean city with its daytime squalor and overheated night life. News of the guerrillas' exploits (still far away) guiltily gladdened him, like the thought of rain after a muggy eternity. And when his fiancée's considerable ardour in private (so delightfully contrapuntal to her prim public mien!) turned out to be matched by certain carapaced certitudes concerning the propriety of what she, he and their country were doing in Cuba – 'Well,' said the blind man on the blazing beach: 'I woke up one day and saw I'd been stopped dead in my tracks.'

The year was '57. Beck was due a month's leave. He took it, endured a world-ending row with the lovely – God, what's her name?! – and came here: to Jamaica, to Port Antonio, and, almost at once, to Her: the gawky laughing nineteen-year-old daughter of two Jamaican schoolteachers, both employed at Titchfield at the time.

Her name I have not forgotten. Her name was Gail.

3

She was girlish and forever laughing, with her limp wrists and intelligent eyes. Her laugh was a single peal of surprised delight. His hands almost encircled her waist. She had eclectically passed HC and was about to enter UCWI. No bar of chocolate he bought her ever quite matched her flawless complexion.

Beck bumped into her, literally, around a corner of the town one drizzly morning. He was already apologising when he saw her – *saw* her – and the words stopped, and the blood drained from his face. Whereupon she glanced away with a wry grimace, then – to her own surprise, she confessed later – stood for him, considering him (at eye level, for she was almost as tall as he) with quiet amusement.

She was nineteen to his thirty-two, and her parents didn't like it. Especially since Beck, not quite believing in his luck – for nothing like this had ever happened to him before – carefully avoided letting slip the least hint of what he might be worth; not that he knew, anyway. When he went to collect her that evening, her father actually refused to speak to him, and her mother looked into his face and her own face closed to a look of unforgiving sorrow.

In the little cockroach-infested cinema at the foot of Titchfield hill, Beck tried to concentrate on the mighty universe of marabunta ants that was urgently eating its way through some South American rainforest with the amplified sound of paper tearing, towards the little cottage in the little Edenic garden where the young Iowa couple (badly advised by their travel agent, it turned out) were tenderly honeymooning. But it was no use; the lively silence beside him was all his thought. When she clapped her hand to her mouth with a stifled shriek, Beck wanted to get up and stride the aisle, laughing. When she leaned into him without a thought, scaredly gripping his arm, Beck knew he would die for her.

They were married in a small ceremony in her grandparents' house in Liguanea. By then, her mother (who was just a few years older than Beck) had grown used to treating him with the casual acceptance of a mother whose family has grown by one; and her father had recovered sufficiently to give an albeit still somewhat gruff speech. When, that night, Beck saw he was hurting her, then saw the blood, a huge desire to impregnate her assailed him. It arrived fullblown out of nowhere, like a gale in a clear blue sky.

'What do you think?' he asked her next morning while they were out strolling, wanting it so much the words came out offhandedly.

'I think you're a brute,' she said conversationally, bending to pick up a pine cone. Then: "Course I'm going to have your child, mister. Why you think I married you?' And she tossed him the cone and ran off, laughing.

Beck followed more slowly, grinning with uncertainty and happiness. To her dying day, he would never understand her.

He had rather negligently informed the Agency that he would not be returning to its employ. Somewhat more tensely, he'd apprised his brother of his news. When the scion wrote sternly back, directing Beck's attention to certain 'unromantic facts of life', Beck cut him off without a second thought. The plan was to reside in Kingston while she did her degree then return to the States. But in her second year she became pregnant.

'We're going,' Beck said when she told him. 'I don't want these local doctors carving you up.'

His young wife demurred strenuously. She wanted to have the baby in Port Antonio. She wanted her mother with her.

'We'll take her,' Beck said; and he saw the light of laughter come on in her eyes as she considered the novel prospect. But then it faded.

'I'm really a homebody, you know,' she told him gently, in a tender moment soon afterwards. 'I know you still don't realise that.'

But to her surprise, her parents backed the plan. The West Indian Federation was creaking and snapping; her father privately opined to his wife that he didn't like the look of Jamaica's future; and the mother needed little encouragement to concede the advantages of a grandchild born in the US. In her sixth month, they flew out to Connecticut.

In Kingston he'd taught her to drive. Now, one morning, he emerged from the house to see his pregnant young wife ensconced behind the wheel. She easily overrode his uncertainty... and was doing quite well, he had to admit, driving on the 'wrong' side of the road for the first time, when at a four-way intersection she turned left, into the wrong lane, and into the path of a sixteen-wheeler. Her startled laugh was the last thing Beck heard, and her shocked look was literally the last thing he saw; for the same impact that crushed her and their unborn child damaged his optic nerve. Beck awoke in darkness, to strange voices and the smell of formaldehyde: a smell that remained for him, to this day, an olfactory synonym for Hell.

'Forty years ago next month,' the blind man on the beach said drily.

He'd stayed close to her parents, talking often on the phone and bringing them over every summer. But eight years ago, the father, seventy-six, had died; at the beginning of this year his

350

widow had followed him; and for the first time Beck felt a need to revisit Jamaica.

'It must be quite different,' I said presently.

'Yes and no,' the blind man said. 'The scent of Port Antonio – it leapt at me. Extraordinary. It might have been yesterday...'

I thought, *The scent of the past.*

But I never said it, because at this point the moonwhite girl came out of the sea.

I had forgotten her – I had been far away – and for a moment she seemed a mirage. Arms folded across bare white breasts, the white torso incrementally rising into sight, as though she were ascending a series of shallow underwater steps... long white waist... white bikini bottom... white thighs...

Beck had grown still.

'Hello,' she said to me, coming up. Then, to him: 'I see you've had a good time.'

I began extending my hand, realised she couldn't take it without exposing herself, and gave a vague salute instead.

'So the water was nice and warm!' The blind man said.

'Yes!' The moonwhite girl looked startled. 'How do you know?'

'You were in so long.'

The girl glanced at me somehow angrily.

'This is Mr Brown, from Trinidad,' Beck said. 'Mr Brown, my wife.'

Sometimes it pays to be fifty-four, not twenty-four: more than once I'd been on the verge of asking him about 'the young couple' in the sea. Involuntarily I glanced around and saw the hirsute, balding guy standing on the little rise beyond the western edge of the beach, talking to the jetsam-burner and watching the smoke rise.

The girl had seen. Her gaze was frankly mocking. 'Hello, Mr Brown,' she said.

'Hi.'

It was all I could trust myself to say in the blind man's hearing.

She dipped into her bag, pulled out a black T-shirt and, turning away, wriggled it on. Returning – 'Ready?' She said to Beck, and he obediently rose, then offered his hand in my direction. I took it.

'Thanks for the company,' the blind man said, in that hearty, dry voice of his. 'I hope I didn't bore you too much.'

'No,' I said. 'Thank you.'

I had the curious impression that behind the dark glasses Mr Beck's 'gaze' softened.

'I'll certainly remember our little meeting,' he said.

I told him I would, too.

The girl slung her bag, folded and picked up the deck chair, and touched her other arm to her husband's hand; and he took it...

Hardly had the white 626 executed a three-point turn and driven out than the hirsute guy – a Lebanese Jamaican, I saw now – crossed the beach to his car. There he stripped and, standing insolently naked, towelled between his legs, then donned a pair of shorts. Then he, too, drove away.

Left alone, I returned to the lounger, picked up *Ada*, found my place and resumed reading.

'...My magic carpet no longer skims over crown canopies and gaping nestlings, and her rarest orchids.'

I read the sentence three times, then gave up trying and lay back. But the variegated loveliness of the eastern shallows was now obscured by a blinding sheen, and I found I no longer wished to contemplate the tossing cobalt-&-white of the open horizon, beyond which, I knew, lay Cuba. I closed my eyes... and was about to open them again when I wondered what it must be like to be blind, and kept them closed.

Darkness. Turgidity. Incipient panic.

But I fought it back, I kept them closed...

...the drifting bursting flecks of light were like a computer's screensaver, or a dying man's dream of the universe...

...and presently this little show was joined by a sound – faraway yet adamantine, trochaic, dull – which, I only gradually realised, was my own heart beating.

THE EDUCATION OF DELROY DUNN

Looking back, Delroy Dunn had to admit it was probably a mistake to migrate back to Jamaica with his young English wife so soon after Sue learnt she would not be able to conceive. How else explain why his pliable, pretty spouse of five years should, within months of being thus doubly uprooted (from nature and from nurture, as it were), abruptly throw propriety and their marriage to the wind, to seek solace in disreputable arms?

Delroy Dunn was fifty-two when this happened. A civil engineer working with various public bodies and private firms amid the inchoate southern approaches to London, he had not done too badly over the years; although, truth be told, he had not done too well, either. In fact, it was his disappointed realisation that the graph of his career had levelled off, a full decade earlier than he'd expected – that, coupled perhaps with his first, obscure intimations of mortality, of the finitude of his time on Earth – that had led him to persuade Sue to close the little estate agency – which she ran with the languor characteristic of her class, showing potential purchasers around this dormer-windowed attic flat or that basement pied-a-terre with a sort of limp-wristed, pleasant vagueness – and fly out with him to the land of his birth and what he construed to her, to them both, as 'a new start'.

Back in Kingston, Delroy Dunn resigned himself to choosing between the job offers he'd elicited from London: fewer and less well paid than he had expected a qualified and experienced returning national to attract. Even so, his modest savings, plus the plump proceeds from the sale of their Croydon 'semi' – both gratifyingly inflated by the prevailing exchange rate – enabled him to purchase quite a spacious monstrosity-in-the-making up in Stony Hill, overlooking the city, with just enough left over to finish and furnish it. The plan was for the Dunns to hunker down meanwhile in cheap rented quarters in Kingston, while either Delroy or Sue made the daily pilgrimage up to Stony Hill to supply, supervise, and each Friday to pay, the taciturn tile-layer, one Mr Edwards, and his sidekick, a dread-locked and bare-backed young painter from whom, Delroy Dunn noticed fondly, Sue seemed to shrink ever so slightly when, perched on a ladder, painting a ceiling while they watched, he abruptly burst into the bellicose gibberish of some snatch of dancehall or rap, or when, carefully putting down his paintbrush and the annealing, ruined rag, he strode insolently past them and out of sight around the house, flinging his wrists and bellowing something about Jah.

But the cramped studio apartment wherein the Dunns camped meanwhile was as dispiriting to them both as their migration was disorienting to Sue, to whom Jamaica had previously meant little more than the memory of an Easter weekend getaway to Montego Bay when she was twenty. And as for her burly and somewhat dour husband – whom Sue had assessed in the early months of their courtship as possessed of an odd mix of worldly competence, a heart of gold, and an incapacity for reflection that bordered at times on, frankly, a contemptible lack of self-knowledge – back in Jamaica, Delroy Dunn was secretly more than a little dismayed to discover how unrecognisable, how no longer felt in his nerves and in his blood, his own country seemed to him after nearly thirty years away from it.

In such isolation, and such unrelieved proximity to each other, amid the anxieties of suspended lives, connubial tempers frayed easily. Once Sue Dunn shocked Delroy by shrieking at him, a sustained harangue that went on for several minutes in nonethe-less perfectly modulated English. (What had been her particular beef? A mere year later, Delroy Dunn could no longer remember; only that at one point he'd made angrily to leave and Sue Dunn had swiftly locked the door, locking them in, and flung the keys out of the burglar-barred window. So embarrassing, the denoue-ment of that little tiff, which co-tenants had had to be summoned to resolve!) And by the time their cantilevered cavern was fin-ished, more or less, and tiler and painter had gone, and the Dunns retreated rather than ascended to their awful eyrie on the hill, Delroy Dunn had begun noticing things.

There was Sue's uncharacteristic alacrity in answering her cell, and her irritating habit of forgetting to switch it on at odd times when she was out. There was the night she came in from some novel book club soirée and headed for the bathroom and stayed there with the shower running for a long time. There were the thirty-four kilometres registered by her nine-year-old Honda Civic's tachometer (because, yes, by now a jumpy Delroy Dunn had begun checking such things) at the end of a day when his young wife, suddenly angry, insisted she had not left home at all.

Most disquietingly, there was the change in Sue's lovemaking.

In their married years in England, Sue Dunn had responded to Delroy's stern strivings in bed with a kind of amused, though not un-athletic, fondness. But now suddenly her lovemaking became both wanton and uncaring, somehow – as if hers were the thrashings of despair.

A time came when the disbelieving husband – horrified, because for all their recent irruptions he still had a real soft spot for his limp-wristed, bleached-blonde, barren young wife – took to parking his second-hand Rav 4 in the city and driving back up to Stony Hill in a rented Sunny with tinted windows.

The second time he did this, Delroy Dunn saw a rusting old car which he thought he recognised parked outside their garden gate. He pulled onto the grass verge, and there sat and struggled for quite some time with the competing instincts of fight and flight, before – suddenly propelled like an automaton, as in the compulsion of a dream – he got out of the Sunny and let himself in through the gate and his own front door.

This was a big mistake. Delroy Dunn had cloudily told himself that Sue had probably summoned the dreadlocked painter to remedy some incompletion or flaw in his performance. Even more cloudily, he'd resolved that if the worse came to the worst (and that was how Delroy Dunn put it to himself: 'if the worse comes to the worst'), he would curtly expel the unkempt brute and unleash a terrific tirade against his terrified wife, at the end of which he imagined her tearfully begging his forgiveness: a little cameo panning out in the couple re-embarking, sadder but wiser, upon a second 'new start' (albeit hard on the heels of the first one). But what Delroy Dunn saw when he opened the bedroom door seared his mind and shrivelled his marriage to a burnt crisp in his heart. Surely the black and white beast with two backs, not bedded but lurching about the room the way a monkey carries its infant, clinging to its belly – *surely*, thought engineer Dunn – and this was in fact his first thought – such a structure was unstable, and had to fall! And he actually stood and stared at the staggering apparition with quasi-professional incredulity for a long moment before – hardly hearing his wife's strangled cry, demitting the room as if shoved backward out of it – Delroy Dunn staggered out of the house in Stony Hill, returned the rented Sunny to its proprietor, cut short the latter's sorrowful explanation as to why a partial refund was not applicable in this case, and got into the Rav 4 and drove, blindly and hard, until in due course the sea, appearing on his right, perforce channelled his course away from the city. By mid-afternoon he was pulling into a gas station in a ramshackle seaside town where, in response to his dull enquiry, the pump man directed him to the house of one Mistress Green.

Mrs Green turned out to be an ample, stern-faced, middle-aged woman in curlers and a scarf who stared through the crack at Delroy Dunn with wordless suspicion for a long time before slipping the door's chain and letting him in. She had not expected any applicants for the room (that was how she put it: 'applicants for the room') so soon, she told him. The room was not ready. But she supposed there was no harm in him looking at it. Mrs Green's delivery was crisp, her accent subtly neutered. Delroy Dunn suspected (rightly, as it turned out – not that he cared) that, like himself, Mrs Green had lived some considerable time in England and now was back home.

The room was large and sufficiently furnished, mainly in old mahogany with the varnish long ago sucked into the grain. Old four-poster bed, table with chair, chest of drawers, various bric-a-brac; in one corner, a veined-with-age porcelain sink. It looked down across the road onto a large bay, in the mouth of which a small, humped, green-clad island was being slavishly burnished by the afternoon sun. In the road below the room's sash window (whose wooden frames looked, to the ex-husband of an ex-real estate agent, suspiciously palpatory under a new coat of white gloss) there laboured uphill now a dented pickup belching smoke with four young men perched on the sides of its tray. They were shouting and laughing and gesturing dismissively at someone Delroy Dunn couldn't see.

'The bathroom is down the corridor,' Mrs Green said. 'The water heater was supposed to be fixed long ago but the wretched man still hasn't come.'

'I have nowhere to stay,' Delroy Dunn said.

'There's quite a decent – ' Mrs Green began. Then, stopped by something – perhaps the bubble of despair that abruptly floated up from the unfocused gentleman standing tonelessly in front of her – she looked Delroy Dunn up and down, then said instead: 'We haven't talked about the rent. I am asking – .'

Delroy Dunn nodded wordlessly, and received next the information that Mrs Green would require a week down in advance.

'But first let me show you the place.'

He submitted to being shown the place. ('This is the kitchen; this is the living room, both living and dining; it's cosier that way, don't you think? This room' – a shut door –'is occupied. That is your bathroom. These are my rooms. And this room I use as a store room, as you can see. Now you can go and bring in your bags.')

Even in his mentally dishevelled state, Delroy Dunn knew better than to confess to being bag-less. He excused himself on the pretext of having to visit an ATM; and when he returned, with a half-empty holdall in one hand, and darkness falling, Mrs Green had bathed and dressed and removed the curlers from her hair, the four-poster bed in his room had been made, and there was a single flushed anthurium lily in a Red Stripe glass on a little lace doily on his bedside table.

He was suddenly, insupportably tired. It was one thing to descend from bustling, familiar London upon noisy, hot and disconcerting Kingston. It was quite another thing to wind up at the end of the world, with black mountains at his back and a black sea gleaming stilly beneath his window. He warded off Mrs Green's gruff enquiry about dinner ('If there's anything you don't eat you'd better tell me now'), and, not bothering to undress or switch on the light, fell back onto the four-poster and stared unseeingly at the sky beyond the sash window where the first stars were just coming on.

A little while later his cell phone rang. From force of habit, he answered it – then lay and listened to Sue Dunn's strained voice saying, 'Delroy? Delroy! Where are you? Delroy, please say something.' To her silent listener, the frightened young English-woman said a lot more. She had reached the part about missing her father – '…so much! You have no idea how much!' – when Delroy Dunn abruptly sat up, pressed the 'Off' button, replaced the redundant instrument on the bedside table and lay back with wide-open eyes in the dark.

His dreams were fragmentary and inchoate and attended by a free-floating horror. At some point during the night it seemed to him that his bedroom door opened and Sue (only, it wasn't Sue) stood there, staring at him for a long moment, before being displaced by a moaning wind with trees thrashing about in it; and when he awoke it was still dark, and raining. A blowing drizzle came and went outside the window, its broken filaments illumi-nated by the eaves lights. The raindrops beaded where they landed, or rolled slowly down the pane.

At his age, Delroy Dunn should have known the unwisdom of lying abed next morning in the old four-poster, pretending to think, to plan, but in fact merely immobilised by misery, while outside his rented room the light turned blare and the day's noises exiled him further from the life he'd unthinkingly assumed he owned. There were the sudden shattering roars of truck and bus, labouring uphill beneath his window. There were the intermit-tent screams of laughter emitted by passing claques of uniformed schoolgirls with the bodies of women. Somewhere an unpunctual cock was maniacally crowing. And so on. But that first morning, unable to rise, Delroy Dunn did just that, masochistically inter-rogating the radiant wrestling match he'd witnessed the day before for proof that his unknowable young wife had been a slut from the start. (She had not.) And it was past 8:30 before a brusque knocking and an equally brusque interrogation by his proprietress ('Did you not hear the breakfast bell? No? That's very strange!') delivered him to the mercy of mundane matters. In the old, linoleum-carpeted bathroom down the corridor (whose toilet featured an overhead reservoir and chain) he was struck by a torrent of icy water that set him violently shivering, and the miniature soap kept slipping from his hand. And by the time he presented himself at Miss Green's dining table, where the lady was in the process of clearing away a used place setting (scrunched up paper napkin, bread crumbs, half-eaten red apple on a saucer with a marmalade smear), he looked tolerably like any other unremarkable, fifty-plus, glumly un-belonging man.

Mrs Green's boarding house was clean, and her meals, though plain, were honest. Yet the place, with its covertly rotting, gloss-white window frames, its stale-varnished mahogany furniture and scuffed wood floors – to say nothing of the ill-green emulsion paint tinting its tongue-and-groove walls – had not escaped the seedy air of the decaying town to which it belonged. Such prints as adorned the living-dining room were as hack as they were eclectic – white tongue of a waterfall protruding from between the green molars of temperate pines; black fishing boats silhou-etted on a livid sea; an effeminate, slender-fingered, semaphoring Christ, his heart blooming astoundingly from his chest cavity – and damp had penetrated the large, framed photograph of the coronation of an unlikely-looking girl. (Hard to imagine, Delroy Dunn thought bleakly, that the dowdy dowager currently presid-ing over British patriotism and pride had once been as young as that that.)

The coffee was good, the grapefruit only tolerably acidic, but Delroy Dunn had never relished eggs fried in oil and edged with a crisp brown lace. Besides, he had no appetite. He mumbled his apologies to a stone-faced Mrs Green, and was on his way back to his room when he pushed open a door – why did he think it would yield a balcony, a bracing breeze and a bright blue vista of the sea? – and discovered too late another bedroom like his own. Too late, because, before he could withdraw, his unprepared gaze had taken in the slender figure of a naked brown girl with frizzy copper hair stretching up to pull something off the top of a wardrobe – an effort that had the effect of flexing her frame along its entire length, from the indented narrow shoulders to the willowy back, with its visible, vulnerable vertebrae, to the sub-stantial swell of her creaseless young bottom, to the barely defined muscles at the backs of her long legs, to the plump convexities at the backs of her young knees, to her arched and elevated insteps.

Words can only describe such a sight sequentially, of course, but Delroy Dunn took all this in with a single shocked gulp of a stare. And as, startled in turn, the figure swung around ('Sorry,' said Delroy Dunn in a sepulchral voice, already backing out, already closing the door), he had a second, epiphanic impression – somehow both blurred and piercingly vivid at once – of a pair of brown breasts, just large enough to drift about, with sallow bikini triangles and startlingly black areolas, with, above them, a pouting nether lip and low-lidded black eyes that had begun widening in what must have been alarm, but which struck the cringing, retreating interloper as amusement at his expense.

'Your other guest,' Delroy Dunn said to Mrs Green later that morning – much later, when his heart had stopped thumping, and the world below his window (comprising various pedestrians – men of the soil and women of the market, mainly – trudging by, morose or waggish, depending on whether they walked alone or in company; the oily gleam of the flat inshore water beyond the road; the forested islet in the mouth of the bay, with beyond it a wind-darkened sea stretching to the horizon, where a queue of white cloudlets was festively scudding along) – had resumed its untenable tenor, though now with a quizzical, underlying tint or tone. 'Your other guest...?'

Mrs Green glanced at Delroy Dunn as though he were scum. 'Ah, yes!' she said with angry gaiety. 'You mean my niece. From Kingston. Student nurse, on secondment to the clinic here in town. You would have met her at breakfast if you'd been on time. Pretty child.' Mrs Green was already turning away when she said this last. But for the metallic rasp in her voice, she might have been talking to herself.

Mrs Green hadn't volunteered a name, and Delroy Dunn discovered he lacked the nerve to inquire it. So when around lunchtime he caught sight of the pretty child in town, where he had sallied forth to purchase a swimsuit (Delroy Dunn had decided to go for a swim), preparing to cross the road ahead of him, in her baby-pink trainee nurse's uniform, with the round white collar, the little white cap and flat-soled shoes, looking left and then right, and then left again (the low-lidded black eyes, the pouting mouth!), he would have passed her with a stiff or sheepish nod had she not seen him and stopped, placing herself squarely in his path and saying up into his face, 'Well, hi again!'

'Hi,' said Delroy Dunn in a voice of doom.

'You *remember* me!' exclaimed the girl. 'I wasn't sure if you would, in all these' – lifting her curled palms to ribcage height, flicking the fingers downward – 'clothes!' And she smiled brightly up at him.

'My name is Delroy Dunn,' said Delroy Dunn.

'I know, Auntie told me... Well, wow, this is so cool! So: what are you doing here? This place is such a dump!'

To Delroy Dunn, it suddenly seemed a mortally tragic question – one that deserved to be answered in all seriousness with the un-condensed story of his once ordinary, recently disappointing, and now completely unreal life. 'Well,' he began – and was saved from making a fool of himself, right there on the pavement of a decayed Jamaican seaside town, when she cut him off, crying over his shoulder, 'Taneisha! Wait for me!' – and then, matching words to action, pushed past him saying, 'I guess I'll see you later', to link arms with a similarly attired young woman: this one shorter, darker, pert-faced, hair in braids.

So that was that. Between them, her perfect nakedness and undaunted insouciance were unbearable. The perky nurse's cap crowning that glory of frizzy copper hair was unbearable. The small mole in the little hollow between her nostril and cheek was unbearable. What was left of his life was unbearable. He had to have her.

Some time later, sitting, wrists on knees, on a towel on the little quarter-moon beach that had silted up the cervix of the bay, the coarse sand blond and damp and cold and not sunstruck, white and fine, and the heaving, seaweed-tormenting water, watched by no eyes but his own, senselessly lunging its creases one by one onto the deserted strand, Delroy Dunn stared at the shaggy green islet in front of him and pictured her face as it would be beneath his, once his no-nonsense strivings – he thought ominously – had induced her to forget her face. He imagined the black eyes widening helplessly, the mouth, no longer pouting, with lips parted – no, stretched wide in a grimace of commingled agony and ecstasy – and the little mole… the little mole… magnified to a Rorschach Blot…

Back at Mrs Green's, he slapped the sand from the soles of his feet, switched on his cell, and cast around the living room for a telephone directory, thinking to deduce from it the name and number of her clinic. He had found a likely contender before he remembered he still didn't know her name. And then he recalled her parting words, and some horrible counterfeit of male *sangfroid* returned to him. 'See you later,' was how he remembered her parting words. Delroy Dunn would urbanely wait and see her later.

He dropped into a living room chair, and was making a tolerable effort at passing the time by leafing through an ancient *National Geographic* (wherein Marco Polo was being belatedly denounced for praising the old Indian custom of suttee, according to which a widow allegedly opted to be burned alive on her husband's pyre) when his cell rang, and the screen showed it was his own number calling.

This time he neither answered it nor switched it off, but let it ring until it stopped. And this time (as Delroy Dunn discovered when, in spite of himself, he checked the voice mail) Susan Dunn left no message.

The impossible child had lied to him, a fraught Delroy Dunn concluded: it was past eleven at night, and still she hadn't returned to the boarding house from the clinic in town. He knew this because, after dinner (which tonight was fried king fish, tossed salad, and a small, slippery serving of the root vegetables his compatriots still quaintly called 'food'), he had positioned himself in an easy chair in the ornament-cluttered but otherwise deserted living room, glancing at his watch in between staring fixedly at the black oblong of night beyond the open double doors, from which the defaulting Lilith had at some point to come. In due course he had fallen distractedly to glossing the archaic prose of a black, termite-ridden hardcover, both untitled and anonymously authored now that its spine and title page had been stripped away: one of the ruined ancient tomes which comprised the boarding house's 'library'. And this was how Mrs Green found him when, without warning, she sweeled imperiously into the living room.

'So, Mr Dunn,' she said archly. 'I see you like reading! Perhaps you would be so good as to give me your opinion on this little poem here' – thrusting at him a notebook page covered in unexpectedly large and loopy handwriting. 'It's just a little nonsense I composed this evening.' And she took up a supervisory position behind Delroy Dunn's chair, leaning over his shoulder to read her own words along with him.

Vaguely Delroy Dunn perused what seemed some sort of pastoral lyric, in which Mrs Green had been hanging out certain 'delicate unmentionables' on her clothesline when a dark dove flew in out of the blue and nestled tingling in her housecoat pocket.

'Very nice,' Delroy Dunn said staunchly, offering the page back to its expectant author. 'I like the part about "the winged glory".'

'Oh, no, Mr Dunn,' Mrs Green said, all but laughing with pleasure. 'You keep it; it's yours!'

Delroy Dunn thought: I have never seen such a transformation.

Delroy Dunn thought: What have I done to deserve this?

Delroy Dunn thought: I am going to have to leave.

For the moment, though, he was alone again, with a night blemished by only a few stars filling the empty doorway. He stared absently at it; then, for something better to do, bent to the black book again.

'The young Justinian, second of that name, mounted his father's throne in 685, when only in his seventeenth year. The accession of this prince was a fearful misfortune for the empire. He possessed the qualities of his grandfather Constantinus in an exaggerated form, being arbitrary, cruel, reckless and highhanded, yet so brave and capable...'

'Hi,' said a bleary voice without the palest ghost of animation in it, and the insufferably late student nurse (she of the lower lip, the lidded black eyes, and the mole!) walked wearily, barefoot, into the living room, an old plastic shopping bag and a pink cardigan in one hand, a pair of brown high-heeled sandals in the other. She had changed out of her uniform and was wearing a white halter-top and a denim miniskirt, and her bare shoulders and face betrayed a post-perspiration gleam, and her once-frizzy copper hair was lank.

'Hi,' said Delroy Dunn stiffly, closing the story of cruel young Justinian on his forefinger. 'I thought – .'

I thought we had a date, he was going to say absurdly; but: ''Night,' said the postcoital, tired child, already wandering off barefoot down the corridor.

Delroy Dunn stared at the black void in front of him until her heard her door gently open and, rather more decisively, close. Then – doing everything by reflex now – he reopened the anonymous tome.

'…He started on his career too young, and might have come to better things if his father had lived for another ten years; but, abandoned to his own devices ere he was well out of his boyhood, he developed into a bloodthirsty tyrant. The Saracens were occupied in civil wars… The Saracens were occupied in civil wars… (The Saracens were occupied in civil wars…).'

The black book was once again returned to the table. Delroy Dunn stood up suddenly and, with a little lurch, set off at funereal gait in the wake of the vanished waif.

'I was thinking,' he said, when in response to his knocking – the first knock too tentative, the second too loud – her door opened partway, and in the dolorous light of a shadeless sixty-watt bulb the pouting mouth and lidded black eyes stared at him. She had changed into an oversized white T-shirt, and nothing else, as far as Delroy Dunn could see.

'What if I picked you up from work tomorrow and we went and had… I don't know… dinner. Tea. Or we could walk, I don't know, by the sea.'

The girl went on staring at him, dull-eyed and damp and young.

'What time is it?' she said suddenly.

He glanced jerkily at his watch. 'Eleven-forty.'

'Eleven-forty.' Her dull gaze went from Delroy Dunn's eyes to his mouth. Then she seemed to shake herself. 'Listen,' she said, with a sudden, odd, funky urgency. 'Why don't we talk about this tomorrow. Okay?'

'Well,' said Delroy Dunn.

And then, because she went on waiting and nothing else came to him to say: 'I'll see you at breakfast, then,' he added. To his own ears it sounded vaguely like a threat.

She did not immediately shut the door, and Delroy Dunn was peering past her, pretending to see what he could see of her room but really to prolong the moment of her standing there, all aura-less and damp and changed-for-bed and young, when she said angrily, '*Don't* come in here! I hate you! Go away!', and a rough young male shoulder bumped past Delroy Dunn, its owner saying entreatingly into the room, 'She's nobody, Kimmy, swear to God! Jes' give it up nuh, Kimmy. Kimmy!', and advancing into the room.

So that was her name: Kimmy!

From the pinnacle of his fifty-two years, Delroy Dunn stared at the sudden drama unfolding before his eyes and heroically and horribly misread it. He was stepping forward to protect her when the dishevelled damsel's glance fell on him and her expression changed. In three strides she had gripped his arm and was pushing him back out of the door, saying fiercely, 'Just leave us alone now, okay? Okay?'

'Well, if you're sure,' Delroy Dunn began with dignity. But here the door was slammed in his face; and next, a movement at the far end of the dim-lit corridor resolved itself into a white-nightied, curlered and scarved Mrs Green. Mrs Green's nightie stopped, startlingly, above her knees, Mrs Green's hands were clasped in front of her groin, and she was staring at Delroy Dunn like a gargoyle.

Delroy Dunn turned and strode off towards his own door; but the landlady, recovering quickly, pursued him, hissing: 'If you think for one moment the deposit – '

' – is yours,' said Delroy Dunn.

For the dismissed hero, the next minutes passed in a blur. He thought he had packed his few newly-purchased belongings, and he had; but he managed to leave behind his cell phone. Getting into the Rav 4, he had a frazzled glimpse of Mrs Green, a burly, gliding ghost in a short white nightie, emerging onto the little verandah to supervise his flight; and, after that, he drove and drove. The glare of Kingston was plainly visible in the night sky ahead before Delroy Dunn realised he was going home.

Realising this made him feel, for the second time in little more than twenty-four hours, suddenly very tired. But with tiredness there came an unexpected wash of relief. They were at rock bottom now, he and Sue, Delroy Dunn thought, slowing the Rav to a recuperating cruise. Caught up in the paw of Time, they had twisted and turned, like separate but equal souls in a purgatorial maze. But now at least, now, at last, they were in a position to make yet another new start.

This was to Delroy Dunn an all-annealing thought. And this in turn would be a far less doleful tale to tell if that was how it had panned out, in the end: with a frightened, forgiven wife and a frightened, forgiving hubby falling gratefully into each other's arms.

But past a certain age life is seldom so comfy. And when, at some indeterminate hour of the night, Delroy Dunn eased into his high driveway at last, it was to find the same rusting old car – a white Corolla, if you want to know – interposed between his Rav 4 and Sue's Honda Civic in the carport, and no lights on in the blackly yawning, cantilevered house for which he had so recently separated out, and fondly threaded onto His and Her key rings, two matching sets of keys.

THE TOCO BAND

1. The Profane Boat

It was a riotous, summery July afternoon with the easterly blowing over thirty knots: driving down to the boat along the finger of land that all but quarantined off the harbour from the sea, the man had glimpsed the tossing whitecaps beyond the dunes on their left, and on their right the furious cats' paws racing away across the dark-crinkled inshore water where they would be sailing. So now he left the jib below deck and tied in a flattening reef in the mainsail for good measure while they were still at the mooring. Then he started the engine and watched the young woman lean over the pulpit and unhank the bow rope, and then, reaching forward and up onto her toes, hang it with a little toss in the high branches of the mangrove.

'Good to see her sailing again!' called a florid English type whom the man didn't know as they slow-motored out of the lagoon. The man thought defensively, 'It's been less than two months'; and he acknowledged the greeting with a grudging wave. It was even more grudging than he'd intended, and he became aware of feeling a discomfort: an enervating sense of oppression, dually centred in his head and solar plexus, which made him burp once or twice, and which he put down to the great, windless heat of the lagoon.

As soon as they had motored out into the harbour and turned east, however, out of the lee of the mangrove and the low bank and clear of the clubhouse and its outbuildings, the wind struck like a fist: under bare poles the yacht listed sharply and the timbre of the diesel acquired a note of muffled straining. The man handed the tiller to the woman, then pointed with a traffic policeman's gesture into the wind. 'Try to keep her there,' he said, 'right there!' And he went forward to the mast and hoisted the fully-battened main, dragging down on the halyard with vigorous, long strokes to minimise the time of the sail flaccidly crashing about. But something was wrong, the sail would not set; and he had to half-lower it again, tie it off, throw off the outhaul – tying in the flattening reef at the mooring he had used the wrong one ('I really have to get to know this boat,' he thought) – and winch in the right one, before hoisting the main again.

All this he did doggedly rather than irritably, as would have been his wont, because by now he was feeling... unwell.

'What's wrong?' the young woman called from the cockpit.

'It's okay!' the man shouted back with an effort, pausing to turn his face to her so the wind wouldn't blow away his words. 'Keep her there!'

He winched the sail up the last foot or two, cleated it off, stood for a moment at the foot of the mast to catch his breath; and now there was a pain in his chest.

Or rather, an ache, for it was not yet pain. But a definite ache. Dead centre, just below his ribcage.

The man thought: *Dammit.* It was a wonderful afternoon, they hadn't sailed in a long time, and he wondered if it was going to be spoilt for him. It occurred to him that perhaps he could burp it away; and he tried, experimentally, once or twice.

'You okay?' the young woman asked a little concernedly when he returned to the cockpit and took the tiller from her and hauled in on the mainsheet, so that the yacht heeled over onto starboard tack and bit.

'Yes,' he said, and he killed the engine, which had already begun to overheat, as it always did after only a few minutes, and now there was only the lovely, residual, liquid rustle of their wake and the low song of the wind in the rigging.

The boat was an old '70s Cal 30, a moderate design that justified its designation, 'racer-cruiser'. Even without the jib, the long-footed, big-roached main drove her well, heeling and righting, heeling and righting, over the flat, goose-fleshed water in the lee of the Palisadoes.

'Do you need me here?' the woman asked; and when the man said no she climbed out of the cockpit and went and sat to windward of the mast, leaning back against it and resting her wrists on her bare knees; and the man thought how at home she'd seemed on the boat from their first sail, just a few months ago. From the cockpit he watched her short black curls blowing without respite in the wind, and glanced from the wind vane at the top of the mast to the cats' paws hurrying towards them across the water, to the big container ship anchored far ahead and to port, at the foot of Long Mountain, on the city side of the harbour. And he thought to himself, *What a glorious afternoon*, and thought that they should really make time to sail more often. And he tried to forget the definite, focused ache in the centre of his chest.

From the foot of the mast, the young woman called: 'Why is the water so black?' and the man glanced over the side and saw it was true. He glanced up at the sky. The sky was a cloudless, hard blue.

'It has to be the angle of the sun!' he called back.

Then he burped, purposely, three or four times – and was perplexed that it made no difference to the pain.

'You sure you okay?' the woman called.

The man nodded. The young woman looked at him for several seconds without saying anything more. Then she turned away and looked at the long, low finger of encircling land with small cars and trucks running along it.

The water was gradually widening between them and the attenuated sandspit to windward as they sailed along, and the man felt a small chop beginning and the boat beginning to judder and occasionally bang. Normally this would not have affected his course, but now it occurred to him that staying in the flat inshore water might ease the pain, and he called to the woman, 'Tacking!', and then waited while she got up and stood in front of the mast, holding onto it with one hand. Then he crossed over to the low side of the cockpit, pulling the tiller down to port with him, and watched the boom lunge overhead and the boat heel over the other way.

For some reason, though, the pain was worse on this tack, and the man felt cold sweat break out on his forehead, and he leaned over the side and vomited.

'Don't you think we should turn back?' the woman said, rising and coming aft to the cockpit.

'No.'

'You sure you want to go on?'

'Yes.'

'What can I do?'

'You could pour me a coke. With ice.'

While she was below, the man tried burping several times. At one point it seemed to help. But then it didn't.

The man took off his T-shirt and threw it below through the companionway hatch. He was sweating profusely now, and the wind drying the sweat on his face and flanks gave him an icy, luxurious feeling.

Back in the flat inshore water, the rustling yacht sailed fast on its big mainsail towards the road, heeling and righting, heeling and righting; the cold coke, when she emerged with it, made him burp some more and felt pleasantly icy in his chest; the sky was a peerless, hard, summery blue; she was with him; and the man thought he would sail till he dropped. There was all that to put against the pain.

★ ★ ★

On port tack their relation to the sun changed and the sea was now a festive, hard blue. But the icy coke had started him burping, and the pain in his chest was steadily getting worse. For the first time, he said under his breath: 'Ah.'

'You're frightening me,' the woman said from where she sat by the mast. 'Please turn back.'

There are two contexts in which a yacht, close-hauled as they were, bears away. One is when it has rounded a windward mark in a race or a windward point of land, or reached the furthest extent on a cruise. The other is in rough seas or with illness on board, in order to ease the boat or its crew. Though the manoeuvre is in each case the same, the first is all elation, while the second is keenly felt by sailors for what it is: a defeat. So now the man registered the young woman's request with a doubly sinking heart. But he knew she couldn't get the boat home without him. And the pain in his chest was her ally.

370

The bow of the yacht wavered, bit, wavered again, sliced up to windward harshly one last time... and then the peninsula ahead of them scythed away abeam as he let the mainsheet run and the boat flattened out, the cockpit seats coming level with each other, the yacht fleeing away downwind with vang and mainsheet straining – and, for the first time, the man felt himself in danger.

Or rather, for the first time it occurred to him that he might die – for, curiously, he felt no fear.

He considered this fact with, sequentially, surprise, relief, and finally with something that, bar the pain, might almost have been delight. How easy and natural it was, once there was no other option, to slip from the land of the living!

'I *knew* it wasn't a big thing!' the man thought, meaning death. And he registered the note of callow triumph but was unable to eschew it, inappropriate as it sounded to his ears. Many times he had been disheartened to think of himself as belonging to a civilisation and an age in which people often seemed to order their whole lives to the dour end of staying alive as long as possible. But death – death, he saw with strange clarity now, as though looking back on life from the other side – death was only a problem for the living.

As it would be for this one sitting by the mast, hugging her knees and glancing around often at the red roof of the clubhouse, still too small and just showing above greenery, if he didn't manage to get them back in.

'Listen,' he said to her, having mercifully to raise his voice hardly at all now that she was downwind of him. 'If you have to get us in, don't try for the mooring. You see that building low down on the hill? Hold the bow on it. Don't let it swing right, because she'll gybe. Stay on it till you're nearly there. Then start the engine... leave the sails up... head for the jetty with the pump... jump ashore and shout for help and try and hold the boat. If you can't, you can't. But head straight in and step off the boat.'

It wasn't much by way of directions, but it took a while to say, because by now he could only speak three or four words at a time.

'Anything else?'

'I love my kids. I would like them to know.'

'I didn't mean that.'

'Stay on the building. Or left of it. Don't let her gybe.'

They were silent again and for a while there was only the long, rustling fricative of their wake and the intermittent, sighed 'Ahs' of the man.

How blue the afternoon is, he was thinking. And then: Oh Christ, this pain! And yet it seemed to him they were somehow connected, and that, the worse the pain grew, the bluer the sea and sky became, and vice versa. And he marvelled that they should grow in lockstep with each other, the beauty and the misery, the blueness and the pain, and each remain itself and not bleed into, not ameliorate nor corrupt the other. The cold sweat was pouring from him now and drying icily, deliciously, in the wind, and he thought again, 'What a wonderful afternoon,' and he wished they could go on sailing. But then he thought, 'It's too late for that.'

It was too late for a lot of things, the man thought; and he wished... but it was pointless...

And at that moment death visited him.

It came as the invigilator of an exam, saying impersonally, without meanness, 'Stop writing. Time!' The man watched as his answer paper, which comprised nothing less than his whole life, was whisked away from in front of him and taken off somewhere to be marked. Then he rose, slightly relieved, but more so perplexed by a novel sensation of vivid inutility. And he stuck his hands in his pockets and wandered out onto the little wooden verandah (the exam had apparently been held in the old Gibraltar Hall) to peer around him, blinking in the sudden glare, and wondering what, if anything, should happen next. Suffused, radiant with inutility.

'How are you feeling?' the woman said.

'Okay. It's only pain.'

'Is it in your left arm?'

'Both arms.'

'Are you thinking you're going to die?'

'I don't know. I don't think so. It would be okay, though.'

'For you, maybe. Not for me,' the woman said; and the man wondered hazily which sense she meant it in.

'When we get abeam of the entrance,' he told her, 'I'll turn into the wind. Drop the sail, okay? Throw off the halyard and drag it down.'

'You'll catch the boom?'

'Yes.'

They were near now, and he pressed the starter with his big toe and was relieved when the diesel racketed into life. 'Okay, stand by!' he called; and he watched her get up, dusting her bottom, and free the tail of the halyard, and unwrap all but the last twist from the cleat. Then she stood there, holding it and looking from him to the clubhouse, and back at him.

He had meant to come perpendicular with the entrance to the lagoon, but now he discovered he couldn't turn his head to tell. In desperation he pushed the tiller hard over, engaged forward gear and stood up, calling, as the sail began to flog mightily: 'Drop it!'

She was silent and quick: the boom dropped into his upturned palm where he held it like a crutch at shoulder height. It was a lot heavier than he remembered, and he sagged under its weight and spilt it onto the cabin roof with a crash that made him wonder if it had broken. The young woman came running back to the cockpit.

'You can't hook it up by yourself,' he said.

'Yes, I can.'

Moments later: 'I don't want people knowing my business,' the man said. 'We're going to the mooring. You have the boat-hook?'

In the lagoon there was no longer the wind, and sweat blinded and burned the man's eyes.

'You'll hand me the stern rope?'

'Yes.'

Assailed by nausea and salt sweat, his vision came and went. When he could see, he engaged forward gear; when he couldn't, he reverted to neutral or reverse. In that start-stop fashion, jerkily, drifting sideways and correcting it, they closed with the finger-pier.

Usually, once she'd snared the stern rope and proffered it to him with the tip of the boat hook, he would wrap it once on the jib winch and then pay it out, taking the strain and finally stopping the boat, while she hurried forward to pluck the bow rope from the mangrove and secure it. But he knew he couldn't manage that now. He'd have to throw whatever loop knot he could make up in time over the winch, and the winch would just have to take it. At the last, he lined up the boat with the pier as best he could, held the tiller between his knees, and threw the rope she presented to him into the reverse loops of a clove hitch.

Then, as the young woman hurried forward (while the boat nosed into the mangrove, the hull settling squatly in the oily, fetid water), he stood and for a long moment stared through tears of sweat at the oddly portentous iconography of the loops on his palm.

They were like a double negative, the man thought. They were like alpha and omega. They were like an ampersand connecting… Oh, all Meaning was there!

Interlude: Havana

'Hak! Ack!'

The exclaimer was a white Cuban woman, fortyish, an orderly on his floor of the Institute of Cardiology and Cardiovascular Research in Havana, Cuba. Flatfooted, narrow-hipped and broad-shouldered, with a wide mouth and forehead, wild grey eyes, and untidy, short blonde hair. Like most of the staff of the hospital she had no English (the man in the bed had hardly more Spanish), but the graphic gestures with which she completed her grotesque little mime were clear enough.

'Hak!': an invisible dagger held in a stabbing grip at chin height and jerked violently downward. This depicted the splitting of his breastbone, the first act of the bypass operation he was scheduled to undergo the following day.

'Ack!': hands opposed at sternum height with fingers clawed, then jerked horizontally apart, while the wide mouth widened further and turned down at the corners in a grimace of commingled effort and horror. That was the forcing open of the ribcage (it would be clamped open) to allow the surgeons to work on the heart.

'Some sense of humour,' the man thought, watching her; and he waited for the substance of her visit to be revealed.

But the female orderly, it turned out, had completed her visit. With a lingering, scornful-significant stare at him, she turned and left the room.

The man returned his gaze to the television on the wall, where the early-morning English language lesson was just beginning. It was being conducted in a classroom setting by a pretty, tense mulatress with straightened hair; and it began with a clip of John Lennon singing 'Imagine'.

> Imagine there's no heaven,
> It's easy if you try,
> No hell below us,
> Above us only sky...

John Lennon, who with the Beatles had achieved his early apotheosis just a couple years after Fidel – and both of them such a long, long time ago! Lennon singing in Havana now, twenty-one years after his assassination, yet suddenly near and vital, alive on the screen: Lennon in his prime, early '70s, the Beatles still an aching memory, their dissolution not yet acquiesced in, with those little rimless glasses and the delicate but sharp features, the very image of manly sensitivity!

It had been a studio production, one of the early music videos, and the camera stayed tight on the famous face while Lennon sang, as though it had been yesterday:

> Imagine there's no country,
> It isn't hard to do;
> Nothing to kill or die for,
> And no religion too...

The man thought he hadn't realised, not until now, what a Marxian song 'Imagine' was. World peace, the Internationale, the people free, delivered from their 'opiate'...

'I will read,' the pretty, tense young teacher said slowly and distinctly, 'while you copy in your notebooks' – she pronounced it, 'yur nott-books' – 'the words of the song.'

And now 'Imagine' – the whole of 'Imagine' – was replayed, one line at a time: for this was a serious teaching programme. After each line, the teacher wrote it in English on the blackboard, speaking it while she wrote. Then, turning to the class, she enunciated it once again.

'Imagine oll deh pee-pol…
Leevin' life een peas…
Yuh may say I'm a dreamer…
Baddam nat de only wan…'

Lennon in Havana. But of course!

And the man in the bed, a child of the '60s like the singer, and finding himself in Havana for the first time as a supplicant, not a scholar, in sickness, not in health – the man thought that there, there on the screen, was both the promise and the failure of his generation, both its idealism and its sentimentality… And what a curious people, he elided, these Cubans were, and how profoundly conservative their regime, in both the best and the worst sense. Imagine playing 'Imagine', John Lennon, in the classroom of the nation, thirty years later! How was that different from driving through the Cuban countryside, subtly unlike and also a lot emptier than the Jamaican bush, and suddenly coming upon a huge billboard in the middle of nowhere proclaiming in Spanish, 'The Fatherland or Death'?

McLuhan had better be right, the man thought, when he concluded that the medium was the message – or many of the best of his generation would have wasted their lives. He was not about to forget that Lennon, the same Lennon of 'Imagine' – the same Lennon on the screen of the Cuban television in the private room on the top floor of the Institute of Cardiology and Cardiovascular Research, Calle 17, Havana, on Monday December 17th, 2001 – had, thirty years before, naively befriended Michael X, the murderous Trinidadian psychopath and conman, giving him succour and stature and quite undermining his compatriots' derisive put-downs.

I hope someday you'll join us…

'Joy-nass!' the pretty, stiffly standing teacher said. 'Joy-nass!'

And the world will be one!

Now they were playing the song yet again; but this time (a different kind of education) the bespectacled features of the Beatles *jefe* had been replaced by inter-cut scenes. Like the 'music video' of the Jamaican national anthem as played in cinemas here in Jamaica, the scenes changed too fast. But there was no mistaking the message.

'No hell below us': shots of American planes, tanks, aircraft carriers, helicopter gunships, all blazing away in the Gulf war... *'above us only sky'*: cut to, yes, a pure blue, empty-lovely sky... *'Imagine there's no country'*: shot of an atlas page of the Middle East, North Africa and Asia Minor, with all the nations differentiated by colour; and then of the cantankerous colours being briskly replaced by a monochromatic, festive green...

'And no religion too': shots of Muslims at prayer, of Bishop Tutu, and finally of some white bishop celebrating mass, the images giving way with the line –

'Imagine all the people' ('Imagine oll deh pee-pol') –

...to a shot of Cubans massed in an arena, waving flags and clapping...

'No need for greed and hunger': longish shot of an opulent Western banquet ('greed')... cut to ('hunger') two poor Afghan children picking at an empty plate in the dirt...

'A brotherhood of man...'

And finally, winding up *appassionato*: *'You may say I'm a dreamer (Baddam nat de only wan!)'*: portraits of – in order – Ho Chi Minh, Mother Theresa, Mandela, Che and Fidel.

When Cuba goes, the man thought wryly, the last specialness in this, our Western hemisphere, will have gone...

★   ★   ★

'Hak!'

The wild-eyed female orderly had returned.

'Ack!' The fisted hands jerked apart, the mouth stretched into a held grimace of strenuous horror.

The man in the bed wondered if she were mad.

This time he looked at her unsmilingly with raised eyebrows, and she gave him a little sheepish-sour grin and left the room.

When, before the day was out, she returned to rehearse her little mime for a third time, the man thought that perhaps he should draw some supervisor's attention to her. But the problem of communication was daunting; he realised he didn't even know her name; and, in a word, he didn't bother. But he would think of her a lot in the pain-wracked, surreal days to come. 'Hak! Ack! Hak! Ack!' His wild-eyed, derisive muse.

3. The Sacred Boat

'Daddy, you don't want to listen to some music?'

It was his younger daughter Saffrey, twenty-five, come from England to be with him in hospital in Havana.

The man struggled to contemplate the question. It was five days since he had undergone bypass surgery, and in that time he had been all caught up in exploring the contours of a pain such as he had never experienced. That first night, the morphine had gifted him with oblivion for all of three hours before wearing off, leaving him frozen in a sort of pre-gasp incredulity, not daring to breathe. (He later deduced that while they were transporting him to the postoperative ward, one of two 1-cm plastic draining tubes they'd inserted through holes cut in his chest had 'worked' and wound up prodding the seam of his split-and-wired sternum: 'Hak! Ack!', as the wild-eyed female Cuban orderly had warned him. But that was later.) In the bed next to his, the only other occupant of the ward was not doing at all well, judging by the sounds he was making, and the man would have liked to see what he looked like. He knew better than to try to turn his head. But now he learnt not to try to turn his eyes, either.

On the second day they pulled the plastic tubes, and on the third day the two electrodes which had been threaded like shoelaces through his heart and tied in untidy knots on the outside of his chest: a precaution, to be used for electric resuscitation if his heart had stopped. And while he gasped each time at the sudden explosion of pain, like a flash of unbearable light, each time the brute constant quotient of agony returned, no more tolerable than before.

So now, sunk in the fog of self-absorption which great pain brings, it took him some moments to focus on his daughter's question; and then he felt a dawning bereavement. Music was part of the world from which he had been exiled by pain. It was one of the pursuits of that happy band of brothers and sisters, human beings in health, in their time on Earth. What had music to do with him?

Yet he saw she was suffering, more than it had ever occurred to him she could suffer on his behalf; and so he checked his intended response and said instead: 'What you have?'

'Kitch, Rudder, Bob Marley. A lotta other stuff you wouldn't like. Xtatik.'

He thought for a moment.

'Kitch.'

And he waited, trying not to wince, while she placed the blue-&-silver, discus-shaped portable CD player on the bedside table, adjusted the headphones over his ears, and pressed 'Play'. Then, as the first chords of 'The Toco Band' rang out in his head, with a lilting gaiety that was both imperious and insouciant, imperious above, insouciant below – then, as from the crevices and cataracts of pain, the rain forests and dry riverbeds of pain, the mudflats and tilting, tentacle-waving night-planes and -plains of pain, the music flowed – the man listened; was staggered; *heard*. And he lay back and closed his eyes so she would not see his tears; because in those first chords, even before the lyrics began, the shining reality of Trinidad had entered his soul.

So it exists! the man thought, staggered by what only incredulity constrained from being joy. Meaning by 'it', Trinidad – meaning not a place, nor even a people, but a particular way of seeing and being in the world, a way unique and novel in the story of the world, disembodied, yet as real as a new object in the world: a bright, disowning laughter.

In his mind, the man protested: he knew only too well what Trinidad was, socially and politically; what it had become. But the great, untrammelled onward-canter of the music swept away such thoughts like a matchbox in a gully in flood. Something waggish and irrepressible and fundamentally benevolent, something that had never been before, was in the world; and the man in the bed thought – and it was part of the same astonishment, the second, stressed beat of his iambic revelation – *and it doesn't exist for us, we exist for it.*

How can that be? He thought wonderingly. And he knew he must, at some point – during his heart attack, or during the surgery there in Cuba, four months later – have been in the surging Gibraltar-straits of death; for otherwise he could not have received what he had just been given.

We come from a country district
all the way up north,
we hobby is playin' music
and drinkin' fish broth…

So sang the dead maestro now; and, as though in Havana the cool December wind had begun thrilling low, complementing and then substituting itself for the Toco band, coming and going, it was suddenly night, and the man was on night's soughing mountainside, along with an inestimable number of his tribe, which was the tribe of Trinidad, and they were dragging the great sacrificial vessel of… Trinidadian-ness… uphill, straining yet humming (unless it was the wind) towards where, far, far above them, the black mountain of History cantilevered away into the ethereal fastnesses, its peak discernible only as a black wedge or womb delineated as a default by a corolla-cone of dense bright stars.

We weathered the storm under pressure
Then decided to form an orchestra…

So it was okay; it had always been okay. If he had fallen by the wayside, as he might easily have done – and as he might, still – the hands gripping the gunwale on either side of his hands would simply have edged towards each other, the fingers spreading slightly, or else new hands would have taken his place; and the sacred boat would have gone right on moving, as it had always been moving, by dint of unimaginable, commingled suffering and elation, by fits and starts, up the black mountain…

For most of the time we gather
alongside the sea…

Heave! said the night wind. And: Again, *heave!* And the man, dropping his shoulder along with the myriad others, leaning into the hill, recalled his daughter, then a mischievous eight-year-old, saying enigmatically on an Easter drive to Maracas: 'When the singing stops, the world will come to an end.' But the singing would never stop, the man knew that now, as he knew the essential goodness of the Trinidadian enterprise, and the rightness of their Golgotha-trek, bearing the sacrificial vessel of Trinidadian-ness up towards the stars. And there in Havana, in a private room on the third floor of the *Instituto de Cardiologia y Cirugia Cardiovascular*, he was reconciled.

> *And now, all around the island,*
> *people want to know*
> *how a little country steelband*
> *could play music so...*

It was all quite simple, preordained. And the singing would never stop. For he and they were not ultimately subjects, not ends in themselves, but the instruments of a high seriousness which used them exaltedly and mercilessly – though he had nearly had to pay with his life for the grace to know it.

The scent of a pine forest came down to him from somewhere far above, where the mountain peak sheared away into the night sky. Around him, softened by night and distance, murmurous human voices arose. Then they died away, leaving once more only the rustle of foliage, the crush and suck of the vessel over the loamy hillside, and the faithful, low song of the wind.

Everything mattered, and nothing mattered, he knew now. And wasn't that a theme for gentle smiles?

He was ready to live. He was ready to die. He threw himself at the black hillside once more, thighs and tendons straining – and felt the sudden cruel crunching as the keel rode over his breastbone.

ABOUT THE AUTHOR

Born in Trinidad in 1944, Wayne Brown read English at the University of the West Indies in Jamaica and lived mainly between the two countries until his death in 2009. His books include *On The Coast* (Andre Deutsch, 1973) which was awarded the Commonwealth Prize for Poetry, and was a Poetry Book Society recommendation; *Edna Manley: The Private Years* (Andre Deutsch, 1976), a biography of the Jamaican sculptress; a second volume of poems, *Voyages* (Inprint Caribbean, 1989); and *The Child of the Sea* (Inprint Caribbean, 1990), like his later *Landscape with Heron* (Observer Literary Books, 2000), a collection of short stories and remembrances. He edited *Derek Walcott: Selected Poetry* (Heinemann Caribbean, 1981) and edited and produced several anthologies of Jamaican fiction and poetry.

Wayne Brown was a Gregory Fellow in Poetry at the University of Leeds, England, a Fulbright Scholar in the US, and a Fellow of Yaddo, MacDowell, The Virginia Center for the Creative Arts, and the Rockefeller Foundation. He lectured in English Literature in the US and at both the Trinidadian and Jamaican campuses of the University of the West Indies. Between 1984 and 2009, some 3,500 editions of his column 'In Our Time' appeared in Trinidadian and Jamaican newspapers; and between February and November 2008 he wrote a weekly column, 'The Race for the White House', which appeared in the Sunday editions of the *Trinidad Express*, the *Nation* (Barbados) and the *Stabroek News* (Guyana). For six months in 2009 he wrote a column called 'In the Obama Era', before returning to his original, wide-ranging column, 'In Our Time'.

Wayne Brown was editor of the literary pages of the *Sunday Observer* and the *Sunday Gleaner* and was the founder-tutor of The Creative Writing Workshop. He also tutored in Creative Writing (fiction, non-fiction and poetry) in the Low-residency MFA Creative Writing program of Lesley University, MA; taught Creative Writing (Poetry) at the UWI, Mona; and taught an online creative writing course for Stanford University. His two daughters, Mariel and Saffrey, live in Trinidad and Jamaica respectively.

ALSO BY WAYNE BROWN

On the Coast and Other Poems
Introduction by Mervyn Morris
ISBN: 9781845231507; pp. 112; November 2010; £8.99

First published in 1972, *On the Coast* was a Poetry Book Society
Recommendation in the UK, and established Wayne Brown as one of
the finest young poets of the post-Walcott generation. It was followed
in 1988 by *Voyages*, a collection that amply showed the maturing of
Brown's remarkable gifts but was rarely available. Now, long after some
of the 'revolutionary' poets are forgotten, it is possible to see that
Brown's work has been seminal in Caribbean poetry, both for its
intrinsic qualities, and for Brown's crucial role as the mentor of a
current generation of Caribbean poets. Part of Peepal Tree's Caribbean
Modern Classics series, this edition restores the original text of the 1972
edition and adds the new poems first published in *Voyages*.

Wayne Brown's poems approach the issues of creativity, finding
meaning, finding contentment and the threats to these human goals
through poems about Caribbean nature (his bestiary of sea creatures
makes him a Caribbean Ted Hughes); through anecdote, frequently
drawing on family life; through poems about favourite artists such as
Neruda, Nabakov, Rilke and the Tobagan poet Eric Roach; through
reflecting on the rewards and pain of remaining in the Caribbean
compared to the loss suffered by those writers and artists who left the
islands.